The Summer I Found Myself

The Summer I Found Myself

COLLEEN FRENCH

KENSINGTON
PUBLISHING CORP.
www.kensingtonbooks.com

KENSINGTON BOOKS are published by
Kensington Publishing Corp.
119 West 40th Street
New York, NY 10018

All Kensington titles, imprints, and distributed lines are available at special quantity discounts for bulk purchases for sales promotion, premiums, fund-raising, educational, or institutional use.

Special book excerpts or customized printings can also be created to fit specific needs. For details, write or phone the office of the Kensington Sales Manager: Kensington Publishing Corp., 119 West 40th Street, New York, NY 10018. Attn. Sales Department. Phone: 1-800-221-2647.

The K logo is a trademark of Kensington Publishing Corp.

ISBN-13: 978-1-4967-2963-7 (ebook)
ISBN-10: 1-4967-2963-3 (ebook)

ISBN-13: 978-1-4967-2962-0
ISBN-10: 1-4967-2962-5
First Kensington Trade Paperback Printing: June 2021

10 9 8 7 6 5 4 3 2 1

Printed in the United States of America

PROLOGUE

The little girl stood in the kitchen in her nightie, broom in hand, looking out the bay of windows. Beyond the porch, beyond the dune grass, a man and woman walked hand in hand along the beach. The hem of her flowered dress fluttered at her knees. The pinks and purples matched the colors of the sunrise, and it made the little girl smile.

She liked being up this early before her mama and daddy rose for the day. Before Mama woke her sisters and they started talking, chatter that wouldn't end until they were asleep in the bedroom the three girls shared. She loved her little sisters, but their constant motion, the nonstop talking, wore on her. She liked the house quiet like this with no sound but the blup, blup *of the percolator on the stove.*

The sunrise she'd watched from the porch that morning had been a good one. There hadn't been a cloud in the sky, nothing to obscure the coming of the new day. Facing directly east, looking out over the Atlantic Ocean, she'd stood in darkness one moment, and the next she was bathed in the golden glow that painted the horizon orange and pink, magenta and rose.

She had watched the sun until it rose fully above the horizon and thought about her big brother, Joseph. They used to watch the sunrise together. He was actually her stepbrother. Mama reminded her of that all the time, but never in front of Daddy. Joseph was Daddy's son from his first wife, who died when Joseph was little. Mama didn't like Joseph's mama, even though she'd never met her. And she was dead. Joseph said the little girl would understand when she was older. He said that a lot, especially before he left.

"Drafted." A big word that she hadn't really understood even when he explained it.

He had been her best friend her whole life and now he was gone. "Drafted" meant you left even though you didn't want to. She didn't even know where he was right now, but Daddy showed her on a globe where the US Allies were. He thought Joseph was probably in France, but he didn't know for sure. He said it wasn't safe for folks at home to know where the troops were; otherwise, the Japs and Hitler would know, too. Daddy knew a lot about stuff like that because he was in a war before. She didn't know much about it because he didn't like to talk about it. All she knew was he was in a place called Cantigny. That was in France, too. A lot of people had fights in France. She asked her teacher at school about Cantigny. Daddy got shot there, and he had to have his leg cut off. That meant he never had to go fight again; that was what Mama said.

The little girl didn't want her brother to get shot and have a doctor cut off his leg. Then they wouldn't be able to run on the beach when he got back. She waited every day for a letter from him so she would know he was safe. She wrote him letters, too, though she didn't know if he was getting any of them.

There was the sound of stirring upstairs and she began to sweep the floor. She heard her mother's low voice, but she couldn't quite make out what she said. It was followed by the deeper rumble of her father's voice. They were probably talking about their day. After breakfast, Daddy would go off to work at the drugstore where he was the town's pharmacist. Then he'd come home for supper. A special supper because it was her birthday and they were having chocolate cake with chocolate frosting. It had been months since they'd had a cake of any sort because of the rationing of sugar and butter, but Daddy said President Roosevelt knew that little girls' birthdays were special. He told her that birthdays were made for sugar and butter.

It was going to be a great day. Because it was summer break, she and her sisters didn't have to go to school. So, after their father left for work, she and her sisters and mother would clean up breakfast, then slip into their swimming costumes. She and her sisters would race across the beach, throw down their towels, and dive into the surf. She loved swimming in the ocean.

Their mother would watch them from beneath her wide-brimmed straw hat on a towel in the sand. She'd read her women's magazines like Redbook, Good Housekeeping, and True Romances and sip lemonade from a jelly jar. Later, she'd pour fresh, icy lemonade for her daughters and feed them crackers. In the afternoon, they'd all traipse back over the dune so Mama could make the cake and later supper. They were having fried chicken; they'd gone to a friend's farm where they got milk, eggs, and sometimes chickens. They weren't supposed to, though, because of rationing, so they didn't do it often. And when they did, they never talked about it to anyone else.

The sounds of her sisters' voices drifted down through the floorboards, and she swept faster. They would all be downstairs in a few minutes. She had swept after supper because that was one of her daily chores, but then she and her sisters had played on the beach after dark, catching fireflies. And even though they'd rinsed their bare feet off in the tub of water at the bottom of the steps, there was still a little grit on the floor. At a beach house, there was always sand on the floor. That was what her mother said.

Making a pile, she fetched the dustpan and swept the sand into it. Then she dumped it into the trash can in the pantry and returned the broom and dustpan to the closet. Next, she turned the flame all the way down beneath the percolator. If she left it boiling too long, the coffee would be too bitter to suit her father, but if she turned it completely off, the coffee would get cold, and he wouldn't like that, either. Wasting coffee was a venial sin in her parents' house. Because of rationing, they couldn't buy as much coffee as before the war. Her father loved his morning coffee, so she was always careful when she made it for him. Mama had stopped drinking coffee, and now she drank mint tea from the leaves she cut in the front yard.

The little girl could hear her mother's voice now from the top of the stairs. She was telling her sisters to hurry along. She'd be making breakfast soon and no one ever missed breakfast unless they were sick in bed.

She dragged a stool across the kitchen and used it to kneel on the counter. Even though she was ten today, she was small for her age. So small that her daddy sometimes called her half-pint. At least he had before Joseph left. Now Daddy didn't tease her much. Maybe because she was the oldest at home now.

She took a mug decorated with yellow flowers and green leaves from the cabinet and set it carefully on the counter. Her mother said the dishes had belonged to Aunt Rose, who was dead now. The house had come fully furnished, dishes and everything. Lenora didn't remember because she'd been a little baby when they moved into the house, but there were reminders everywhere of the aunt she'd never met: furniture, sheets, dishes, knickknacks. There were so many of them that she felt like she knew Aunt Rose. Joseph said he always thought of Aunt Rose when they set the table.

She looked out the windows at the ocean again as she climbed off the counter. Thinking about Joseph made her sad. She missed watching the sunrise with him. It made her feel so alone, standing on the porch in her nightie by herself. So alone, she sometimes thought about asking Mama to get up early and watch it with her.

She knew that her mother would never get up to see a sun

come up, though, so she never asked. *Mama didn't like the beach. Daddy had inherited the house from Aunt Rose when she died of the consumption, whatever that was, and that was why they lived here. Not because Mama loved sunrises, the beach, or even the house. She complained a lot about the house and talked about moving inland all the time. To her daughters, never to Daddy, though. Out of his earshot, she complained about the sand, about how drafty the house was in the winter, and she constantly worried about hurricanes.*

The little girl dragged the stool back across the hardwood floor. Of course, she could just sleep in like everyone else. She couldn't feel lonely tucked into bed with her two sisters. But she couldn't do that because she promised Joseph she'd watch the sunrise without him until he came home.

She heard the neighbor's dog bark, quickly followed by the sound of a horse and wagon. The milkman. Mr. Tull used to come in a truck, but he didn't have the gasoline for deliveries because of gas rationing. A lot of folks in Albany Beach couldn't afford milk delivery anymore, but they were lucky because their daddy made a decent living as a pharmacist. People still got sick; they needed medicine, war or no war. That was what Mama said.

Savoring the last few minutes of her time alone, the little girl walked to the front door to meet Mr. Tull and got their quart of milk. As she walked, feeling the cool floorboards under her bare feet, she decided that someday she'd live here in this house with her children and she would get up every morning to see the sun come up with them.

1

All this happened, more or less.

Ellen stared at her screen, then backspaced.

~~All this happened, more or less.~~

She groaned, closed her laptop, and rested her forehead on it on her desk. She'd been teaching creative writing to college students for half her lifetime. But she couldn't write.
A hack.
That's all she would ever be. That was what her father, the great southern American writer Joseph R. Tolliver told her when he read the first short story she'd ever had published.
He'd seen himself as a modern-day Hemmingway.
She could still picture him in his walnut-paneled office that looked as if it came off a movie set. It was the office where one would imagine an iconic writer would work, with floor-to-ceiling bookshelves, worn Persian rugs, and wainscoted walls. An antique walnut desk, leather couch, and crystal decanter of scotch on the coffee table rounded out the depiction. Her father

looked like he belonged on a movie set, too. Or maybe a play: wool sweater, pipe between his teeth, messy hair that always seemed to need a trim. He was so spot-on that he was more the caricature of a successful male novelist from his generation than an actual person.

She had been twenty-two the day he said it. Fresh out of college with a squeaky-clean undergrad degree in literature and the dream of being a novelist like her nothing-is-ever-good-enough father.

Did every girl from the South grow up with daddy issues?

Her father had suggested she follow a different career path sooner rather than later. That way, she wouldn't have to find a roommate or marry to have someone to pay the bills when she failed at her chosen career. She went with the latter. She also took his advice to go back to school so she could get a *real* job. First a master's degree in education, and now she was halfway through her doctorate. She'd never intended to teach undergrads APA formatting for this long. She'd expected to *pay her dues* and become established as a writer by the time she was thirty-five at the latest. A real writer. That was what she wanted to be when she grew up.

She lifted her head and took another sip of wine, fighting the urge to down it. Her Siamese cat watched her from the shelf above the desk. Her blue eyes were unblinking. Her tail swished. She was judgy, even for a cat.

"'There are two means of refuge from the misery of life,'" Ellen quoted aloud. "'Music and cats.'"

The cat stared.

"Albert Schweitzer." As if the cat would recall the quote with that little hint.

If the cat knew the scientist, she gave no indication.

Ellen opened her laptop again. It was time to stop goofing around. She'd wrapped up her spring classes and turned in her grades. Twelve fails, sixteen As, and her other one hundred and sixty-seven students fell somewhere in between, so she'd done her job. This summer, she was only teaching one online class.

The light class load would give her the time she needed to get her family's beach cottage up in Delaware ready to sell. And time to get started on her novel. The one she'd been planning to write for the last two decades.

Okay. Going on three. But who was counting?

Ellen flexed her fingers, opened her laptop, stared at the screen. She knew she couldn't start her novel with Kurt Vonnegut's words, but she'd been hoping for a little inspiration. Using them as prompts.

Her hands found the keyboard.

All happy families are alike. . . .

There was something about Tolstoy's words that touched her. And rattled her at the same time. It was the word "families" that made her eyes scratchy. Both of her parents were dead now. Her brother was being held hostage by his new wife. Her son was gone, flying all over the world with his job. They had been her family. Who was her family now?

Her phone vibrated.

"Saved," she told the cat.

It was Lara, her best friend in the world. Her only I-can-tell-her-where-the-body-is-buried friend. "Hey," Ellen greeted.

"Hey, sister by another mister."

Ellen reached for her wineglass. Just hearing Lara's voice lifted her spirits. They had been best friends since Mrs. Carter's second-grade class and not marriage, jobs, divorce, children, nor geography had ever come between them. "I'm so glad you called. We haven't talked in what, two weeks? I know that's as much my fault as yours. I should have—"

"I can't talk long, Ellie," Lara interrupted. "I just wanted to give you the news before you read it in one of my mother's Facebook posts. It's back."

Ellen froze, her glass in hand. One she'd stolen from her mother's beach house the previous summer. Not exactly stolen. The beach house in Delaware was hers now and with it the mismatched wineglasses and other assorted dishware. Her brother had gotten their house on Magazine Street in New Orleans and promptly moved his new wife (#4. Is she not worried?) and baby in. Ellen's new niece, whom she doubted she'd ever see.

"What's back?" Ellen switched screens on her laptop so she could go to Facebook. "Not that stray cat that was using your flower beds for a litter box?"

Ellen was a cat person. Lara dog. Lara complained all the time about neighborhood cats in her yard. Ellen complained about dogs. Dogs that pooped on her front lawn. Cats, at least, buried their gifts.

"The Big C."

"The what?" Still not following, Ellen mistyped the word "Facebook" in the search bar, and it sent her flying out into space, landing on a site where she could spin a wheel and win money. Win money? She tried to key in the social media website again.

"Didn't you watch the Showtime series? In 2010, 2012 maybe? *The Big C*, Laura Linney, Oliver Platt?"

Ellen sat back in her chair after fat-fingering the word "Facebook" again. She needed more wine. Just a half a glass. One-point-five glasses a night and never a drop more. The rule helped keep her weight under control. And kept her from joining the rolls of all the great alcoholics, her father being one of the most outstanding achievers. "Never heard of it. I don't know who those people are."

"You don't know who Laura Linney is?" Lara sounded as if she were taking it personally. "Okay, I get Oliver Platt, but *Laura Linney*? Ellie? How big a rock do you live under? *You Can Count on Me, The Truman Show, Love Actually* . . ."

A big rock evidently, Ellen thought as she listened to Lara tick them off. She hadn't heard of any of those movies.

"*Mystic River, The Life of David Gale*, the sitcom *Frasier*—"

"Bingo. I know that one," Ellen cut in, relieved the rock wasn't *that* big. "But I still don't know Laura Linney. I'll Google her. Laura Linney," she said, typing in the search bar again. "*L-a-u-r-a*—how do you spell 'Linney'?"

"Ellie, it doesn't matter." Lara was obviously frustrated with her. Nothing new there.

Ellen typed. "*L-i-n*—"

"The *cancer*. The cancer is back."

Lara's words took the wind out of Ellen and she sat back hard in her chair. "Oh, Lara," Ellen breathed. A soft, sorrowful, "Sorry," escaped her lips. "How bad?"

"Bad," Lara said, sounding oddly cheerful.

2

Wearing a path on the carpet in front of her desk, Ellen listened as Lara rattled off the details of her diagnosis and treatment plan. Ellen knew the vocabulary: "carcinoma," "invasive," "ductal." She'd been through it with Lara a decade before. Then Lara said the word that really hit home: "metastasized."

Ellen's heart was pounding, and she felt light-headed. She couldn't process what Lara was saying.

This cannot be happening.

In December, they'd gotten together for the weekend in Philadelphia to celebrate Lara's tenth anniversary of being cancer-free. They'd seen the musical *Cats*, taken Lara's younger daughter to dinner at the City Tavern, and visited the Liberty Bell. How could the cancer come back after all of these years? How could Lara be sick again? Her Lara, her anchor in a storm. Her only anchor keeping her from drifting into oblivion.

"Wait. I don't understand," Ellen interrupted. "You have bone cancer?"

"Technically, it's secondary boob cancer. I already said that. The little bastard cells dug in elsewhere."

Every time Lara said "boob cancer," it made Ellen cringe. It seemed disrespectful to her. To the disease, to the physicians and scientists who were fighting to treat and find a cure, to those who had lost a loved one, and certainly to those diagnosed. She had brought up the subject before. Lara had not reacted well. She'd said something along the lines that "if she was the one who'd had her boobs cut off, she had a right to call them what she wanted." As Ellen recalled, Lara had used the *f* word in there somewhere. The *f* word was a bone of contention between them.

Bad choice of phrasing, considering the circumstances.

Lara's cursing had been an issue since they were in middle school. Ellen would never, ever use that word and Lara threw it around like rose petals. Neither of them had ever been able to budge in all these years.

Ellen pressed the heel of her hand to her forehead and took a long, slow breath. If she started hyperventilating, Lara would be pissed. "But you did everything the oncologists said. More than they advocated. You had the bilateral mastectomy and the chemo. And it's been years. Over ten years." Her voice wavered.

"Sucks to be me." Lara was so matter-of-fact. "It comes back sometimes, Ellie."

As if she was talking about a freckle or a boomerang.

"What's the research say? What's the prognosis?"

"I don't know."

"You didn't Google it?" Ellen asked, her voice squeaking. Had the diagnosis been handed to her, she would have been looking it up on her phone in the oncologist's parking lot.

"Didn't Google it. Work's been crazy. We're shorthanded. I told you, Sam tore his Achilles tendon playing tennis."

Sam her ex.

Maybe two exes back?

Ellen was still trying to work through the idea that Lara hadn't even done any research on her diagnosis yet. She took a breath, fighting to stay in control of her emotions. Lara was so composed. So pragmatic. How could she be so darned calm? Bone cancer . . . that was bad. "Did . . . did you have symptoms?"

"Meh. My leg hurt a little. Remember, I told you my lap times were sucking?"

They were both swimmers. They had been on swim teams together through elementary school, middle school, and high school. Lara had competed in college, too, but at that point Ellen had said good-bye to her competition days. It was just too stressful. However, she still swam at her local YMCA three times a week. Mondays, Wednesdays, and Fridays, 12:30 to 1:30. Two thousand five hundred yards, no more, no less.

"Lara! That was almost two months ago." Ellen practically yelled when she did the math.

She could hear water running and splashing. It sounded as if Lara was washing dishes. Who washed dishes at a time like this?

"That was April," Lara defended. "It's May. April was last month. Come on, Professor. Stay with me."

"And it will be June in a week." Ellen used the tone she used with freshman students. "That will be two months ago."

"Tomato, tomato," Lara said, pronouncing it first as Americans did with a long *a*, the second time the British phonation making the vowel short.

Ellen closed her eyes for a moment, gripping her cell phone so tightly that her fingers were cramping.

No, no, no. Lara couldn't have cancer again. Lara couldn't get sick and die and leave her.

Ellen wouldn't let her. Then she thought about Vera and Chastity. Lara's poor daughters. "Have you told the girls?"

"Not yet. Chastity has one more final—Anatomy and Physiology II with a lab. The class is a bitch. I still remember it. I scraped by with a B minus. Vera's in Paris. Work."

Ellen had never been to Paris. In fact, never been out of the country except for the time she and Tim went to Cabo. She'd hated it. All those fresh fruits and vegetables on the buffet. How did she know if they'd been washed properly? And it had been challenging to get a glass of Chardonnay. Or any white wine. All the drinks were frozen in plastic cups with fruit in them. And the rooms, though they appeared clean, had bugs in them. *Cockroaches.* Tim had said there were bugs in the tropics; it was just a way of life. Ellen had been happy when the week was over, and she'd told him at the airport on the way home that she'd never go again. She hadn't.

But he had. With his new girlfriend.

"Are you going to call the girls, see them?" Ellen asked, trying to focus on Lara and her family and not herself. This wasn't about her. Ellen knew that. Even though it was. Because if she had to say who she loved the most in the world, who she had *ever* loved most (and she knew she wasn't supposed to), it would be Lara. "Do you want me to come over so we can tell them together?"

"I'll just call them. I want to keep the whole thing low-key."

"You want to keep your *bone cancer* low-key?"

"My bones, my choice," Lara quipped. "I don't want the girls thinking they should come home or anything ridiculous like that. Chastity has that summer internship at Penn Medicine starting in a week. She's worked too hard to give it up for me."

"But you said you're going to have to do chemo again."

"Looks like it." She sounded more annoyed than anything else. "Different drugs. A lot has changed in ten years. Or so I'm told."

"Oh, Lara," Ellen sighed. "It was so awful for you last time."

"Right. Which is a problem."

An understatement.

Lara went on. "I'd like to think I could do this alone—"

"Do it alone?" Ellen interrupted. "You are not going through chemo *alone.*" The last time, the girls had been so young, only ten and eleven then, that Lara's mom, Marie, had moved in with them for six months. She'd driven Lara back and forth to the

hospital for treatments and cared for the girls. Ellen had gone up to stay with her every couple of weeks, giving Marie a break.

More like giving Lara a break from her own mother.

The sound of something shattering exploded in Ellen's ear and she pulled the phone back for a second. "You okay?" she asked.

"Fine. Filling the dishwasher. Broke a wineglass. Aw, damn it. And it was the one with the starfish on it. Remember, we got them at that little shop on the avenue in Albany Beach. You got the sand dollar. I'm trying to hurry," she went on. "I've got a date tonight. *Raul.*" She said his name in some weird, fakey accent that didn't exist anywhere in the world. "A drug rep that comes into the office. He's darling."

Lara was a physician's assistant who worked at an urgent care facility in the Philadelphia suburbs. Unlike Ellen, Lara loved her job. Ellen was envious. She couldn't imagine being excited to work each day.

"Hell," Lara muttered.

"You okay?"

"Cut my finger on a piece of glass." Lara made a sucking sound.

She was a physician's assistant, and this was how she treated wounds?

"Should you have it looked at?" Ellen fretted. "Do you need stitches?"

"I'm fine. I'll use some superglue if I need to. Listen, I have to jet. We can talk more this weekend. I just wanted to tell you that I had the scan, saw my oncologist, and now the diagnosis is official."

"You should have told me before it was official."

"I didn't want to worry you."

Always the cavalier attitude.

"Ellie, we'll talk." Lara's tone softened. "But I've got to grab a shower. We're going to a pub I like. It's trivia night." She sounded as if it were an ordinary Friday afternoon.

As if her world wasn't collapsing around her.

"Okay, I'll let you go in a second. But back to the Big C," Ellen said, stroking the cat sitting on her desk. She was feeling a little steadier. Her synapses were firing again. "You said you'd prefer to do it alone, but what? What were you going to say?"

"I was going to say, but let's face it." Lara sounded like the new diagnosis of bone cancer was an inconvenience—like the dry cleaning not being ready. "I'll need someone to drive me to treatments, feed me, though no food for four to six weeks might be the diet I've been looking for. Oh, I know what I wanted to tell you!" Suddenly she sounded excited. "I'm thinking about getting one of those cold caps. Have you read anything about them? They basically freeze your head during each chemo treatment. I don't know all the details yet. But it's supposed to block the poison they're pouring into your veins. Keep it from reaching the hair follicles or something. It costs an arm and a leg, but what the hell. I just got my hair the length I like it. I found a new guy to cut it. *Also* costs an arm and a leg, but not as many legs as the cold cap."

All of this talk of chemo, Ellen was feeling overwhelmed. She took a long, deep breath. In through her nose, out through her mouth, as her bestie rattled on. "You can't do this alone, Lara," she managed finally.

"I'm not having Vera or Chastity hold my hair while I barf. If I'm lucky enough to still have hair. Which is why I need to come up with a plan before I tell them. I can hire a caregiver, but also an arm and a leg, and I'm going to have to take a leave of absence, so I actually need to make a budget."

Something Ellen had been telling her for years. Lara made half of what Ellen made, and she still rented her town house, took exotic vacations, and thought nothing of spending three hundred dollars on a pair of patent-leather flip-flops.

"I'll come there, then," Ellen said. "And stay with you. I've only got one class this summer. I was planning on working on my book, but—"

"Nope," Lara interrupted. "You're going to Albany Beach for the summer. You're not putting it off any longer. You should have gone last year after your dad died. You said the insurance and other shit was costing you an—"

"An arm and a leg," Ellen chimed in, and they said it together.

"I don't want any fuss." Lara was drinking something now. A cocktail before she went out? "From you or my girls. Or my mother. Mom's having her hip replaced in two weeks, so even if I wanted her to come, which I don't, she can't. She's needed a new hip for years."

Ellen walked to the window to look out into her backyard. The hydrangeas were already blooming. She brought cuttings from the house in Albany Beach. They were the blue/purple kind. She loved them, but for some reason seeing them brought tears to her eyes. "You can't do this alone, Lara," Ellen said softly. "I won't let you."

"I'll figure it out."

Ellen turned away from the window. "Come with me to the beach," she blurted.

She had no idea where that had come from. She wasn't an impulsive person. She was the polar opposite. She never made reckless decisions. She never even bought fresh raspberries at the farmer's market unless they were on her shopping list.

"What?" Lara was as shocked by the invitation as Ellen was.

"Come with me," Ellen repeated. "To Albany Beach. There's the new hospital there. Chemo is chemo, right? Your oncologist can write the prescription, and someone can administer it in Albany Beach. How long will your treatment be?"

"Four to six weeks, then possibly radiation."

"Okay." Ellen's thoughts were firing a thousand a second. "You can sit on the porch of the beach house, watch the tide go in and out, and rest. And I can clean out the house. Top to bottom. There's a hundred years of stuff in that attic." She sounded almost as animated now as Lara. "You'd be doing me a favor if you came for the summer. You'll keep me on task. It would be like when we were kids and had sleepovers all the time. We'll paint each other's nails and do face masks."

"You don't paint your nails. Or use face masks."

Ellen ignored those points. "It will be one big, summer-long sleepover."

"Sounds heavenly, except for the part where someone will be injecting venom into my veins and I'll be barfing like a girl on spring break in Fort Lauderdale."

"We can do this, sister by another mister." Ellen was surprised by how positive she sounded. She was terrified, of course. To have the responsibility of taking care of Lara.

What if the chemo didn't work? What if Lara died?

"Hmm," Lara mused. "I guess I could come there. I won't be working for a while, so I suppose it doesn't matter where I go for treatment. As long as it's not Sierra Leone," she added. "I read an article while sitting in the oncologist's waiting room waiting for my sentencing that said Sierra Leone has the worst medical care in the world."

Ellen dug down to her toes for every bit of strength she could muster. "You're coming to the beach with me, Lara. We'll make it work."

It has to.

3

Ellen pulled into the driveway on Pintail Lane and came to a full stop. Gripping the steering wheel of her Toyota, she stared up at the house looming over her.

Nothing looked different from the last time she'd been there, though the hydrangea bushes needed trimming. Aside from that, the guy she paid for lawn care was doing a good job; the grass was cut, mulch had been spread in the flower beds, and the driveway had recently been edged.

The house was a classic style for the mid-Atlantic coast in its time period. Built in the 1920s, it was a square box, elevated on pilings with wide porches on the street side and ocean side. White, with dove-gray shutters and trim. On the front porch were four white Adirondack chairs. Chairs that had been there as long as she could remember and would have ordinarily seemed inviting to her. The house had been in her mother's family since the forties when her great-grandfather bought it.

The house still had the original white clapboard exterior, the only one on their street. Everyone else had long ago gone with vinyl siding. "Vinyl is final," her neighbors had told her. Especially when renting it out. But Ellen's family didn't rent their house, never had. Either a family member occupied it, or it sat empty.

Still holding the steering wheel in a death grip, Ellen fought the urge to back out of the driveway and drive home to Raleigh. She hadn't come last summer after her father died, except for a long weekend. She'd driven up intending to clean out the house. But she hadn't been able to do it. She'd stayed two days, then packed up her car and driven back to Raleigh.

The house was haunted.

Not by her parents.

By Tim. By the last events of her two-decade marriage.

Ellen took a breath.

It had been the beginning of the end.

Who was she kidding?

It had been the end of the end.

She didn't even have to close her eyes to see the scene that she was afraid would be forever seared in her brain. She had been loading dishes into the dishwasher, waiting for him to come home. He'd gone out to buy beer and wine and had been gone more than an hour. The trip should have taken fifteen minutes. She had texted him, but he hadn't replied. She had even tried to use the locator she had set on her phone to see where his phone was, but apparently he'd turned it off again. She had just been contemplating calling the hospital or the police looking for him when he walked in the door carrying her favorite Chardonnay and a six-pack of Dogfish Head beer that was brewed locally.

"Where have you been?" she asked, spinning around, a dirty plate in her hand.

He set the beer and wine on the granite counter that separated the kitchen from the eating area. "I went to the liquor store."

She looked at her watch. "An hour and seventeen minutes ago."

"I ran into our neighbor down the street. Eric? He asked me

if I wanted to have a beer. I had a beer with him. What's the big deal?"

"The big deal"—she waved the dessert plate at him—"is that I didn't know where you were. You could have been in a car accident."

The dishes were pretty white ones with yellow buttercups on them. They'd been in the cabinet for as long as she could remember. Completely out of style and starting to show wear. Half of the dinner plates were chipped and several bowls and salad plates were long gone, but she didn't care. She liked them.

"I didn't get into a car accident. I had a beer with a friend after weeding flower beds all day!" He hooked his thumb in the direction of the front yard.

"But I texted you."

"I saw that when I got in the car. I missed it. I'm sorry." He walked over to the sink and picked up a salad bowl and placed it in the dishwasher.

"You could have texted me when you saw my text."

"I was going to be home in six minutes."

Ellen leaned over and moved the bowl he'd just placed in the dishwasher to the other side, facing it inward so it would get thoroughly clean.

"What are you doing?" Tim asked.

She added the buttercup plate that was still in her hand. "Loading the dishwasher."

"I just put that bowl in there. Why did you move it?"

"Because that's how you load the dishwasher."

He folded his arms over his chest. "I'm sorry I didn't call you or text you when I decided to have a beer with Eric. Okay?"

"If you had been in an accident, how would I have known?" she demanded.

"My grandmother always used to say that bad news has a way of finding you."

"That's not funny." She slid out the top drawer of the dishwasher and began to load the silverware, grouping the tea-spoons, then the salad forks.

"Ellen, we've talked about this. I'm forty-seven years old. I can stop for a beer with a friend on the way home if I like."

"It's a Friday night. We don't go out on Friday nights down here. A lot of people drink and drive on the weekends. We said we wouldn't go out on weekends when we're down here in the summer."

"No, you said we shouldn't go out on the weekend because there are more accidents with people drinking and driving." He ran his hand through his short salt-and-pepper hair. "'Those who would give up essential liberty, to purchase a little tempo-rary safety, deserve neither liberty nor safety.' Ben Franklin."

"I know who said it," she snapped. He was always throwing quotes at her. She was an English professor, too.

"I'm not going to give up living my life because I might make a wrong decision or something bad might happen. You never want to try anything new, do anything fun—"

"You're mad because I told you I didn't care if you had a coupon that I was not parasailing? I told you, I just read about a man who—"

"Enough, Ellen." Tim's voice had had an edge to it she hadn't recognized. He hadn't exactly sounded angry. Frustrated maybe. Fed up. And just *done*, she would realize much later.

In hindsight, she should have paid more attention. Maybe if she'd realized how upset he was, she could have diffused the conversation.

Maybe she'd even still be married.

He stood there, his arms hanging at his sides. Her Tim. The man she had married shortly after college graduation. The man she had shared a bed with for more than two decades. "I'm done," he repeated.

"Me too." She picked up a sponge to wipe up any water that might have splattered from the sink. "I don't want to fight."

"No, I mean, I'm done, done, Ellen." He exhaled heavily, and she remembered feeling a weight that seemed to lift from his shoulders settle on hers. A weight she'd been carrying since that night when he had said it.

Divorce.

He'd asked her for a divorce that night. Irreconcilable differences. He wanted to live his life, have fun, explore, experience, and she wanted to hide in her little, well-structured box. He said he didn't love her anymore. That she was a good person, but not the right partner for him. He told her that maybe she had never been the right one. And that he hadn't been the right one for her.

At first, she'd been angry. Then sad. And now, more than a year later, she just . . . she didn't know how she felt now.

Lost?

"Ellie? You okay?"

Lara's voice brought Ellen back to the present. She glanced at Lara in the passenger's seat, feeling as if she were being sucked out of a dark tunnel, back into the light. "Fine. Good." She forced a cheery smile and lifted her foot off the brake. "One of the shutters looks wonky." She pointed vaguely in the direction of the row of windows on the second floor. "Does it look wonky to you?"

Lara removed her aviator sunglasses and stared at the house. She was wearing jean shorts and a tank top with a ball cap pulled over her long, lush blond hair. The end of her ponytail stuck out from the back of the cap. She could have easily passed for a woman in her mid-thirties rather than her mid-forties. "I don't see a wonky shutter." She lowered her cell phone to her lap. "You sure you're okay?"

Ellen eased the car into her parking spot and put it into park. "Peachy. Come on. Let's unload so we can take a walk on the beach before sunset."

4

Ellen rolled over in bed and stared out the bay of double-hung windows that faced the ocean. She had the best bedroom in the house now. The room that had once been her great-grandparents', then her grandparents', and later her parents'. Actually, her mother's; her father had rarely ever come to Albany Beach. It felt strange to call the room her own, to call the beach house her own. To know she no longer had parents or grandparents, that she was the adult here, now somehow made her feel . . . untethered. A little bit like an imposter. She was too adrift to be responsible for anything.

She closed her eyes for a moment, trying to enjoy the moment of quiet before the busy day she and Lara had planned. It was their last weekend of fun before Lara's chemo began on Monday, and they intended to make it a three-day weekend. Lara had a whole list of things she wanted to do, including sunbathing on the beach (she swore she'd wear 50 SPF and reapply often), swimming in the ocean, and going shopping. And at some point, they were going to the Crab Shack for steamed blue claws, covered in Old Bay Seasoning that she knew she wouldn't be able to eat once she started treatment.

A breeze drifted in off the ocean, carrying the briny scent of the water, the call of seagulls, and the rumble of a sand-cleaning machine. The sun had just risen, and Ellen had missed it. She thought she'd set her phone to wake her at five so she could go for a walk or at least enjoy her coffee on the back porch. But the phone hadn't gone off, and she'd blissfully slept.

Realizing Ellen was awake, her cat rose from the end of the bed, stretched the way a cat stretched with every limb, muscle, and tendon, and then slinked toward Ellen. The cat rubbed against her, purring loudly, and Ellen stroked the soft white and gray fur on her back. "And how's my Nefertiti this morning?" she asked softly.

Tim had said it was a silly name for a Siamese cat. That half the female Siamese cats in the world were probably called Nefertiti after the female pharaoh, but for once, Ellen hadn't cared what her husband thought. *Husband at the time*, she reminded herself, trying not to let herself get down first thing in the morning.

She'd had a Siamese kitten named Nefertiti as a child. Her brother had let it out of the house, and it was killed on the street in front of their house. Eddie had always sworn it had been an accident, but she still secretly held it against him. Even if he hadn't let her kitten out the front door on purpose, his carelessness had put her in a Nike shoe box in their pet cemetery in the backyard.

The cat pushed at her hand and meowed for further attention.

"Shhh," Ellen whispered. "We'll both be in trouble if we wake her."

Lara was not an early riser when she didn't have to be up for work. She was not an early riser, particularly after drinking half a bottle of vodka. They'd sat on the back porch the night before, eaten sweet chili Doritos, and drunk adult beverages as, since they were middle schoolers, they had always called anything with alcohol in it. Lara had her vodka and soda, Ellen an entire bottle of Chardonnay. Ellen had worried she'd have a hangover after overindulging, but to her surprise, her head was clear. Probably because of the liter of water she'd chugged before bed.

The cat curled up against Ellen's side and continued to purr as she closed her slanted blue eyes until they were nothing but slits.

"Nope, no making yourself comfortable," Ellen murmured. "I've got places to go, people to see. Your aunt Lara has big plans for today. She thinks I need to go shopping to buy *dating* clothes."

The night before, she and Lara had covered a myriad of topics. Ellen had tried to keep the conversation light. The hours were ticking down until Lara started her first treatment. But Lara had been on a mission. Between 8:00 p.m., when they returned from a walk on the beach, and midnight, when they'd dragged themselves to bed, Lara had told Ellen in detail why it was time to make changes in her life. And she had a whole list of suggestions:

- Stop obsessing over her ex [she wasn't]
- Stop talking about writing a book and just write it [easy for her to say]
- Stop whining and get the attic clean [no rebuttal]
- Finish profile and start online dating [no way]
- Break some rules [that was Lara's MO, not hers]
- And start finding happiness within herself instead of from others [the hardest thing to hear. Maybe because three-quarters of a bottle of Chardonnay in, which was why she had argued the most vehemently over this one.]

Ellen knew deep down that Lara was right. She needed change. To change. She wanted her life to be more than just getting through each day, checking tasks off a list. She wanted to have something to share in her Christmas letter besides all of the wonderful places her son had traveled during the year for his job. Shoot, she wanted to be so busy enjoying her life the way Lara was that she didn't have time to write a Christmas letter. Lara hadn't even sent out Christmas cards in years!

What freedom. To not send out Christmas cards and be okay with that.

But just the idea of it seemed so unattainable.

Ellen exhaled and stretched to reach her cell without disturbing the cat. She checked her alarm. She *had* set it. But for 5:00 p.m., not a.m. She began to close apps and found Facebook was open. When had she been on Facebook? Then she vaguely remembered, after crawling into bed, flipping through Tim's vacation (with his new girlfriend) photos for an hour. The one with him zip-lining through some treetop canopy had made her angry and brought tears to her eyes at the same time.

She groaned and flopped back on her pillow. Nefer continued to purr.

Was Lara right? *Was* she obsessing over Tim?

A sound downstairs made her lower her phone to her chest.

Was Lara up already? Had she gone for a run? She wasn't kidding about getting the most out of her last day before she was *dead man walking*. A phrase she had not had to explain to Ellen. Ellen had read *The Green Mile*.

The night before, over a dinner of steamed shrimp and kale salad, Lara had been bemoaning the fact that she wouldn't be able to run for a while. Months probably. Or never again, depending on how her treatment went. Maybe she was heading out for a final run.

Ellen gave the cat a gentle push. "Up."

Nefer made a little cat sound but didn't move.

"Up," she told the cat again, then extricated herself from beneath the light blanket she'd slept with.

Rain had come in the evening before and cooled the temperatures enough to turn off the upstairs air conditioning. Ellen had been chilly when she'd gone to bed. She padded barefoot across the hardwood floor to the master bath. Initially, there had been no bathrooms on the second floor, but her grandparents had turned one of the five upstairs bedrooms into two full baths and a walk-in closet for the master bedroom. According to the real estate agents Ellen had spoken with, the additional full baths would bring tens of thousands of extra dollars to the selling price.

Ellen brushed her teeth and then headed down the hall. The smell of coffee wafted from downstairs. Lara must have already run if she was brewing coffee.

Ellen heard dishes rattling as she walked down the steps. Lara was up early, making coffee and doing the dishes they left in the sink? Who was this creature, and what had she done with Ellen's Lara who could sleep until noon and leave dirty dishes in the sink quite happily for a week?

"You're certainly up—" Ellen froze when she reached the kitchen.

Someone *was* washing dishes, but it wasn't Lara.

Ellen held her breath. For a moment, she felt disoriented. This was her house, her kitchen, but standing at the kitchen sink was not her tall, lithe Lara, but a tiny wizened woman in a flowered housecoat.

"He . . . hello?" Ellen said.

"Good morning." The woman went on rinsing the suds from the glass Lara had used to abuse her body with vodka the previous night. The woman was barefoot, which somehow didn't fit with the housecoat.

Ellen's first thought was that someone had broken into the house to rob her. But this woman obviously wasn't stealing anything. She was washing dishes! Was she a . . . diversion? Were the thieves elsewhere in the house?

"Can . . . can I help you?" Ellen asked, slipping her hand into her pocket to find her phone. *What should she do? Call 911?*

"I don't think so, dear. Coffee is almost ready." She looked over her shoulder and smiled. She had big, shiny white dentures.

Ellen's heart rate slowed a bit. The woman seemed harmless.

But if you had a burglary ring and you were using an older woman to distract the occupants of the home while you stole their big-screen TVs and diamond stud earrings (hers were only a quarter carat each, but they had been her mother's) wouldn't you choose a nonthreatening grandmotherly type?

But that whole scenario was ridiculous. People didn't rob houses with their grandmother in tow. And there was no crime to speak of in Albany Beach beyond the occasional stolen kid's bike (usually taken by a drunk father of three) and teenagers TPing someone's house.

Ellen's gaze strayed to the stove where the smell of coffee brewing was coming from. It was an old percolator, making a strangely comforting sound. *Blup, blup.* She also noticed that a second and third burner were on.

She had never seen the percolator in her life. The woman at her sink made Ellen wonder if she was losing her mind. It was as if she were in someone else's house rather than the other way around. The percolator she didn't recognize made the argument even stronger.

Ellen didn't know what to say. But obviously, she had to say *something. Do* something. This woman was trespassing. She might be dangerous. The idea sounded logical, but the fact that the stranger was washing dishes and making coffee suggested otherwise. And there didn't seem to be anyone else there. Was the woman lost? Confused? Both?

"Do . . . do I know you?" Ellen asked.

The little old lady with a slept-on helmet of snow-white hair laughed. "Very funny, Doris."

Doris? Ellen didn't know a Doris. No one named Doris lived on the street. "What . . . what are you doing here?"

The older woman sighed, turning away from the sink holding a dish towel. The dishes done, she dried her hands. "Dishes.

Always dishes to be done, isn't there? Would you like some coffee? I don't think Daddy will mind. He's still sleeping. We could pour ourselves a cup and sit out on the porch. It rained last night, but just for a little while. The chairs are dry enough." She took one of the coffee mugs with the yellow buttercups that had come with the house and poured into one and then the other.

"You left a couple of burners on," Ellen pointed out.

The woman stared at the stove for a moment, seeming surprised to see the circles of blue flames. She turned them off. "You missed the sunrise. A beauty." She offered Ellen one of the mugs.

Not knowing what else to do, Ellen accepted it. It smelled heavenly. She wondered if it was safe to drink. "Where did you get that coffeepot?"

The woman arranged the dish towel just so, took the other mug of coffee, and walked through the kitchen. Ellen followed her through the screen door, onto the porch. The back door was open, the point of entry she guessed, though how she wasn't sure.

A bottle of Chardonnay the previous night or not, Ellen knew she'd locked the back door when she and Lara went to bed. And she'd checked the front, too, even though she knew she'd locked it when they came home from the liquor store. Living on the ocean side of the house the way they did, she tried to keep the front door locked at all times.

"I was ready to wake you and ask you where you'd put it." The older woman sat down in one of the Adirondack chairs on the back porch. She was so small that when she slid back, her bare feet came off the floor. "Found it in the back of the pantry in an old cardboard box. The coffee grinder was a little tricky. I usually grind it in a mill. You just turn the handle. Nothing fancy like that electric thingy." She shrugged as if it were all a great mystery and took a sip of her coffee. "Good," she remarked.

Not yet sure what she should do next, Ellen looked into her cup. It appeared safe to drink. And the older woman was drinking hers. While Ellen was staring into the cup of coffee a stranger had made for her in her own house, trying to decide what to say next, a voice called from the beach, just on the other side of the dunes.

"Granny? Granny, where are you?"

"Oh, good grief," the woman muttered. She got to her feet, with surprising pep, and took a last sip of her coffee before setting it down on the wide chair arm. "I'd better go, else there will be heck to pay."

Ellen watched her go down the back steps. Then jumped up and leaned over the railing to see which direction the woman went, but she was gone. Just like that, just gone, in her housecoat and bare feet.

As if she had never been there.

As if she didn't exist.

As if none of it had happened.

Ellen looked at the coffee in her hand, proof it had.

5

Lara dropped into one of the faded white Adirondack chairs on the back porch. She stared at the other chairs, thinking they needed to be painted. And that they ought to be bright colors.

She reached for her vodka and tonic. She'd made it the minute Ellen walked across the dunes to pick up some trash that was caught in the sea grass. If Ellen knew she was having a second drink before dinner, she'd bitch. Ellen had been reading up on chemo and was getting hung up on all the don'ts, including the no alcoholic beverage warning. Ellen's thought was that Lara should abstain before treatment to "get a head start." Lara's feeling was that she should eat and drink more since it was likely she'd be skipping meals and cocktails when the chemotherapy drugs kicked in.

The intention was to reduce the cancer cells in her femur. Her secondary cancer was osteolytic, meaning the breast cancer cells were breaking down and thinning her bone. Her oncologist hadn't come right out and said so, but there was no cure. The doctor had hopped, skipped, and jumped over and around

Lara's direct questions about her prognosis the way doctors did. Particularly when it wasn't good news.

"I can't answer that until we see how you respond. I'm hopeful, but we'll just have to wait and . . ."

Dr. Gupta had twitched her nose when she said it. Lara liked her and she thought she was a good oncologist, but the woman had an annoying habit of twitching her nose like a little rabbit. She did it when she was nervous. When she had bad news. Or didn't want to answer a question.

"Treatments have improved so much over the last decade. . . .

"We'll see how you do and then we'll have a better idea. . . ."

Blah, blah, blah.

Lara could have called her on it. She'd considered it. She'd done it before but had decided, in the end, what was the point? Her prognosis was unknown. She might survive this bout of cancer or she might not. That was the truth, no matter how positive the doctor tried to sound.

She sipped her vodka and tonic, enjoying the tang of the fresh lime. She liked a lot of lime and none of that juice out of a plastic container that looked like a lime bullshit. She'd bought a dozen freshies at the market. And a big bottle of expensive Finnish vodka at the liquor store. She planned on drinking a lot of vodka before she had to make the dead-man-walking stroll into the oncology unit Monday morning.

She sat back in the chair and breathed in the salt air, raising her face to catch the last of the sun's rays. Through the open windows of the house, she could smell the curry in the Crock-Pot that she'd put on in the morning. She hoped the recipe would turn out, as she'd never made it in a Crock-Pot. Ellen needed an Instant Pot.

But Ellen needed a lot of things right now and an Instant Pot was pretty low on the list.

Now that they were there and settled, Lara was glad she had made the decision to come to Albany Beach. She probably could have managed at home. She had friends who could give her rides to chemo, stop by to check on her, drop off food she would never eat. She could have Gatorade and barf bags delivered. And new head scarves if the damned cold cap didn't do what it was supposed to do. She could have made living alone work. But Ellen needed her. The chemo was just Lara's excuse to be there, at this point.

Because she was worried about her. In light of the Big C diagnoses, more than she was before. More even than she was worried about her girls. If she died, she knew her girls would be okay. She had done her job. As she saw it, a parent's primary role in his or her child's life was to prepare him or her for life without a parent. And Ellen's parents had done a shitty job. So the task had been passed on to her. Ellen was Lara's responsibility, and she felt that on a cellular level.

Lara didn't want to die. She didn't think she was going to bite it on this go-round, but she wanted to be smart about playing the odds. Ducks in a row and all that. And Ellen was at the front of the line right now. She was floundering, squandering her life, and as her best friend in the world, Lara believed it was her obligation to make sure Ellen was okay, just in case she *did* end up in an urn on one of her daughters' bookcases.

"I don't know how this much trash can end up on the ground!" Ellen called up to the porch as she crossed the dunes. She was wearing jean shorts, but they were a good three inches too long. And not the hip, Bermuda style, the grandma culottes style. Ellen had nice, muscular legs, not skinny string beans like her own. Lara made a mental note to grab a pair of decent shorts for the next time they went shopping.

"Look at this." Ellen held up a plastic grocery bag bulging with trash. "And I collected this much yesterday. Where are they getting plastic grocery bags? They're supposed to be banned in Albany Beach."

Lara sipped her drink, refusing to allow littering in town

to bug her. She had bigger problems today. Like Ellen's senior citizen shorts and the color of the chairs on the porch. "Black market!" she called down.

Ellen crossed the path to the steps. "Very funny," she said. "Want to go for a walk? Tide's going out."

"After I finish my drink."

She came up the steps, looking at the drink in Lara's hand, but wisely said nothing. "Dinner smells good. When will it be done?"

"No clue. I'm used to doing it in an Instant Pot. How did you not get on that bandwagon? I thought every U.S. citizen had one."

"Instant Pots are pressure cookers," Ellen warned as she reached the top step. "They can be dangerous. Our neighbor in New Orleans had one blow up on her. She's lucky it didn't kill her."

"Pressure cookers were dangerous in 1963 when they went on the stovetop and they had one of those little things on the vent that wiggled as the steam came out." Lara made a rapid motion with her hand.

"A pressure valve." Ellen walked into the house with the garbage and came back without it. "We drinking already? It's early."

"I don't know if you're drinking yet, Miss Chardonnay, but I am."

Ellen plucked her cell from her back pocket and checked the time. "I don't usually have my wine until later."

Lara leaned back in the chair and closed her eyes. "Come on, live a little."

Ellen stood there in obvious indecision. Lara could almost hear her thinking. She knew Ellen wanted the wine, but she was so strict with all of her arbitrary rules that it was hard to get her to budge. "Go on," Lara urged, opening her eyes to study her best friend behind the cover of her sunglasses. "Pour a glass of wine. Enjoy a cocktail with me. I doubt I'll be imbibing next week."

"Maybe I will," Ellen said noncommittally. She leaned against the rail to look out over the ocean. "Hey, crazy question."

"I love crazy questions. They often require crazy answers."

"Did you . . ." Ellen stopped and started again. "Have you seen an elderly woman hanging around the house?"

"*This* house."

"Mmm-hmm," Ellen intoned.

"No." Lara took another sip. "Okay, I'm going to bite. Why do you ask?"

Ellen hesitated and then went on. "When I came downstairs this morning, there was . . . there was an old woman in the kitchen. Making coffee."

Lara sat up straighter, immediately intrigued. "You're kidding?" She made a face. "Why was she making coffee?"

"I have no idea. She found an old percolator in the pantry. I walked downstairs, and there she was, making coffee." She pointed toward the kitchen. "I don't know how she got inside. I still don't."

"Holy shit," Lara said.

Ellen turned around and leaned back, resting her elbows on the rail. "It was pretty obvious she has dementia. She thought this was her house. She kept calling me Doris."

"What did you do?"

"She was only here a few minutes. I probably should have called the police—"

"Call the police?" Lara demanded. "Why would you call the police? Why didn't you wake me up? I could have had coffee with the crazy lady, too."

"That's not very nice."

Lara smiled. It was brave for Ellen to have had such an experience and not completely flipped out. "Next time she comes, wake me up."

"I doubt there will be a next time. She must live nearby. A child was out on the beach looking for her."

"So you had an adventure. In this house." Lara lifted her chin. "Bet you could use that in your book."

"I don't know about that." Ellen exhaled, crossing her arms over her chest.

Which drew Lara's attention to the T-shirt Ellen was wearing. "That's what we need!" She pointed at Ellen's shirt. It featured a row of brightly colored chairs in the sand that was almost identical to the ones on the front and back porches. "That's what colors the chairs should be."

"What are you talking about?" Ellen looked at her shirt and back at Lara again.

"These chairs." Lara tapped the arm of the one she was sitting in and picked up her glass. The lime juice and tonic were refreshing as they went down her throat. The vodka was heavenly. "They're dingy. We should paint them. Beachy colors like hot pink and teal and tangerine."

Ellen pursed her lips. Lara knew that look. Ellen was wrestling between wanting to explain why the chairs had to be white and wanting to go along with what Lara said. Because of the cancer.

"Wouldn't they be beautiful?" Lara prodded. "I want mine to be purple. A rich purple like plum. Or eggplant. And yours can be a pretty green. Mint green, maybe. You've always liked that color. It will go with your hair. Green looks great on redheads. You look good in blue, too."

Ellen tugged on her ponytail. "It's not exactly red anymore. It's kind of a mousy brown."

"So buy a box of hair dye." Lara gestured with her vodka and tonic.

"I've considered it. I've got a few grays." She continued to fuss with her hair. "But shouldn't I go to a hair salon? Get a professional opinion? Let a professional color it?"

"Well, you could, but it will cost you a hundred and fifty

bucks. We can get a decent box at the drugstore for twelve." She swirled the ice around in her glass, debating whether or not she was going to make herself a third. It wasn't like she needed to worry about the calories; the chemo was going to take care of that. And she wasn't driving anywhere tonight.

"You really think we should paint the chairs?" Ellen crossed her arms over her chest, studying the one she usually sat in. "Different colors?"

"Absolutely. White is boring," Lara declared. "And you said yourself on the drive here that you're bored with your life. You need a little excitement, Ellie."

"And you think painting the Adirondack chairs will add some excitement to my life?" Ellen asked, clearly not believing it.

"It's a start." She used her fingernail to peel up a fleck of paint. "You don't want anyone sitting in flaky paint, do you?"

"Who's going to sit in the chair beside you and me?"

"I don't know." Lara shrugged. "Maybe I'll make a friend at chemo. You wouldn't care if I brought a friend over, would you?"

"Of course not."

"Better yet, maybe *you'll* have a friend over. One of the male species."

Ellen cut her eyes at her. "I think I'll have that wine now."

6

Ellen thought she was prepared for Monday morning when she had to drop Lara off at the hospital for her first chemotherapy treatment. She wasn't.

"You sure you don't want me to go inside with you?" Ellen pulled up to the curb. There was a blue and white sign directing patients and visitors where to go. One of them was *Oncology*. She'd been up since 5:00 a.m. pacing. Fighting the what-ifs.

What if this treatment didn't work?

What if Lara died?

Ellen hung on to the steering wheel for dear life. "I brought my laptop. I have some papers to grade, and I need to set up a new fall class on writing the short story that I'm teaching. I can sit with you, or sit in the waiting room, or—"

"Nope," Lara injected, grabbing the bag they had packed together the night before. She heaved it onto her lap and tucked in the end of the fleece blanket Ellen had bought her. It had different kinds of dogs all over it. Lara loved dogs, though she didn't have one right now because her sixteen-year-old corgi had died in the spring.

Just as well. Who would care for it now?

Ellen bought the blanket because she remembered from the last time Lara had chemo that she said she'd been cold all the time. Wearing that crazy cold cap she'd rented, Ellen guessed Lara would be frozen. She had to wear it for an hour before chemo started and then for three hours after she was done. The hospital had a storage freezer to keep the ice packs cold during treatment, but they also had to have ice bags at home.

There were extra socks and a zip-up hoodie in the bag, too. Easy access to the port Lara had put in her chest before she left Pennsylvania. A chemo spigot, she called it.

"Go home. Get to work on that attic." Lara looked over the top of a pair of enormous blue plastic sunglasses. "And I expect to see results."

Ellen groaned. "I'd rather stick hot pokers in my eyes."

"It's only fair, Ellie. I have to have drain cleaner pumped through my veins, you have to suffer, too."

"Or just come inside with you." Poised now to actually have to go into the attic, Ellen would have rather sat in the hospital. Or anywhere else on earth. It wasn't the cleaning that bothered her. She was a hard worker and she loved mindless tasks. She could just pop her earbuds in and listen to a book or a podcast. But going into the attic meant sorting her parents' and grand-parents' possessions.

And her own emotions.

And she would be the first one to admit that she wasn't good at that.

"Nope," Lara said. "Absolutely not. Already told you. I don't need you for the treatments. I need you at home when we get to the barfarama portion of the—"

"*Barfarama?*" Ellen shook her head.

While Ellen didn't actually see an eye roll behind Lara's ri-diculous glasses, she sensed one.

"Stephen King. Hello. His novella *The Body*? Made into the iconic movie *Stand by Me*? Richard Dreyfuss narrates?"

Ellen shrugged.

"And you call yourself a student of literature." Lara exhaled in a great huff, imitating her own mother.

Or possibly Ellen. Lara said Ellen sounded like her, huffing and puffing but never coming out and just saying what she wanted to say.

"Back to the attic," Lara redirected. "You're going home and starting on it. No more excuses, Ellie. You're here; you've got the boxes and the tape, the Bubble Wrap. You've got your little *Where the hell did it go?* notebook to record donations. It's time to put on your big-girl thong—"

"I do not wear a thong!" Ellen tried not to sound indignant, but it came out that way.

And maybe just a little self-righteous.

And prudish.

"I don't know how you walk around all day with that dental floss between your butt cheeks."

"Another thing we're going to have to work on. You want to get a date, you want to get laid, you've got to toss those cotton granny panties."

This had been an ongoing subject of conversation since they arrived in Albany Beach. Lara had it in her head Ellen needed to date. Online. And have sex with some stranger/practical stranger. Just *thinking* about going out on a date gave Ellen hives.

"I don't want to get laid. *You* want me to get laid. And I do not wear granny panties. They're hipsters. One hundred percent cotton." Ellen had gone from indignant to defensive.

No one had a right to criticize a woman's choice of undergarments.

Not even Lara.

Did she?

Lara lifted her perfectly shaped brows above her ridiculous sunglasses. She'd bought them at Burke Brothers, the five-and-dime on the boardwalk, the evening before when they'd gone on a hunt for frozen custard. The variety store had been there since she and Lara were kids and was still run by the same family. The Burkes had a house on the beach over on Mallard, the next street over. Ellen passed it most mornings when she went for her walk. It was one of those big, rambling beach houses that had been there since the turn of the twentieth century, one of the few houses that survived the hurricane in the forties.

Lara was still staring her down.

"I don't wear granny panties," Ellen repeated firmly.

"We're going shopping again next Saturday if I can drag myself away from the toilet and we're getting you some nice, lacy undies and some decent bras."

Ellen touched her chest. "What's wrong with my bras?"

Lara pointed her finger at her. "Are you wearing a sports bra right now? Like you're fourteen? I'll bet you a tub of Thrasher's French fries you're wearing a sports bra right this minute. White," she added as if that were an offense on its own. "All white. Not even so much as a swoosh."

Ellen had put a clean white sports bra on this morning. She liked them. Her breasts were small, she didn't need much in the way of support, and sports bras were more comfortable than conventional bras. What did she care? No one ever saw her in her underwear.

Was that why her husband left her? Because she wore cotton hipster underwear and sports bras?

"You're being ridiculous. I don't need new underwear."

"Aha! You *are* wearing a sports bra. You owe me a tub of Thrasher's." Lara opened the car door. "And I get them when I want them. Not when it's convenient for you. If I want them at eleven on a Friday night, or eight a.m. on a Tuesday, you're buyin', sister by another mister." She cackled with glee as she got out of the car. "I'll call you when I'm ready to go. I imagine it will be four or so. We've got to do the whole intake thing first. Then I've got to wear the stupid cap."

"I am not buying new underwear," Ellen told her, leaning over so she could see Lara standing on the sidewalk. "And I'm not going on any dates."

The car door slammed, and Ellen watched her stride toward the doors, limping slightly because of the cancer. But into the lion's mouth she went, a bounce in her step.

7

Grace slid back in the Adirondack chair until her purple Nikes no longer touched the floor. Taking her time to get situated, she gazed over the porch rail, absorbing the view Lara had described. The account was accurate in the visible details but didn't portray the less tangibles. The way the ocean view made her feel rejuvenated and eager for whatever life had in store for her. One would think that staring out into the Atlantic Ocean would make Grace feel small and insignificant, but this porch miraculously had the opposite effect. The moment she pulled up into the driveway and stared up at the white house, she knew her life had changed forever. However long forever was going to be. And she was waiting on pins and needles to see how.

The porch steps led down to a path that crossed the dunes and joined the wide, sandy white beach. Beyond the sand, she could see the great expanse of the ocean that was the bridge between the homeland she was born to and the one that adopted her as a newlywed.

"You're absolutely right," Grace told her new friend. She reached over and patted Lara's hand. "Breathtaking view. I don't think I've seen a better one, and I've been a lot of places in the world over the years."

"Traveled a lot?" Lara leaned back in her chair.

Grace couldn't see Lara's eyes behind the enormous blue sunglasses, but she could see the young woman's face relax. It had been a hard day for Lara. The first day always was, even if one was a repeat offender, as Lara had called herself when they were introduced that morning. Grace knew that from personal experience and from watching folks come and go at the hospital. Walking into the infusion room for chemo was a death of sorts. But it could also mean a new life.

"I traveled quite a bit when I was younger. My husband was in the air force."

"Career man?" Lara didn't move a muscle.

"Career officer," Grace answered. "A navigator. Can I get you something? A glass of water? A few crackers, maybe?" She touched Lara's hand again. Folks needed physical contact when they were going through chemo. Something else she had learned on her journey. "You're looking a little piqued."

"Headache."

"From the cold cap. To be expected."

"And my chin hurts like a bitch. The strap was as tight as a noose." Lara rubbed the spot under her chin. She'd finally just taken the thing off. "Sorry about the language. That's not going to offend you, is it? Because if it is, you should probably try the porch next door. Their language is cleaner. Though they have terrible taste in dinner music."

Grace chuckled. "I'm not offended. I can throw a swear or two around when it's needed. My husband, Charlie, might have been a fly boy, but I always said he could swear like a sailor."

The screen door to the house opened, and a woman with reddish-brown hair and bright blue eyes walked out onto the porch. She was a pretty woman, mid-forties. Dressed in the uniform of the day for most folks in Albany Beach: shorts, a

T-shirt, and flip-flops. She was cute, though her shorts were long for a woman of her height with such nice, muscular legs.

"Oh, you have a guest. I thought I heard voices. You scared me, Lara. You didn't tell me when you texted that you had a ride home, that your friend was coming in. You're lucky I didn't come down here with a baseball bat."

"Grace, Ellen." Nothing moved but Lara's lips as she introduced them. "Ellen, Grace."

Ellen smiled at Grace, but it was obvious that she had caught her off guard. Grace had asked Lara if she should phone ahead when Grace offered to give her a ride home and Lara invited her to sit on the porch with her. A call seemed appropriate considering this wasn't Lara's home. Lara had said, from behind *People* magazine, that it was unnecessary to call. Any friend of hers was a friend of Ellen's.

The look on Ellen's face suggested otherwise.

"It was so nice of you to drive Lara home," Ellen said to Grace. Then to Lara, "I could have picked you up. I thought that was the plan?"

"Grace offered. I was telling her about the beach house and how beautiful the view was from here. I wanted her to see it."

"Ah." Ellen folded her arms over her chest. "You two met in chemo."

She was using that fake pleasant voice people spoke with when they were uncomfortable but were trying to cover it. Grace didn't get the feeling it was her per se that Ellen took issue with, just the situation. She struck Grace as the type that made a plan and preferred to stick to it. Grace could appreciate that. Following through with a plan was so much more comfortable, easier than taking detours. But it had been her experience that the detours were the best journeys in life.

"Affirmative," Lara said, still unmoving.

Ellen looked at Grace.

Grace knew what she saw: a seventy-five-year-old woman

who looked eighty-five. Thin, sprouts of gray hair shooting out from beneath the scarf tied around her head, shorts and T-shirt too big and baggy on her shrunken frame. Wrinkled face, black-and-blue hands from the IVs. She looked like she was dying. A fair assessment.

"I like your shirt," Ellen said.

Grace quickly gauged that she was one of those people who always thought before they spoke. Not Grace. She didn't have enough time left on this earth to waste it, trying to pick the right word or phrase every time she opened her mouth. She looked down at her T-shirt, not even sure which one she had put on that morning. It had become her thing at the hospital, to wear T-shirts that had a message. Today her red shirt featured a pair of boxing gloves and read *Patriarchy Isn't Going to Fight Itself.* Grace had bought it because she liked the boxing gloves. It reminded her of her father, who had been a boxer when he had been in his early twenties. But now she liked the message, too. It got people talking during their treatments, took them out of their pain, physical and mental. Her shirts often prompted interesting conversations from both sides of the aisle. And the occasional fight. A man named Isaac had gotten into a shouting match with the man getting treatment in the recliner next to him over the Equal Rights Amendment and its purpose. Isaac had thrown a cookie at Vern. Isaac had gotten no freshly baked cookies the next day.

Grace smoothed her wrinkled T-shirt that she'd retrieved from the dryer that morning. "Thank you."

Ellen was still holding the screen door open. "Can I . . . would you like something to drink, Grace? I just made iced tea."

"I'd love some iced tea. So would Lara."

"I don't want any iced tea." Lara was still in the same position in the chair, her head tipped back, the sunglasses covering a good portion of her face.

"She'd love some," Grace answered for her. "Is it sweetened or unsweetened? I do love a good sweet tea."

"Unsweetened. I don't know how to make sweet tea."

"I thought Lara said you were from North Carolina and this was your family's summer house. A southern girl who can't make sweet tea?"

"My mother's family was from here, but I grew up in New Orleans, where my father was from. I went to college in North Carolina, married there, and then just"—she shrugged—"stayed."

"Married?"

A dark storm cloud came across Ellen's face. "Divorced." The word came out pained, and Grace instantly regretted asking. This would have been a topic better discussed after she and Ellen got to know each other better.

Grace smiled. "Unsweetened will be fine. Do you have any of those little yellow packs of sweetener? Not the blue ones. They make your iced tea taste like the inside of a lab beaker."

Ellen looked at Lara. "She needs to stay hydrated," she said softly.

Grace wasn't sure who she was speaking to. Just herself, maybe. Grace talked to herself all the time. It made her son crazy. It made him even crazier when she talked to his dead father. "Just bring her some cold tea. I'll be sure she drinks it."

The screen door had barely closed behind Ellen when Lara said, "What if I didn't want iced tea?"

Grace leaned back and closed her eyes to catch a few rays. "You'll drink it anyway, luv."

8

Ellen pulled the casserole dish out of the oven. The chicken divan smelled amazing, and the bread crumbs were browned perfectly. She'd made the sauce herself, no canned-soup short-cut. She set it on the stove and turned off the oven. "I made rice," she said. "Brown. I hope that's okay."

"It's fine."

Lara was sitting at the counter looking at her phone.

Tim had helped Ellen pick out the granite. She'd been so overwhelmed with all of the kitchen renovation choices that three-quarters of the way through the process she was all out of decisions. At the time, she had thought it was silly of her father to want to renovate the kitchen, even if it was chic 1970s décor. He was an old man. An old, sick man. An old, sick alcoholic.

"Who gives a flying fart how he spends his money?" her brother, Eddie, had said.

Flying fart.

Eddie had a colorful vocabulary. Creative, Ellen would give him that.

"I doubt we'll ever see it," Eddie had said. "I'm laying bets he'll leave his money, the houses, and his royalties to the Audubon Society, that or Freckles." Her father's old beagle.

Eddie was wrong on that. Their father left them everything, neatly divided up so there were no disagreements. The only issue had been Freckles—neither Ellen nor Eddie wanted him. But Freckles resolved the issue on his own. He lived exactly two days after his master departed the earth. Missed him so much, the old dog had just laid down in his expensive plaid dog bed, closed his eyes, and never opened them again. For which Ellen, who wasn't good with dogs, would be eternally thankful. She had no idea what she would have done with the dog, and her brother certainly wouldn't have taken Freckles. His new wife, Chantelle, had allergies. Which extended from dogs to the rest of Eddie's family. Ellen had understood why she hadn't liked their father—no one did—but she never knew what she had done wrong, why Chantelle didn't like her. Why she had never seen her new niece, now seven months old.

While the casserole cooled and thickened, Ellen got a glass of water for each of them: no ice for her, plenty for Lara. "It was nice to meet your friend, um . . ."

"Grace," Lara filled in when Ellen paused, unable to remember her name.

"That's right, Grace. She seems very nice. Very . . . *contemporary* for her age. British, right? I noticed a slight accent."

"Came when she was in her early twenties. Married an air force guy." Lara was texting. Smiling.

Ellen wondered if it was her new boyfriend. The drug rep. Her new squeeze, not boyfriend. Lara had been insistent on that matter, despite the fact that he'd called her every day since they arrived in Albany Beach. And he'd sent her flowers that morning. Two dozen yellow roses. Lara had taken them to her bedroom.

Ellen was glad Lara had the diversion.

She took two plates from the cupboard and set them on

the counter. Tim had always wanted to donate the buttercup dishes. He went so far as to pick out dishes in a store that were white with starfish on them—nautical-themed tableware was appropriate for a beach house, he'd said. But she'd refused to give up the buttercup china. She couldn't. There was something about them that she loved, that she treasured. She didn't even know why. But she'd already decided that when she left the house in September the dishes were going with her. She'd lost so much. She wasn't losing the dishes.

Lara set down her phone.

"Raul?" Ellen asked.

"Yup."

Ellen grabbed forks from a drawer. "You should invite him to come down."

"Nope. You want me to pour you a glass of wine?"

"I can get it myself."

"I think I can manage to pour wine." Lara got off the stool.

Ellen hesitated. She didn't want Lara to exert herself. But then she understood Lara's need to be as normal as possible during her treatment. "I finished off the last bottle. More in the pantry."

Lara was back a minute later, a bottle of Chardonnay in one hand, a bottle of Malbec Lara had brought her from Argentina in the other. "Red or white?"

"Um . . ." She considered having Lara open up the Malbec. She loved Malbec, but she stuck to white because red stained clothes, couches, and teeth. "I'll go with the white. I'm saving the Malbec for a special occasion."

Lara looked at the bottle. "Seriously?" She shifted her gaze to Ellen. "I went to Argentina six years ago."

Ellen turned back to the stove. "You can throw an ice cube in since the wine isn't chilled."

Lara returned the Malbec to the pantry, poured the glass of wine, and set it on the counter near the stove. She leaned over to sniff the casserole. "Smells good."

Ellen retrieved a serving spoon from another drawer and then went to the refrigerator to get the salad she'd made earlier. "You think you can eat a little?"

"Probably not, but I'll have a bite."

"I made the salad you like with the mandarin oranges and pecans." Ellen closed the refrigerator door with her hip. "You want to sit here or on the porch?"

Lara gave a laugh. "Silly question. Porch of course. One of my friends at chemo, Amara, says this sounds like a place of healing."

Ellen cut her eyes at Lara. "*Healing?* What did she mean?"

"I don't know." Lara shrugged. "Some mystical bullshit." She picked up a plate and put a tablespoon of chicken divan casserole on it. She added a spoonful only slightly bigger of the salad.

Ellen picked up her plate. "So chemo went okay today?"

"Yup."

"And . . ." Ellen scooped casserole onto her plate, covering one of the bright yellow buttercups. "The new oncologist give you any . . . instructions? Things you should be doing? Resting . . . not having too much company?" she added.

Lara narrowed her gaze. "Are you fu—" She caught herself. She knew Ellen didn't like her using that word. "Are you talking about Grace?"

"I just didn't know if . . . you should be . . ." Ellen hesitated. "Resting. Having people over can be tiring."

Lara set her plate down with a clatter. "Ellie, you just said you wanted me to invite Raul here. How would that be different than having Grace, or anyone else I meet at chemo?"

Ellen realized she'd errored in starting this conversation. Maybe made a mistake in even thinking it. But it was too late. She was already hip-deep. "I don't know." She pushed her own plate onto the counter beside Lara's. "I just don't know that you should be having other sick people over."

"No? What else shouldn't I be doing, Mom?"

"You shouldn't be using artificial sweeteners," Ellen blurted. "And Grace shouldn't be, either."

"And why's that?" Lara asked. Deadpan.

"Because it causes cancer."

Lara got a funny look on her face and then started to laugh. A big belly laugh.

Realizing how ridiculous what she had just said was, Ellen laughed, too. And wrapped her arms around her best friend in the world and hugged her tight.

9

Ellen stood at the kitchen sink looking out the window onto the porch, trying not to eavesdrop. But she couldn't help herself. She was fascinated by the conversations that took place regularly on her porch now. It certainly wasn't what she had expected in a cancer support group when Lara had announced (not asked) she was sponsoring one. There on Ellen's porch.

She had anticipated Lara and her friends would talk about their illnesses and treatment and how they were feeling about it all. Instead, they seemed to chat about everything but that. In the last two days, Ellen had heard conversations about the cases before the Supreme Court, everyone's all-time favorite chocolate bar, and the possibility of life in other solar systems. She heard lengthy discussions on a nurse's bad toupee, a nearly extinct animal called a Vancouver Island marmot, and an argument about professional football quarterbacks' pay. Lara and her friends talked about where in the world the best sunsets could be seen, the worst cold cereals and their favorite movies directed by James Cameron. They seemed to talk about everything *but* the elephant in the room. Their cancer.

They seemed so . . . happy. And Ellen was a little jealous.

Which turned immediately into guilt. How could she be jealous of people with cancer?

What was wrong with her?

Each day they came, they invited her to join them, but the guilt that wracked her kept her from doing so. Or at least enjoying herself when she was among them. She just didn't know how to balance out the juxtaposition of their dire situations and the positive outlooks on life these people had.

Ellen needed to get moving, anyway. She didn't have time to chat with strangers. She needed to finish what she was doing in the kitchen and grade some papers submitted online by her students. She was supposed to be loading the lunch dishes into the dishwasher, but she was just standing there, letting the water run, listening. She'd served chicken salad finger sandwiches to Lara and her guests.

When Ellen pulled up in front of the hospital that afternoon to pick up Lara, Grace had been with her. She'd had a fender bender and her car was in the shop. An elderly African-American gentleman had gotten into the car with the women.

"Pine, our Uber driver, Ellen," Lara had introduced as she lowered herself into the front passenger's seat of the car. "Ellen, this is Pine."

Ellen had adjusted the rearview mirror to get a look at her latest fare. Since Grace's accident the previous week, she'd been dropping Lara off and picking her and her cohort up each day. Pine was new. He was small and thin and wearing a T-shirt emblazoned with an American flag. He wore a pair of large, dark wraparound sunglasses. Not the cool kind you saw teenagers wearing, the kind your optometrist gave you to wear home after an eye exam.

"Ma'am." Pine nodded and then searched for his seat belt.

Lara had sat back in her seat and put down her window. She seemed to be in a constant state of nausea. Then she grabbed her blanket and pulled it over her. She was also cold, but usually just when she was still wearing her ice cap. Instead of remaining at the hospital for the three hours after her treatment, she was wearing it home each day. They changed out the ice packs when they got to the house. Ellen had already taken the ones they kept in the freezer and placed them in a cooler with dry ice.

Ellen had handed Lara her sunglasses that she'd left on the seat of the car. The first time she had seen Lara in the blue ice cap that looked something like the protective headgear wrestlers wore, it had upset her. It was just part of their life right now. The cap, so far, was working. Lara's hair was as beautiful and thick as always.

"Nice to meet you, Pine." Ellen smiled at him and readjusted the rearview mirror. "Anyone else coming?" she asked Lara.

"Amara will be by after a while. Her niece is dropping her off. You'll like her. And Alex might stop by if she can sneak out."

Ellen had looked at Lara. She'd meant the comment sarcastically. How many elderly cancer patients did Lara think she could have on the porch at one time? "Sneak out?" she asked, not liking the sound of that one bit. Was Alex sneaking out of an old folks' home? She'd read about senior citizens doing that.

But Lara had given no further explanation. She just lifted her hand, gesturing forward. "Home, James."

So Ellen had driven Lara and her friends home. Fed them lunch and cleared their plates. Once the dishes were done, she thought, turning off the faucet, she'd go up to the attic and drag a couple of boxes down to the living room to sort. It was getting too hot in the attic to work anytime but first thing in the morning.

Ellen added two more plates to the dishwasher and closed it as she listened to the sound of Pine's voice. It was a deep, thunderous voice for a man of small stature. And he was always laughing. And telling jokes.

"Knock, knock, Ellen," Pine had said as she pulled out of the parking lot and onto the street.

Caught off guard, Ellen had said, "Who's there?"

"Cows go," he'd answered.

"Cows go who?" she had asked, playing along.

"No, silly, cows go moo." Pine had slapped the seat, cackling with pleasure. "Get it? Moo, not who?"

Grace had laughed with him and gazed out the window. "I just love knock-knock jokes. It's such an American thing."

Pine was talking about his wife outside on the porch now, his voice drifting in through the screen.

"Best thing that could have happened to me after I came back," he was saying. "My first wife, Loretta, was the daughter of a preacher man. Met her in Mobile, 1969. Just come back from the war and I was messed up in the head," he was saying. "But she set me right. We married three months to the day after we met."

"Ah, true love." Grace sounded like a dreamy schoolgirl. "It was the same for us. Barrett's father and I met in a pub. He was stationed at RAF Upper Heyford near Oxford. I went home to his flat with him that night."

"No, you did not," Lara said with a laugh. "You little hussy. What year was that?" After a little nap in her chair, she seemed to be feeling pretty decent today. It felt good to see her more like herself than she had been the last few days. She looked more like herself now with the cold cap replaced by a ball cap.

"Same year Pine met his wife, 1969. He had to return to the United States three months later and he asked me to marry him. My parents forbade me. Said they'd disown me if I ran off with a bloody American."

"And you did it anyway," Lara said.

Pine cackled with glee. "Good for you, Grace."

"So did they?" Lara asked.

Grace glanced in her direction. "Did they what?"

"Did your parents disown you?"

"They did, but only until we had Sophie. I showed up at the door when she was nine months old and they let me in. They pretended nothing had happened between us."

"Wait, so you have a daughter, too?" Lara asked. "For some reason, I thought Barrett was your only child."

"Sophie was our first." Grace's voice changed. "She died when she was twelve. Epileptic seizure."

"Oh, Grace. I'm sorry."

Ellen watched Lara reach between their chairs and take the older woman's hand. "I didn't mean to pry," Lara said. "And I didn't mean to make you sad."

"No, no, it's okay. It was so long ago that sometimes it seems like a dream. Talking about her feels good. What kind of mother would I be if I didn't keep her memory alive?"

Lara squeezed Grace's hand again before letting go. "I cannot imagine losing a child. You'd have had to carry me off to the loony bin."

"Not when you have another child, sweet. When you have another child, you can't let yourself fall apart. Sophie was gone, but I still had Barrett. Barrett deserved my attention, my love. That he survived and Sophie didn't wasn't his fault. He was just a baby."

Ellen was surprised by the tears that welled in her eyes. She didn't consider herself an emotional person. She had never cried watching a commercial, nor had she gotten teary when her only child had headed off to kindergarten or moved out of the house after graduation. She had barely cried the night Tim told her he wanted a divorce. But here she was crying, listening to a woman she didn't know talk about a child who had died decades years ago.

Ellen wiped her eyes with the kitchen towel she'd dried her hands on. So maybe she was human, after all. That was something Tim had said once, in the first days after he had announced he wanted a divorce. When they were discussing finances, who would buy out the house from whom, who would make which car payment and such.

He had called her cold, inhuman. A robot. And it had hurt. It still did. She wondered if he said things like that to his girlfriend.

Ellen hung her head. Lara was right. It wasn't healthy to be dwelling on what had been said, done. It was over. In the past. Tim had found another woman. And he was happy. She saw that on every social media post. He was so happy! The overuse of exclamations in his posts was proof of that.

Lara said she needed to unfriend him. Continuing to be a part of his life, even online, was keeping her from moving on with her life. Growing. Ellen saw her point, but . . . she hadn't been able to do it. She *couldn't* let go. He was the father of their son. She had known him since she was nineteen. He—

The doorbell rang, and Ellen stiffened. She took a deep breath and headed for the foyer. If it was Rick, the UPS guy, she was ready for him. She was dressed, makeup on. And she was liking the haircut she'd gotten; her hair was still long enough to pull back in a ponytail, but it looked smoother and healthier. To make her feel good. Now if she could only be bold enough to dye it red, the color it had once been . . .

Rick's family had lived in Albany Beach area for more than a hundred years. His grandfather had been a milkman there during the war. Rick had lived down the street his whole life and Ellen had known him since they were kids. They'd played together every summer until they were too old for playing and then they had moved in the same summer crowd. She'd had a crush on him all through high school and had made out with him at a party just before she began her freshman year of undergrad. After that, they lost touch, married, had children . . .

Divorced.

The word still stuck in her throat when she was forced to

say it. Think it. She was divorced, something that happened to other people, but not her.

But it *had* happened to her.

Rick was still good-looking, still not the brightest bunny in the hutch, and still a fun guy. Also divorced for the *third* time, he'd told her when asking about her marital status the other day. If she hadn't known better, she would have thought he was flirting with her while delivering a box with six bottles of nail polish and a silk pillowcase for Lara.

She opened the door, smiling for Rick.

It wasn't Rick.

A slender teenage girl stood at the door. She was wearing a pair of large cat-eye sunglasses, bits of inky black hair poking out from under a pink fedora. In each hand she carried a small cardboard box from the local bakery of donut holes.

"Hi," the teenager said, her voice deeper than Ellen had expected from such a wisp of a girl. "I'm Lara's friend, Alex. She's expecting me?" Her voice went up at the end of the sentence as if she wasn't quite sure if Lara really was expecting her.

Alex.

Someone had mentioned her in the car. Alex was who was hoping to come by if she could sneak out. Ellen had imagined an elderly gentleman trying to slip out of his assisted-living facility. It made a lot more sense that *this* Alex would be trying to sneak out. Though Ellen couldn't tell for sure how old she was, she was pretty sure she wasn't eighteen. Ellen's rapid powers of deduction also told her that this teenager was being treated for cancer at the hospital. That was the commonality of all the folks sitting on her porch right now.

So now she was harboring runaway teenagers with cancer?

"I brought donuts." Alex held up the boxes. Despite the fact that it was in the mid-eighties outside, she was wearing white jeans. And a Hawaiian-style shirt in hot pinks and purples and greens that looked too big for her. In her ears, beneath the brim of the pink hat, were earrings that looked like plastic bananas.

Ellen opened the door farther. "Come on in. She's on the back porch." She watched the teen walk by, platform flip-flops snapping as she walked. Her toenails were painted a bright, creamy Pepto-Bismol pink.

Ellen walked behind Alex. She wore a pink Hello Kitty backpack.

"This way?" Alex asked.

"Right through there." Ellen pointed. "Through the kitchen."

Alex used her hip to open the screen door and walked onto the porch.

"Alex!" Pine exclaimed, sounding as if he had just won a million dollars. "You made it!"

"Alex, darling," Grace said.

"Alex!" Amara, whom Ellen had just met, greeted. "We were waiting for you."

Amara wasn't much bigger than Grace and was equally thin. She was wearing baggy, knee-length purple shorts and a bright flowered tank top with a yellow silk scarf on her head.

Lara got out of her chair and wrapped her arms around the teenager, who had just arrived, in a big hug. "I guess this means you managed to escape?"

"Nina Flowers saw me go out the back door, but she pretended she didn't. I think she's ready to see me check out. I get in the way of her watching her afternoon telenovelas." She held up the boxes in her hands. "Look, I brought donuts. Well, donut holes because I know none of you are going to eat a whole donut."

Lara took a box from her hand. "I'm not eating a donut hole. I'll just puke it up."

"Maybe not." Alex handed her the other box. "But even if you do, it will taste good going down, won't it?" She slung her pink backpack off her shoulders. "Or you could lick off the sugar. That's what I used to do."

Lara put the boxes on a teak table between her and Pine.

Pine opened the box and peered in. "I don't know if I can, but they sure look good. Are those chocolate rolled with coconut?"

"Mimi Imfurst saved a dozen of them for me. She's the lady at the bakery. I told her how much you like them."

Ellen knew everyone who worked at Leeder's Bakery. She didn't recall anyone named Mimi. Someone new, maybe.

"Well, in that case, I'm having one." Pine took one from the box. "I don't care if I do puke it back up."

"There's Boston cream, too, Lara." Alex took one from the box and waggled it in front of her. She was almost as tall as Lara. "Just for you," she sang.

Lara stared at the donut hole, then, to Ellen's surprise, took it from the teen's fingers. "Thanks, Alex. You're the best."

"Amara?" Alex asked, taking the box over to Amara.

Amara, Ellen had learned, had been born in India and had been a pediatric nurse in a Boston hospital for thirty-five years. She'd been married a very short time and her husband had died. She never married again. After she retired, she became a volunteer, sitting with children at night, reading to them. She had dedicated her entire life to sick children before she'd had to give it up when she'd been diagnosed with pancreatic cancer. Unable to continue to care for herself, she'd moved to Albany Beach to live with her great-niece.

"Just a bite, sweetie." Amara took a powdered donut hole from the box.

"Grace?" Alex said.

"Love the glasses." Grace scooted forward slowly in her chair.

"Amazon," Alex said. "I got a purple pair with tassels, too. They're arriving tomorrow."

Grace took a donut hole in each hand and popped one in her mouth. "Wait, one more," she said, her mouth full of donut as she grabbed another. "Your parents don't mind you ordering things?"

Alex frowned. "I've told you this before. I'm their only child, Grace. Dying of a brain tumor. My parents are attorneys with more money than sense." She smiled a lopsided grin. "You think they're going to deny me some cheap plastic sunglasses?"

Grace narrowed her gaze. "You shouldn't be manipulating them that way, Alex."

The teenager grinned. "I know."

10

The second time Ellen found the old woman in her kitchen, she wasn't quite so startled. Obviously, she couldn't allow it to continue, but she was hesitant to involve the police.

Ellen walked toward the stove where the coffee was percolating, unable to resist the heavenly scent. There was something about the rhythmic *blup, blup* of the coffeepot that was ... soothing.

The woman was wearing a different flowered housecoat. This time her thin hair was in pink foam rollers. She was barefoot again.

"What are you doing here?" Ellen asked.

"Making coffee."

Realizing there were unused burners on, again, Ellen walked over and turned them off. They were lucky she hadn't started a fire. "Where did you find that coffeepot?" Ellen had hidden it in the pantry just in case the woman found her way into the house again.

"Pantry. Behind boxes." The woman took two mugs from the cupboard.

Ellen watched her pour the coffee. "How did you get inside? The doors were locked."

"Get inside? I just got up." She eyed Ellen, suspiciously. "You're not Doris."

"No."

"What's your name, dear?"

"I'm Ellen." She set her cell on the counter. She almost said, "And *I* live here. I own this house." But she didn't. Instead, she accepted the cup of coffee. "What's your name?"

The woman smiled. "Lenora." She poured herself a cup. "It's nice to have you here, Ellen. Would you like to join me on the porch? It's pretty this time of morning before the sunbathers flock to the beach."

Ellen stepped back to let her pass.

Lenora led the way onto the porch, this time having to unlock the door.

What if Lenora really had slept in the house? But where? There were just four bedrooms upstairs. Surely Ellen or Lara would have heard an intruder.

Lenora crossed the porch, her cup in hand, and went to the rail. "The paint is peeling," she remarked. "You should scrape it and paint it. She's a good house. You need to take care of her." She spoke as if the beach cottage were a living, breathing thing.

"I . . . I know. I just haven't had time." Ellen hesitantly took a sip of the coffee. It was hot and strong and delicious, just like before. "I've been cleaning out the attic. And my friend Lara is sick and—" She stopped herself. Why did she feel as if she needed to make excuses for herself? To a stranger? To an *interloper*?

"A wire brush, a little paint, and she'll be beautiful again." Lenora leaned forward on the rail and breathed deeply, closing her eyes.

The look of contentment on Lenora's face made Ellen smile. The older woman obviously loved the beach. The house, too. Watching her at the porch rail, Lenora seemed like she belonged there. There seemed to be some sort of symbiotic relationship between her and the house. Ellen wasn't very spiritual. She didn't usually think of things that way, but at the moment, it seemed to be an accurate assessment.

Lenora turned to Ellen. "Please. Sit down. A cup of coffee is better when you're sitting than when you're standing. My daddy always said that. When coffee was rationed during the war, he only had a cup a day. No matter how busy the store was, he always sat for his morning coffee."

Ellen remained standing and studied Lenora. She had to live nearby, maybe on the next street over. Ellen didn't know everyone in the neighborhood. There were always houses being bought and sold now. And then some were rented out.

Lenora looked so feeble. How far could she have walked to get there? And in a housecoat, bare feet and rollers. Surely someone would have seen her wandering. Was someone looking for her again? Ellen wanted to ask Lenora where she lived again but had the feeling the response wouldn't be helpful.

"Going to be another warm day," Lenora remarked, taking a seat. "What are your plans? Going for a walk? Will you sit on the beach?"

"Oh, I don't have time for that. I've got a lot to do. I have to take my friend to the hospital every day for chemotherapy. And I've been cleaning out the attic. There's decades of stuff up there."

"You don't have time to take a walk on the beach? Fiddlesticks! You ought to be ashamed of yourself."

Against her will, Ellen found herself intrigued by Lenora. For a woman her age, she seemed so happy. It had been Ellen's experience that the older people got, the grumpier they got, and usually with good cause. Aging was no picnic. How could Lenora be happy? She obviously had memory loss, confusion. Wasn't it scary not to know where you lived, who people were? But looking at her, now perched on the chair, her toes barely touching the porch floor, she didn't appear to be a person suffering.

"A gift like this?" She motioned over the rail, in the direction of the beach and the ocean that stretched out, as far as the eye could see, beyond. "It must be appreciated. Every day. And swallowed up and absorbed into your being." She made a fist with her tiny hand. "You must take it in greedily."

Ellen took another sip of coffee. "Do you walk on the beach?"

"Every day," the older woman answered. "Sometimes in the morning. Sometimes after supper."

"Does . . . someone go with you? Your . . . husband, maybe?"

"Lester?" Her face lit up like a schoolgirl's with her first crush. "Oh, Lester and I love to take romantic walks on the beach at sunset. You know how we met, don't you?" Lenora leaned forward. "We were star-crossed lovers. The Montagues and the Capulets had nothing over our families."

"Granny?" came a child's voice from somewhere outside. The same voice Ellen had heard the last time Lenora had been there.

"Granny! Where are you? Mom says we're having pancakes for breakfast! With chocolate chips . . ." The last bit was said in a way that made it obvious it was a ploy to draw Lenora out.

Ellen met Lenora's gaze. A part of her wanted to ignore the child. She imagined if they were quiet, he or she would walk right by the house, not seeing them on the second-floor porch.

"Oh, darn it," Lenora muttered. "That's Brayden." She took a last sip of coffee as she stood. "Who names a boy *Brayden*? He's going to be teased his whole life. My great-grandson," she explained. "They should have named him Lester. Now's there's a good name." She set down her coffee mug. "I best go."

Ellen moved away from the steps to let her pass. "Where do you live again?"

At the top of the stairs, Lenora turned to look at Ellen as if she had just said the silliest thing. "Why, I live here, of course."

11

Eyes closed, Grace lifted her chin and took in the delicious heat of the sun that warmed her fragile bones. She breathed deeply, taking in the salty ocean that had a hint of Thrasher's French fries on the finish. In her mind's eye, she saw the edge of the worn porch rail and the creaky steps that led down to the sand and over the dune to the ocean's edge. The tide was coming in, bringing with it white foam and the afternoon's tourist debris. She remembered the sort of things she saw when she was still able to walk the beach at sunrise. She imagined a paper cup, a gum wrapper, a cap from a suntan lotion bottle, washing in, then drifting out with the pulsing tide. With her eyes closed, she could see past the porch rail that needed painting to the line of the horizon and beyond. She envisioned London and the pub outside the gates of the British Museum where she'd first met her Charlie. She remembered his tweed sweater, his sharp military haircut, his beautiful mouth—

"Ninety-one degrees," Pine announced loudly. "Going to be ninety-one today. That's what the weatherman said this morning. Weather *lady*. Alexa. I just say, 'Alexa, what's the forecast today?' and she tells me."

Grace opened her eyes and adjusted the red plaid blanket on her lap. Just then, the wind picked up and blew sand in her face. She closed her eyes, blinked, and rubbed the right one. "Bloody hell!" she muttered, glancing down, running her hand over the blanket. "Anyone seen my eyelashes?"

"Oh, dear, lost them again?" Amara rose so slowly from her chair that Grace felt guilty for saying anything. She had an extra pair in her bag. Two pairs for ten bucks at the drugstore if she used her military discount. "Don't bother, darling." She looked at Amara, who was at least ten years younger than she was and moved like she was fifteen years older.

"Not a bother." Amara had the sweetest voice. Just what one would think a nurse should sound like. Grace could imagine being a frightened, sick child being greeted by that voice. A voice that probably healed as well as any drugs or surgery. But it was also a voice that easily took command of any situation. Silk and steel, that's what her mother said a woman had to be made of, and Amara sure fit the bill.

"I don't know why you wear the damned things," Pine groused good-naturedly.

"Because I'm ugly without eyelashes," Grace snapped. Then she felt guilty. It was a mean thing to say. None of them had eyelashes. And in her mind, they were all beautiful.

Amara felt around on Grace's blanket for the errant false eyelashes. "I don't see them." She put her hand on Grace's bony knee and slowly lowered herself to the porch floor. Also in need of paint.

"Amara, stop fussing. It's fine. I have more."

"Maybe they're down here."

When Amara lowered her head, Grace adjusted her friend's bright magenta head scarf. It was Tuesday. Tuesday was magenta. Grace's favorite was the peacock-blue one with the paisley print. Fridays. Sent from India by one of Amara's aunties. Grace didn't know if she was actually an aunt or not. Amara called all of her female relations in her native country Auntie.

"Oh, for the love of Pete, Amara." Grace clasped her friend's shoulder. "Get up off the floor before you hurt yourself. We'll have to call the paramedics if you fall."

Amara slowly, what looked to be painfully, came to her feet. "Sorry. Don't see them." Squinting, she peered into Grace's face. "You sure you lost one?"

"Of course I'm sure." She closed her eyes and touched the left side of her face. "Demi wisps here." She touched the right. "Nada here. Naked as a newborn."

"Newborns are born with eyelashes."

Grace cut her eyes at Pine. "You're in a mood today."

He laughed. "Just telling you the way things are. You're beautiful to us, with or without eyelashes."

"It's fine, Amara." Grace patted Amara's hand as she slowly lowered herself into her chair.

The screen door squeaked, and Grace looked up to see Alex carrying a tray of glasses of iced tea. She was wearing fake eyelashes, too. Alex had gone with Grace to the drugstore to buy them. That was where Grace had gotten the idea to begin with. From Alex. Alex had worn them even BC. *Before Cancer.* Alex wore a different pair every day, and they never *ever* looked natural. Grace had had no idea there were so many styles of fake eyelashes. Today Alex was wearing ones with little rhinestones along the eyelids. Grace adored them.

Almost as much as she adored the fifteen-year-old.

But Grace had demurred and gone with the more natural-looking demi wisps.

"Tea is served," Alex announced with great aplomb. She was carrying a tea towel with a sand castle on it draped over her skinny forearm like a waiter.

Grace reached for the glass offered and scowled. "We're going to work on your British accent, luv."

12

Ellen stood in the pantry, hands on her hips, looking at her handiwork. She'd always done a superficial cleaning whenever she came and went, but today she'd done some rearranging on the shelves where food was stored. She made sure anything that would be appealing to mice was sealed in quart-sized Ball jars her mother had always kept for that purpose. She rearranged items used frequently, keeping the baking goods in one place, canned fruits and vegetables in another. But like the attic, there was plenty of junk that had been there for decades.

She wasn't surprised that Lenora had found an old percolator. Considering the things squirreled away in there, she wouldn't have been surprised if Lenora had found a Volkswagen Beetle in there. There might still be one, but the pantry wasn't a one-day project.

The room was a reflection of the time period the house had been built. It was eight by ten feet with floor-to-ceiling wooden shelves painted a pretty green. On one side of the pantry, mostly at eye level, the cans and jars of food were stored. Then there was a section of things like trash bags, aluminum foil and plastic wrap, and such. Toward the back was where all the cleaning supplies were kept. But on the opposite side of the pantry, the deep shelves were lined with cardboard boxes that looked like they were older than Ellen. And lots of big cans with lids that featured advertisements for potato chips. They had been there as long as she could remember. In the back corner, near the only window in the pantry, aprons hung from a hook. They needed to be gone through, too. Tossed out probably, but she'd save that for another day.

"Ellie?" Lara called. "Where are you?"

"Pantry!" Ellen called, looking at several rings of keys in her hand. She had no idea what some of them went to and she'd have to try them one by one in the house's main doors. A project that would also need to be done another day.

Lara stuck her head through the doorway.

"I thought you'd gone to bed." Ellen hung the keys back on their hook. "You okay?"

"Fine. I fell asleep, but then I woke up and now I can't go back to sleep. I'm going for a walk on the beach." She walked back into the kitchen. "Come on."

Ellen picked up a trash bag of stuff that wasn't worth keeping or donating. "I have a choice?" she asked, knowing very well what the answer would be.

"Nope." Lara opened the door to the porch.

Ellen flipped off the pantry light and followed with the bag of trash. She left her flip-flops on the porch. At the bottom of the steps, she deposited the bag in the dumpster she kept outside the laundry room. She found Lara waiting for her on the path that went over the dunes.

It was after nine o'clock, and the sky was dark. Ellen could hear the waves crashing on the beach. "You sure you want to walk? You seemed really tired today."

Lara slowed, waiting for her to catch up. "In another week I won't have the energy to walk all the way down to the water. So I better go now."

Ellen tried to think of something that would make Lara feel

better. "Cheer up. If you get so you can't walk, I'll rent one of those wheelchairs with the big wheels and roll you out."

Lara laughed. "Over my dead body."

Ellen laughed with her, glad to see that Lara still had her sense of humor. Of course, she'd expected nothing less. Lara was an amazing woman with strength beyond her own comprehension. She chose a path and then threw herself headlong onto it. Nothing deterred her. When she'd decided she wanted children, but not a husband, not even a baby daddy, Ellen had been afraid for her. How would she care for a child alone? Raising her son had been the hardest thing she had ever done, and she'd had Tim to do it with her. And even though he hadn't been the husband she had hoped he would be, he'd always been an amazing father.

Unsurprisingly, Lara had launched herself into motherhood at top speed with no brakes. And succeeded in ways Ellen never had been able to. Lara was a friend and a mother to her two adult children now. Lara adopted her daughter Vera as a baby, and a year later, when her social worker called to say that Vera had a newborn half sister being put up for adoption, Lara hadn't hesitated. She'd called Ellen that night on the way to the store to buy newborn diapers. And had never looked back.

Lara was what people call a fighter. And she was so darned stubborn that it seemed to Ellen that she made things work out by sheer determination.

That's how she would get through this chemo. Ellen was sure of it.

"How's Vera?" Ellen asked, changing the subject. Vera had called after dinner when Ellen was cleaning up the meal Lara hadn't eaten.

"Great. Looks like she'll be in Paris at least another two weeks working, and then she's thinking about taking another two weeks off to see the sights."

They had crossed the dunes and were walking through the soft sand. Ellen slowed. She could tell that Lara was getting winded, but she knew her well enough to know she wouldn't admit it. At least not yet. They had been through this together before. And Ellen knew that Lara's acceptance of her limitations, while she was being treated, would come. But not yet.

Was it a form of denial? Maybe. But Ellen would give her that, at least, for now.

"She's okay not being here with you?" Ellen went on.

"No. But I threatened filicide if she came home early. I told Chastity the same thing."

Ellen smiled, a lump in her throat. Lara's mothering style could be a little heavy-handed, but it worked for her. And it obviously had worked for her daughters because they adored her. "Think about if you were in their place, wouldn't you want to come home?"

"Ellie, I can't do this in front of them again," Lara answered in a small voice.

Ellen heard her sniffle in the darkness.

"I told Vera I had you to take care of me." Lara reached out and took Ellen's hand. "And that what she could do for me, what she and her sister could do for me, was live their lives."

They walked hand in hand until their feet hit smooth, wet sand and the waves were so loud that Ellen had to raise her voice to speak. "I get it. I just don't want you to be too hard on them."

Lara squeezed her hand and let go.

Nothing else needed to be said. And for once, Ellen was content with that.

They turned and headed south along the shore, the town to their backs, the water lapping at their bare feet. There were a few people on the beach, but they were far enough away that it felt as if Ellen and Lara had the whole place to themselves.

As they walked, Lara looked to their right at the houses and condos they passed as they got farther from the center of town. "Ever wonder what's going on up there?" she asked.

Ellen gazed at the lights twinkling in the windows. An ordinance kept the condos from being higher than three floors, which gave Albany Beach the feel of yesteryear. Voices floated off the balconies. Someone was playing the Beatles, and she heard laughter. A party. "I don't know. Sometimes, I guess." She looked at Lara. "What do you imagine?"

Lara studied the condo they were passing. "See that one single light—in the white stucco building?"

"Yup."

"That's Leopold and Gertrude's place."

Ellen giggled at the names.

"They've gone to bed. She's reading a British spy novel. He's reading golf magazines. He hates coming to the beach, but she loves it. So they stay in their condo every other week. He plays golf at the public course across the highway and wishes he was home at the country club. She sits on the beach all day in a bathing suit with a skirt, under an umbrella." Lara held up one finger. "And imagines how much better life will be when he kicks the bucket. She's going to move here full-time and get two cats."

Ellen groaned. "That's terrible."

"Wait, wait. There's more. Gertrude is waiting for Leopold to die so she can be with his younger brother, who she's always loved. You see, his brother Albert never married, and still holds out hope that he and Gertie can be together someday."

"Albert and Leopold?" Ellen laughed. "Have you been watching *Victoria* again?"

Lara looked at her. The moon hadn't risen yet, but there was enough ambient light that Ellen could see the mischievous look on her face. "Maybe I have. I love that show! Albert and Leopold are good names!"

"Good point." Ellen indicated the next building, where there were a bunch of young men on the balcony playing music. She could practically hear the beers being chugged. "How about that one?"

Lara spun a wild, fanciful tale of a couple of friends who had just been released from a Mexican jail by their wealthy parents. By the time she had finished, she and Ellen had turned around and were walking back to the house.

They talked as they made their way back. Not about anything important. Ellen told Lara about the student taking her online English course who was going to be a problem. She'd already gotten an email from her boss saying he'd had a complaint from the student's mother.

Lara told her about a hot oncologist she'd met at the hospital and her plans to *shtup* him. Just as soon as her eyebrows and her pubes grew back.

They arrived in front of the house a short time later and stopped so Lara could catch her breath before they had to cross the soft sand again. As Lara breathed hard, Ellen watched the blue-green fish wind sock with its sequin belly whip in the wind on the flagpole jutting from one of the porch's support beams. She'd bought it two summers before after she'd walked past the house twice before she was able to find it. From the shore, all of the homes looked alike in the dark.

"Ready to go up?" Ellen turned back to Lara.

To see her stepping out of her shorts.

Her panties came next.

"What are you—"

Lara dropped her T-shirt in the sand. She wasn't wearing a bra. "What does it look like I'm doing?"

Ellen glanced around, panic in her chest. "Someone will see you."

Lara shrugged and started for the water. "Probably not." She looked one way and then the other. "There's no one out tonight."

"That guy." Ellen pointed north.

"He's walking away. Come on. Let's go skinny-dipping."

"I am *not* going skinny-dipping. And you shouldn't, either. Lara, you're weak. You know how rough this water is. You'll drown."

Lara stood there naked. "Then you better come in and swim with me. Keep me from drowning."

Ellen looked up and down the beach. "You're going to get arrested. And I'm not bailing you out if you do."

"No, I'm not, but yes, you will. You won't let me miss chemo tomorrow." Lara looked at her. "Come on. You told me you want to be more daring."

"I don't remember saying that."

"But you want to. I know you do." Lara walked toward the water.

Ellen stood there for a moment. She hadn't been skinny-dipping since she was twelve, when she and Lara had gone swimming in a friend's pool at night at a slumber party. She still remembered how naughty it had felt.

And freeing.

"If I drown, it will be your fault," Lara threw over her shoulder.

Ellen hesitated, then grabbed the hem of her T-shirt and pulled it off. She added it to Lara's pile of clothing up on the dry sand.

Lara whooped as the cold water hit her, and she turned and watched Ellen. "Take it off, baby!"

Ellen shimmied out of her gym shorts.

A moment later, she was in the water, splashing past Lara. The water felt warmer than it did during the day because the air temperature was cooler. But it still felt cold. White water rose and rushed toward them.

"Wave!" Ellen shouted as she took a breath and dove. She heard Lara squeal just as she went under.

When Ellen popped up, she was relieved to see Lara only a few feet away. Her wet blond hair shimmered in the darkness. She was fine.

"You're cheating!" Lara accused, paddling toward her. "You're in your underwear!"

"Five minutes," Ellen warned. "Ten max, and then we're going up to the house."

"That's not skinny-dipping!" Lara complained, treading water beside her.

Ellen used her hand to squirt water in Lara's face the way they had done when they were kids.

"But it's a start," Lara said, obviously pleased, despite her protest. "And I'll take it."

"Incoming!" Ellen shouted as another wave rose in the darkness, the white surf barreling down on them. As she went down, she felt a little shot of adrenaline go through her.

She was swimming in her underwear in the ocean. In public!

So maybe Lara was right.

Maybe she could change.

Maybe she wanted to.

13

Amara gazed over the porch rail and breathed in deeply, letting the salty air fill her nostrils, then her lungs, and finally her soul. From this spot on the porch, she could see a patch of the ocean between the blades of sea grass that had been planted to prevent erosion. She concentrated on the motion of the waves, and her thoughts drifted.

She would never tell anyone, but sometimes when she got contemplative like this, she thought about walking out into the water. She thought of it often these days, especially at night when she lay in bed beside her great-niece. She thought about walking beyond the surf's frothy waves until she was waist-deep, then shoulder-deep in salt water. She would enjoy the feel of the hot sun on her face and the cold water on her skin. She might swim a little until she was out beyond the breakers. Then she would let herself go. She'd float for a while like the pieces of fast-food trash she often saw go by, and then just . . . sink. It would save those who cared for her the pain of seeing her shrivel away into nothingness. Save herself the pain. And then she would know at last the answer to man's greatest question.

Was this it or was there more?

Amara didn't know what she believed about the afterlife. Was there one? And if so, what? Where? When she was younger and full of answers, when she had read to children and rocked those babies from the NICU in her arms all night long, she had been so sure there had to be more. But now as her time grew shorter, she wasn't sure. Her brain and her heart were too conflicted between her husband's Christian beliefs of heaven and hell and the Hindu dogma she grew up believing in: samsara. Rebirth here on earth. What if they were both true? What if Christians went to their heaven and Hindus were reborn? Where did that leave people like her who believed in both? Or neither? What it came down to was that she wanted to be with Casper after she died. If that was his heaven, she was fine with that. But if she was going to be reborn on earth, she wanted it to be here on this beach. Because this was where she felt closest to Casper and to herself.

Amara felt most at home when she could see the ocean. Being invited by Lara to join the others on her porch had changed her life. The view from this chair was so picturesque, it was beyond description. And she hadn't had to drag her sorry self across the great expanse of the shore to see it. Lara's open invitation made Amara happy to be still alive, happy that just when she thought life had nothing new in store for her, another door had opened. In this case, the door to the chemo unit. The door to new friendships and laughter and comfort. Comfort to give and be received.

Amara's gaze shifted to Grace. "Put that ice pack back on your head," she reprimanded.

"I'm fine." Grace's tone was short. She was in a grumpy mood. She'd not had a good day.

"You're not fine. You've got a lump the size of a goose egg on your head. It's already turning black-and-blue." Amara pointed at her. "Put that ice pack back."

"It's not an ice pack. It's a bag of peas. It's demeaning to sit here with a bag of peas on my head. And I've never seen a goose egg," Grace added indignantly. "I don't know if that's big or small."

Amara removed her sunglasses, giving her friend the eye. "We can call your son to take you back to the hospital and have that looked at. That's what the police wanted to do."

"I don't need to go to the bloody emergency room." Grace reluctantly raised the bag of peas to her forehead. "And nobody needs to call my son and worry him." She looked away, obviously annoyed with Amara. "Worry him to death. What if he were to hear the news and have a heart attack?"

"Oh, my." Amara was immediately concerned. "Does he have a heart condition?"

"No, but what if he did?"

Noticing that Grace's head scarf had shifted, showing her bald forehead that was beginning to sprout gray hair, she checked her own. "You're being dramatic."

Grace leaned toward Amara and said in the sweetest voice, "Would it hurt your feelings if I were to tell you to mind your own business, luv?"

Mulling that idea over in her head, Amara slid back in her chair and put her sunglasses back on. She shifted her weight, trying to get comfortable. Every movement was painful. She'd grown so thin in the last six months that it felt as if needles poked into her flesh wherever she sat. Or lay down. Or walked. Or breathed. She inhaled deeply, distancing herself from the pain. She knew she'd be relieved of it soon. But not today.

Today wasn't the day.

Amara redirected her thoughts. "How are you feeling today, Lara?" she asked, keeping one eye on Grace to be sure the bag of peas remained on her head.

"Okay," Lara exhaled. She was sitting in her chair, her head thrown back, her big sunglasses perched on her nose. And today she was sporting a neon-pink beanie pulled down over her head. She always left chemo feeling cold, no matter how warm and humid it was outside.

It was the cold cap she had been wearing, Amara supposed. She didn't understand Lara's attachment to her hair, but maybe that was because she'd lost hers when she first started treatment for her pancreatic cancer. After that, she had chosen to shave it. Which was coming in handy with her latest round of chemo. There was little hair to clean off her pillow in the morning and the shower in the evening.

Lara was a beautiful woman. Inside and out. The first thing that caught Amara's eye when they met was her long blond hair that so far wasn't falling out because of that silly torture device. And her big brown eyes. A lovely young woman. But she was even more beautiful on the inside. Such a kind and loving heart. And fun. She knew how to keep up people's spirits in chemo, and not just the patients'. She was one of those rare people who seemed to be able to take the emotional temperature of everyone in the room and gauge what each needed. And somehow provide it. At the hospital, that meant the nurses, too, and the occasional oncologist who popped in. She remembered everyone's name and their story. She knew the questions to ask. She knew when to talk and when to just listen.

A remarkable woman.

But Amara already knew that. Lara had brought them together, hadn't she? Brought them here to the porch. Given them a purpose she was just beginning to sense. One that was too much in its infancy to speak of aloud, but one she could feel in the air. She thought Grace felt it, too.

"Would you like a little something to eat, Lara? I imagine Ellen has some soup in the refrigerator. Or maybe just a few crackers? She bought those crackers you like."

Lara rolled her head from side to side. "No food. Just iced tea. Is Ellen home yet?"

"Not yet, luv," Grace put in.

Lara sighed. "Where's Alex when you need her?"

"Her grandparents were coming," Grace explained. She was painting her fingernails a sparkly gold color. "She said she'd be here as soon as she could."

"The rich grandparents or the dumb ones?" Pine, who had looked like he was sleeping, but apparently he wasn't, asked.

"Don't know," Grace replied.

"I can get iced tea for you." Amara slid slowly forward in her chair, willing her jellylike limbs to move.

"You sit. I'll get it." Pine rose and adjusted the floppy bucket hat he wore to keep the sun off his face.

"I can do it." Amara gripped the chair, trying to shift her weight forward so she could get to her feet.

"No need in both of us getting up and I'm going that way anyway." Pine shuffled toward the screen door. "I've got to drain my lizard again, ladies."

The screen door slapped shut behind him, and the women on the porch all burst into laughter.

14

Ellen followed the sidewalk down the main avenue of Albany Beach, taking in deep breaths of the scent of freshly made caramel corn and enjoying the warmth of the sun on her face. Overhead, she heard the familiar cry of seagulls, scavenging for bits of popcorn, French fries, and cotton candy tossed or dropped. Reaching her destination, she stopped in front of the new bookstore. The building had previously housed a shop that sold clothing with inappropriate slogans, salt and pepper shakers shaped like blue claw crabs, and other junk tourists loved. The shop was newly renovated with exposed brick walls and high ceilings. Coffeehouse-type music drifted from hidden speakers. The bookshelves were built from mismatched wood: some old, some new, some pine, some walnut, but somehow it worked. Whoever had designed the space had good, if not eclectic, taste. And it was a nice bookstore.

If there was one thing she knew, it was bookstores. When she was young, back when her parents had managed some sort of affable relationship, her father had often taken his family to local book signings and readings. He would have her mother dress her and her brother up and sit them in the front row.

Looking back, Ellen realized now that it was all for show. (He had always driven separately or ordered a car and never included them in the dinners and cocktail parties that followed. Sometimes he'd not even returned until the next day.) Ellen had, however, always been allowed to pick out a stack of books that he would buy for her. That was one credit she had to give her father begrudgingly. He gave her a love of books, of reading.

Scanning the shelves, she quickly discovered that the store had an excellent selection and was set up to encourage comfortable shopping. Integrated between bookshelves were places to sit and flip through pages before making a purchase. The shop also had a little coffee shop where you could order a latte in a real mug and have a cookie or a lemon bar while narrowing down your selection of books.

The thermometer had hit ninety degrees by noon, and the blast of air conditioning felt good on Ellen's sweaty face. She immediately found the nonfiction area and stood in front of the shelves hand-labeled with purple curlicues reading *Creative Writing*. She searched the titles for one she *hadn't* read. She'd become an expert over the years with the technical side of how to write a novel. Such an expert that Lara, trying to be helpful, had suggested maybe she should write a how-to book. She didn't tell Lara that it was hurtful when she said things like that. Did Lara not have any more confidence in her than her father had had? Ellen was struggling with the opening pages. The opening lines.

The first page is the hardest.

That's what Ellen kept telling herself. Day after day. Week after week. Year after year. But now she was motivated. She wanted to be a writer, and she was finally going to make it happen. Yes, like her father. Though, ideally, *not* like him. She was confident she could be a successful writer and not be a sonofabitch to everyone in the human race: friends, family, fans, the FedEx driver.

The only thing holding her back from becoming a novelist was that she didn't know *what* to write. She was without inspiration—as her father had pointed out many times. Technical crap didn't matter; it was all in the muse, according to him. His claim to fame (one of his supposedly many) was that he had never read one piece of how-to drivel in his life. He just sat at his desk and wrote novels. And won awards. Made the *New York Times* best-seller list and was featured in newspapers and magazines.

So what was wrong with her? She was his daughter, his progeny, and she had his nose. Surely she had one good book in her. She was an excellent writing instructor, excellent at technical writing. She'd helped two colleagues get their doctorates. She'd read a thesis over and over again, making corrections and suggestions until it was a good, solid paper.

She glanced at the floor-to-ceiling wall of books. The next shelves over featured self-help books, and she eyed them wondering if she needed to slide over to that section and check them out.

A customer in her early thirties, pushing a baby stroller while sipping a frozen coffee drink, passed by and Ellen pretended to read a book jacket.

Before Lara's cancer returned, Ellen had intended to spend the summer at the beach house, cleaning it out and preparing to sell it. But now with the real threat of losing Lara, Ellen wanted more from this *summer vacation*, as a co-worker back in Raleigh had called it at a staff meeting. She wanted to take this time to think about her life and make some changes. Try to figure out what she wanted and how she could get those things. Could she have those things.

Nothing like the threat of death to make you look at life.

Ellen had started a journal again and she wanted to remember that phrase to write it down. Journaling was something many writers did, a way to plant the seeds of ideas for books, scenes, conversations. She'd tried a couple of times before, but the exercise always went quickly by the wayside. In the past, she'd found herself simply recording what she did that day. Worse, what she ate. Even worse yet, what the cat ate. It had been pathetic.

She'd brought a new leather-bound book specifically made for journaling with her to the beach. Everyone on the Internet said that it was important to the process to handwrite the entries. However, she had quickly discovered that she hated handwriting anything, even in a forty-nine-dollar Italian leather-bound journal. It hurt her hand. And she couldn't read her own handwriting, it was so terrible. When she tried to go back and read what she'd written, it was like a word search puzzle. At that point, Ellen had been tempted to give up the idea of the journal altogether, but she didn't want to be a quitter. Not anymore. No one wrote a novel by hand anymore, anyway, not even the great Joseph R. Tolliver, she rationalized. So she'd started "taking notes" on her laptop.

To get into the swing of entering something each day, to get her creative juices flowing, she'd been jotting down the contents of the boxes of junk in the attic. On the day of Lara's first chemo treatment, Ellen had learned that the purge was going to be even more interesting than she'd anticipated. In the first twenty minutes of her attack, she discovered that there were no boxes labeled accurately. A *BOOKS* label didn't mean a box was full of books. It didn't even mean there were books inside. A box labeled as such might be full of old bedsheets and shower curtains, and a tuna fish can, minus the tuna. Every box was a crazy mix of worthless objects. Her favorite so far held a heart-shaped candy box filled with buttons, a broken toilet seat, two mismatched dirty socks, an empty tissue box, a bunch of magazines including a *Playboy* from 1977, and the pièce de résistance? A set of dentures missing the front two teeth. Top *and* bottom. Neither of her parents wore dentures. Nor her grandparents, for that matter. Now *that* had been journal worthy.

Logging the contents of some of the boxes had helped her, leading her to write other things. Most of it was rubbish, but amidst the rubbish, she saw a sliver of hope. She'd started writing down thoughts she had throughout the day that she wanted to contemplate later. The night before, she had written an entry that she found intriguing.

What Do I Want? For Me?:

had been the header. Beneath it, she noted,

In no particular order:

Clean the crap out of the beach house
Save Lara's life
Lose 7 pounds
Write a novel
Make a friend I can call on a Friday night
Read *Ulysses*
Be happy

The last one had caused her to pause and she'd gone back to it several times after she wrote it. Now she had it memorized.
She wanted to be happy?
Was she *unhappy*? What *was* unhappiness in a world where you could order your favorite tea online and have it delivered before 6:00 p.m.? With free shipping. How could she live in a world of gel nail manicures, nitro brews, on-demand movies, and Botox and be unhappy?
Maybe "discontented" was a better word for her state of mind. She had a job, a roof over her head, and food to eat.
But she wanted more. And it wasn't free overnight shipping.
So what was it?
What would make her happy?
What made any human being happy?
It was too big a question for right now. She needed to get home to be with Lara. Lara caught a ride home from the hos-

pital with her new friend Grace again. Which was troubling on
several fronts. Should one chemo patient be driving another?
Then there was the matter of Grace staying the afternoon,
sometimes until supper. It wasn't that Ellen didn't want Lara
to have friends. It was good for her to have someone to talk to
while she sat at the hospital for hours, getting her chemo, a polar ice cap on her head. And she had told Lara she was welcome
to bring anyone over. But it hadn't occurred to Ellen that Lara
would bring *more* sick people into the house.

Having the responsibility of caring for Lara was one thing.
Ellen felt capable of doing that. She'd spent weekends with her
when she was going through chemo last time. She could do
CPR and operate an automated external defibrillator. (Did she
need to buy one for the house?) She knew what to do for nausea
and the little things like throwing Lara's favorite blanket into
the dryer to warm it for her before she curled up on the couch
for a nap.

But caring for someone else was entirely different. What if
something happened? What if one of Lara's chemo friends had
a medical emergency?

Grace looked like she was half-dead already. Ellen had noted
in her journal:

Grace Faulkner
Age: 100+?
Diagnosis: Stage IV non-small-cell lung cancer
Prognosis: 6-12 months to live

Grace was an old woman to begin with, a skinny, wizened
thing with deep wrinkles on her face and tufts of gray hair
peeking from beneath her head scarf. (Ellen had no idea how
her hair was growing. She hadn't rented a cold cap for three
thousand dollars and wasn't paying daily for dry ice. Ellen had
asked.) Grace reminded Ellen of Granny in the TV show *The
Beverly Hillbillies*—a TV show her grandmother had liked

when Ellen was little—in looks, not personality. Ellen worried that Grace could fall. She could go into cardiac arrest. Stop breathing.

And then there was Amara. She'd taken notes on her, too. On all of them.

> **Amara Linder**
> **Age: 61**
> **Diagnosis: Pancreatic cancer with mets to her liver**
> **Prognosis: 2-6 months to live**
>
> **Pine Abbott**
> **Age: 72**
> **Diagnosis: Non-Hodgkin's lymphoma**
> **Prognosis: Excellent**

And then there was the teenager. Ellen had asked her outright what she was being treated for and then had been so flustered, she hadn't known what to say. It hadn't occurred to her that the girl could be terminal.

> **Alex Brittingham**
> **Age: 15**
> **Diagnosis: Ependymoma, a form of brain cancer**
> **Prognosis: Borrowed time [Alex's words, not hers]**

Just thinking of all of the things that could go wrong with Lara's friends made Ellen's pulse increase, and suddenly she was sweaty again. She needed to get home to be there to call 911 if anyone had a medical crisis. She didn't want anyone dying in her house. On her porch. That wouldn't be a good selling point.

Ellen checked the time on her phone. It was after two. She needed to get going, but she needed a book first.

The sound of rock music blared suddenly from over the speakers startling Ellen, and she glanced around.

"Sorry about that!" a man hollered from somewhere in the store as the music got quieter.

Ellen peeked around a shelf of books to see who had disturbed the peace, as it was. Weren't bookstores like libraries? You were supposed to keep your voice down. And certainly the music.

Unable to locate the man, she returned her attention to the books, running a finger along the paperback spines, skipping over the hardbacks. She knew the chances were slim she would read the whole book, so she didn't usually spend money on the hardbacks. For a small beach town bookstore, there was a fantastic selection of how-to books. How to: find your muse, self-publish children's books, self-publish *adult* literature. She raised an eyebrow. Whoever acquired the books for the store was undoubtedly daring. She wasn't interested in writing erotica, aka porn, but the title intrigued her. Looking one way and then the other to be sure no one was watching her, she pulled it from the shelf.

She skimmed a few pages, found it was remarkably similar to any other how-to-write guide, and put it back. Five minutes later, she'd managed to find three books she had never read, including one on how to self-publish a first novel.

It never hurt to be prepared.

Carrying the books in the crook of her arm, she headed for the checkout counter located at the coffee bar. Halfway there, a table covered in brightly colored paperbacks caught her eye. A sign announced *Summer Reading* in the same curlicue script with a big sun drawn coming up from behind the words. There were a couple of classics, books she guessed were maybe summer reading for high schoolers: *A Raisin in the Sun*, *The Scarlet Letter*, *Romeo and Juliet*. But there were also titles featuring covers with brightly colored beach umbrellas, waves carrying starfish and sand dollars to the shore, and beach chairs in the sand. The ocean was prominently featured in the background of each one. The covers had graphics that made you smile even if you didn't want to.

The music boomed again, and Ellen glanced around. Was that Pink Floyd? She felt secondhand embarrassment for the employee who had selected the music. It was not bookstore appropriate. Summer help? Probably a teenager. In the summer, the population of the little beach town nearly doubled, springing from fifteen hundred to three thousand, and that was only within the town limits. When the new hospital was built, new neighborhoods popped up on the west side of Route 1. Or had the developments come first? Chicken or the egg?

The music receded to a more appropriate level, though the psychedelic rock song continued to play. Still, she couldn't see the employee. Wouldn't the bookstore owner be furious if he or she knew employees were not doing their job? No one was greeting shoppers at the door or keeping an eye on the exit to be sure there was no shoplifting.

She picked up one book after another and read the back covers: two sisters who reunite in a South Carolina beach resort after forty years without communication, a widower who comes to a sleepy beach town in New England to toss his wife's ashes into the ocean and finds new love, a grandmother who brings her grieving granddaughter to the beach where she grew up, hoping it will give them both peace.

Deciding what the heck, it *was* summer, the perfect time for light reading, Ellen added the one about the widower to the books in her arms as well as the one about the grandmother. As she approached the register, she spotted a row of Amish romance novels on an endcap and scooped two up without even bothering to read the cover copy. Lara loved romances, all kinds from the famous kinky bondage series to the sweet religious ones. No matter how hard Ellen tried to get her friend to try something different, she refused. She said they were pure escape and that was why she read them.

With an armful of books, Ellen approached the counter and looked for a clerk, a barista, *someone*. She set the books down harder than she needed to, thinking the sound would alert the clerk to be minding the register.

Nothing.

She leaned to her left to peek through a half-open door to an office or maybe a prep area for the coffee. An antique bakery case displayed assorted delicious-looking pastries, and a glass jar beside the register was filled with homemade biscotti meant to tempt shoppers. She was certainly tempted. She loved biscotti, especially the kind with chocolate on the top.

The aroma of strong, fresh coffee wafted through the air.

Still, no one came.

"Hello?" she called tentatively.

When no one answered, she looked for a bell. Maybe they were short staffed? It must be hard to keep part-time employees when there were so many summer part-time jobs.

"Hell-o!" she called louder.

"Chill," came a male voice from the back room.

It was the same voice she had heard before. Some kid left to run the shop.

The music got quieter, then louder, then quieter again.

A man with sun-bleached blond hair stuck his head out the door, tilted it, as if trying to gauge the music. Then he ducked back into the room.

Ellen shifted her weight from one foot to the other impatiently. She checked her watch. She really needed to get home. "Excuse me!" she called. "I'm ready to check out."

"Be there in a sec!" he called.

She waited.

A second passed. Another. Then. Thirty. A full minute passed, and still, she waited. She glanced behind her. There were a few customers milling around. Two girls who looked to be in their early twenties sat across from each other at one of the café-sized table and chairs, reading magazines and drinking enormous frozen coffee drinks.

Ellen huffed. She debated whether or not to return the books to the shelves and leave. This was not the kind of service a new store should be providing in this town. A bookstore was open year-round. The owner needed to play to the folks who paid property taxes in Albany Beach.

Ellen was about to call out to the clerk and tell him as much when he walked through the doorway. Her first thought was that she was surprised the man was playing rock music rather than the Beach Boys. He looked like he could have come off a book cover with his messy chin-length blond hair and tan. He was older than she expected. She'd envisioned someone college age, maybe even high school. There were a lot of teenagers scooping ice cream, frying potatoes, and tending to arcade games in Albany Beach.

The clerk looked to be in his late thirties. And was good-looking . . . as in movie-star good-looking. As in Brad Pitt in his *Legends of the Fall* days. Bit of scruff on his chin and all. Had a casting director wanted a good-looking lead male character, this bookshop man would have been him.

He wore a faded orange T-shirt that advertised a West Coast surf shop and baggy cargo jeans. On his feet, a pair of worn leather flip-flops. He looked as if he'd stepped from the pages of one of Lara's romance novels and Ellen immediately felt awkward.

"In a hurry?" he asked as he reached across the counter for her stack of books.

She froze. "Um . . . I didn't see anyone who could help me. I . . . imagine your boss likes having someone out front." *To keep his customers from walking out the door with the store,* she thought.

He studied her with a funny look on his face. Then he said, "Nah, the boss is cool. I was hooking up a new sound system.

For some reason, I couldn't get it to stream." He scanned the bar code on the first book. "Got it now." He pointed upward, and she followed his gaze to a black speaker mounted on one of the open beams. "Like this station?"

"Is that Pink Floyd?" she asked.

"Nope." He rang up the next book.

She waited for him to tell her who the band was. He didn't. Finally she said, "Who is it, then?"

"King Crimson. Pink Floyd was more of a psychedelic rock band. King Crimson was progressive rock."

"Ah," she said.

The intricacies of rock music were not something Ellen was well versed in. She'd played the cello as a child because her father had insisted and it was easier for her mother to go along than to argue with him. Ellen had taken lessons for six years and never learned to play anything that wasn't awful. But she liked music. She liked rock music. Just not in a bookstore. It somehow seemed . . . sacrilegious maybe?

"You know King Crimson?"

He seemed so pleased that she considered for just a second saying she liked the band. He had the strangest, most beautiful eyes. They were so pale they looked more gray than blue. The word "haunting" came to mind.

Haunting gray eyes. She would add the phrase to her journal when she got home.

Her gaze flitted from the beach boy to the menu written in chalk on a board behind him. He was waiting for her response. What did she say? If she told him she knew the band, how would she respond if he asked her what her favorite song or album was? Then she'd be caught in the lie.

Why did she care? He was a clerk in a bookstore. Probably ten years younger than she was.

"Um . . . no," she said, her voice sounding strange to her ear. "I'm not familiar with them."

"British band," he told her. "Opened for the Stones in Hyde

Park in '69. That was their first big break. Once upon a time, they considered hiring Elton John to sing with them."

"You like Elton John?" she asked, trying to shift the conversation away from King Crimson. Elton John she knew.

He held her book on self-publishing and opened his arms wide. "Doesn't every Brit?"

He didn't sound British. He sounded as all-American as . . . she didn't know what. A Beach Boys tune played in her head. *Brian Wilson?*

"Dual citizenship. My mum is British, and my pops was an American." He scanned the book on characterization. "Good one. Paper bags are twenty-five cents each."

"You read it? I have to pay for a bag?"

"Read it before I ordered copies for the store. A lot of garbage on writing out there. Most customers bring their own bags. Plastic bags were banned last year." He leaned down to look at the cash register to see what he'd rung up. "You should bring your own next time. Here for the week?"

"I live here." Not exactly a lie. She lived in Albany Beach *right now.* For the summer. "I don't need a bag," she told him. "I'll carry them."

He shrugged. He had broad shoulders and muscular biceps. *Of course he did.* "Suit yourself." He rang up the next writing book. "We've got a group of writers who meet here on Tuesdays. One p.m. Anyone's welcome."

She stared at a knot in the wooden countertop. She'd never joined a writers' group before. Her first thought was that she didn't need a group of women sitting around wishing they could write a novel. She could do that on her own. And her father had never had anything good to say about writers' communities, online or in person. Of course, he'd never had anything good to say about anyone or anything.

So why was she still doing what her father said?

Maybe checking out the writers' group wasn't such a bad idea.

"Tuesdays?" she repeated, then felt stupid. He just said that. Why was she suddenly all jittery?

Somewhere in the back of her mind, she knew why. She recognized the little bump up in her heart rate. The uncomfortable, exhilarating feeling that she hadn't felt in a very long time. *Attraction.*

She was attracted to this kid who played rock music in a bookstore.

He reached across the counter. Lara's book was next. Suddenly she wished she hadn't picked it up for her. What would he think? She wanted to snatch it off the counter before he picked it up and mumble something about grabbing the wrong book.

But then he picked it up, and it was too late.

Maybe he wouldn't notice what kind of book it was, she told herself, scrambling for her emotional self-preservation. How many books a day did he ring up? They were probably all the same to him. Maybe—

He looked at the cover. "This what you want to write?"

15

Ellen locked gazes with him. Her first impulse was to blurt out that none of the fiction was for her, but for a friend. A *sick* friend. A friend with cancer.

But another part of her, a tiny sliver of her soul, wanted to defend herself and her choices. What right did he have to judge what she read? And he *was* judging. She could hear it in his tone.

She was pathetic.

She *wanted* to defend herself. It was what Lara would have done. Lara would have argued with him just for the sake of argument.

Ellen just didn't know *how* to defend herself in this situation. She had no problem waiting in line at the grocery store, with ten people behind her, to get a price check. If the ramen noodles were on sale for ninety-nine cents a pack, she wouldn't pay one-ten. She just asked for a price check.

But in this case, she didn't know what to say. How to say it.

What she needed was a clever comeback. To put him in his place, as her grandmother used to say.

Only Ellen couldn't come up with one. She never could in

the moment. But she knew from experience that she'd have thought of plenty of snappy comebacks by the time she got back to the house.

Instead of a snappy retort, she said, "No, it's not what I want to write. At least I don't think so," she threw in. Then she congratulated herself for being brave. Brave for her, at least.

"Hmm."

The beach boy gave her the total for her purchase, and she reached into her crossbody bag for her wallet. The sooner she was out of here, the better. What did she care what this kid . . . well, he wasn't a kid, but— Anyway, what right did he have to judge what she and Lara liked to read?

She fumbled in her bag for her wallet, and when she didn't feel it she slung the small leather bag around, yanked it open, and peered inside. She was starting to sweat. She could feel her armpits getting clammy. Why was she letting this guy get under her skin?

To her horror, there was no wallet in her bag. She dug around again, which was ridiculous because it was a small bag. Her wallet wasn't there.

Had she been robbed on the boardwalk? There had been nothing in the weekly papers about pickpockets, but they could be anywhere, couldn't they? "I—" She looked up at him.

Then she realized where it was, and she closed her eyes in horror.

She'd taken her wallet out earlier when she'd needed her card to place an online order. It was sitting on the kitchen counter.

How could she have done such a thing? She had never left her wallet home in her life.

She could feel her cheeks getting hot as she looked up at him. Sweat was beading on her forehead. "I . . . I don't have my wallet with me. I must have left it at home."

"I hate it when I do that." He shrugged. "So next time you're in, pay for them then."

"What?" She drew back. "No . . . I . . . I'll leave the books here, run home and get my wallet, and—" She exhaled, flustered. "I am so sorry."

He pushed the stack of books across the counter. "Take them. Pay another day."

"You're just going to *give* them to me?" She gave the stack a push back in his direction. "I can't do that."

"Why not?" He picked up a reusable cup advertising a brand of boogie board from beside the register and took a sip from the straw. "You're good for it, aren't you?" He narrowed one eye comically. "You're not going to like skip town without paying."

"No . . . no, of course not. But . . . but your boss. I'm sure he or she wouldn't want you selling books on credit."

He leaned against the counter, obviously amused. He wrinkled his nose. "I think he's cool with it."

She tucked a piece of hair behind her ear. It was damp. "I wouldn't want you to get in trouble. You could get fired for something like this."

"I don't think so— What's your name?" He sucked on the straw again.

"Ellen."

"Well, *Ellen*, since I am the boss, I get to say who takes books out of this store and who doesn't." He gave her stack a little push back in her direction.

"You . . . you're the boss? You mean the manager."

He looked at her over his cup. "Owner." He flashed a smile that made him even more handsome than he already was.

"Oh . . ." She knew she had that deer-in-headlights look on her face. The owner? He didn't look like he owned anything more than an old surfboard. "Well . . . um . . . nice store." She grabbed the books. "I'll be back tomorrow to pay. Is tomorrow okay?" She took a step back.

"Tomorrow will be fine." Again, the smile. "I look forward to seeing you, Ellen."

She turned around, clutching the stack of books to her chest. "Thank you."

"You sure you don't want a bag? I can add it to your bill!" he called after her as she went out the door. Again, the amusement.

"No bag!"

Outside on the sidewalk that was bustling with tourists in bathing suits and sandy flip-flops, she decided to walk home along the beach rather than the sidewalk. She was still flustered, and she thought the walk would do her good.

It was a decision she regretted within two blocks. The sun was high in the sky and hot, and while she wore a ball cap, she could feel its heat on the back of her neck. She was roasting.

And she was wearing sneakers. Not the best choice for walking on sand, especially not with the beach so busy. The local schools were out, and it was the first full week of summer for those folks. Most of the rentals in town were fully booked, according to the local newspaper. Lugging her pile of books, she was rethinking the characterization purchase because it was heaviest, but she slogged on, telling herself that walking was good for her thigh and butt muscles. Swimming was good for her, but a workout like this was better, she told herself.

Sweat trickled down between her breasts and her shoes filled with sand. She pressed on. Only five more blocks.

There were beach chairs and umbrellas everywhere, kids on rafts and boogie boards. Seagulls squawked over her head, and she prayed no one was feeding them. Tourists always thought that feeding the seagulls scraps from their snack bags or coolers was fun or cute or something—until they had bird poop in their hair.

Ellen would be annoyed if one of those flying rats pooped on her new ball cap.

She slogged on, the fine white sand more like quicksand with each step she took.

Two blocks from the beach house, she spotted a group of sunbathers gathering at the shore, shading their eyes as they gazed out into the water. She stopped to have a look and catch her breath.

"Porpoises," a woman in a strapless yellow bathing suit and enormous straw hat told Ellen. She pointed.

Ellen followed her line of vision. "Atlantic bottlenose dolphins," she corrected.

The woman gazed at her over her rhinestone sunglasses. It looked like someone's BeDazzler had gone haywire. There were so many sparkly gemstones weighing down the frame that Ellen seriously wondered how the woman kept the glasses on her face.

"Dolphins have elongated beaks and cone-shaped teeth," Ellen said, the teacher coming out in her. "Porpoises have smaller mouths and spade-shaped teeth."

"I can't see their teeth." The woman sounded suspicious of the facts. She rubbed her shoulder, which was terribly sunburned, with marks from the straps from a bathing suit worn previously.

Looking at the red, bubbly skin made Ellen shudder. She always wore an SPF of 50 or higher and frequently reapplied, depending on how long she was outside. She wore sunscreen on face, chest, and hands year-round at the recommendation of her dermatologist.

Ellen shifted her stack of books from one arm to the other and wished she'd coughed up the quarter and bought the paper bag. "A dolphin's dorsal fin—the one in the middle—is curved. A porpoise's is triangular. Dolphins are thinner, too."

The woman didn't respond, but as Ellen walked away she heard her tell someone else, "See the porpoises. There are five of them."

By the time Ellen spotted her house and cut across the sand toward the back porch, her T-shirt was soaked with sweat. From the water's edge, she could see people on the porch.

She sighed. Grace had stayed.

So it was a good thing she had skipped the grocery store and come straight home.

"Hallo, luv!" Grace called from the porch when she saw Ellen. She waved. "I see you've been shopping."

Ellen forced a smile as she trudged up the steps, squinting in the bright light. *Was Grace holding a bag of peas to her forehead?*

"I hadn't been to the new bookstore yet. It's very nice," Ellen said. "There's a coffee shop there, too."

"I hear it's good coffee." Grace smiled up at her. She had a fuzzy blanket on her lap.

It was ninety degrees, and she needed a blanket. Ellen worried about her. If she got any thinner, she would blow off the porch in a gust of wind. Ellen wondered where her family was, what her story was. Didn't she have anyone to care for her? Did she not have anywhere to go? Was that why she sat on the porch with Lara each day?

"I wouldn't know if it is good, though," Grace went on. "I don't drink coffee, and I certainly don't drink it for four dollars and fifty cents a cup."

Finally reaching the top step, Ellen set down the pile of books and sat down to remove her sand-filled sneakers. As she pulled them off, she glanced at Lara in one of the chairs. "Thank you so much for bringing Lara home." She dumped the sand over the railing and watched it fall.

Ashes to ashes, dust to dust.

It could be applied to so many situations. Most people didn't even know where the phrase came from. It was the Book of Common Prayer, not the Bible. Her father had taught her or bullied her well. She had a useless wealth of quotations to recite to anyone willing to listen.

Ellen peeled her socks off and dusted the sand from her bare feet. It was even between her toes. As she got up, she couldn't resist asking, "Is that a bag of peas on your head?"

Grace lowered it and had a look as if it were the first time she'd seen it. It would have been funny under other circumstances.

"It sure enough is!" Grace said.

Ellen couldn't tell if Grace was pulling her leg or really didn't know she'd been holding a bag of peas to her forehead.

"Put it back," came Lara's voice from behind her big blue sunglasses. She was wearing a yellow scarf over her cold cap, tied beneath her chin. She slowly removed her glasses.

The books and her sneakers forgotten for the moment, Ellen looked from Lara to Grace and back again at Lara, waiting for an explanation.

"Ice pack," Lara explained, sitting up.

"You hurt yourself, Grace?" Ellen asked. "Here? Did you fall here at the house?" The already high cost of her homeowner's insurance policy crossed her mind. If she had to file a liability claim, it would go even higher.

This was just what she had been afraid of when she expressed her concern about sick guests at the house. In the world of litigation that they lived in, she could be held responsible for an accident on her property.

"I'm fine," Grace insisted. "Just a little bump."

Not an answer.

Ellen looked at the two women sitting side by side in the Adirondack chairs. She wanted to know what happened to Grace. She'd have to get Lara alone to find out. "Could I get you something? Some iced tea? A snack? I have grapes and crackers and cheddar cheese."

"Please," Lara groaned, holding up her hand. "Can we not talk about food? Amara's getting us iced tea. You should sit down and join us."

As if on cue, the screen door swung open and Amara, wearing a magenta silk scarf over her head turban-style, came out carrying a bamboo tray that had been in the pantry. She had four glasses of iced tea and a little sugar bowl filled with yellow packets.

Ellen turned to Lara. "Could I talk to you for a minute?" She tilted her head ever-so-gently in the direction of the house.

Lara exhaled as if just breathing took great effort. "Sure. I've had to pee for the last hour anyway. I was just trying to work up the energy."

Ellen scooped up the books and went into the kitchen, holding the door open for Lara. "It's nice that you're making friends," she said quietly. The windows were open. She didn't want the others to hear her. "But is it . . ." She stopped and started again as she slid the pile of new books onto the island. She felt sweaty and gross. She needed a shower. Or better yet, a swim in the ocean and then a shower. "Is it okay with their doctors, their family, for . . . for them to be here every day?"

Lara limped through the kitchen toward the powder room, sliding her sunglasses up on her head. "Are you asking me if they have a *doctor's note* to sit on our porch?"

She looked like crap. Her skin was splotchy, and she was already beginning to lose weight. Then there was the limp that almost seemed worse than it had been when they arrived. Had the cancer in her leg spread, or was it her exhaustion that made it look like the limp was worse?

Lara didn't often take a tone with Ellen. Now she wished she hadn't said anything. But how could she not say anything? Lara's friends were obviously ill. They seemed sicker even than Lara. Of course they were sick. They were taking chemo treatments that were killing off the cancer cells but killing healthy cells at the same time.

Lara went into the bathroom, leaving the door open. "You said it was fine if I brought someone over. Amara, Grace, Pine, Alex, and I have formed a cancer support group. They're my support, Ellie. You can't kick them off the porch. I need them."

Ellen took a breath. She'd revisit the issue of all of these sick people on her porch another time when Lara was feeling better.

Instead, she changed the subject. "What happened to Grace's head? Did she fall?"

Ellen heard Lara peeing.

Lara never closed the door when she used the bathroom when they were alone together. Never had. Ellen always did. Always had. Further evidence of how confident and casual Lara was. How cool and relaxed.

All things Ellen had never been.

It was no wonder Tim left her. No wonder he was happier without her. Happier with the new girlfriend. The evidence was all over social media. Ellen had spent an hour in bed the night before looking through all of his Facebook posts. He was grinning in every photo.

"Did Grace fall?" Ellen repeated.

"Car accident."

"She had a *car accident*?" Ellen said it louder than she intended. She swung around to face the bathroom door, lowering her voice to a harsh whisper. "On the way here? With you in the car?"

"Yup." Lara flushed.

"Are you all right?" She stepped into the bathroom doorway as Lara pulled up her gym shorts.

"Fine," she pshawed. "It was just a little fender bender coming out of the parking garage."

"Did Grace get her car out of the shop already? I thought she had a fender bender last week and it was in the shop."

Lara shrugged. "She borrowed her son's car."

Ellen cocked her head. "She wrecked her son's car, too?"

"It's not *wrecked*. The hood just needs to be straightened out. And maybe the bumper replaced?"

Ellen crossed her arms over her chest. "You shouldn't be riding with her."

"You should come outside and join us. Amara just told us a hysterical story about her uncle and an elephant. And then Pine, not to be outdone, was telling us about coming face-to-face with a bamboo pit viper in Vietnam." She met Ellen's gaze with bloodshot eyes and smiled mischievously, reaching out to grab her hand. "Come on. Please? They're here for you, too."

Ellen drew back. "For me?"

Lara met her gaze. "They're such amazing people. They have so much to share. Just being with them makes me feel . . . I don't know. Like I can do anything. Be anything I want. You don't want to miss the magic, do you?"

16

Ellen came down the stairs with a beach towel rolled up under her arm and a pair of goggles in her hand. She'd changed into an old bathing suit, pulled a swim cap over her head, and slathered up with sun block. The lotion gave a little bit of a white cast to her skin, but she cared more about carcinoma than looking like a ghost.

Lara had really wanted her to join her and her friends on the porch, but she needed a swim. She needed the exercise and time to think. She did her best thinking while swimming laps in the YMCA pool at home, and she was finding that she liked the open-water swimming even better. There was something about the cold, salty water that she found grounding. And freeing. This was the first summer she'd ever felt completely at ease swimming in the ocean with nary a worry of sharks or anything else that had once been in her nightmares. After a swim and a shower, she'd planned to return to the bookstore and pay the beach boy.

She still couldn't believe that the hunky guy owned a bookstore. Though the more she thought about it, the more she could see his personality in the eclectic shop—the mismatched wooden bookcases, the old-style travel posters, and ads for books on the walls. The coffee shop.

He'd said she could come back and *pay her tab*.

As if she had been in a bar in the middle of the day.

Once she paid beach boy what she owed him, she'd be in the right state of mind to join Lara and her *support group* if they were still there.

Halfway down the Craftsman-style staircase, Ellen heard the doorbell ring. Probably another package delivery. Lara placed online orders almost all the time. It was her hobby, she explained. She was getting deliveries every day, via the US mail, UPS, and private delivery sometimes more than once a day.

The mail had already come, which meant it was probably UPS.

Ellen wasn't answering the door for Rick. Not in her bathing suit and a swim cap. It was one thing, someone seeing her like this on the beach, but she wasn't answering the front door. If she didn't, Rick would leave the package.

She paused on the staircase. She didn't want him to see her through the sidelights of the door. What would he think of her if she was standing right there and didn't open the door for him? He'd think she was trying to avoid him, which she wasn't. Well, she *was* right now, but she wasn't . . . long-term. She had toyed with the idea of a little innocent flirting with him. Just for . . . practice. To see what it felt like. It had been a very long time since she had flirted with a man. She was pretty certain she'd be poor at it, but she wanted to give it a whirl. But not like this. She'd be too self-conscious. She wanted to be fully dressed, a little makeup on, and her hair in some semblance of order, minus the latex swim cap.

She waited a full minute, giving Rick time to leave the package at the door and go down the porch steps. Then she started down the stairs again. Just as she reached the bottom step, the doorbell rang again.

Ellen froze.

It rang again.

And then again.

Did the package require a signature? What was Lara ordering that needed to be signed for? Surely not more nail polish. What if it was from one of those sex-toy places? Would Rick think it was for Ellen?

Would that be a bad thing? she wondered. If Rick thought she was a woman who could take care of herself, as Lara put it.

Then she was surprised that thought had gone through her head. A month ago, it would never have occurred to her to think such a thing.

She hesitated in indecision. She supposed she could wrap her towel around her.

Then she saw a face in one of the sidelights. He held his hand on his forehead, shading his eyes as he tried to see inside. It was definitely a man.

The bell rang yet again. This time, he held his finger down, and it rang and rang.

"Ellie! Doorbell!" Lara called from the back porch.

Ellen strode to the door, wrapping her towel around her, and yanked open the door. "Rick, what are you—"

It wasn't Rick.

Of all the gin joints . . .

Of all the people on earth who could have been at her door, this man wouldn't have made her top one hundred guesses. She would have sooner expected her ex, who was in Costa Rica right now zip-lining through jungle canopies with his girl toy and tossing exclamation marks around on his Facebook page. Ellen would have sooner expected her dead grandmother, who she knew for a fact was dead because her ashes were at home on her bedroom bureau. Along with the ashes of both of her parents and her grandfather.

It was the beach bum.

He seemed as surprised to see her as she did him. "Oh, hey. Ellen." His look of wonder turned into a grin. He wore wraparound sunglasses, the kind that made cool, attractive, younger men look even cooler and more attractive.

Ellen didn't know what to do. She was tempted to close the door. Lock it. Run straight through the house, out the back, and into the ocean. She wanted to dive in and never resurface.

No, no, no. Her hand flew to her swim cap. *This wasn't happening.* She wasn't ready!

While changing into her bathing suit, she had gone over, in detail, her next encounter with this guy. She planned to go after her swim after she showered, dressed, and put on makeup so artfully that it would look like she wasn't wearing any at all. She'd pay him and then she was going to say something intelligent to the gorgeous man who probably knew he was gorgeous. Something profound. Something that would make him feel guilty for dissing the books she had bought. Exactly what she was going to say she didn't know yet.

Her next thought was to wonder why he was here. Had she told him she was coming right back? Another ripple of panic went through her. He'd said to pay him the next time she was in the store. Had she told him no, she'd be right back, and didn't remember saying it?

Did she have a brain tumor and she just didn't know it yet? Was this her first symptom, the one she'd be telling an oncologist about in a few months?

But that was ridiculous. Of course she didn't have a brain tumor. Lara had breast cancer. She couldn't have an inoperable brain tumor at the same time. The fates weren't that cruel.

And even if she *had* said she'd be right back, which she knew she hadn't, how would he know where she lived?

"I'm looking for my mom?" he said.

Ellen stood there, frozen. The idea of running away was looking better by the second. *His mom?* "Sorry?"

So he wasn't there about the money she owed him. But apparently he wasn't there to apologize for his behavior back at the store, either.

This was almost funny.

It would have been one of those funny scenes had it been in a rom-com or a book and not her life with her covered in white sun block, wearing an old competition swimsuit that was worn thin across her bottom. And a swim cap that made her look like she had a condom on her head. That was what her son had once observed.

To have Rick see her looking like this was one thing. But this Adonis, this was another.

"*Who* are you looking for?" she asked him.

"My mom. The police called. She was in an accident. She isn't answering her phone." He made no attempt to *not* look at her, obviously amused by her getup. "She's not at our place. I checked. Then I went to the hospital. A girl named Alex said she might be here. With someone named Laurel? Alex gave me your address."

Was Grace his mother? He was too Caucasian to be Amara's son. Unless, of course, he was adopted. But Lara had said that Amara didn't have any children. Her husband had died only a few months after they married, and that had been more than thirty years ago.

"A *Lara* lives here," Ellen corrected. "Sorry, *who* are you?"

He laughed. "You know very well who I am. You were in my bookstore today. You owe me a thousand dollars." His tone was playful.

She raised her eyebrows, almost enjoying herself now. "A *thousand* dollars? That's a lot of interest. I owed you ninety-seven dollars and thirty-two cents when I left."

"Barrett Faulkner." He took off his sunglasses and offered his hand. "My mother is Grace Faulkner. A British lady with a lot of opinions. Wrecks cars. Can be nosy, bossy, and opinionated." He rocked his head one way and then the other. "Also, unfortunately, often right."

So the beach bum, *Barrett Faulkner*, was Grace's son. And she lived with him. For some reason, Ellen found that touching.

And incongruous with the assumptions she had made based on his looks. A man taking care of his sick mother.

Ellen didn't take his hand. (What if her hand was slippery from the sun block she'd just applied?) Instead, she opened the door a little farther. "She's here. Come on in." She pointed through the dark, cool house. "Straight through. Back porch."

He walked past her, shamelessly eyeing her up and down.

If she didn't know better, she might have thought he was flirting with her.

He pointed, a sparkle in his gray eyes. "Nice look, by the way."

Ellen was tempted to swat him with her towel, but it was cocooned around her and there was no way she was dropping it.

"Mum?" he called, using the British pronunciation as he headed in the direction of the porch. "Grace?"

Ellen closed the front door behind him and followed. She dropped her goggles on the kitchen counter.

Barrett pushed through the screen door. "Mum." He stopped. "There you are. Thank God. I was afraid I was going to have to start checking the morgues."

Grace held a glass of iced tea in her hand. If she was surprised to see him there, she didn't show it. She looked more annoyed than anything else.

It was a pretty glass. Ellen had found a whole box of them in the attic and Grace had noticed them on the kitchen table and declared they couldn't be donated. Not such a treasure. They were tall and slender and frosted with an intricate silver and turquoise design. Ellen had been so fascinated with the glasses that she'd Googled them and discovered they were very popular in the 1960s. They were often used to serve a Tom Collins, which, Ellen had learned from Mother Google, was basically a gin and tonic with lemon.

"Barrett." Grace raised a bag of green beans to her forehead. Someone had switched out the thawed peas for the new frozen vegetable. "What are you doing here?"

"What am *I* doing here? What are *you* doing here?" he asked. "You're supposed to be at home resting."

"I'm resting here," she answered, lifting her pointy chin.

"Got it. Busy day. What with you going to chemo, then getting in a car accident. In *my* car. You didn't tell me you were taking my car to the hospital. I thought you got a ride with someone else."

Grace sniffed the air. "How did you know about the car?"

"The police called the store to let me know where they were towing the car." He stood in the doorway, holding the screen door open. He sounded more like her father than her son, right now.

Ellen watched from behind him, clutching her towel around her.

"They weren't supposed to call you," Grace said tartly. "They were *supposed* to call me. I gave them my phone number." She set down her glass and the bag of green beans and dug in her bag beside her chair.

"It's *my* car!" He raised his voice, but there was no temper behind it.

"*Technically*, it's mine. Was mine. I gifted it to you. I'll take it back and then it will be mine."

"Indian giver," he retorted, his tone still perfectly pleasant.

"A terrible phrase," Grace chastised. "It's racist."

Barrett ignored his mother's last comment. "How could anyone call you? You're not answering your phone. I called you over and over again, Mum. You're supposed to pick up when I call, right? We talked about this," he chastised. But it was obvious that he was relieved. That he loved her.

Which annoyed Ellen a little because it was easier to keep him a one-dimensional character. Beach bums didn't love their mothers; they loved themselves. Right?

Wrong.

Ellen realized that, like her father, she was making assumptions that just weren't true.

**We need to fight the genetic inclination to be who we
don't want to be.**

"So how about I take you home, Mum?" Barrett asked.
"We'll go home and get you into bed."

Ignoring her son, Grace pulled a flip phone from her bag,
opened it, and studied the screen. She pulled off her sunglasses
and squinted at it. Still unable to see the screen clearly, she dug
into her bag again and came up with an eyeglass case. Everyone
watched as she put on her yellow reading glasses. "Bloody hell,
they did call." She sighed and closed her flip phone. "And you
called *seven* times?"

"I told you, I was worried about you." He opened his arms
wide in a gesture. "You stole my car!"

Grace rolled her eyes. "It's not like I was pulling a Thelma
and Louise."

Mother and son were talking over each other now.

"I was just coming here."

"I didn't know what to do."

"I called the hospital to be sure you hadn't been admitted."

Grace dropped her phone into her bag and got to her feet.
"See you tomorrow, ladies? Gentleman?"

"See you tomorrow, dear," Amara said.

"Bye. See you." Pine and Alex.

"Ciao, darling," Lara said. She'd sat up in her chair when
Barrett walked out onto the porch; she liked a good-looking
man as much as the next woman. But now she leaned back
again, adjusting her sunglasses.

It seemed to take forever for Grace to retrieve her bag. Barrett made a move to help her, but then she shot him a look so
fierce that it was a wonder he didn't turn to stone. He backed
off, hands up as if he were being robbed.

Which it turns out he *had* been earlier in the day.

Was it grand theft auto if you'd once owned the car?

"I have to use the ladies'," she told her son, ducking beneath
his arm that spanned the doorway. Today she was wearing a

yellow T-shirt that read *Woman Up*. She handed him her flow-ered canvas bag. "I'll see you at the car."

He turned in the doorway to watch her take one tiny step after another through the kitchen. He slung her bag on his shoulder as if he carried a woman's flowered tote all the time and looked down at Ellen. "I wish someone had called me," he said under his breath. "You should have called me. She should have gotten checked out at the emergency room. I talked to the responding officer. She refused treatment."

Ellen walked with him toward the front door. "How was I supposed to call you? I didn't know she was your mother. I came home from town, and she was here on my porch with the others. It's a cancer support group."

He opened the front door and made a face. "Huh. First I've heard about her joining a support group. My mother's not usu-ally a joiner. Too conventional for her. When I was a kid, I was dying for her to join the PTA at my school, but she refused. I think she called them fascists." He stopped, considering the idea. "Which makes no sense at all, does it?"

Ellen shrugged, taking care to hold on to her towel so it didn't fall off.

He walked out onto the front porch and turned back. "I'd be lying if I said I was totally okay with this. My mother is com-ing here every day. She's . . ." He paused. Again, considering his choice of words before he spoke them. "Fragile right now."

The tenderness in his tone made her uncomfortable, maybe because she was concerned about Grace, too. And trying not to be. She studied her bare feet. "My friend Lara's been taking chemo at the hospital, too." She looked up at him. "She says it helps to be with others who are going through the same thing. That the normalcy of sitting on our porch together makes the whole situation seem a little more bearable."

"She pulled right out in front of someone and then hit a sign. Before she even made it out of the hospital parking ga-rage. Obviously, she shouldn't be driving. I've been saying that for weeks." He massaged his temples with his thumb and fore-finger. "I've offered to drive her to the hospital time and time again, but she refuses. Clinging to her independence as long as she can, I guess. But now both our cars are in the shop. I've got a motorcycle, but I can't drive her around town on a Harley. I had to borrow a friend's car to come looking for her." He shook his head. "I don't know what I'm going to do with her. I can't stay home and babysit her all day."

Ellen hesitated, torn. She still wasn't crazy about the idea of cancer patients turning her home into a hangout, but if it helped Lara, how could she say no? And Grace was her friend. If Lara wanted Grace here, if she wanted Attila the Hun here at the cottage, Ellen knew in her heart of hearts that she would move heaven and earth to make it so. "So maybe she should come here after her treatment. How about if Grace rides from the hospital with me?" she asked. "Any day she wants to come, she can ride here with us and you can pick her up later. Or . . . your wife could pick her up."

The moment the words came out of her mouth, she realized it sounded like she was fishing for personal information on him.

Which she was.

"Divorced," he said.

"I'm sorry."

"Don't be. She was a bitch."

He smiled down at her and the strangest sensation came over her. He was divorced. Meaning single. And an intriguing juxtaposition of a man. Good-looking with at least half a brain in his head. Devoted to his mother. And . . . fun.

But he's younger.

Drop-dead gorgeous.

Out of your league.

She pushed those thoughts aside. He'd said something, and she'd missed it. "Pardon?"

He didn't answer right away, which made her uncomfortable. But she also liked that he thought before he spoke. It added to the intrigue.

"I said maybe that's the best choice. Her riding here with you when she leaves the hospital."

"It is?"

"Absolutely. If that's what she wants. I'm not her keeper. But she has to answer her phone when I call. When I call to check on her and she doesn't pick up—" He let the sentence go unfinished. "I don't think she'll be driving anymore, but that conversation . . ." He shook his head.

"It's going to be tough," she said, looking up at him. She hesitated and then asked, "Grace isn't going to get better, is she?"

Tears welled in his eyes as he slowly shook his head no. "A one-way ticket south," he murmured.

Tears filled her eyes, which made her more uncomfortable than anything that had happened between them. Including showing up to make a hundred-dollar purchase without any money.

"Thank you, Ellen," he said, then turned away. But at the bottom of the steps he surprised her by turning back again. "You should come."

She knitted her brows. "Come where?

"To my store."

"To pay you. Right. I was going to go for a swim first, but I can get dressed and—"

"I don't care about the money," he interrupted, sounding as if she had just accused him of running over the Easter bunny crossing the street. "You should come and check out our group at the store. The writers' group. Tuesdays." He pointed at her. "I'll be expecting you next week."

And then he was gone.

17

Ellen sat on the edge of her bed, staring at her bare toenails. She had noticed that all of the women today, including Alex, wore toenail polish.

It was Alex who was making Ellen rethink the whole toenail polish thing. Alex was just on the threshold of womanhood. Did Alex, at fifteen, know more about living than she did?

Ellen only had a professional pedicure a couple of times in her life, and that had always been when she was with Lara for a girls' weekend and Lara had refused to take no for an answer. And Ellen had always chosen clear polish. She didn't even own nail polish remover, except the bottle she kept in the garage to dissolve glue.

Looking down at her bare toes, she wondered if she was missing something profound. Most women kept their toenails polished and seemed to get great pleasure from it. Coloring one's nails dated back as far as 3200 BC, when Babylonia warriors colored their nails before going off to war.

Mother Google was all-knowing.

What if she was missing out, not having her toenails painted?

Ellen grabbed her phone and walked out of her room, going down the hallway to Lara's. She tapped lightly on the door that was slightly open. "You still awake?" she asked softly, in case she *was* sleeping.

"Unfortunately!" Lara called.

"Okay if I come in?"

"Of course."

Ellen pushed open the door. Lara was propped on a pile of pillows—she'd brought her bedding with her, so she'd be more comfortable. The bedspread was an explosion of purples and greens and yellows, and there must have been a half a dozen throw pillows on her bed, of varying sizes in the same colors. Ellen had exactly two pillows on her queen-sized bed. And her sheets were white. As she was standing there, looking, Lara in her bed seemed like another road sign similar to the toenail polish.

Was this an indication of a life not lived? Really *lived?*

"How you feeling?" Ellen asked from the doorway.

"Like shit." Lara set down her phone.

"Can I get you something?"

Lara smiled and patted the place beside her in her bed. "Come lie here with me."

Ellen kicked off her flip-flops and climbed into bed. She arranged a green floral pillow and a solid purple one behind her and lay back beside Lara.

"I'm glad you came," Lara told her, closing her eyes. "I was lonely in here, but I didn't have the energy to get out of bed."

Ellen turned her head to look at her. "I should go. You need to sleep."

Lara's hand shot out and she caught Ellen's wrist. She opened her eyes. "Don't leave me. Talk to me. I just spoke with Chastity on the phone. Her internship is *fantabulous*. She wants to visit me. We argued. Tell me something so I can get my mind off leaving my girls orphans."

"That's not going to happen," Ellen responded, her voice catching in her throat. "You're going to beat this. And she should come see you."

"Beat it?" Lara released her death grip on Ellen's arm and looked up at the ceiling fan spinning lazily overhead. "You do understand that cancer cells are your own cells? They're not some foreign invader. My body is trying to kill itself. I'm trying to kill myself." She frowned, thinking on that for a moment. "Well, sort of." She looked over. "But the prognosis for stage four breast cancer is—"

"The cancer in your bone can be managed," Ellen argued. "You can't give up."

"Give up?" Lara laughed, but there was no humor in her voice. "I'm not *giving up*, Ellie, I'm just being pragmatic. My girls could be without a mother, a year from now, twenty years from now. It doesn't matter when." She jabbed at Ellen's shoulder. "Which is why it's time to get your shit together. And I'm serious."

Ellen looked at her, feeling her brow furrow. "What?"

Lara smiled, her tone softening. "You know I love you, maybe more than I love anyone or anything—except my girls and mint chocolate chip ice cream."

Ellen laughed, afraid if she didn't, she'd tear up.

She still teared up.

But she didn't fight it.

She'd spent her entire life trying not to cry.

But this *was* love, wasn't it? Tears. They went hand in hand with laughter.

"I've been thinking a lot on this, Ellie, and my mind is made up." She turned slowly, as if every muscle hurt, which they probably did. "And because I love you, because my girls love you, I want you to be my backup singer. Ready to take the mike, should need be."

"Backup? I'm a terrible singer."

Lara grabbed her hand that rested between them, ignoring

what Ellen had thought was a clever retort. "I want you to be Vera and Chastity's backup mom. You don't have to do anything now, but if I croak, you have to be their mother. You—"

"You're not going to—"

"Ellie, be quiet and let me say this." Lara took a deep breath and went on. "You have to send my girls Trader Joe's gift cards and make pancakes in the shape of elephants for them when they come home for the weekend and you have to tell them when they're screwing up their lives. That's key. And you have to hold my grandbabies in your arms and give them butterfly kisses on their cheeks." Her big brown eyes with the black shadows beneath filled with tears. "And you have to love them. They'll be fine if they know you'll always be there for them if they need you, knowing you love them unconditionally."

Ellen was so overwhelmed by emotion that she couldn't speak. She wiped at her wet cheeks. She and Lara hadn't had a conversation like this since her cancer had come back. They hadn't had this kind of conversation since her original diagnosis. "I don't know what to say," she whispered.

"Nothing. You don't have to say a thing." Lara reached out and tucked a lock of Ellen's hair behind her ear. "Because I know you'll do it. If it comes to that. In the meantime, you need to get yourself on track."

Ellen stiffened, her tears drying up. "I wasn't aware I was off track." Her phone vibrated, and without thinking she picked it up. A Facebook post from Tim. She opened it. A snapshot of him and Genevieve grinning in front of a boarding gate. *Next stop, Mexico City!* the caption read. Comments immediately began to appear from his friends. Friends who used to be *their* friends. Sort of.

"What's that?" Lara reached for Ellen's phone.

"Nothing." Ellen pulled it away.

"Nothing?" Lara leaned farther, half on top of Ellen, and took the phone from her hand.

Ellen had locked the screen, but the minute Lara lay back,

holding the phone, tapping it, Ellen knew that was silly. Lara knew her passcode. It was identical to Lara's own phone passcode, her ATM PIN, and her electronic keypad on her back door.

Rob Lowe's birth year.

They'd both had a thing for him in middle school. Still did. Ellen had watched *West Wing*, start to finish, half a dozen times over the years. And she and Lara had just watched *St. Elmo's Fire* at Christmas.

"Lara, give it to me."

"Please tell me you're not still following Tim on Facebook?" Lara demanded. "This is what I'm talking about when I tell you, you need to get your shit together."

Ellen rolled onto her back and stared at the ceiling fan.

"Why are you still doing this to yourself, Ellie? We talked weeks ago about you unfriending him."

"He's my husband," Ellen whispered.

"Not anymore he isn't. He's moved on, and the who, what, where, and when of that is no longer of consequence. Ellie, he's with someone else. And I don't say this to hurt you, but he's happy."

Ellen took a shuddering breath.

"And you deserve to be happy again. But this?" Lara shook the cell phone at her. "This is not making you happy. This is making you sad. And angry, and it's keeping you from everything you could be. All the things you could do."

"We were married for more than twenty years. He . . . he's the only person I've ever had sex with."

"Not true. Iggy. Senior prom."

Ellen rolled her head to look at her. "I don't think there was penetration."

"You thought there was at the time. You were petrified he hadn't gotten the condom on right and that you were knocked up."

Ellen didn't know why, but she laughed. Laughed to keep from crying. "He never got his teeny weenie anywhere near my who-ha. He came all over my leg. And now, I'm half-wishing he'd found his way. Then at least I could truthfully say I'd had sex with *two* people in my lifetime. No one is ever going to have sex with me again."

"Yes, they are. You're smart, you're pretty, and you've got a nice ass."

Ellen closed her eyes and rolled her head back and forth.

"You're going to finish that profile on that online dating app that you started months ago and—"

"I did that when I was home in Raleigh. I'm not driving to Raleigh for a quickie."

Lara giggled. "Sweetie, you can change your location on the app."

"I'm not having sex with a stranger."

"Yes, you are."

"No, I'm not."

"Fine," Lara said. "How about with someone you know? Our favorite UPS driver. Rick."

"He might have cooties. Or worse."

"Good point." Lara thought for a moment. "How about Grace's son? He's hot. Fit. I bet he's a tiger in—"

"I am not having sex with Barrett. He's ten years younger than I am. He's a baby."

"Eight years. I asked Grace."

Ellen's eyes flew open. "You *asked* Grace?"

"I was cool about it. She had no idea I was asking his age for you."

"His age doesn't matter because I'm not having sex with him!"

"Fine." Lara spoke as if she was making a big concession. "No sex with Barrett tonight." She offered Ellen's phone.

Ellen met her gaze. "Do it," she whispered. "Unfriend Tim for me."

"Oh, no. I'm not doing it. You have to do it yourself." Lara passed her the phone and lay back on her pillow. "I'm tired. I think maybe I'll try to get some sleep." She looked at Ellen. "You know I love you, right? I'm not just picking on you for the fun of it. Though it is fun sometimes."

"I know," Ellen murmured, getting out of bed. She pulled the purple top sheet up over Lara. "Call me if you need me. I'll leave our doors open."

"Okay, sister by another mister." Lara suddenly looked exhausted.

At the door, Ellen turned back. "Can I borrow some of your nail polish?"

Lara's eyes were closed, but she smiled. "Sure. Basket in my bathroom. Fingers or toes?"

"Toes."

"Go with the purple. No, wait." She opened her eyes. "Blue."

"Don't push it," Ellen warned.

18

The next morning, the first thing Ellen saw when she got out of bed was her shiny, pink toenails. Pink was the closest she had been able to find to neutral in Lara's collection. They made her smile when she studied them while she sat on the toilet.

Had I known toenail polish could make me this happy, I'd have started wearing it years ago.

Then she moved on to more serious thoughts. The conversation the previous night with Lara had hit her hard. It had taken her hours to fall asleep. Lara wasn't going to die, but what if she did? Lara was right. It was time she got her shit together. For Lara's girls. For herself.

And Lara was right about unfollowing Tim on social media. Ellen was only making herself miserable. And prolonging the pain. She needed to rip off the Band-Aid. Today. But first she needed coffee.

Ellen found Lenora in her kitchen again.

As before, the older woman was barefoot, in a housecoat. Should she call the police? Maybe the local police station rather than 911? But Lara said she would disown her if Ellen called them. She said she'd still love her but would have to disown her.

"Does your family know where you are?" Ellen asked with a sigh.

"Not early risers," Lenora responded. Then she shrugged. "And where else would I be this time of the morning?" She pointed to the coffeepot percolating on the stove. "I'm making coffee. Oh! And we have cinnamon rolls."

Lenora waved a large, serrated knife.

"Careful," Ellen warned, cringing as the older woman drew the knife dangerously close to her.

Lenora set the knife on the counter and rose up on her tip-toes to retrieve two plates from the cupboard. "Wait until you taste them. They're yummy." She beamed.

Ellen wanted to argue that her family *would* miss her. Then she wondered if her house was the only one Lenora was breaking into. She only came sporadically. Was she making coffee for everyone on the street?

Ellen set down her phone on the countertop and walked over to the stove. All four burners were going on high. "You need to be careful with the stove, too," she warned. "This is dangerous."

If Lenora heard her, she gave no indication. She was busy arranging two cinnamon rolls on the buttercup luncheon-sized plates. "Made these fresh this morning."

They looked to Ellen like the homemade cinnamon rolls from Leeder's Bakery on the avenue. The white cardboard inside the plastic grocery bag also seemed amazingly similar to the box Leeder's put their pastries in.

"Should I heat them up?" Lenora asked, tapping her chin. "I think we can spare the coal to stoke up the oven a bit."

Ellen shook her head. "I think they'll be perfect." She glanced out the window. "Been raining long?" she asked. Though the sun had already risen, it was cloudy outside, and she could see light rain falling on the porch rail.

"Since before the sun came up."

The elderly woman's hair wasn't wet. "You walked here in the rain?"

"Umbrella," Lenora answered. She carried the two plates with the cinnamon rolls to the side of the counter where there were stools and set them down. "Want to go out to the porch or sit here?" She headed back to the stove for the coffee.

Ellen glanced out the window again. The chairs were probably wet, plus she imagined it was cool out. Lenora didn't look dressed for cooler weather. Of course, she shouldn't agree to sit anywhere with Lenora. If she wasn't going to call the police, she should at least tell her to go home. But Lenora had already made the coffee, and she'd brought cinnamon rolls, and sitting down with her once more seemed harmless. "Let's sit here," she answered, pulling out a stool.

"Okeydokey."

Ellen carried one cup of coffee to the counter while Lenora carried the other. They sat side by side. "Do you want a fork?" she asked Lenora, starting to get off the stool.

"A fork? Who needs a fork?" Lenora picked up the cinnamon roll with cream cheese frosting that was as large as her hand and took a big bite. "Mmm," she said with gusto. Her mouth was so full, Ellen could barely understand her. "So good."

Ellen stared at the frosted cinnamon roll on the plate in front of her. It looked amazing. It also looked like six hundred calories. Easily. She didn't usually eat treats like this. But maybe she'd have just a bite. It would be rude not to have at least a little of Lenora's cinnamon roll. That she made . . . or bought from the bakery.

Or possibly stole from someone else's house.

Ellen took a tiny bite and then closed her eyes with pleasure. It was sweet and cinnamony and just a little chewy. She heard herself moan. "I can't possibly eat all of this."

"See, I told you it was good."

Ellen chewed for a long moment, savoring it. "I don't think

I've ever tasted anything so good." She swallowed and opened her eyes. This was what Lara referred to as orgasmic food. She chose not to share that with Lenora.

The older woman grinned at her, bits of white icing on the corners of her mouth. "Eat what you want and save the rest for your husband."

Taking another bite, Ellen reached across the counter, retrieving two cloth napkins. She handed one to Lenora and wiped her own mouth. "No husband."

"Dead? Divorced? Never saw the need for one?" Lenora asked, her voice muffled by the napkin.

Ellen had to smile at the last option. She took another bite, this time a big one. "Divorced."

Lenora studied Ellen. "I should have guessed. I see it on your face. Fighting over money? Child support?"

Ellen took a sip of coffee, giving herself a moment before she responded. The subject of Tim was an awfully big hot button to hit this early in the morning. "No fighting. He was perfectly fair in the split. More than fair," she added. "And . . . our son, he's twenty-two. He works for an airline. A flight attendant. We just had the one child."

"Good for you. I wanted a houseful of children until I had them. Pain in the buttocks most of the time." Lenora took another big bite and washed it down with a swallow of coffee. "Why does talking about your divorce make you sad?"

Ellen pushed the plate back, exhaling. She wasn't used to people asking her such pointed questions. But somehow, it felt okay. She felt as if she wanted to answer. "It wasn't my choice," she said slowly. "The divorce."

"He cheat on you, the scoundrel?"

Ellen couldn't help but smile at the word "scoundrel." Did anyone use that word except in Lara's romance novels? "No. No one cheated."

"A drinker? A druggy? Couldn't keep a job? Ran up the credit cards?" Lenora pressed.

Ellen shook her head slowly. For a woman who thought she'd made coffee on a coal stove, Lenora seemed to think pretty clearly on some subjects. Ellen wondered what it must be like for Lenora. It had to be hard to be with it one moment and not the next.

But Lenora never seemed upset. In fact, she was always happy. Content. But how was that possible, to be so untethered and be okay with that?

Ellen cleared her throat. "He was none of those things. But I . . . I thought we would be married forever."

"Doesn't always work out that way. You still in love with him?"

It was on the tip of Ellen's tongue to say yes because that was what she was supposed to say, wasn't she? But she didn't say it. Instead, she thought on the matter for a moment. "Good question. I don't know. I guess I love him. How could I not still love him? We'd been married since college. He's the father of my child." She hesitated and then went on. "But I don't think I'm *in* love with him anymore."

"Sounds like you're living too much in the past. People think marriage is for everyone. It isn't. They think it's forever. It's not always." Lenora covered Ellen's hand resting on the counter with her own. It was small and wrinkly with protruding blue veins. "You've got to live in your today. Not worry about the past or the future. Life's too short for regrets of the past, or for fear of what might happen. Time to let go of that husband." When she said it, she released Ellen's hand and went back to her pastry.

They sat side by side in comfortable silence: Lenora scarfing down the huge cinnamon roll, Ellen sipping her black coffee. When Lenora had eaten the entire roll, which was *bigger* than her hand, she got off her stool. She was so small, she had to hop down.

"I best be going. I've got shopping at the market to do." Lenora carried her mug and the plate to the sink. "Leave the dishes, dear, and I'll do with them when I get back." She toddled across the kitchen, past Ellen, and opened the door to the back porch.

Ellen couldn't imagine Lenora was going to the store in bare feet and a housecoat. Maybe she was just going home?

"Let me drive you," Ellen said, purposely leaving out the word "home." "You'll get wet."

"I won't melt. And I've got my umbrella. It's on the porch." She gave Ellen a big, beautiful smile and went out the door, closing it behind her.

Ellen considered following her. She could speak to her family. Obviously, Lenora couldn't be allowed to continue to break into her house. Did her family realize she was going into people's homes uninvited?

Ellen glanced out the kitchen windows but didn't see Lenora. Maybe she had gone around the house and to the street? Slipping her phone into the pocket of her sleep shorts, she walked through the house and out onto the porch. No Lenora.

She went back into the house, debating what to do. Should she have a talk with Lenora's family and get it over with? But it was Lara's last day of chemo for the week, and Ellen needed to shower, get dressed, and put a load of laundry in. She'd ponder what to do about the old woman later.

At the counter in the kitchen, she picked up her plate with the cinnamon roll, debating whether to wrap it up for another day or toss it so she didn't eat any more. At the sink, she set the plate down and stared at it. She was dying for another bite. Maybe two.

"Live in the present," she said. "I'll worry about the size of my butt another day."

Live in the present.

The words reverberated in her head. She took a big bite, licked her fingers, and as she chewed savoring the taste, the smell, and the feel of the pastry in her mouth, she pulled out her phone.

She opened Facebook and stared at the screen for a moment. **Time to move on.**

The message was coming from every direction in the universe. Even from strangers breaking into her home.

She took a deep breath, unfriended her ex-husband, and finished off the cinnamon roll.

19

Ellen picked up a cardboard box of donations from the attic floor, remembering to squat, not lean over, and carried it down the stairs. It was after four o'clock. Almost quitting time. Over the weekend, she and Lara had sat on the beach, their feet in the water, and talked for a little while about what Ellen could be doing to *get her shit together.*

More accurately, Lara talked. She had been in one of her bossy moods. Ellen just listened.

Lara thought Ellen shouldn't spend all of her time grocery shopping, cooking, cleaning, and grading papers, that she needed to schedule time for herself. Lara suggested, no, *insisted* Ellen stop working on the attic during the weekends. And that she give the writers' group at Barrett's bookstore a chance.

Ellen was okay with taking weekends off from the attic. She didn't like the hours she spent working there. It gave her too much time alone to think. To go over in her head all the mistakes she had made in her life. She was still on the fence about the writers' meetings.

Her father had always said that writers' groups were a waste of time and space. He said the writers who met with other writers weren't really writers. He said those people knew that; that was why they attended group meetings instead of writing. They preferred to *talk* about writing rather than getting down to the terrifying business of it. He said writers' groups were for the uninspired, the untalented.

He'd been wrong about almost everything.

Was he wrong about this, too?

Reaching the first floor, Ellen set the box beside the front door. She'd load it into the car in the morning, where the box of *good junk* could join the others she'd already carried out. Today she'd bagged up a lot of trash and boxed a lot of donations, but she'd also discovered a couple of treasures. She found a tiny framed cameo of her grandmother when she was in her twenties, a letter written to her grandfather from his mother when he was stationed in Italy during WWII, and the best discovery of the day was a birthday card she'd made for her mother. Her handwriting was barely legible. She must have been in first or second grade at the time. On the front, she'd scrawled:

Hapy Bday, best MOM Evar

Inside, her six-year-old-self had signed her name and drawn what looked like a cat . . . or maybe a lobster, and a green blob on a string. Possibly a birthday balloon. Ellen didn't remember making the card, and it had made her eyes scratchy. The card reminded her of how much she had adored her mother as a child, how good her mother had been to her and her brother. Thinking back now, she realized how hard her mother had tried to make up for the fact that she'd married and subsequently bred with an ass.

It was hard to believe she'd been gone two years.

Ellen wished she'd seen that more clearly when her mother was still alive. Being a parent was sacrificial. Hard. Loving another human being was hard. But her mother had never had difficulty showing her love. Even when it hurt. She'd loved her husband and given herself completely to him, to her love for him. Even though Ellen knew she must have wondered if he ever loved her back.

Ellen straightened slowly from lowering the box and massaged the small of her back. She'd intended to work another half an hour or so. She'd found a tin box that looked like it had once held saltine crackers filled with old photos. She was going to sort them. But maybe instead, she'd pour herself a glass of wine and join Lara and her friends for *cocktail hour*.

None of the members of the porch support group were supposed to be imbibing while on chemo. Interestingly enough, Grace had a drink every afternoon. A stiff one. Stiffer than Ellen could handle. Grace liked a gin and tonic with fresh lime. The other day, Ellen had found Lara leaning against the kitchen counter, looking as if she were about to pass out, trying to make Grace a drink. Ellen had volunteered to make it. Lara had shown her how and Grace had declared the drink the best she'd ever had. She'd especially liked the little paper umbrella Ellen had added on impulse. She'd found a little Baggie of them in the pantry. Something Lara had brought down years ago for a weekend stay when they'd made daiquiris from fresh strawberries they'd picked at a farm.

The sound of male laughter caught Ellen's attention. It was Pine. He had a unique voice and laugh that she recognized at once. Hearing him made her smile. Then she heard more laughter: Amara's, Grace's, and Alex's.

Ellen wondered why they were laughing so hard. She walked through the house, kept cool by closing the blinds in the afternoon. As she approached the back door, she realized the laughter wasn't coming from the porch, but farther away. She stepped out into the hot, humid afternoon and squinted. An hour and a half ago, Lara, Alex, Amara, Grace, and Pine had been sitting on the porch discussing the best flavor for shaved ice. There was talk of a *field trip* to get shaved ice from a little place on the boardwalk. Ellen, however, got the feeling no one was serious about going anywhere farther from the porch than the bathroom. Not until they wandered home and Lara came inside to push the food Ellen made for her around her plate.

Ellen swung open the screen door. Not only were Lara and her friends missing from the porch, but so were the Adirondack chairs.

Kidnapped?

That was the first thing that came to mind, which was ridiculous, of course. Who would kidnap a bunch of cancer patients? And if someone *did*, they certainly wouldn't take their chairs with them.

Ellen leaned over the porch rail. Lara was sitting in the sand, her big straw hat beside her, and she was giggling the way she had (they had) as middle schoolers. Knees drawn up, she sat beside a plum-colored Adirondack chair that looked suspiciously like one of Ellen's *white* porch chairs. Amara sat on the sand beside her in a sparkly teal sari, beside a fuchsia-pink chair.

A man she didn't recognize looked up and waved. There was a spray can in his hand.

That was when Ellen caught the scent of wet paint.

They had painted her chairs?

"Are those *my chairs*?" Ellen hollered down, making no attempt to cover her exasperation.

Lara, Grace, Pine, Alex, Amara, and the stranger stopped what they were doing and looked up.

"Sure are!" Lara called, a challenge in her voice.

Ellen watched the newcomer shake the spray can and paint a band of orange across the back of the white chair nearest to him.

"Have you ever seen anything so beautiful?" Alex hollered up.

The teenager's smile was so big that Ellen couldn't resist smiling back. And Ellen felt her resolve crumble. Who cared what color the chairs were? If they brought joy to a *dying* teenager, how could she care?

Alex had on a pale pink wig, not the long hot-pink one she'd worn the previous day. This one was pixie cut. She was wearing a pastel-striped sundress that emphasized her gaunt body.

Ellen felt sick to her stomach. She couldn't imagine being Alex's parents. Of course, she couldn't imagine being Alex, either. To be a girl on the brink of womanhood knowing she wouldn't live to be old enough to drink or vote. Or marry or have a baby.

Lara had told Ellen that Alex had stopped treatment around the time she had started hers. It wasn't working; it was only making her sicker. Lara said Alex had wanted to stop sooner, but she had continued for months for her parents' sake. To give them a chance to get accustomed to the idea that the treatment wasn't working and what that ultimately meant. Now Alex went to the oncology department to help Grace pass out cookies, fetch blankets and what have you for patients having treatment. That's what Lara had said. It hadn't made sense that Grace was passing out things while getting her chemo treatment. She couldn't be wandering around during the infusion, could she? But Lara had gotten a phone call from her daughter Vera in Paris, and by the time she was off the phone Ellen had forgotten about it.

She made a mental note to ask Lara about it later.

"Do you like this shade?" Alex hollered up, pushing her clear cat-eye sunglasses up on her head. She shook the can, and it rattled. "It's called cotton candy." Sunlight reflected off the rhinestone eyelashes she was wearing.

Ellen leaned on the rail. "It's exquisite. It matches your hair," she told the teen.

Alex opened her arms wide, looking up at Ellen. "*Right?*" she called up, grinning. Her inflection included a question mark after the word, the way Ellen's freshman students pronounced it.

"What color would you like?" Alex pointed to the only chair from the back porch that was still white. "I'll paint it for you."

"Let her paint it herself, Miss Divine," Lara said. She called the teenager that sometimes. Why, Ellen didn't know.

"I've got some other colors." Alex indicated her Hello Kitty backpack. "I thought you might like the green. But Grace called dibs on it."

Ellen's gaze shifted to where Grace stood, painting the seat of her chair an emerald green. The paint was so uneven that it looked tie-dyed. "I don't know," she said, kicking off her canvas sneakers and walking down the steps to the sand. "I don't need a chair on the porch."

"Yes, you do," Lara told her, settling her hat back on her head. "These are for you, for your support group."

"For *my friends*," Lara answered. "That includes you. Oh. Meet Shorty." She indicated the unfamiliar man.

Shorty was tall, six-three, six-four. In his sixties, she guessed. Broad shouldered with big hands. Like the others, he was thin and gaunt, looking as if he were a small man wearing a large man's body. Like many of the others, he had no eyebrows, and Ellen suspected no hair beneath his ball cap. The ball cap read *FDNY Ladder #3* on it. She knew that fire department from the news. They'd taken on heavy casualties on 9/11.

"Shorty, this is Ellen. Our hostess with the *mostess*." Lara turned back to Ellen. "Shorty was a paramedic in New York City. A first responder when the Twin Towers went down." She spoke the words as matter-of-factly as if saying he had been a preschool teacher. "Pine and Shorty's wives met each other in the hospital cafeteria and introduced the guys to each other."

"Nice to meet you," Shorty said, nodding to Ellen. He had a deep voice with a slight Brooklyn accent. "I sure appreciate your—" He coughed and cleared his throat. "Hospitality."

Sean "Shorty" Lewis
Age: 61?
Diagnosis: Mesothelioma
Prognosis: Terminal

"Alex, what other shades of paint do you have in your magic bag?" Lara asked.

Ellen watched Lara pick up a glass with a piece of lime floating in it. It looked a lot like the gin and tonic she'd made for Grace the other day, except that it wasn't pink. Grace liked her pink gin. Apparently, it was a British thing. "Are you drinking *gin*?" she asked.

Lara looked at the glass as if it were the first time she had noticed it in her hand. "I hope not. It's supposed to be vodka."

"But you're not supposed to have alcohol," Ellen protested. "It's right in the guidelines in your packet. You'd know that if you'd read it."

"Why would I read it? I have you to read my *guidelines*."

"They're written for a reason."

"You're about to get the tall man, Ellie." Lara took another sip, a defiant look in her eyes.

The tall man. That's what Lara called her middle finger when she flipped it. A clever phrase. She'd have to add it to her journal, which seemed to be evolving. Several times now, she'd added bits and pieces of conversations she'd had on the back porch. Or conversations she'd overheard.

"Don't push," Lara warned.

Ellen harrumphed but didn't say anything more. They'd talk about it after everyone went home. As she turned back to Alex, she noticed Pine, whose chair was navy blue, watching her closely. It was unnerving, his dark-eyed stare.

"Let's see what I've got." The teen dug into the backpack.

"You think it's okay to be spray-painting them down here?" Ellen directed her question to Lara. "You don't think the wind will carry any of the paint onto the beach? Onto sunbathers?"

Lara sat back until she was under the shade of the porch and swirled the ice cubes in her glass. "Who cares?"

"How about summer pool?" Alex asked.

Ellen wished she'd grabbed her sunglasses. The glare was so

bright she had to shade her eyes to see what Alex was holding up. It was another can of spray paint. "Sorry?"

"*Summer pool.* That's the name of the paint color." Alex shook the can in her hand, popped off the lid, and walked over to the white chair. She painted a band of a tropical turquoise across the back of the chair. "It's pretty, isn't it?" Alex narrowed her gaze. "It will make your blue eyes look even bluer. You have amazing eyes, you know."

Ellen blinked, taken off guard by the compliment. "I do?" Her first impulse would have been to argue the point. But instead, she smiled and said, "Thank you."

"Colored contacts?" Alex asked, still studying Ellen's eyes.

"Um, no. My mother's eyes. Born with them."

"Cool." Alex pushed the paint can into Ellen's hand. "Give her a try."

Ellen held the can for a moment, then pressed on the top and sprayed the arm of the chair a nice, even coat.

"Very pretty," Amara declared, shaking her own can.

"Keep going," Lara encouraged.

Ellen was surprised by how much fun it was to do something so impulsive. The more she painted, the better she felt. The long day alone in the attic faded, and she enjoyed the feel of the warm sand under her bare feet and the afternoon sun on her face.

Alex drifted back to her chair.

Pine started telling a funny story about one of Gwen's granddaughters insisting he and Gwen try one of her beauty face masks. The teenager had put them on her grandparents and then taken the photo. It wasn't until their granddaughter emailed the photo of them that they realized the moisturizing masks had animal faces printed on them: the granddaughter a unicorn, Gwen a panda bear, and him a pink pig. He told them Gwen had gone to the drugstore to make copies of the photo and he would bring it another day to show them.

Someone said she was hungry and Amara, busy painting her chair fuchsia, began talking about the food she'd had at a three-day wedding she'd gone to in India. Ellen was still painting, listening to Amara's story, when a male voice called from the side of the house.

"Mum? You here?"

This time Ellen recognized the voice immediately. At least she wasn't in a ratty bathing suit, covered in sunscreen.

"Back here!" Grace called.

Barrett walked around from the side of the house and stopped near the stairs. "I rang the doorbell, but no answer."

"We're painting Ellen's chairs for her."

Barrett looked at his mother's green chair. "I can see that."

"I have to get this leg; then I'm ready to go," Grace told her son.

"You're going to need another coat," Alex warned, pointing at Grace's chair. "It's streaky."

"Looks tie-dyed to me," Grace answered. "I like it."

Barrett looked to Ellen. "You're putting them to work, I see. Excellent. Maybe it will keep them out of trouble."

Ellen gave her can a shake and continued spraying. "Something like that."

He was quiet long enough for her to sneak a glance at him. He was watching her. She tucked a piece of hair that had come loose from her ponytail behind her ear and tried to concentrate on her painting.

At thirty-eight, he is eight years younger than I am.

She couldn't get the thought out of her head.

"You didn't come last Tuesday," he said.

When Ellen realized that he had moved closer, she looked up, spooked for a second. Did he know what she was thinking? "*Tuesday?*"

"The writers' group. I thought you were going to come."

He sounded disappointed, and Ellen didn't know what to say.

"You should come tomorrow," he told her. "We're talking about characterization."

She tentatively met his gaze. Swallowed. "Maybe I will."

"Are we going or not, Son?" Grace asked, handing her paint can to Alex. Today her T-shirt read *A woman's place is in the House and Senate.* "Because if we're not, I'm getting Ellen to make me another gin and tonic."

"We're going. We're going." Barrett glanced at Ellen again but didn't say anything.

When he walked around the corner of the house and out of sight, Alex clasped her hands to her chest. "That man is *gorgeous,*" she declared. "Please tell me you're going to hit on him, Ellen. Because if I weren't bald, I'd do it in a second. I don't care if he is an old guy," she added.

Pine burst into laughter, and to Ellen's surprise, despite the inappropriateness of Alex's comment, she threw back her head and joined him.

20

Ellen stood on the busy corner of Albany Avenue and Rodney Street, staring in the window at a display of chocolate-covered strawberries on wood skewers.

Strawberry Kabobs! the sign read. *Buy one, get one free!*

Lara loved chocolate-covered anything, but especially strawberries. She wondered if Lara would eat one if she bought it.

Lara had struggled to get up that morning to go to chemo. Her nausea, which seemed to have no rhyme nor reason, hadn't been bad, but her exhaustion had been overwhelming. She'd had to stop and sit on the edge of the tub to brush her teeth. Ellen wondered if the whole painting the chairs activity had been too much for her. For *The Porch.*

That's how she had begun thinking of Lara and her friends. She had written it in her journal:

> Collectively the people who sat there every day are The Porch.

At first, it had seemed foolish, maybe even dangerous, to Ellen for a support group to meet at someone's home. But as she had watched the interaction between Lara and her friends, she'd realized that their friendship might be as vital to their recovery as the drugs they were receiving intravenously. Lara's friends adored her. She adored them—something Ellen might have been jealous of under different circumstances.

She always had secretly disliked having to share Lara with others: friends when they were kids, later boyfriends, Tim, even their children, her son, Lara's daughters. Maybe because Ellen had always worried Lara would like someone else better. Love someone else more.

It seemed petty now. Seeing how much Lara's friends liked her, loved her, made Ellen's chest tighten, her breath catch. Lara deserved that love. She needed it right now and anything Ellen could do to facilitate it she was going to do her darnedest to try.

Ellen made a mental note to come back to the candy shop to get the chocolate-covered strawberries later and walked on. It was almost one o'clock. She was going to be late.

If she went.

She hadn't made a final decision. However, she had brought a legal pad and pen to take notes. In case she decided to stop by. She'd made the mistake that morning in telling Lara she was considering going, and Lara had made plans to catch a ride home with Pine and his wife after her treatment. Grace wasn't driving anymore. Not even now that her car was back from the shop. Her son had taken her keys and royally pissed her off, according to Grace. *Good for Barrett*, Ellen had thought when Grace told The Porch she'd been grounded.

Ellen slowed her gait as she approached the bookstore. Suddenly she felt self-conscious. She was afraid she hadn't dressed appropriately. What did a real writer wear? Her father had worn tweed vests and an Irish cap.

She didn't own anything tweed.

She'd changed her clothes three times before settling on cropped white jeans and a mint-green T-shirt with fluttery short sleeves. She'd added flip-flops to look casual. And she'd blown out her hair and put on mascara and lipstick.

She halted in the middle of the sidewalk that was teeming with tourists. There were people in a rainbow of colors, from all walks of life. Some wore bikinis; others, jeans and tank tops. A man in his seventies walked past her, bare chested in tight red jammers. The sun was hot on her face and the air smelled thickly of boardwalk food and suntan lotion.

Was this a mistake? How could she call herself a writer? She hadn't written a word of her novel that she hadn't erased. The closest she'd come to writing since she arrived in Albany Beach was her journaling.

But she was enjoying her journaling more by the day. Her entries were sometimes just phrases, sentences. Thoughts to ponder or to go back to another day. She'd thought she'd start fleshing out a plot for her book, but instead, she found herself writing down observations about herself and those around her.

> Do we all have to come to terms with our own mediocrity?
> Do I?
> Why does the old lady think my house is hers?

That morning, thinking about Pine, she'd asked herself the question:

> Why are some people so happy all the time?

Even though his prognosis was decent, Lara said his chemo was really wrecking him this round. It was his third series of treatments for his non-Hodgkin's lymphoma in the last two years. He looked bad. Worse. Even in the week since Ellen had met him, she had noticed it. He was weak. His skin was splotchy, and he was sometimes unsteady on his feet. But he was always the life of the party. He was always the first to get out of his chair to get something for someone else on the porch. And he talked about his wife as if she were the most beautiful, smartest, most fascinating woman on earth. He talked about all of his family that way, too: his oncologist, Lara, the guy who came to the house to fix his cable TV. His enthusiasm for life was remarkable.

Ellen checked her watch. It was three minutes after one now. If she didn't go to the meeting now, she'd be interrupting. Which would be rude, especially since it was her first time.

She took a deep breath and walked toward the bookstore.

And walked right past the door.

She didn't stop until she reached the iconic Thrasher's French fry stand.

"Help you?" a young man with his head shaved on one side and a tattoo of what looked like a toad—maybe a frog—on his earlobe asked her from behind the counter.

He was wearing a hairnet over his head, and she took a moment to appreciate a twenty-year-old who was comfortable enough with who he was to shave one side of his head *and* wear a hairnet. She couldn't even make a decision to dye her hair the color it had been when she was a child.

"No thanks." She smiled, gripping her bag, and walked back toward the bookstore.

And walked by the door again.

This time she made it to the candy store before she came to a stop, letting a lithe young thing in a yellow bikini, talking on her cell, brush past her. A man with a corgi on a leash walked by her going in the opposite direction. He was hurrying to keep up, so maybe the corgi was walking him.

Ellen wiped her brow. She should have worn a hat. She had intended to, but her hair looked nice for once. She didn't want to have hat hair the next time she bumped into Barrett. She thought that after the meeting she might pick up another book so that she could go to the front register and see him.

She groaned. She was sweating profusely now. Second-guessing the decision not to wear the hat and to wear jeans. They were hot as all get-out. She should have worn shorts.

She wiped her brow again and slid her canvas bag back up over her shoulder. Maybe she'd go next week. And dress better. Shorts and a tee would be fine. Summers at the beach were always casual. She—

"I saw you walk past the store," a deep voice said from behind. "*Both* times. You may as well come in. You've been found out now."

She whipped around. Looked up.

It was him.

One corner of Barrett's full mouth turned up in a one-sided grin.

Ellen didn't know what to say.

"Oh, come on in." He opened the door and held it for her.

For a split second, Ellen seriously considered tucking her head down and walking away. As if she hadn't seen him, heard him.

"You're running up my air-conditioning bill." He sounded amused. "Come on." He cocked his head. "We won't bite. They're nice people." He leaned closer as if to take her into his confidence. "Except for one guy. You'll know which one soon enough."

He offered a genuine smile and Ellen's heart took off, beating like crazy. She walked through the door, into the bookstore. The heavenly smell of freshly brewed coffee clung in the air. "Sorry I'm late," she managed.

"You're not." He followed her. "We say one o'clock so those who need to make small talk can do so before we move on to business. And so Josh will actually be on time occasionally. You'll meet him, too. We don't officially start until one-thirty."

Ellen noted that Barrett had referred to when *we* start. Was it a figure of speech, or did he run the meeting? How did that work? Did they have speakers and he served as a facilitator?

The inside of the store was darker and cooler than outside.

Much cooler, and she gave a sigh of relief. She inconspicuously checked the armpits of her T-shirt. Luckily, they weren't wet yet. She'd made it inside just in time.

"We're back here." He walked away. "My new guy, Tyler, will take orders if you want a coffee or a pastry. Just be patient with him. He's not a born-and-bred barista, but he's getting the hang of it." Again, he lowered his voice as if . . . as if they were friends, he could share things with her. "I hired him as a favor to his grandmother. Kid's had a hard go of it. No dad. Mom's in rehab again." He wound his way between bookshelves. "We've got a Vietnamese iced coffee on the menu now. It's good. If you like that sort of thing."

He stopped at a glass door. Behind it was a small meeting room. There were half a dozen people sitting around a table. She could faintly hear their voices, but not what they were saying. The conversation was upbeat and mingled with laughter.

"I . . . I didn't realize there was a meeting room back here," she said, hoping her voice didn't sound as off-kilter as she felt. This was strange, Barrett acting as if they were friends. She wasn't quite sure what to make of it. Was he just being nice to her because his mother sat on her porch and drank her iced tea most days of the week?

"This is nice," she said. "Letting them meet here."

He rested his hand on the door handle. "I sell books." He shrugged. "I should support other writers, right?"

Other?

"So . . . you're like a facilitator?"

He pushed open the door, making a face. "No. I'm a member of the group."

"You're *a writer*?" She hoped she didn't sound as surprised as she felt.

He rocked his head one way and then the other. "Some days more than others. I just sold my twenty-third teen romance. Went with vampires this time." He winked at her.

And she smiled.

21

Lara watched Ellen emerge from the surf, tugging on the seat of her old bathing suit. She looked good, better than she had when they arrived in Albany Beach. Which was nice because Lara knew she herself was looking worse by the day.

Ellen had gotten a little sun, giving her a healthy glow, even wearing her 50 SPF. And she looked leaner. She hadn't needed to lose weight, but she was more muscular now. Healthier. It might have been Lara's imagination, or maybe wishful thinking, but the lines around Ellen's mouth seemed less defined.

"Well, I didn't drown," Ellen announced, tossing her goggles into the old canvas L.L.Bean bag she always used for a beach bag.

The bag read *Paatricia Pigg*, stitched in puce green. Ellen had bought it off a sale table years ago while they were vacationing in Maine and had gone to the flagship store. It amused Lara that Ellen was frugal enough to buy a high-quality bag that had lasted years of abuse on the beach, including being carried off on the incoming tide on more than one occasion, at a discount. Ellen didn't care if it had someone else's name on it, even misspelled, even a name like Patricia Pigg. The entire rest of the vacation Lara had called her Pat Tricia, or Ms. Pigg. She still called her that once in a while.

"Glad you didn't drown," Lara answered, looking up at her. She'd removed her hat to take in the warmth of the last rays of the day. She didn't care if one of the items, the many items, on the DO NOT list in her chemo packet warned against sun exposure. The heat made her feel as if she was still alive, at least on the outside, even as the chemo tried to kill her. She was cold all the time now, between the cancer and the cold cap, and had become a heat-seeking creature. Like Ellen's Siamese cat. Lara had read somewhere that it was possible that cancer patients were always cold because their temperatures were lowered by the cancer cells to make their environment more hospitable. *The little bastards.* Was it not enough that the cancer cells were eating up her bones? They had to make her cold, too?

"Lifeguards are off duty," she told Ellen. "And there's not a chance in hell I could have saved you, not even if the water only came to my knees."

Ellen picked up a blue and white starfish towel off her beach chair. "I wouldn't be much of a swimmer if I could drown in knee-deep water."

Lara held up her hand. It felt like lead. "I'm just giving you the facts."

Ellen stood in front of her, drying off, blocking the view of the outgoing tide. "You want to go in and have something to eat? I made chef's salad, but if you're not up to that, there's still some chicken noodle soup in the freezer. You said the other night that was good on your upset stomach."

Lara pushed her sunglasses up onto her head. The sun was low in the sky behind her now; she didn't need them. "Let's sit here a while longer."

Ellen dropped into the low chair and stretched out her legs. She smelled like suntan lotion and the brine of the ocean. Lara loved the smell. It reminded her of all the days, as a child, that she had spent on this beach. The first time she had come, she had just turned nine.

Her parents had never had a problem shipping her off to stay with Ellen for a few weeks each summer. "Better the Tollivers deal with you than me," her mother had always said. Lara also suspected that part of the draw had been that she could tell the women in her golf foursome that her daughter *practically lived* with *New York Times* best-selling author Joseph R. Tolliver. Somehow, she thought it added to her social status.

Every time Ellen's dad had had a new book release, Lara had been forced to ask him to sign multiple hardbound copies. Thankfully, she had never had to ask him directly. She rarely saw the mean bastard of a drunk. He didn't eat dinner, attend events, socialize, or go on vacation with his family. He spent all of his waking hours in his office, sometimes his sleeping ones, which seemed to work out just fine for everyone. Ellen's mother, who had been a darling, had always taken care of the personal autographs when Lara's mother forced her to ask for them.

Ellen brushed Lara's hand. "You should try to eat something. You're getting skinny. *Skinnier*," she corrected. "You have to keep up your strength."

"I have an idea, Ellie." Lara took care to be sure her tone was just right. She didn't want to bitch at Ellen for caring about her, caring *for* her, but she also had to make it clear that sometimes she needed to do things her way. She needed to do what was best for her own mental health rather than Ellen's or anyone else's. "Let's not talk about my cancer anymore today. My treatment, either." She waved her hand as if she could magically erase it all. "None of it. I—"

When Ellen started to interrupt, Lara held up her hand, stop sign style. "And don't interrupt. I don't have the patience for it today. I know what you're going to say, so save it. I'm not talking about denial here. Well . . ." She cocked her head. "I'm thinking *temporary* denial. Let's just sit here and talk for a few minutes about something else." She turned to her friend. "I know. Let's talk about you. Tell me more about your writers' meeting. Better yet, about Grace's hunky son."

Ellen squirmed and looked away. Together, they watched two women in their fifties, both in tankinis and sun visors, walking hand in hand.

"Look," Ellen said. "She's wearing my suit. The green one I just bought."

Over the weekend, she and Ellen had gone shopping. They'd only gone to three stores before Lara had had enough and needed to go home for a nap. But she'd enjoyed herself. She'd made Ellen buy the bathing suit, some new undies (though Ellen had put her foot down on the thong style), and a cute denim miniskirt. And Ellen had finally bought a pair of jean shorts of the appropriate length. Lara was presently scheming to toss the old, baggy, knicker jean shorts, forcing Ellen to wear the new pair. She was just waiting for the opportunity. And the energy to go down to the lower level where the once-a-garage laundry room was located.

Ellen lifted her chin in the women's direction, her tone thoughtful. "They look happy, don't they?"

"Maybe it's the suit," Lara quipped. But then she smiled at her friend, appreciating the tenderness in her voice. Ellen gave the impression to many that she was cold and unfeeling, but Lara knew better. Ellen was full of kindness and compassion. She just wasn't always comfortable showing it.

Ellen laughed and dug two refillable water bottles from her bag: one green, one purple. She held up the purple one. "Drink. You're going to get dehydrated again, and then you'll be consti-pated again, and then—"

"Enough already." Lara snatched the bottle from her.

"I thought you said no interrupting today."

"You can't interrupt me. I can interrupt you. I'll drink. See me drinking?" She made an event of flipping the spout and making sucking sounds like a guinea pig. "Tell me about the meeting. I want to know everything about Grace's son. I want all the sordid details."

"No sordid details to be had." Ellen took a drink from her water bottle. "It was, you know, a meeting. A discussion, an exchange of ideas." She raised her shoulder and let it fall. "It was . . . nice to talk to other writers. We discussed how to go about creating three-dimensional, fleshed-out characters. They all use storyboards." She made a face. "I've tried it, but I haven't had much luck. It seems like busywork to me." She glanced at Lara. She hadn't put her sunglasses back on, so Lara could see her eyes. "You know what a storyboard is?"

"Don't care," Lara answered, stretching out her leg. *The* leg. The one with the cancer. It hurt today. "We'll talk about that later. What I want to hear about is Barrett. You said he was nice to you."

"He was." She sounded suspicious. "I don't know why."

"*Why?*" Lara slipped her water bottle into the cupholder on the beach chair. "Because he's a human being and human beings are generally nice to each other." She leaned closer and smiled. "Do you think he likes you?"

"Are we in middle school again?"

"Do you like him?" Lara sat back, winded from that little bit of exertion. She had told Ellen the low-slung beach chairs were fine, even though she had to sit in the sand to reach the seat practically. Now she was having second thoughts. Standing up from this position, she feared Ellen would need a crane to lift her. "You think you should ask him out? I think you should ask him out."

Ellen looked at her as if she had grown a horn in the middle of her head. Which only egged Lara on. "You should ask him out for a drink. Or over for a drink." She grabbed Ellen's forearm. "I'll go hang out with Grace."

"Hang out with Grace? Both of you are in bed at seven o'clock."

Lara thought for a moment. "Good point. Okay, I'll close

my door. And turn on my sound machine. With my bedroom door and yours closed, you can have all the wild sex you can stand. I'll never hear a thing." She smiled slyly. "I bet he's good in bed. He's got the kind of hands a man who's good in bed has."

Ellen frowned, lines popping up on her forehead. Lara had warned her time and time again that they'd turn into wrinkles if she didn't cut it out.

"What does that even mean?" Ellen demanded,

Lara refused to give in to her naysaying. "You should ask him out. Grace says that since she sold her house and moved in with him, he doesn't have much of a social life. Like someone else we all know and love." She made an event of cutting her eyes at Ellen. "He works long hours at the bookstore, cooks, cleans, shops, takes care of her, and writes. That's it. Grace is worried he'll become a hermit once she's gone."

"Wait, wait, go back," Ellen said waving her hand. "You knew he was a writer and you didn't tell me?"

"I didn't?" Lara thought for a moment. "I guess I didn't. Chemo brain. Alex says we should use that excuse whenever possible. She says we've earned it. Poor kid. If anyone knows, she does. Did you know that she was diagnosed when she was ten? No school, no friends, in years, just hospitals. That's been her life ever since, and to what end?"

"I know you said she stopped treatment," Ellen said soberly. "Is there nothing anyone can do?"

"Alex said it was a death sentence from the get-go. All the chemo, they even tried some sort of radiation, nothing worked long term. That's why they finally stopped chemo. The tumor shrank for a while, but then it started growing again. The docs' bags of tricks are empty."

"I can't imagine being her parents. I know you said she was an only child." Ellen gazed out at the lapping blue waves. "I'm surprised they let her out of their sight."

"It's pretty much the opposite. She rarely sees them these days, and only in passing. They're both fancy attorneys. They work long hours and travel a lot. They have a live-in house-keeper, and she's responsible for taking care of Alex. Not that Alex needs anyone to take care of her."

"You have got to be kidding me. If she was my daughter, I'd do anything to spend every moment I had with her. What horrible people."

Lara exhaled. "That was my first thought, too. But Alex is cool with it. She says she thinks her parents are learning how to live without her now, so they'll be prepared when she dies. It's Alex's opinion that this way it's easier all the way around for everyone, including her."

Ellen turned in her chair. "She said that?"

"Pretty savvy kid. Beyond her years in a lot of ways. I guess she's had to be. Having terminal cancer and being transgender, I can't imagine—"

Ellen swung her head around so hard, it was a wonder it didn't snap off. "What did you just say?"

Lara looked at Ellen. "I said Alex has had to be strong, being dealt such a shitty hand—cancer and being born in the wrong body." She stared at Ellen.

Ellen had a look on her face as if she'd just been told the world was indeed flat, that cats were actually dogs, that the Girl Scouts of America had just decided to stop selling thin mint cookies.

"She's *transgender*?" Ellen whispered.

Lara nodded slowly. "Yup. You didn't know? Of course, I guess why would you know? Alex was born with a penis, but she identifies as female."

"Alex is a boy?"

Lara tilted her head one way and then the other. "Yes, and no. She was born with male genitalia, so her birth certificate says she's male, but she said she always knew she was a girl from the first time she had self-awareness. Her parents gave her a typical response, told her she wasn't a girl, tried to keep her from wearing girls' clothes, playing with toys they thought were *girly*. Obviously, it didn't work."

"Did she . . . Did Alex have a sex change operation?"

"Too young. And with terminal cancer, it doesn't really make sense to—" Lara's voice caught in her throat and she picked up her water bottle, giving herself a moment as she took a drink. She made a habit not to dwell on the idea that her friends were in different stages of dying. Because they were living now and living well. She reminded herself all the time of that.

She'd only known Alex a short time, but she adored her. The kid had it together better than most adults. She was funny, sweet, articulate, and just plain fun to spend time with. She had such a unique outlook on the world. She wasn't in the least bit angry or resentful of her situation, not being transgender, having terminal cancer, or having parents who couldn't emotionally deal with the impending loss of their only child. And Alex still had so much to give. Lara had met her at chemo, not because she was taking treatment but because she visited the infusion department often. She helped Grace, passing out cookies, fetching blankets from the warmer, and just offering her big, bright smile, fluttering her long, sparkly lashes, and sporting her crazy wigs.

"Alex isn't going to live long enough to have the surgery," Lara said when she found her voice again. "She has to be over eighteen to consent for herself."

"So . . ." Ellen was obviously thinking. "Her parents ended up agreeing to let her be a girl?"

"I don't think they so much as *agreed* as just decided to ignore it."

"That's terrible," Ellen whispered.

Lara sighed. "I know. But Alex has told us all that she's come to terms with it, so we need to." She reached for her water bottle. "How did we get on this subject? Back to hunky Barrett. You need to get laid."

22

"What have you got for us today for show-and-tell, Pine?" Amara asked, settling down in her chair after her third trip to the bathroom. Once upon a time, she might have been embarrassed by her frequent trips to the lavatory, but she was long over that. Age and illness had a way of reminding one what was important and what wasn't. She had always thought she had a good idea of what mattered and what didn't, but losing her beloved so soon after they married had refined her ability to choose the gems from life's rocky stream bed.

Besides, Lara had gone to the bathroom several times before excusing herself to lie down on the couch in the cool darkness of the living room. Grace had offered for them to "all clear out," but Lara had been adamant that they stay, promising to be back in an hour.

"What have I got?" Pine chuckled. "What have *you* got? Gotta be someone else's turn besides mine."

Pine had started bringing little things to share with them in the hospital, even before joining them on the porch there at Ellen and Lara's. The first time Amara had sat beside him in chemo, he'd pulled an Indian arrowhead from his bag and shown it to her. He'd told her he found it when he was a boy hunting arrowheads with his father. "We'd go whenever it rained," he'd said. "Back in those days, you could walk out into any field in Delaware after a rain, find the highest point, which ain't all that high here"—he'd winked at her then—"and you could find an arrowhead or pottery. Even a stone hatchet blade," he had told her. "My daddy found one once up in Kent County."

"No, you go first. You always have the best show-and-tell. Don't you think Pine should go first—" Amara had meant to direct her question to Grace, but Grace had fallen asleep. She was sitting in her newly painted green chair, gripping the arms, her head flung back, her mouth wide open. "Alex," Amara finished. She set her gaze on the teenager.

She had liked Alex the first time she met her. The business of being male, being female, didn't matter to Amara in the least. She found it exasperating that Westerners were so caught up in such matters. Maybe it was because in the Hindu religion into which she'd been born, souls were believed to be reincarnated into various bodies until moksha—final release from death and rebirth. Hindus didn't believe souls were male or female. For that reason, gender had never mattered all that much. She didn't care if Alex was male or female. She was just Alex.

Alex looked up from her cell phone. "Sorry I wasn't listening. Bianca Del Rio was throwing some serious shade Adore Delano's way."

"I have no idea what you're talking about, dear." Amara smiled. "I was asking you if you thought Pine ought to share what he brought for show-and-tell." She glanced at Ellen, who looked nervous sitting on the edge of her chair, which was a nice aqua color. When Lara had gone in the house to lie down, Ellen had come out to join them. Lara had joked the day before that her friend liked keeping an eye on them. That Ellen was afraid one of them would die on their porch. Amara had to agree it was a reasonable possibility but certainly nothing to fear. She wished Ellen weren't so uncomfortable every time she joined them. Ellen just didn't seem to know how to relax and be present with those around her.

"Sure." Alex lowered her phone to her lap. She was wearing a yellow sundress and a pretty brunette wig that looked like it could have been her own hair. Even her faux eyelashes were natural looking today. "What did you bring? That old rucksack you showed us last time was so cool."

"Got photographs," Pine said. He pulled them out of his bag and held them up, splayed in his hand, as if they were playing cards.

Alex sat up. Amara noticed, out of the corner of her eye, Ellen perk up with interest.

"There I am. Nineteen years old." Pine plucked the photo from the array in his hand and passed it to Amara.

She sat back in her chair and studied the black-and-white photograph. It was square with wide, white borders. Black-and-white, with *AUG 1968* printed at the bottom in processing. She had seen this type of photo from the sixties before, though she hadn't immigrated to the United States until the seventies, when she'd gone to college. The photo was faded, so faded that it took a moment to register who the solemn young man in a floppy-brimmed bucket hat, standing in front of what appeared to be a latrine, was.

"You?" Amara asked, looking up at Pine.

Alex rose to have a look at the photo, and Amara passed it to her.

"Yes, ma'am. Drafted into the good ol' US of A Army in January 1968. Boot camp at Fort Dix, and then before I knew what hit me, I was in Vietnam." He pronounced the country to rhyme with "man." "I was posted at Long Binh, an army post northeast of Saigon."

Amara glanced up at Ellen. "Would you like to see?" She started to get up, but Ellen shot out of her chair, taking the photograph from her hand.

Ellen stood there in a baggy pair of shorts and an old Rolling Stones 50 & Counting tour T-shirt and studied the photo. On the back of her shirt, there was a list of tour dates and cities with the year *2015* printed on it. She wore the shirt all the time. Lara had one, too. They had attended the concert together in Philadelphia, Lara had told them. Amara didn't care for Mick Jagger or his antics, but she always had liked the song "Angie." Her husband had loved the Rolling Stones. They had danced to "She's a Rainbow" at their wedding.

"Wow," Ellen said quietly, still staring at the photo in her hand. "You were just a kid." Amara heard heartbreak in her voice.

"I was." Pine, a small man, perched himself on the end of his chair and passed another photo to Amara and the last to Alex. "Didn't think so at the time, of course." He pointed to the photo in Amara's hand now. "Good-lookin' boy, wasn't I?" He cackled.

It was Pine again, but he looked years older in the photo Amara held. He was standing in front of what looked like a hole in the ground. The photo was dated two months later than the first. In the final photo, dated December 1968, he was naked from the waist up, wearing a Santa hat, automatic rifle lying across his lap.

Ellen continued to stare at the photo in her hand. "What did you do there?"

"Look, he's wearing a Santa hat holding a gun," Alex said, sounding half-afraid, half-exhilarated.

"M14," Pine told Alex. He looked to Ellen and chuckled. "Was supposed to be infantry, but I ended up a rat."

"A rat?" Alex asked with disgust.

"A tunnel rat," Ellen whispered. "My son did a report in high school on the American and Australian tunnel rats." She looked to Alex. "They went down into the underground tunnels the Vietcong had dug to travel undetected, so they could sneak into cities, villages, and military installations."

"The Vietnamese went underground?" Alex asked, leaning over to look at the photo Amara held up for her.

"They did, clever little bastards that they were. 'Scuse my French." Pine lowered himself back into his chair. "And we went in after them."

Amara handed the photograph to Alex and picked Pine's bucket hat up off the porch rail. "Put on your hat. You're going to burn."

Pine grinned, running his hand over his shiny dark head. He didn't have a single hair. No facial hair, either. "You know, darker-skinned folks like you and me don't burn the same as white. Don't get skin cancer like 'em, either."

"Put on your hat," Amara ordered. "I told Gwen that if she let you stay for the afternoon, I'd be sure you took your pills on time, that you'd eat, drink your water, *and* wear a hat."

"Has to do with the melanin in your skin. It's what makes me darker than you." He directed his comment to Alex.

"Nonwhite ethnic groups still get melanoma, Pine." Amara pressed the hat into his hand.

"That the nurse coming out in you?"

Amara's response was quick and clipped. "It's the you-better-do-as-I-say-or-I'm-going-to-tattle-on-you in me."

"You women. Always ganging up on men." He took the hat from her and pulled it down over his head.

Alex handed the two photos to Ellen and went back to her chair and her cell phone.

Ellen was still studying the photos, now all three. She looked up at Pine. "How do you get to be a rat?"

"I was small, and you see me. In those days, I was as skinny as Alex. No offense intended, sweetheart," he said in the teen's direction.

Alex was looking at her phone again and didn't glance up. "None taken."

"I know you had to be small to fit into the tunnels safely. Five-five or under, right?"

"Somethin' like that." Pine rested his hands on his knees.

"I meant . . ." Ellen hesitated. "How were you chosen to be a tunnel rat? You're not white."

Pine cackled with glee. "No, ma'am, I am not. Though likely I am somewhere in the family tree. My ancestors came from Central Africa, brought on a slave ship into Charleston. Lived in the Carolinas until the emancipation. I imagine a little white blood found its way into the family tree," he said with amusement.

Amara watched Ellen watch Pine.

"But I see what you're getting at. We trained together in Fort Dix, but for the most part, black men didn't fight with whites in the Vietnam war. We were *separate but had an equal opportunity to die.* And black men weren't welcome among the rats, but I told 'em—" He tickled himself and couldn't speak for a moment. "I told 'em I was Mexican." He slapped his knee. "Which wasn't even a lie because I spoke a little Spanish because my grandmother's neighbor was Mexican. Abuela Luisa taught me how to make a decent tortilla and say the sign of the cross in Spanish." He crossed himself. *"En el nombre del Padre, y del Hijo, y del Espíritu Santo.* Amen." He shook his head. "Abuela Luisa's been dead fifty-some years, and I still remember. Still say it that way sometimes, too. She was good to me. She and my grandmother both. My grandmother raised me, but you could say both of them did."

"Thank you for your service," Ellen said softly, handing the photos back to him.

"Don't look so down in the dumps!" Pine exclaimed, accepting the photos. "'Cause I was wrong."

"You were wrong?" Ellen asked.

Amara smiled to herself but kept quiet. She knew what was coming. She'd asked him herself the origins of his name the first time they had met, sitting side by side in the chemo lounge, waiting to go inside.

"My name!" Pine slipped the photos back into the bag beside his chair "Did I never tell you how I got my name?"

"You didn't," Ellen said, sitting down in her blue chair.

"So, first day I set foot in the godless jungle, I just *knew* the only way I was getting out of there was in a pine box. I went on about it so much that the guys started calling me Pine." He shrugged, grinning. "Turns out I was wrong, but the name stuck anyway."

23

Ellen lay in her bed with her arm tucked behind her head. She was holding her iPad in front of her, trying to decide which photo of herself she liked. The answer was easy—none of them. Her cat slept curled up beside her. It was too hot to have a furry cat pressed up against her, but she'd pushed the Siamese off multiple times, and eventually, she gave up.

"These are all terrible," Ellen mumbled as she looked at one taken the previous Christmas when they had been making cookies at Lara's. It was a candid shot that Lara's daughter Vera had taken and sent in a text. Love this, Auntie Ellie! When the photo had been taken, Ellen had been talking to someone, probably Lara, and was laughing, her head tilted back a little, a wineglass in her hand. Her hair looked decent, though it was just in a messy ponytail. But she looked . . . happy.

It had probably been the Chardonnay.

She squinted, pushing her reading glasses up on her nose to take a closer look at the photo.

Where had that double chin come from? She'd never had a double chin before. Using both hands, she moved the iPad closer. Then she made the photo bigger by grabbing the corner and stretching it. On her first try, the photo was too tall for the width and gave her laughing face a bit of a creepy, funhouse look. Or maybe a serial killer look.

Fixes the chin problem, though, she thought.

But like many solutions, it was only temporary.

When she sized the photo correctly, the chin was back. Or was it more of a neck waddle?

She used her thumb to stroke beneath her jawline. She couldn't feel any fat hanging down, but she obviously had some. It was right there in the photo.

She thought about getting up to check it in the mirror. But then she'd have to disturb the cat.

Maybe a different photo?

She went back to her photo gallery and flipped through more photos of herself. Interestingly enough, one of her father from his younger years was included in the mix. When the photo app had sorted them, it had made the mistake. It was interesting. She'd never thought she looked like her dad, but she saw it now in this old photo of him. It had been taken on the front porch of the beach house a decade ago, at least. She wondered when.

He'd rarely come to the beach. Even though Ellen had spent nearly every summer there for as long as she could remember. Years went by without him joining his family staying in Delaware for the summer. He had not come when she and her brother were children, and he hadn't come when they'd had children of their own. Joseph R. Tolliver always preferred to remain in New Orleans.

Work.

On the rare occasion when he *did* grace them with his presence, it was because he was on an East Coast book tour and her mother had insisted he stay a night or two while passing through. She always hosted a fancy cocktail party when the famous writer Joseph R. Tolliver was in Albany Beach. Ellen remembered being eleven or twelve, sitting in her pajamas on the staircase, listening to the clink of glasses and adult conversation and laughter. She remembered seeing her father standing in the foyer and talking with Judith Burton, the town's mayor. There had been something about the way he whispered into her ear, the way she touched his shoulder and looked up at him, that had made Ellen uncomfortable. She'd been too young at the time to understand appropriate boundaries for men and women married to someone else, but when she got older she recognized the behavior of a scoundrel. She didn't know if her father had ever cheated on her mother; maybe he hadn't, maybe he just liked the attention, but thinking about it, even now, brought a bad taste to her mouth.

She clicked the *No, this isn't Ellen* pop-up, and her father's face disappeared.

Good riddance.

She found another photo of herself that she semi-liked, taken the previous summer. She was in her kayak on the Roanoke River near her home. Her son, Christopher, had taken it from another kayak. He'd surprised her by coming to spend the night when he had an unexpected layover. It had been taken from far enough away that she liked the photo. Her arms looked long and lean as she pulled the paddle through the water, and the overgrowth on the bank behind her was gorgeous.

And no double chin.

She uploaded that photo and went back to the one Vera had taken in her mother's kitchen. If she touched it up a bit— removed the chin flab—it'd be a good photo. She wondered if it was ethical to touch it up, though. Because if it was okay to touch up her photo, that meant it was okay for someone else to touch up his. Right?

Ellen heard a knock on her doorframe. She always kept her door open in case Lara needed her during the night. "Hey," she said, quickly lowering her iPad, screen down, to the bed. "You okay?"

"Fine. Well, fine except for, you know, the cancer." Lara shrugged and made her way to Ellen's bed. She looked like a bag of bones dressed in sweat pants and a hoodie with sheepskin booties on her feet. Her gorgeous blond hair, still gorgeous and still plentiful, was piled on top of her head in a messy bun. "I'm lonely," she said, coming to the side of the bed, her arms crossed over her chest. "Scooch over."

Ellen picked up her iPad and scooted over, displacing the cat that meowed and took off.

"Whatcha doin'?" Lara asked. She got into bed and settled back on Ellen's two pillows.

"Nothing."

"Nothing?" Lara raised her eyebrows, which were mostly penciled in now. After almost a month of chemo, her eyebrows and eyelashes had fallen out. As had her pubes, she'd informed Ellen the previous evening when she had managed to find the energy to shower. "Nothing? Looks like something. Let me see." She tried to take the iPad from Ellen. "Please tell me you're not stalking Tim again."

Ellen held the iPad to her chest. "I'm not."

"You said you'd unfriended him. You agreed it's unhealthy and not helping you move on."

"I did, and I do," Ellen insisted.

Lara managed to wrangle the iPad out of her hands. "Then why are you— Oh." She cut her eyes at Ellen. "The dating site? Nice. I like this picture of you." She was looking at the chin photo. "Is this the one you uploaded to the site?"

"I didn't upload anything. I'm not even sure I'm going to do this."

"Oh, you're going to do this. Great photo. I'll add this one." Lara tapped the screen a couple of times. "Done. But you need a couple of photos." She swiped the screen and brought up the array of Ellen photos. "This one in the kayak is good, too. Now you need just one more. Hmm. How about this one?"

"Give it back. I don't want to do this right now. I don't want to do it at all," Ellen protested.

"Okay. How about *this* one?" Lara lifted the iPad for her to get a better look but kept a death grip on it.

Ellen took one look and shook her head. "Nope. I look fat."

Lara enlarged another. "This is a good one. Great smile."

"Hell no. I'm in a bathing suit!"

Lara swiveled her head to look at Ellen. "You little potty mouth, you," she said, obviously delighted.

She was as surprised as Lara was to hear the curse word come out of her mouth, but she wasn't ready to say so. She ignored Lara's question. "Not that photo."

"But you've got a cute figure," Lara argued. "Why not show it off?"

"I don't like it. Absolutely not."

Lara pointed out two more. Ellen nixed both.

"Fine," Lara said with a huff. "Two is enough to get you started. Now let's see what you wrote in your profile."

"This is a bad idea." Ellen crossed her arms over her chest, protectively. "An awful idea. I haven't been on a first date in like . . . twenty-five years."

"Let's see. Ellen, forty-six—"

"But I'm going to be forty-seven in September." Ellen cringed. "Should I say forty-seven?"

Lara looked at her as if she'd just asked if they should jump off the roof. "No, you don't say you're forty-seven. You're not."

"But I'm almost," Ellen fretted. "I don't want anyone to think I'm trying to mislead them."

Lara rolled her eyes. "'Forty-six, English professor. Enjoys swimming, kayaking, riding bikes, and taking walks on the beach at sunset.'" She looked at Ellen. "That's it? You're a writer for heaven's sake. You couldn't do better than that. *Likes to walk on the beach at sunset?* So does everyone else on the planet. Ellie, the point of your profile is to tell guys who you are."

Ellen looked away.

What if I don't know who I am?

She didn't have the nerve to say it out loud. Lara must have read her mind, though, because her face softened. "This is the easy part. How about if I write it for you?"

Ellen hesitated. She liked the idea of Lara writing it, but she didn't know that she trusted her. "You'll write a rough draft and let me look at it?"

"Sure. I'll do it on my computer and email it to you. You can make changes as you see fit and then upload it and get this ball rolling. You already answered all of the questions, right? Income level, religious preferences, activity preferences, what you like on your hamburger?"

Ellen stared at her for a moment. There must have been a hundred questions, but she didn't remember anything about what she liked on a hamburger. Then she saw the look on Lara's face and she laughed.

"Got ya, Ellie." Lara poked her in her stomach.

"Very funny." She took the iPad from her and stretched to set it on the nightstand. Tim's nightstand. Or it had been. She hadn't brought herself to put anything on it. There was just the lamp and even that she hadn't turned on.

But it was her nightstand now. Both of them were. And she could put what she wanted on it. Just setting it there gave her a strange sense of independence.

And something akin to well-being.

Ellen rolled back toward Lara and pushed up on one elbow. Lara was resting back on the pillows. Her eyes closed.

"Feeling sick?" Ellen asked, rubbing Lara's arm.

"No. Just tired."

"Question."

"Answer."

"Did you hide a key to this house somewhere outside?"

Lara opened her eyes. "What?"

"I keep meaning to ask you, did you hide a key to the house?

In the seashells in the front flower bed, under a flowerpot. I don't know."

"No, I don't even know where my copy of the key is," Lara told her. "Why?"

"Lenora."

"Ah, the old lady."

"I made sure the doors were locked before I went to bed, and this morning at sunrise, there she was again." She gestured. "Standing in my kitchen, barefoot in her housecoat, making coffee. Waiting for me."

"Is that so bad? Having someone make coffee for you?"

"She's breaking into my house, Lara. That's illegal."

"She's not stealing anything; she's not destroying property. What's the problem?"

"What's the *problem*?" Ellen stared at Lara. "The problem is that this isn't her house. She obviously has dementia. She turns on the stove and forgets to turn it off. *Multiple* burners. What if she gets hurt or . . . or—"

"Dies on your kitchen floor while she's making coffee for you?" Lara asked.

"That's not funny."

"Just asking. You *have* expressed concern about someone croaking while we're on your watch."

Ellen frowned. "I can't keep letting her break into my house. But I can't figure out how she's getting in."

"You ask her?"

"She won't say. I don't even know if she knows." Ellen rolled onto her back and watched the ceiling fan spin. "I think I'll follow her home next time she comes and talk to whomever she lives with. Do you think that's what I should do?"

"Better than calling the police, I guess. But then what if you tattle on her and then they lock her in a closet and starve her? It would be your fault."

"That's a terrible thing to say," Ellen sputtered.

"Just something you should consider."

"You don't think there's anything wrong with her breaking into my house at dawn and rifling through my pantry?"

Lara opened her eyes for a moment and smiled a sleepy smile. "I think it could be a hell of a story to tell your grandchildren someday."

24

Ellen grabbed a grocery bag from the passenger's side of her car. As she closed the door, another car pulled into the driveway. A red Honda she didn't recognize. But she knew who it was before he got out of the car. There was an American flag sticker in the corner of the windshield and a bumper sticker that read *Honor Our Heroes/Thank a Veteran*.

"Pine!" she called.

He was leaning into the car, talking to someone. The glare of the afternoon sun was so bright that she couldn't see who it was. Then he stood to his full height of five-foot-three (he swore he'd once been five-four and a quarter but shrank with age) and called to her, "Ellen, you have a sec? I want you to meet my better half!"

Ellen smiled and walked down the driveway. She had liked Pine the first time they had met, but after his show-and-tell the other day she hadn't been able to get him out of her mind. How had he been able to survive the Vietnam war as an African-American when they had been disproportionately drafted, assigned to combat units, and killed in Vietnam? How had he been able to reconcile those tragic facts and move on with his life, build a new life when he returned home? And now he had cancer? It just didn't seem fair. And yet he always saw the glass half-full; no, no matter what the experience, he seemed to see every glass as entirely full.

The driver's side door opened and an attractive woman in a green sundress got out. She whipped off her sunglasses to reveal striking blue eyes that were all the more noticeable against her mocha-colored skin. She had gorgeous natural hair she wore pushed back off her face with a green headband. And she was noticeably younger than Pine. Early fifties maybe? To Pine's seventy-something.

Ellen wasn't sure what she had expected, but this woman wasn't it. The funny thing was, she was okay with that. In fact, for the first time in as long as she could remember, she was pleased that she had been wrong. She was pleased with the un-expected.

"Hi." Ellen shifted the canvas bag of groceries to her left shoulder and offered her hand. "It's nice to meet you.

"Gwen." Pine's wife shook her hand. It was a warm, firm handshake. "I'm so glad I finally got to meet you. I've been dying to come in and say hello, but *someone*"—she indicated Pine with a tilt of her head—"wanted his support group to be his own. I guess he spends so much time with me that he needs to get away."

"That's not it and you know it, Gwen." Pine took from the car the gym bag that he always carried and came around to join them. "I thought it was a good way for you to have some time to yourself." He turned to Ellen. "As you can tell, I've got a sassy one here. But I love her all the more for it."

He put his arm around his wife and kissed her cheek. She saw overwhelming love in their gazes and unconditional acceptance. It was so sweet and struck Ellen so deeply that she blinked behind her sunglasses.

Gwen looked into Pine's eyes and smiled in a way Ellen realized, in an epiphany, that Tim had never smiled at her. Not ever. Ellen knew Tim had loved her at least once upon a time, but he had never loved her the way Pine loved Gwen.

How had she never seen that? How had Ellen lived with a man, loved him, made love to him, and picked up his dirty underwear off the floor and not realized that she and Tim were not a good match?

The moment of clarity was numbing. But also strangely freeing, she realized as a sense of relief washed over her. Tim had been right. They didn't belong together. She and Tim were not well suited to each other. Not in this phase in their lives, at least. And it wasn't her fault. It wasn't Tim's.

Sometimes things happen that aren't anyone's fault.

"I wanted to thank you for allowing the group to meet here," Gwen went on. "Pine spends so much time here, I feel like you should claim him on your tax return." She laughed. "He told me it was a meeting, but I feel like he and his friends have turned your place into a second home. I . . . I wanted you to know how much it means not just to the folks on your porch but the loved ones caring for them."

Like with Pine, Ellen took an immediate liking to Gwen. She was as friendly and happy as Pine. And there was a sparkle in her eyes that didn't seem to belong to a woman with a husband sick with cancer. "I don't mind at all," Ellen told them both. "I brought Lara here to take care of her while she goes through treatment, but most days, I feel like she's taking care of me."

"I hear you," Gwen said. "This one wants to make me breakfast every morning, even though he doesn't eat before he goes to chemo. And he rubs my feet every evening after work."

Ellen cut her eyes at Pine. "You've never offered to rub my feet."

"Didn't know you liked your feet to be rubbed. 'Sides, we're just getting to know each other," Pine teased. "I wouldn't want you to think I was getting fresh." He chortled at his own joke.

Gwen shook her head as she reached through the open window of the car and pulled out an envelope. "I should probably apologize right now for anything Pine has already said or will say." She offered the envelope. "This is for you. I was going to have Pine give it to you, but now I can give it to you myself."

Ellen accepted the envelope.

"It's just a little something from us," Gwen explained. "To thank you. It's a gift card for By the Sea, that new restaurant on the avenue. Have you been there?"

Ellen clutched the card, touched the couple could be so thoughtful. "I haven't." She looked up at Gwen, who was taller than she was. "You didn't have to do this."

"We wanted to. And we like supporting local businesses when we can. The chef there is the wife of one of my colleagues. They came from the Boston area. She knows her seafood. The crab bisque is to die for."

Ellen looked at the white envelope in her hand. She couldn't believe Pine and Gwen had bought her a gift card. She was dying to try the new restaurant. Of course, who was she going to go with? Lara was barely eating. She'd told Ellen on their way over to the hospital that she was going to start dumping her dinner into the toilet and cut out the middleman.

"One of your colleagues? Where do you work?"

"The hospital."

"Gwen's a doctor." Pine beamed. "Hospitalist. That was how we met. I was fixing medical equipment in a hospital up north. She was doing her residency."

"I'm Pine's second wife. His first wife passed suddenly when they were young," Gwen explained. "We've been married for twenty years. But I'm sure you know all of this."

"No, no, I didn't," Ellen answered. "Pine's been holding back on me."

He smiled and adjusted his big plastic sunglasses. "I like to be a man of mystery."

They all laughed and Gwen reached out and squeezed her husband's hand. "I have to run. It's my day off, but I have to go into the hospital for a meeting." She turned to Pine. "Pick you up at six, babe?"

"That'll be just fine." Pine kissed his wife good-bye and shuffled up the driveway.

"Thank you again," Ellen said as Gwen got back into the car. "You really didn't have to—" She chuckled. "This was so nice of you."

Gwen had her sunglasses in her hand. "Thank you for keeping an eye on Pine. I used to worry about him at home alone all day long when I work. But I don't worry now. Because he has you."

Ellen stood in the driveway and watched Gwen back onto the street as she tried to process what she'd just heard. Pine's first wife had died suddenly?

How could a man still smile the way he did?

25

Alex sat on the porch in her cotton candy chair and checked Twitter on her phone. She had tweeted that she'd uploaded a new video on her YouTube channel. A bunch of people had replied and a few had retweeted. This one was how to use an under-eye concealer that looked natural, even without full makeup. She had terrible dark circles under her eyes from all of the drugs she had taken. She'd stopped the drugs, but the circles were still there.

But not with a good concealer and setting powder.

Alex scanned her tweets. "Oh my God!" she squealed, coming out of her chair. She flapped her free arm. "Chelsea Piers just retweeted my YouTube link!"

She beamed at Grace as the woman settled herself carefully onto a pillow on her chair. "A retweet like that will get me *thousands* of new followers. I'm going to be famous!"

Grace smiled sweetly. "I have no idea what you're talking about, darling." She pronounced the last word with a heavy British accent. "But I'm happy for you."

"YouTube?" BeBe exclaimed from his dark blue chair. "What the hell is that? I hear my grandchildren talking about it." Alex had secretly been calling Pine BeBe. After BeBe Zahara Benet, one of her heroines.

BeBe won the first season of *RuPaul's Drag Race*, Alex's favorite show of all time. Based on the contestants over the years (she knew every single episode of every season by heart), Alex had nicknames for everyone on the porch. Pine wasn't from Cameroon like BeBe; she'd asked him. But Pine said he didn't know exactly where in Africa his relatives had come from, so Alex figured it was possible. Maybe Pine and BeBe were related!

"YouTube is a platform where you can be seen," Alex explained to Grace. She spent a lot of time on the porch explaining things to adults, but she was cool with that. She liked that they actually heard her when she spoke. Being a teenager with terminal cancer was tough. No one wanted to get to know you, because you were going to die. "It's where anyone, even someone like me, can be seen and heard."

Pine leaned forward the way he did when he listened carefully. It was one of the reasons she loved him. Because, unlike her parents, he asked questions and paid attention to her answers. He was genuinely interested in whatever she had to say, whether it was about how she could prepare her parents for her death or the right shade of blush. Pine wasn't like a lot of adults whose interest in someone else was based on their own likes and dislikes. Alex knew Pine cared because *she* cared.

"Platform?" Pine blustered. "I'm with Grace. I got no idea what you're talking about."

Alex thought for a moment. It was hard explaining things to adults sometimes. Especially those old enough to have had to turn a dial to make a phone call back in the old days. "Okay, it's not TV, but it's *like* TV. Anyone can turn it on to watch a video or subscribe to a channel you're interested in."

"So you can watch CNN or Gwen could watch her shows?" Pine asked. "She loves the ones where people want to buy a house and you see their three choices and then, at the end, they tell you which one they bought. Only it's never the one you would buy."

"*House Hunters*," Grace said. "I watch it, too. I like the international ones. Sure are some good buys in Portugal these days."

Alex paused to think as she sat down again and scooted her chair back a bit. She didn't want to block Lara's sun. Lara had fallen asleep in her chair while trying to catch a few rays. "It's sort of like that, only it's not broadcasted the way TV is, so I don't think you can watch CNN or a network show like *House Hunters International*. Unless maybe it's a clip someone put up. There are famous people on YouTube, but mostly regular people posting stuff they want to share with the world. Anyone can have a YouTube channel. You just record and upload."

"Upload?" Pine turned to Shorty. "You followin' this crazy talk?"

Alex didn't know Shorty very well. He was quiet, but when he spoke he had this deep voice that she imagined had been comforting to his patients. Shorty had been a paramedic before he had to retire because of his cancer. He'd been at Ground Zero on 9/11 when the World Trade Center towers fell.

And he had the cancer to prove it. Mesothelioma.

Alex had done some research on cancer on 9/11 first responders. They had a 41 percent increased rate of leukemia, 25 percent for prostate cancer, and their risk of thyroid cancer was double that of the general population. Plus they had an overall increased cancer rate of 9 percent. At least, according to Wikipedia.

Pine's wife, Gwen, and Shorty's wife, Brenda, had met first. Shorty wasn't doing any treatment. He just went to the hospital for doctors' appointments and scans. Brenda had told Gwen about how her husband hated the support group he'd attended in a conference room at the hospital. The wives had introduced their husbands to each other, and Pine had invited Shorty to join their group on the porch. And now he came three or four days a week.

Alex had been wearing her candy striper outfit the first time she met Shorty and Brenda, and Brenda had complimented her on it. Alex had made it herself. Copying it from old photos she found on the Internet. Candy stripers had been volunteers, girls, who wanted to be nurses. They volunteered in the hospital, getting water and newspapers for patients, checking on families, and whatever. There was no such thing anymore. Most of the volunteers Alex knew in hospitals were senior citizens and they wore turtlenecks under their smocks. No turtleneck for her. No one looked good in a turtleneck. (Bald men particularly. Didn't they know it made them look like big, walking circumcised penises? They grossed her out.) *Anywho*, she'd sewn a cute pink denim utility skirt and a pink and white pinafore that looked like it was right out of the fifties. Brenda had recognized the outfit and told Alex she had been a candy striper when she was a teenager. She became an accountant instead of a nurse, though.

"I'm sorry. I don't know what you're talking about, Miss Divine," Pine said.

Alex loved it when he called her Miss Divine. When any of her porch friends did. She didn't tell many people her secret name, but now, with her YouTube channel trending, she could become a household name and everyone would know. Sooner rather than later, she hoped, since she had an expiration date, the actual date to be determined.

"It's like TV, but it's not?" Pine looked to Shorty for confirmation.

"I've seen YouTube," Shorty said. "My brother-in-law emails me links to videos of miniature schnauzers wearing sunglasses, floating on blow-up rafts in pools, and sitting in high chairs in a bib and stuff."

"Schnauzers?" Pine gave a long whistle. Then he drew back, studying Shorty. "You like schnauzers?"

Shorty shook his head. "I don't even like dogs."

"So why's your brother-in-law sending you videos of them?"

"He likes schnauzers. He's got two of them of those little ones. I guess he thinks it will cheer me up. I'm partial to cats. I have the sweetest little calico. Her name is Suzy. She sleeps with us in bed at night."

"Schnauzers in swimming pools." Pine looked at Alex. "I don't guess I'd have much use for YouTube if it's dogs in sunglasses in people's swimming pools."

Alex laughed as she got up from her chair again. She'd dressed casually for an afternoon on the porch, with a possible field trip down to the water, if she could get anyone to go with her. She was wearing white linen shorts and a cute little pink and white crop top. Her parents' housekeeper who was the maid, cook, and babysitter had tried to stop Alex from leaving the house in the crop top. Her name was Maria. (Unoriginal for a Hispanic housekeeper, right? But her mother was Maria before her. And her mother before her. Alex had asked.) But Alex called her Nina, for Nina Flowers, the first runner-up from season one of *Drag Race*, and Maria let her. Probably because Alex was dying. It was amazing the things she got away with because she was basically on death row. Nina let her do all kinds of things Alex's parents would disapprove of if they knew about them. Like binge-watch *Buffy the Vampire Slayer* all night and eat BBQ pork rinds until she puked. Alex wasn't sure why Nina had put her foot down on the crop top. Nina said it was indecent or something like that. Alex didn't speak much Spanish and Nina didn't speak much English, so she wasn't sure. Determined to wear it anyway, Alex had climbed out of her bedroom window.

Alex walked over to show Pine her cell phone. "You don't have to watch schnauzers if you don't want to. You can watch anything. Like *literally* anything. I bet there are hundreds of videos of calico cats. Probably wearing sunglasses, floating in pools." She touched the screen and brought up her own channel, then unmuted the phone. Hearing her own voice made her cringe but not enough to stop uploading content.

"Hey, friends," Alex heard herself say. "Thanks for stopping by. I can't wait to show you my foolproof way to get rid of those black circles under your eyes while still looking natural. I like natural, don't you?"

Alex mouthed her own words.

"So you know the drill. Give me a thumbs-up and subscribe." Alex did a thumbs-up, mimicking herself on the screen. "Notes about the products I'm going to use are linked below, so let's get to it."

"That you?" Shorty asked, leaning closer so that he could see the screen. He pulled off his big wraparound sunglasses.

"That's me."

"I like your top." Pine glanced up at her. "You look pretty in yellow."

Alex turned the screen so she could check herself out again, then turned it back for Shorty and Pine. "You don't think it makes me look sallow?"

Pine guffawed. "You crack me up sometimes, girl. If I say you look pretty, you do."

"I like that color hair," Shorty complimented. "The pink's a little wild for me. Of course, in my day, I wore things my grandparents didn't like." He indicated the wig she was wearing today. "I like the light brown hair. It's pretty. Shows off your green eyes."

It was the most Alex had ever heard Shorty say at one time and she smiled. Like any girl, she liked someone saying she was pretty, and she knew Shorty meant what he said it. He wasn't being a creeper. Blowing smoke up a girl's skirt.

Alex liked that phrase. "Blowing smoke up your skirt." She'd read it somewhere. It wasn't a phrase that was applicable very often.

She'd have to figure out a way to work it in next time she made a video.

26

Ellen's phone vibrated in her back pocket, and she stood up, relieved to have any excuse to take a break from weeding flower beds. It was too hot to be weeding, and she was ready to call it quits for the day. She looked at her phone to see who was calling.

Tim.

Tim? She stared at the screen, then pulled off her sunglasses. It was definitely Tim.

The phone continued to vibrate in her hand.

Why was her ex calling? Wasn't he vacationing with his girlfriend somewhere in the world? She didn't know when he was supposed to return to the States. Since she'd unfriended him, she'd lost track of where he was and what he was doing. When she'd talked to her son the other day, she hadn't asked him a thing about his father.

And it had strangely been a relief.

She slid her sunglasses back on. It was a butt dial, right? It had to be a butt dial. They hadn't spoken in months. A moment later, the missed call popped up, but Tim didn't leave a voice message.

It had to have been a butt call.

She felt a flutter of panic in her chest. Was she supposed to call him back? What if something had happened to their son?

But if it had been an emergency, Tim would have used the signal, she thought as she talked herself off the ledge.

He knew the signal. He would have called three times in a row. And if he had needed to speak with her for some other reason, he'd have left a message.

Sometimes a butt dial in life is just a butt dial.

She slid the phone back in her pocket, slowly, pleased with herself. Pleased she'd been able to resist answering. Resist calling back.

Catching movement out of the corner of her eye, she turned to see Barrett crossing the lawn toward her. She'd seen him pull into the driveway in Grace's Mini Cooper, now back from the body shop, to drop her off after a doctor's appointment. He'd walked his mother to the front door and helped her up the steps.

Grace had thrown a fit on the porch the other day about her son not letting her drive. She'd paced back and forth, reminding them (because Barrett wasn't there) of how she had given birth to him, fed him, clothed him, sent him to boy scout camp, and this was what she got in return. Then she'd dropped into her chair, tired from her tirade, and admitted it was probably time to surrender her keys. She just hated giving up the independence she felt when she had them in her bag.

Ellen tugged her ball cap down, then rubbed her nose with the back of her hand. She usually wore gardening gloves, but she couldn't find them. Which was so unlike her. She rarely misplaced anything. A place for everything and everything in its place: keys on the table near the front door, car sunglasses in their case in the console, shorts in the bottom right-hand drawer of her dresser. But shortly after she'd arrived in Albany Beach, she'd begun misplacing things. And it was getting worse. She felt scattered all the time.

The day before, she'd looked for her grocery list for ten minutes. She kept it pinned to the refrigerator so she could grab it on the way to the store. She'd found it eventually, upstairs in Lara's bathroom. For some reason, she'd had it in her hand when she carried Lara clean bath towels upstairs and left the list on the sink when she put them away. She didn't remember doing it. Having Lara and her friends there was making her scatterbrained.

She didn't like feeling out of control.

Did anyone like feeling out of control?

"Dropped Mom off." Barrett pointed in the direction of the house. He was wearing a pair of khaki shorts, a T-shirt with a parrot on it advertising the Margaritaville restaurant in Biloxi. And what she saw now as his signature wraparound sunglasses—the cool kind, not the Pine kind. He was looking pretty darned handsome, she had to admit, though it pained her. She's never had a thing for big guys who towered over her with their broad shoulders. She didn't like men with long hair . . . well, his wasn't *long*, but it was longish. All that said, the fact of the matter was, she was attracted to Grace's son.

Ellen picked up a bunch of dandelions and dropped them into her weed bucket. She'd been weeding around her purple hydrangeas. Even though the beds were well mulched, weeds still seemed to be able to take purchase. "How is she today? Alex was concerned. I didn't get the details, but I heard them whispering on the porch when I took them something to drink. I guess Grace wasn't feeling well at chemo today."

He halted and gazed out at the street. "Mum, she's—"

Ellen was taken back by the emotion in his voice and gave him a moment. Gave them both a moment.

She had become attached to Grace, even though she knew she shouldn't. Grace was old and sick, and she wasn't going to live long. But the older woman was such an interesting person, with her feminist T-shirts and talkative nature. Grace was always asking questions of the folks on the porch and was quick to put them to Ellen. They were questions that Ellen had to think hard about before she answered. Questions she often contemplated late into the night and into the next day. Sometimes the questions were simple, like what Ellen's perfect day would be like, but Grace also asked things like how she thought others saw her or if she could change one thing about herself, what would it be.

"What does her oncologist say?" Ellen asked.

"Good question." The moment had passed and so had the vulnerability in his voice. "I don't know because she doesn't let me talk to anyone on her care team anymore."

"Could you call her doctor and see what you can find out?"

"Tried that. She removed me from her HIPAA forms and threatened legal action if anyone shared medical information with me . . . or the Savior, I think she told the staff." He exhaled slowly. "Her body, she says. Her right."

Ellen didn't know what to say. She watched a honeybee buzz around one of her huge hydrangea flowers. Standing there with Barrett made her feel awkward and uncomfortable. At the same time, it made her weirdly happy that he'd bother to walk across the lawn to say hello to her.

"Guess I need to get to the store." He slid a hand into his shorts pocket. But made no move to go.

Ellen waited, wondering if he was expecting her to say something.

He pushed a clump of dirt with the toe of his flip-flop. "Coming to the meeting at the store tomorrow?" He locked gazes with her.

She rubbed at her nose again, worried there was still dirt there.

"I think the topic is transitions," Barrett went on. "But we're also going to have anyone read a piece of their work they're struggling with. Get some opinions. I've been going back to this one scene in my book that I know isn't quite right. I thought I might bring it along. Just in case no one else brings anything."

"Your new book about vampires?" she teased lightly to gauge his reaction.

He nodded. "My editor's not expecting it until October first, but I work so much at the store and with Mom—"

"I can imagine," Ellen said.

She thought about the first time they'd met when she'd bought books from him. The sound of derision he'd made as he noted her selection of fiction. "So-o-o . . ." She drew out the word. "You write YA books, romances, vampire romances, and you don't approve of romances for women?"

He tilted his head. She couldn't see his eyes because of his sunglasses, but his posture suggested confusion. "I don't have a problem with romances."

"Obviously, you do. You made fun of my selection the first time I was in the store. I bought some romances."

"Ellen." He gestured with open hands. "I didn't make fun of your romances."

She took a step toward him, one hand on her hip. "Yes, you did. As you rang up one of the romances I was buying, you made fun of it."

"What did I say?" He still sounded as if he had no idea what she was talking about.

Panicking a little, Ellen tried to remember his exact words. She couldn't.

Had he actually said something? Now that she was recalling their conversation from two weeks ago, she wasn't sure he had said something. But she'd been sure he'd made fun of her. "It . . . it was your attitude when you asked me if that was what I was going to write."

"Why would I make fun of romances? I *write* romances." He gave a little laugh. "And not even romances for adults. I write romances for fifteen-year-olds. And I sell them in my store. I sell more romances than anything else. That's what keeps me in business in this town." He stood in front of her, his hands on his hips, his voice almost apologetic. "Ellen, I don't know what

I said to give you that impression, but I assure you, I was not making fun of the books you like to read."

She was tempted to clarify that the romances had been for Lara. The beach books with the sand dollars on the cover were for her. But then she realized she was doing exactly what she'd accused him of. And she did read a romance occasionally. And she liked them. She just didn't think a college professor was supposed to like romances; the daughter of the great American writer Joseph R. Tolliver certainly wasn't. As a teenager, she'd hidden her books the way her friends hid cigarettes and condoms to keep her secret from her father, who would have belittled her. "You *sounded* like you were dissing them," she said. It was one of Alex's words. "Diss." For some reason, Ellen liked it and had added it to her lexicon.

"Ah." He sounded as if he'd had an epiphany. "So it was my *tone*." He hesitated. "Well, I think you read me wrong. I didn't mean to *diss* your choice in reading. Or writing. I apologize if I offended you."

He said it as if he meant it.

Ellen chewed on her lower lip. "I'm not writing a romance."

"Okay. Fine. What are you writing? You didn't say at the meeting when you introduced yourself." He waggled his finger at her. "You were cleverly evasive as I recall."

"I don't know exactly how it would be classified," she heard herself say. "Just general fiction. You know. About life. People."

He was quiet for a moment. This pensiveness she saw today didn't jive with the beach bum persona she'd attached to him.

"You should definitely come tomorrow," he said at last. "Bring something to read."

She felt a moment of panic again. "I . . . I don't know if I have any transitions scenes to share."

Who was she kidding? She didn't have any scenes at all. All she had was her weak attempts at journaling. Ideas scrawled across the pages. Not even a solid premise, plot, or characters. Right now, she had more notes about the men and women on the porch than potential characters. "I'm . . . early in the process. I'm not ready to talk about my book."

He shrugged. "You should come anyway. Hey, you've got some dirt on your face." He reached out and brushed her cheek, then turned away. "Maybe we can grab a cup of coffee after the meeting!" he called over his shoulder.

Ellen watched Barrett walk across the grass toward his car, rubbing her cheek where he touched her.

Had he just asked her on a date?

27

"I want to see that video of you." Grace scooted forward in her chair. "I don't think I've seen this wig."

"Yes, you have. I wore it last week with the polka-dotted jumper."

"You wore a sweater in this heat?" Grace asked quizzically.

Alex cocked her head. "No, I wasn't wearing a *sweater*. It's like a one-piece dress that goes over a top."

Grace pressed her hand to her forehead. "I knew that. It's just that the British call a sweater a jumper."

Alex carried her phone to Grace so she wouldn't have to get up. Grace was having a bad day. She'd had to sit down several times at the hospital. Alex had handed out cookies and water and fresh barf bags for her while Grace rested in the volunteers' lounge, which was like a big closet. But there was an old upholstered chair in there, and Alex had pulled Grace's feet up onto a table and made her lie back and rest. She was worried about Grace. For a while, she'd seemed better. She'd been able to eat again, and she'd gained some weight. But, of course, Grace wasn't going to *get* better. Alex knew that. Grace certainly knew it. She suspected everyone else on the porch knew it. Except maybe Ellen.

And Alex assumed Grace's son didn't know.

"Want me to rewind it for you so you can watch?" Alex asked Grace. "Maybe get some tips?"

"No need. I've lived this long with dark circles under my eyes. I'm not doing anything about it, now."

"Yoo-hoo! Sorry I'm late," came Amara's voice from under the porch. She was just arriving. She'd come in the back way.

"We're up here!" Alex called down.

Amara began to climb the steps so slowly that it was hard for Alex to watch. Halfway up the open staircase, Amara stopped and leaned on the rail to catch her breath.

"Amara!" Grace called. "Wait until you see this. Alex is on TV."

"It's not TV," Alex corrected.

"Wait until you see how pretty she looks," Grace went on. "She's teaching people how to do makeup."

"If I die on these steps," Amara called up, "just bury me in the sand. Be cheaper!" She took a breath. "You know what a cremation will run you these days? It's outrageous."

"Sure do." Shorty rose from his chair and leaned over the porch railing to gaze at Amara. "Brenda and I made the arrangements last year. So my son and daughter wouldn't have to."

Pine shook his head. "I just can't get over how you can see stuff like that on your phone. It's like a little TV. Computer, I guess."

"It is a little computer," Alex agreed. "Amara, let me get your bag." She handed her phone to Pine and went down the steps. When she reached Amara, she considered moving behind her. Amara looked kind of wobbly like she might fall down the steps and break her neck. Adults were always warning against breaking your neck. Personally, Alex didn't think it would be a bad way to go. Not if you just hit the ground, your neck snapped, and you were dead. No pain, no good-byes, that stretched into months or years.

Alex rested her hand on Amara's back and eased the bag off her shoulder. Amara was struggling to breathe and sweat had broken out on her forehead.

"You okay?" Alex whispered.

Amara looked up at her since Alex was taller. "I'm fine. Thank you, sweetie."

"You want to take a break. Sit for a sec?" Alex asked her.

Amara shook her head. "No. I can do this."

Alex let her go. Because she knew what it felt like when you had no control over your own body, your own life.

Amara finally made it up to the porch and Alex went around her to move her chair a little closer.

"There you are, Amara," Lara said, looking over her sunglasses. She'd woken up while Alex was on the steps. "Christ on Wheels. You look like shit."

"Don't take the Lord's name in vain," Amara reminded her. "Some people are offended by that."

"You need something?" Lara asked, ignoring Amara's reprimand. "Something we can get you?"

"A new body," Amara quipped as she eased down into her chair.

Alex set Amara's bag down beside her chair.

"I can't watch anything on my phone," Pine told Alex. He had his phone out of his pocket and was comparing the two.

Alex tried not to laugh. Her BeBe had a flip phone. "Because you don't have a smartphone." *A flip phone!* She smiled.

"I used to take pictures with it, but the camera's busted," he went on. "And it's a pain in the butt to text. That a swear, Amara? Am I allowed to say 'butt,' or do you prefer 'buttocks'?" he teased the old Indian woman.

He didn't wait for her answer. It was his way of throwing shade. That's what they called it on *RuPaul's Drag Race* when you made fun of someone or criticized them. Pine wasn't exactly criticizing, but Alex liked the phrase, so she had broadened the definition to suit her needs.

"I try to text my grandchildren sometimes, but it's too hard having to push a button one, two, or three times, depending on what letter I want. Takes so long, I forget what the hell I'm doing." Pine looked at Amara again. "That was a curse."

"I'm bringing a jar, and every time someone curses, they have to put a quarter in it. A dollar for the *f* word." Amara eyed Lara. "We can use it to pay for someone's cremation."

"The question is whose?" Lara asked. "Do we go with financial need or do we pick a name out of a hat?"

It was all spoken in fun. That was why Alex loved The Porch. She didn't care that her friends were a lot older than she was. They knew what was what with their cancer, but they never got melancholy like people around them without cancer did. On this porch, Alex felt like she could breathe. She didn't feel like that anywhere else. Certainly not at home.

"Look, I almost have the same phone." Shorty pulled his out of his pocket. Another flip phone. "Mine's red is all."

"How old are those things?" Alex asked in horror.

Pine laughed. "You know, I've got a mind to have one of those iPhones." He pointed at Alex's.

"I was just thinking the same thing," Shorty said.

"You should get one!" Alex told them excitedly. "You too, Amara. Grace. We should all get the new iPhone together. It just came out and it is amazing! You won't believe what the new camera can do. The video experience on the babe is so badass—" She caught Amara giving her the eye. The other day, she'd threatened to put soap in Alex's mouth for calling some girl she used to know a *c* word. Amara said it didn't matter if the girl was a *c* word, it wasn't right to use that kind of language. Ever. "Sorry, Amara," she said quickly. "I'll bring the quarters tomorrow."

"It's all right, sweetie. As long as there's a learning curve."

Alex nodded, not entirely sure what that meant.

"I think I like that idea," Shorty said. "And Alex can show us how to work them."

Alex turned around, surprised that it was Shorty who spoke up first. "You really want to get one?"

"Sure do. I wouldn't mind using that fancy camera to take photos of the birds at my bird feeder. You wouldn't believe how many hummingbirds I have right now. You think that fancy camera in the phone would take photos of my hummingbirds? Good enough so you could see them?"

Alex slid to the edge of her chair, excited. "I bet it would take beautiful photos. And then you could add them to text messages and you could send us pictures of your birds."

"Didn't know you were into birds, Alex," Shorty said, amused.

"What do you think, Pine? You think you'd be interested in a new phone?" Alex asked him. "If you had an iPhone, you could take pictures of schnauzers and send them to your brother-in-law. If you have one. Do you have a pool? If you did, I bet we could get a blow-up raft and you could float a miniature schnauzer on it." She laughed, knowing she was being silly but enjoying the moment.

"I guess he could put his cat on that raft. I don't know that she would like it that much. I bet his brother-in-law would be surprised to get that photo, though." Shorty laughed. "Shoot, you could send them to my brother-in-law. I'll give you his email."

"You boys are getting new cell phones?" Grace asked. "I want a new cell phone." She looked at Alex. "How much do they cost?"

"Oh, what do you care, Grace?" Pine asked. "Word around town is that you've got more money than Midas himself."

Grace frowned. "I don't know where you got that nonsense from."

"I don't know how much they cost," Alex said. "But I can look it up."

196 / *Colleen French*

"Do we have to go to a store, or can we just order one of those phones and have it mailed to our house?" Shorty asked. "It takes a lot of energy to go into a phone store."

"You can order them right from Apple." Alex was so excited. She couldn't believe they really wanted new phones. And they wanted her to help with them. "I bet they would be here in a few days."

Shorty nodded slowly, a smile on his face. "I think I'll get one if nothing else just to annoy my children."

"Your children wouldn't want you to have a phone?" Pine glanced Shorty's way. "Why not?"

"Like I was saying the other day. They don't want me spending any of my money, 'my money' being the operative words."

It was Alex's turn to frown. "Why? It's yours, right?"

"My kids don't see it that way. Well, it's mostly my daughter and her greedy, beady-eyed husband. They've got it in their heads that what's mine is theirs. Or will be once I'm dead. My daughter and son are from my first marriage. Brenda and I never had any children. Wanted them. It just didn't happen for us. My daughter, Amber, thinks that when I pass everything what's mine should become hers and her brother's and I should leave Brenda out of my will. I've told her that's not going to happen, but she won't listen to me. She keeps saying she thinks Brenda and I should move closer to her so she can take care of me. I think it's all about her taking care of my money."

"Sorry to hear that," Pine said quietly. He nudged Shorty's knee. "I mean it. . . ." He hesitated. "Hurts, don't it? When the people you love aren't who you hoped they would be."

Shorty looked out over the rail at a blue and green kite with an orange tail making a slow circle over the beach. "They're still my kids. I still love them."

Pine pressed his hands to his knees and leaned forward, looking at Shorty. "Of course you do, buddy."

Everyone was quiet for a moment, and then Amara cleared

her throat. "If everyone else is getting a new phone, I am, too. I don't care how much it costs."

Alex jumped out of her chair, clapping her hands. "If everyone is getting a phone, I'll get one, too!"

"Your phone is practically new," Lara pointed out. "Your parents aren't going to give you a new phone."

Alex pushed her yellow-framed sunglasses onto her head, careful not to mess with her wig. "Sure they are." She laughed. "I can have anything I want. I'm a fifteen-year-old dying of brain cancer."

28

Ellen waited quietly in the semi-darkness, observing Lenora. The older woman stood at the porch rail, captivated by the sun appearing on the horizon. Fearful of getting too close to the window and being caught, Ellen couldn't see Lenora's feet, but she guessed they were bare.

Ellen didn't know why she was worried about Lenora catching her. She didn't know what it was about the woman that fascinated her, but she was bordering on obsessed. Ellen wondered why Lenora kept coming there, to her house. What was it that she got from her early morning cat burglar behavior? Of course, she wasn't a burglar because she didn't steal anything. That was Ellen's logic and why she had decided not to call the police. What were they going to do with her? Arrest her?

Lenora didn't do anything wrong beyond her habitual breaking and entering. She just made coffee.

Taking care to be quiet, Ellen had measured coffee she had ground the night before into Lenora's percolator and set it on the stove. It was starting to smell heavenly in the kitchen and she hoped Lenora couldn't smell it through the closed windows.

Each night Ellen closed all of the windows—to slow the

honest people down. That's what her grandmother had always said. She said you couldn't keep criminals out—if they wanted in bad enough, they'd break a window, jimmy a door. Closed and locked windows kept people from just happening to walk by, see a window open, a house dark, and perpetrate a crime on impulse.

Lenora's breaking and entering was certainly not impulsive. Her routine was too repetitive. Ellen had hoped to be up early enough that if the elderly woman showed up, she could see how she was getting inside. The previous morning Lenora hadn't come and, disappointed, Ellen had ended up watching the sunrise alone.

Why had she been disappointed? Lenora didn't belong there. It wasn't her home.

The sunrise's first golden light glowed on the horizon, and Ellen, forgetting Lenora for a moment, watched captivated, from the kitchen sink. As the sun rose above the ocean's horizon, darkness gave way to light. No matter how many times Ellen watched a sunrise, she was still surprised by how quickly the daylight came. It was as if it was pitch dark one moment and then light the next.

As the sun came up again with the promise of a clear, cloudless, hot day, Lenora gave a sigh that sounded musical. Then she walked to the door that led from the back porch into the kitchen and eating area.

Ellen watched from the window as the elderly woman took a key hanging on a piece of red yarn from her housecoat pocket, opened the screen door, and unlocked the door.

"So you *do* have a key," she said as Lenora walked inside.

"Of course I have a key." Lenora eyed Ellen as if she'd said a ridiculous thing.

Ellen looked at her sternly. "You told me you didn't have a key."

Lenora drew herself up until she was every bit of five feet tall. "I said no such thing."

"Liar, liar, pants on fire," Ellen wanted to say. Which surprised her. And amused her just a smidge.

Where had that come from?

Ellen always prided herself on how she maturely handled any situation, keeping emotion out of it because emotion never solved anything.

But it is what makes one human, isn't it? Emotions that aren't always logical.

She tucked the thought away to contemplate it later when she added it to her journal. She held out her hand. "I'm afraid I'm going to have to ask you to give that to me."

"Give you what, dear?"

Lenora had a way of doing this to Ellen. Setting her just slightly off-kilter. "You know what. The key to my house."

"I don't have a key to your house." Lenora smiled sweetly, slid the key into her pocket, and walked to the stove, her small, bare feet silent on the hardwood floor. "Going to boil over if you're not careful. Then Daddy will be angry with us, Doris. 'The less we waste, the less we will lack in the future,'" she said, obviously quoting someone. She turned down the flame beneath the percolator and then went to the cabinet to get coffee cups. It was the same routine every time Ellen found Lenora in her kitchen. "That's not from the Bible. Did you know that?"

Ellen watched Lenora, not sure what to do. It hadn't occurred to her that the older woman wouldn't give her the key when she asked for it. "Lenora, you can't keep walking into my house. You can't have a key to my house." Her tone started out forceful but quickly lost its intensity. By the last word, she sounded apologetic.

"I like your new hair color," Lenora responded. She went on as if she hadn't heard Ellen ask for the key. The funny thing was, her method worked well. She easily steered the conversation away from things she didn't want to talk about.

"You do? I did it last night. I've never dyed my own hair

before. Never had it dyed." Feeling self-conscious, she tugged at her ponytail. "It's not my natural hair color anymore."

Lenora laughed and drew her hand over her cap of snowy white hair. "And you think this is? . . ." She paused as if she had delivered a line in a play, her timing impeccable. She gave time for the comment to settle on Ellen, for her to realize the truth of it, that people changed inside and outside. Then she went on.

"I used to be a redhead, too. A little redder than yours. I hated it when I was a child. Kids called me Carrottop in school. And Redheaded Woodpecker." Her eyes grew misty then. "But my Lester, he loved it. He said it was my hair that had given him the courage to speak to me the first time we met. He said he'd always known he was going to marry a redhead and then there I was one day, standing in line in front of him to buy a movie ticket. *The African Queen.* He was alone, too. So we sat together and never sat apart again until he died."

Lenora's eyes were open, but Ellen could tell that she was lost for a moment in the memory. "His grandmother had red hair and so did our daughter Lillian. Her daughter has red hair, too, and so do three of my great-grandchildren."

"You really think it looks all right?" Ellen asked. She hadn't intended to color her hair. Maybe she had thought about covering the grays, but certainly she had never thought to dye it this bright. No, that wasn't true. She'd wanted to be brave enough to do it. She still didn't know what had made her put the box of hair color in her basket when she took a shortcut down the hair care aisle of the drugstore where she had gone to pick up a few things for Lara.

"I wouldn't say it looked nice on you, dear, unless I meant it." Lenora seemed to return to the present time and place, or her version of it. "It suits your coloring. Your hair was red when you were younger?"

"A duller red. Reddish-brown," Ellen answered.

"You look fantastic. Younger."

"Thank you," Ellen said softly. Then she looked away, not quite comfortable with the older woman's compliments.

Even though she secretly craved them. Didn't everyone?

Lenora returned her attention to the coffee. "I didn't have time to make muffins this morning. I picked blueberries yesterday and meant to make muffins this morning. Joseph loves my blueberry muffins with the streusel topping. I'm expecting him this morning, so I can't dally long."

"Your brother?"

"Aren't you funny." Lenora chuckled. "*Our* brother." She stood on her tiptoes and took mugs from the cabinet.

Ellen wondered if she should have gotten the stool for Lenora to make it easier for her to reach. But that didn't seem like a good idea. She could imagine having to call Emergency Services and report that a woman who had broken into her home had fallen off a stool and broken her hip while making Ellen coffee.

"Where does your—*he* live again?" Ellen asked, thinking she'd make another attempt to get her key back in a minute. Where had the key come from? She never left a key outside and Lara hadn't, either. Only neighbors down the street, Susan and Buck, who lived full-time in Albany Beach, had a copy. They were the unofficial neighborhood watch and had copies of keys for several part-timers. Ellen so appreciated them keeping an eye on her place that she sent them a big holiday basket of dried fruit, smoked salmon, crackers, and nuts from Harry & David every year.

"Our brother lives here with us of course," Lenora said as if it were the silliest question she'd ever heard.

The fact that she had just told Ellen she had to go soon because her brother was coming didn't seem to occur to her.

"Here you go." Lenora poured a cup of rich, dark coffee. "Let's take it out on the porch, don't you think?"

As Ellen walked over to get her coffee, Lenora poured her own. "I'm sorry about the blueberry muffins," the older woman said.

"Actually . . . I have a little something," Ellen said, then immediately felt silly.

Why was she making baked goods for someone breaking into her home?

At five-thirty in the morning!

She walked over to the antique freestanding wooden icebox her mother had bought at a yard sale decades ago. They used the top where the ice had once gone as a bread box. "Do you like banana bread? I made it; I didn't buy it."

"You made it?" Lenora said with such joy that Ellen was glad she had stayed up after Lara went to bed and made the bread from bruised bananas she'd frozen.

"I added chocolate chips," Ellen explained as she carried the mini loaf wrapped in foil to the counter. "The small ones, so they don't sink in the batter and burn on the bottom." She looked up, realizing that may have been a mistake. She always tried to take allergies into consideration whenever she made food to share with others—nut-free and gluten-free.

Lara said her recipes were sometimes taste-free as well.

"You're not allergic to chocolate, are you?"

"I'd sooner be with the good Lord than be allergic to chocolate!" Lenora clasped her tiny, frail hands. "I love banana bread with chocolate chips! It's my favorite."

"I love it, too," Ellen admitted as she took out a small cutting board and a serrated knife. "I know it's not good for me, but I make it anyway sometimes. I feel my waist expanding every time I eat a slice. Shoot, every time I bake a loaf."

"That's utter nonsense," Lenora declared, watching Ellen slice off several pieces from the mini loaf. "You're young and beautiful." She stepped back to take Ellen in. "And such a nice figure. You have a nice bottom. You take good care of yourself. Which is good. We all should." She took a sip of coffee. "God only gives us one body, you know."

When Lenora had used the word "beautiful" to describe Ellen, Ellen halted with the knife hovering over the banana bread. She didn't know if anyone had ever said that to her. Not her mother or father. Not Tim. Not anyone. Ever. And she knew she wasn't beautiful, but she had always thought she had a memorable face. In a good way. And she never thought she was necessarily *un*attractive. But no one had ever called her beautiful . . . until today.

And she had a nice bottom? Ellen almost giggled. Lara said the same thing, only in more colorful language, but hearing it from a stranger . . . well, practical stranger. It made her smile.

Ellen put a slice of banana bread each on two dessert plates that matched the old coffee cups. "Do you think I could see Joseph sometime?" she asked Lenora.

Lenora hesitated. It was obvious she was contemplating the question. Ellen wondered if she was trying to absorb the fact that if Ellen was her sister Doris, then she obviously would have known Joseph. She would be his sister, too. But maybe the Joseph she was talking about wasn't her brother. Maybe Joseph was another great-grandson. Or someone else she lived with. Or maybe there was no Joseph, had never been a Joseph.

Lenora lifted her gaze to Ellen and smiled. "I'd like very much for you to see him. I'm expecting him anytime."

Ellen picked up both plates of banana bread and headed for the back porch. She'd come back for her coffee. "That's wonderful that he'll be here soon. Where's he coming from?"

"France, of course." Lenora's face lit up. "Daddy says he'll be home as soon as we beat Hitler."

29

Feeling self-conscious for a multitude of reasons, Ellen crept along the sidewalk, remaining far enough behind Lenora that, she hoped, the older woman wouldn't realize she was there. Ellen had intended to change out of her old gym shorts and sleep tee before following her, but when Lenora made the decision to leave she didn't have time to go back upstairs. After finishing her coffee and banana bread, Lenora had taken the back staircase from the porch with surprising ease and then slipped around the side of the house.

In the early morning light, Lenora walked down the sidewalk, her gait spry. Ellen continued to hang back. She planned to find out where Lenora lived, since the woman refused to tell her, and then speak with whoever cared for her. Obviously, Lenora couldn't continue to wander the streets alone.

A white toy poodle mix yapped from the driveway Lenora passed two houses ahead of Ellen, and the elderly woman stopped on the sidewalk.

Afraid Lenora would see her, Ellen darted behind a flowering butterfly bush and peered through the branches. She felt ridiculous, but not ridiculous enough to come out of hiding.

"It's okay, Bitsy. It's just me," Lenora said to the dog, giving him as much attention as she gave Ellen when they spoke. "You remember me. Lenora. I'm sorry, but I didn't bring any treats for you today."

The dog gave a yip, but it was only halfhearted, and then he wagged his tail. Lenora was obviously not a stranger to Bitsy. Which was a good thing because Bitsy could be mean. The other day, the dog had bitten Rick when he was delivering a package. He'd told Ellen about it at length. Right before he'd asked her to meet him for a drink at The Frog Pond downtown. She'd said no, of course, but she'd secretly been pleased. It was hard for her to believe that someone could be *remotely* attracted to her, so his invitation had been good for her ego. Maybe she might have that cup of coffee with Barrett this afternoon after their writers' meeting.

Maybe.

If she found the courage.

"How about if I bring you something tomorrow?" Lenora talked to Bitsy as if he were a friend. "How would that be? Hmm? Some nice blueberry muffins. I plan to bake them up today. Fresh blueberries I picked in Grandma's backyard yesterday."

Bitsy's owner, Mrs. Campbell, walked out onto her front porch in a yellow terry bathrobe, her hair in rollers, carrying a ginormous plastic cup advertising a weight-loss shake. She waved to Lenora. "Good morning. Have a good walk on the beach?"

"That I did!" Lenora called back.

Ellen wondered if Lenora was lying on purpose or if she really couldn't remember the hour she'd spent on Ellen's porch. Lenora's loss of memory was an interesting thing. There seemed to be no rules to it. It was completely random. Sometimes when talking, Lenora thought she was a child again. The next minute, she thought it was the 1940s and the Japanese had just bombed Pearl Harbor. Other times, her mind was sharper than Ellen's.

How did a person stand to always be in such mental chaos?

"I forgot to bring Bitsy a treat," Lenora told Mrs. Campbell. "But I'll remember tomorrow. "

"That's okay. He's getting fat anyway. George says I feed him too much. I say I feed George too much." Mrs. Campbell, a woman as wide as she was tall, sniggered. "That shuts him up."

The two women chuckled, and Ellen got the impression that conversations like this had taken place before. Mrs. Campbell, Aretha, Ellen thought her first name was, didn't seem to be in the least bit concerned that Lenora was wandering the streets in bare feet and a housecoat.

"Sounds like a man," Lenora shot back. "They've got a lot of opinions."

"That they do," Mrs. Campbell agreed. "See you tomorrow." She took a sip of her coffee and then called, "Come on, Bitsy. Inside, boy!"

Bitsy gave one more halfhearted bark and then turned to trot up the driveway, onto the front porch, and into the house with his owner. Lenora continued down the sidewalk. Ellen followed her and began to feel a little bit like a stalker. A stalker in gym shorts that were way too short for a woman her age. At least she'd taken the time to run a brush through and pull back her hair this morning before she came downstairs. She wouldn't frighten little children.

Lenora continued her walk, seeming intent on her destination. Ellen hoped it was home.

As she made her way down the street, the old woman waved to several neighbors and picked up a basketball from the side of the road and rolled it onto the lawn of a new green house with a basketball hoop in the driveway. She also picked up an empty soda bottle and a piece of paper that some inconsiderate person had left behind and she tucked them into her pocket with Ellen's house key. If she knew Ellen was following her, she gave no indication.

Walking away from the beach, Lenora stopped, looked both

ways, crossed the street in front of her, and walked onto the next block. Ellen continued to follow her staying well behind. They had almost reached the end of that block when Lenora picked up a newspaper at the end of a driveway and walked toward the house.

Ellen recognized the house. It was one of her favorites in all of Albany Beach. She had been inside it once years ago on a Christmas house tour. The nineteenth-century house dated further back than her own and was a two-story, square monstrosity with a full widow's walk on the third floor. The style, usually only seen in coastal towns, featured a railed rooftop platform with an enclosed cupola. Supposedly the architectural element was built for wives of mariners so they could watch the ocean for the return of their husbands—husbands who sometimes never returned, leaving the women widows.

With the newspaper tucked under her arm, Lenora walked up the sidewalk to the gray, weather-stained front porch. The front door opened, and a woman dressed in scrubs stepped onto the porch. She had bright red hair. "How was your walk, Granny?" she asked as Ellen stopped at the end of the driveway.

"Excellent," Lenora responded, practically bouncing up the steps. "It's going to be another hot day. We best draw the curtains now before the day heats up the house."

From the sidewalk, Ellen watched the exchange. Now that she was here, she had second thoughts about her mission. It was apparent her granddaughter knew that Lenora left the house in the morning. And maybe Lenora was taking a walk on the beach some mornings, because she didn't break into Ellen's house every morning. Ellen hated to be the one to curtail her walks, but she couldn't let Lenora continue to break into people's houses.

Could she?

Taking a breath of resolution, Ellen walked up the driveway. She was halfway to the house when Lenora's granddaughter spotted her. "Good morning," Ellen said, raising her hand in a quick wave.

"Good morning," the woman in the scrubs answered. She was freckled and tall, her red hair lighter than Ellen's. Likely in her early forties.

"I live two blocks up, oceanside. Ellen," she said.

At the sound of Ellen's voice, Lenora had swung around. She didn't look surprised to see her, though.

Had she known all along that Ellen was following her?

"Ellen, this is my sister, Doris," Lenora introduced.

The woman in the scrubs smiled, friendly enough, but obviously wondering what her neighbor wanted at six-forty-one in the morning. "Miranda," she said. "I'm Lenora's granddaughter. And my great-aunt, Doris, this morning." She winked at Ellen.

"My Lillian's daughter. And my *favorite* granddaughter," Lenora announced, grinning.

Miranda cut her eyes at her grandmother and then looked back at Ellen. "Don't listen to her. She fibs. She tells my sister the same thing when she's here to visit. And my cousin."

Ellen hesitated at the front steps. She had rehearsed what she was going to say to Lenora's caretaker. She was going to explain what Lenora had been doing and make it plain that it was Lenora she was concerned about more than the breaking and entering. But now, standing there, she felt like a tattletale. A snitch. A rat. Once she told Miranda what her grandmother was doing, that would be the end of Lenora's sunrise outings. And the sunrise wouldn't be the same here at two blocks off the beach.

Mirada crossed the porch. "It's so nice to meet you finally. I'm sorry I haven't come by to say hello. I keep meaning to, but with work—I'm a nuclear med tech at the hospital—and the kids home for the summer . . ." She pushed a stray tendril of red hair behind her ear, making a face that suggested being overwhelmed. "We had talked about making you a pie or a quiche or something. I just haven't gotten to it."

Ellen looked up at her, taken off guard by the fact that Miranda knew who she was. Lenora must have mentioned her to her granddaughter. In what context? Surely Miranda didn't know that her grandmother broke into people's houses. The comment about the pie or quiche suggested that Miranda thought Ellen had invited Lenora into her home.

Both Lenora and Miranda smiled at her.

Suddenly she felt terrible. Maybe Lara was right. Lenora wasn't harming anyone by coming into the house to make coffee once in a while. Ellen hadn't seen her do anything unsafe to suggest the older woman wasn't capable of walking the two blocks between their homes.

Lenora turned to Ellen, who stood at the bottom of the porch steps. "Nothing Doris and I like better than to sit on her porch and watch the sun come up. We have a cup of coffee together, don't we, Doris?"

Miranda gently touched her grandmother's elbow. "Granny, she's not Aunt Doris. Your sister's gone. She's your friend Ellen."

Lenora shrugged. "I knew that."

If Ellen was going to rat out Lenora, this was her chance.

Before she could say anything, Lenora spoke again. Her voice was as smooth as the honey she had talked about harvesting at her cousin's farm. When that harvesting had taken place, six months ago or sixty years ago, or ever, Ellen didn't know.

"Would you like to come inside and see the house?" Lenora asked. "It's not as pretty as yours, but you'd like it."

There was a sparkle in her eyes that made Ellen think the elderly woman knew exactly what she was doing. Manipulating her and keeping a secret from her granddaughter.

"Of course. Please." Miranda stepped back and waved Ellen in. "Come in and have a cup of coffee. I have a dental appointment this morning, so I'm going into work late." She plucked her cell phone from the pocket of her scrubs and checked the screen. "I don't have to leave for another half hour."

"Have coffee with us," Lenora coaxed, moving to stand beside her granddaughter. "We've got a fancy machine that sounds like a dragon." She leaned toward Ellen. "The coffee isn't as good as at your house. But I bet there are chocolate donuts. The kind with sprinkles."

Grandmother and granddaughter waited for Ellen's response.

"I'm sorry," she said, "I can't today. My friend Lara, who's living with me right now, has a chemo appointment this morning. I take her. I just wanted to be sure that Lenora made it home safely."

"Oh, gosh. I'm so sorry." Miranda's face was awash with compassion. "Is she going to be okay?"

"She is." Ellen swallowed hard, feeling like such a jerk. But Lenora couldn't be allowed to break into people's houses. "Miranda, I think there's been a bit of a . . . miscommunication. Lenora's been . . . letting herself into my house." The last words came out in a rush.

"*Granny!*" Miranda's eyes widened. "You swore you were walking on the beach with Granddad." She looked back at Ellen. "I'm so sorry. She goes for her walks and gets confused sometimes."

"She somehow has a key to the back door."

"Do not," Lenora said.

Ellen looked at Miranda, feeling like a complete heel. "I think it's in the pocket of her housecoat," she whispered.

"I can *hear* you." Lenora was obviously annoyed now.

"If you have Ellen's key, Granny, you have to give it back."

"Don't have it." Lenora raised her arms as if she were under arrest. "Check my pockets."

Miranda exhaled and reached over, squeezing the pockets of the flowered housecoat. "Sorry, no key."

Ellen didn't know what to say. She knew she hadn't imagined seeing Lenora unlock the door and then put the key in her pocket. Had she hidden it somewhere on the way home? She'd been out of sight the first half a block.

"I really am sorry," Miranda said to Ellen. "We have an alarm system, so we know when she leaves the house, but my kids are home for the summer and they keep turning it off."

"It's fine. Really." Ellen began to back down the steps. "It's not that I don't enjoy Lenora's company. I just want her to be safe."

"I'll talk with her," Miranda promised.

"Thank you. It was nice to meet you." At the bottom of the porch steps, Ellen called up, "Good-bye, Lenora!" and waved.

Lenora stuck out her tongue and made a loud raspberry.

30

Ellen glanced down self-consciously at the cup of coffee in front of her. The bookstore had been so busy by the time the writers' meeting was over that there had been no place to sit. Shoppers and browsers had taken all of the small tables in the café area. She wasn't surprised; it was common for tourists to duck into shops in the afternoon to escape the beach's heat. And good for business. Like many coastal towns, Albany Beach depended on the income of tourism and welcomed the strangers who swarmed their streets in the summertime. Seeing there were no available seats, Ellen had suggested they just do it another time. Barrett had said, "No way," and suggested they sit outside where there were a few additional tables on the sidewalk.

So now here they were, sitting across from each other at a wrought-iron table so small that her knees nearly brushed his. But they were out of the sun, thanks to the well-placed new awnings, and there was plenty to see in the parade of beach-goers in skimpy bathing suits and inappropriate T-shirts. From where they were sitting, Ellen could smell Thrasher's French fries and Fisher's caramel popcorn, the staples of beach life in Delaware.

"You didn't bring anything to read today." Barrett wrapped his hand around a chipped handmade mug that was obviously from home. In front of him was a piece of key lime pie he'd taken from the pastry case in the coffee shop. He'd offered her a piece, too, but she'd declined. She was too nervous to eat.

She was *so* nervous.

Her armpits felt wet, and Ellen had to consciously keep her hands in her lap to prevent herself from checking the underarms of her T-shirt. "I didn't have anything to share."

He sipped his caramel cappuccino with a heaping portion of whipped cream on top. He was full of surprises. He wrote teenage romance novels and drank froufrou coffee.

She kept her eyes down as she took a drink of her black coffee. Overhead she heard the call of a seagull, and hoped no one was feeding them nearby.

"Struggling?" he asked, shaking his head as he took a big bite of pie. "Been there. Sucks."

She stole a glance at him. "You could say that." She didn't have the nerve to tell him she wasn't just struggling with transitions, the topic of conversation at the meeting earlier. She was struggling with coming up with the premise for her book. A plot. She had stopped and started her book so many times that she'd lost count. Her ideas always looked good on paper, but when she started actually writing it all fell flat.

He took another sip of his coffee and a bite of pie. A silence stretched between them that made her feel uncomfortable. Lags in conversation were always awkward for Ellen. She wondered if the person she was talking with was waiting for *her* to say something. Barrett didn't seem to mind, though.

He looked relaxed. He wasn't waiting for her to say something necessarily. He was thinking, maybe getting ready to say something himself. In the meantime, he was enjoying his coffee, his pie, and the afternoon sunshine.

As she watched him, an epiphany hit her square in the face.

Maybe silence between two people didn't have to be uncomfortable.

With Tim, with anyone, she always felt as if she needed to fill the silence with words.

Ellen relaxed a little in her chair and took a sip of her coffee, taking a moment to savor the bold, smooth taste. It was excellent coffee, the kind that was good black. She'd probably pay for the caffeine when she went to bed tonight and couldn't sleep. But she didn't mind because she was having coffee with a man who was not her husband, a man who had not only asked her if she wanted to have coffee with him but also not taken an out when she offered it.

She lifted her gaze.

He watched her, tilting his head. "I like your hair this color. It suits you."

She knew she blushed. "Thank you," she managed, eyeing him over the rim of the blue Le Creuset mug.

"I hope you don't mind me saying so. I never know when to mention things like that to women. It seems like compliments are often interpreted as criticism."

She frowned. "How so?"

"People—not just women, that's not fair—assume that if I say something like I like the color of your hair, it means I didn't like your hair the color it was before."

She felt heat rise in her cheeks, and it wasn't the sunshine. She raised her hand ever-so-slightly in a *pick me* gesture. "Guilty. Or I have been." She hesitated and then went on. "I'm so uncomfortable in my own skin sometimes, so critical of myself, that I assume others see the same faults."

Again, it took him longer to speak than she was used to, but she forced herself to be patient because she wanted to hear what he had to say.

"I believe we're all guilty of that at times. As far as being uncomfortable in our skin, I don't think that's always a bad thing.

We can use that emotional discomfort in our writing. It can be a way to build a bridge between our readers and us," he said thoughtfully. "It's our vulnerability that makes us human, isn't it? And it's through vulnerability that we're able to connect, able to love. And hate," he added. "And all those emotions in between."

She mulled that idea over for a moment. He had an interesting point.

"So back to your writing—" He held up a finger. "Not all that good a segue, I know."

She laughed.

"Don't be offended," Barrett warned, "but you didn't say at the meetings. Are you published?"

"I am. A lot of academic stuff over the years. As I said, I'm an English professor. But I've also sold short stories. I've sold a couple to *The New Yorker, The Atlantic*, and *The Georgia Review*." The moment the words came out of her mouth, she wished she hadn't said them. She didn't want him to think she was bragging. That she, the great Joseph R. Tolliver's daughter, boasted of her accomplishments.

"Wow. Impressive."

She gave him a quick smile, one she wasn't feeling.

"What kind of stories were they?"

She thought for a moment. It had been more than a year since she'd sold a short story. She hadn't even submitted one since her father died. She guessed that it was because she had decided it was time to take the idea of writing a novel more seriously. Maybe because he was gone and she didn't have to feel like she was competing with him. Of course, she would always be. If she did manage to write a book and manage to publish it, everyone would compare it to her father's work.

She didn't have a chance.

Yet she still wanted to write a novel. Why?

When she met Barrett's gaze again, she saw that he waited patiently for an answer. "They've all been stories of relationships, family," she heard herself say.

He nodded. "Well, you must be good at it. *The New Yorker? The Atlantic.*" He gave a low whistle. "If you're struggling, maybe you need to go back to your roots. Write a novel about relationships. About family. One of the best pieces of advice anyone ever gave me was to write about what I know. What I know here." He tapped the breast pocket of his faded T-shirt.

Ellen lifted her mug to her lips. *Great advice.*

The problem was, what *did* she know?

31

Ellen and Lara sat in their beach chairs in the space between the back-porch steps and the dunes, enjoying the last rays of the day's sunshine. The porch gang had just left, and while Ellen hadn't been able to coax Lara into having something to eat, Lara had agreed to sit on the beach—as long as they didn't have to walk over the dunes. She was too bushed for that.

Ellen had thought about telling Lara about following Lenora home the day before and her talk with Miranda, but she decided to keep it to herself, at least for the time being. She'd tell Lara at some point, of course, but she didn't want to upset her right now. Or argue with her. She just wanted to spend some stress-free time with her best friend.

Lara dug her bare feet into the warm sand. Her toenails were bright blue. "Okay, so tell me. How was the date with Grace's son?"

So much for a stress-free conversation.

"It wasn't a date. We both went to the meeting, and then we had coffee together and talked about . . . you know, writing stuff."

"Um-hm," Lara intoned. "Right. No. Wrong. The meeting

was an excuse for him to ask you out. It was a date, Ellen. Your first date since you've been single." She sounded pleased with herself. As if she had arranged it.

She hadn't arranged it, had she?

"It wasn't a date," Ellen repeated firmly. "And it was fine. It was . . . nice." She smoothed her ponytail. "He likes my new hair color."

"See! I told you!" Lara reached over and squeezed her arm. "I *told* you, you look fantastic. I'd give my left boob to have your hair. Well . . . if I still had a left boob. A real one anyone would want. It makes you look younger, more vibrant. If I were a lesbian, I'd ask you out in a hot second. No, I'd do you. I'd do you for sure."

Ellen rolled her eyes behind her sunglasses and checked her cell. She'd been hoping to hear from her son. The last time she had talked to him, he'd said next time he had a layover in Philadelphia or Baltimore he'd come to see her. She hadn't seen him in two months.

"Are you going to go out on another non-date?" Lara pressed. "Maybe out for dinner? Ooh, you could use the gift certificate to By the Sea that Pine and Gwen gave you. A movie? A romantic walk on the beach?"

Ellen scowled and balanced her phone on the arm of her beach chair. "He's not interested me. And— And I'm not interested in him."

"You're not?"

Ellen didn't say anything. Because she kept telling herself the same thing, but she didn't know if she believed herself or not, either.

"Fine." Lara snatched Ellen's cell off her chair and entered the four-digit passcode.

Time to change the passcode.

"Hmmm. Let's find someone you'll like."

"What are you doing?" Ellen took a drink from her water bottle.

Lara swiped and tapped. Then looked up. She was wearing a ball cap to cover her dirty hair and her big sunglasses to cover her bloodshot eyes. "What's your credit card number?"

"What?"

"Never mind." Lara returned her attention to the phone. "I'll use mine."

"What are you—" Ellen tried to grab her phone, but Lara leaned just out of her reach.

"Expiration date," Lara mumbled to herself. "Three-digit security number and . . . there. Bam." She looked up, smiling. "You're live."

"I'm live where?" Ellen could feel her forehead creasing.

"On Find You a Man dot-com. Oh, look. The algorithms have already kicked in. The site is already making suggestions." She drew back her head as if smelling something putrid. "Ewww. No." She swiped. "Nope." She swiped again, then, "Hey, he's cute." She held up the phone to show Ellen a photograph of a man. "Nonsmoker. Exercises three to four times a week like you. And he doesn't want children. So that'll work out."

Ellen snatched the phone from Lara's hand. "You're fired."

Lara laughed. "From what?"

"You're not my friend anymore. You're fired."

"You can't fire me, sister by another mister. Come on," Lara cajoled. "You love me. You know you do."

Ellen looked at the screen. There was a photo of a guy who looked to be around her age. Attractive. Graying. A nice smile. "How does this work?" she asked suspiciously. Against her will, she could feel her interest rising. Not necessarily in this guy, but in the idea of maybe going out on a date. Maybe she *could* do it. After the first uncomfortable minutes with Barrett, the conversation had gone pretty well.

"It's easy."

Before Ellen could stop her, Lara snatched the phone back. "Start with the matches they've suggested. I think they give you like ten a day. Check out his photo." She held up the phone, but still out of Ellen's reach. "Read the highlights and then hit the X or the checkmark."

"The checkmark?" Ellen said, half-intrigued, half-petrified.

"Yup." Lara hit the checkmark with a flourish.

"And then what?"

"Nope. Nope. . . ." Lara paused. "Hm. Here's a possibility. Not classic good looks like Barrett, serious receding hairline, but you don't care about that, right?" She hit the checkmark. "I kind of have a thing for bald men. Sir Patrick, Patrick Stewart à la Jean-Luc Picard. *Star Trek: The Next Generation*, not that weird *Star Trek: Picard* series. Hot." She looked down at Ellen's phone again.

"Give me that." Ellen put out her hand.

"Or what? You going to take away my dinner?" Lara teased.

"I'm going to take away your eyebrow pencils," Ellen snapped, only half-kidding.

Lara drew back as if Ellen had slapped her. "That is cold. I have cancer. You can't take a cancer girl's eyebrow pencils away. But if you do, I'll use a Sharpie."

The cold cap was working for the hair on Lara's head, but her eyebrows had fallen out entirely. Along with her armpit hair, the hair on her legs, and the hair in her nether regions. She'd just been telling Ellen that morning that she was pleased the hair on her legs was gone, but she was in official mourning for her eyebrows. She did such a good job drawing them on that from more than a foot away Ellen couldn't even tell they weren't real.

Ellen continued to hold out her hand.

"Fine. But don't be a chickenshit. Okay?" She slapped the phone into Ellen's hand.

Ellen stared at the screen. "I can say yes or no to these ten choices today? What does that mean?"

"The guy sees you might be interested, and if he is, he can message you. Of course, you could just message someone you're interested in."

"That is not going to happen." She studied the photo on her screen. The guy's Labrador retriever took up more of the frame than he did. She hit the X.

Lara leaned back in her beach chair. "The choices are infinite. Well, depending on how far away you want to go. Oh!" She leaned forward. "But there's this Discover screen where you can see who's in the immediate vicinity. If you're looking for a hookup."

Ellen pulled off her sunglasses. "A hookup? Really? Do I seem like a hookup kind of girl to you? Did you lose your mind in the shower? Did it go down the drain with your eyebrows?"

Lara laughed and pointed at her. "Good one!" She seemed genuinely tickled. "But hey, don't knock it until you've tried it. It's very freeing. A hookup. Meet a guy for a drink, and if you're both attracted to each other?" She shrugged. "Why not?"

Ellen slid her sunglasses back on. "I am not having sex with a stranger." She swiped to look at the next suggestion. Also with a dog. She hit the X. "Where are the cat guys?" she asked. "Why do all of these guys have dogs in their photos?"

"They think women will be more likely to give them a wink."

"A wink?"

"It's like the checkmark. To say you might be interested."

"I'm confused." Ellen was starting to feel overwhelmed. "Do I wink or check?"

"Either-or."

Ellen dropped her phone to her lap. "I can't do this."

"Yes, you can."

Yes, I can, Ellen told herself. *If I want to.* She picked up her phone again. "A red heart just popped up. In the top corner. With a numeral one in it."

"Oh!" Lara clasped her hands. "Someone liked you!"

"Someone *liked* me?" Ellen stared at the phone in her hand. "How do I know who?"

"Select the heart and the likes will be listed with a profile pic for each"

"Then what?"

She shrugged. "If you're interested, like him back, or better yet, message him."

Ellen stared at the little heart in the corner of the screen and smiled.

Someone liked her. . . .

32

Amara watched Pine ease into his Adirondack chair beside her. He didn't seem like himself today. He was moving slowly, his voice not quite so full of energy. She kept thinking about the photos of him in Vietnam that he'd shared with them. She wouldn't have recognized him had his name and the date not been at the bottom of the old black-and-white photos. While small in stature, he'd been broad chested and muscular then, with a big smile and his whole life ahead of him. This Pine lowering himself into a chair with a cushion Ellen had brought him was only a shadow of the man in the photo.

"How are you doing today, Pine?" It was just the two of them at the moment. Lara and Grace were inside, Shorty had an appointment, and Alex was . . . somewhere, and expected later in the day.

Amara patted Pine's hand. His skin was darker than hers, rich and chocolatey. Her husband Casper's skin had been almost the same shade. For some reason, she found that comforting.

Pine chuckled. "Still on this side of the grass, so I'm great." He let himself drop the last few inches and exhaled heavily.

"What you got there?" He pointed to the cardboard box on her lap.

She adjusted her broad-brimmed sun hat. The new hat was one of her favorite possessions, bought on the boardwalk in one of those cheesy stores with all the junk for tourists. Across the street from Grace's son's bookstore. It had little plastic fuchsia petunias on the hatband. She wore it over her green scarf. "My new phone. It came yesterday. UPS." She lifted the white box to show him the front. "I got the big one so I can read texts without my glasses. My niece Lilly asked me if she could have it when I'm dead. I said no. A ten-year-old doesn't need a phone."

Ordinarily, Amara would have given her great-niece anything she asked for. They were, after all, roommates. In fact, they shared the same double bed. And they were best friends, according to a story the little girl had written in school the previous spring. It was supposed to be about a hero in her life. Amara's niece said Amara was in good company. It had been a toss-up between her and Wonder Woman. Amara still wasn't leaving the phone to Lilly in her will. Instead, she was leaving her a stock portfolio.

Pine eased back in the chair and closed his eyes.

"You look tired," Amara said, patting his hand again. "Maybe you should take a little nap."

"Not that tired." He opened his eyes. Blinked. "Let's see it. I ordered mine online. Picking it up at the store tonight on the way home."

Amara tore the plastic off the white box, removed the lid, and lifted the new iPhone as if it were as precious as a newborn baby.

She and Casper had never had the chance to have a newborn baby, but she'd held so many in her arms when she'd volunteered in the NICU. Some had lived, some had not, but they all had been precious to her. She'd been there to hold them when their parents couldn't and to love them because she could.

Pine gave a loud whistle of appreciation. "She's a beaut!"

He leaned over to have a closer look. "What color do they call that?"

"Rose gold," she answered proudly.

Leaning over the arm of his chair, he studied the new phone in her hand. "I got the space gray." His brow beneath his bucket hat furrowed. "I don't know what makes it *space* gray. Gwen says that's just what they call it. Her laptop's the same color." He studied the box on her lap. "You turn it on yet?"

"No. I'll let Alex do it. Lilly wanted to do it for me. She's good with technology. She fixes her mother's iPad and computer when something's wrong. But I told her that Alex was taking care of it. She seemed a little miffed."

He leaned back and started patting his pockets. Pine lost things all the time.

"What are you looking for?" she asked.

"Sunglasses. I know I got 'em here somewhere. Wore them over in the car. Gwen went back into the house to get them for me."

Amara reached into his bag he'd put between their chairs. "Here you go." She offered him the case.

It took Pine so long to get the glasses out and put them on that Amara had to sit on her hands to keep from putting them on for him. But she knew that it was important for Pine to do some things on his own, even when he struggled. It was important to all of them. When he had them on, she took the case from the arm of his chair and dropped it into his duffel bag.

Footsteps sounded on the steps, and Lenora walked onto the porch. She was spry for a woman her age. Amara had noticed that the other day when she'd appeared on the porch out of nowhere. Today she was carrying another plastic grocery store bag.

"Bra goes under your shirt, Lenora," Pine pointed out to her. His tone was nonjudgmental. He had bigger fish to fry. They all did.

Lenora looked down at her bra over her madras plaid shirt. "Darn it," she muttered. "I knew that."

"Pretty, though," Pine complimented. "I like the lace."

Lenora smiled and slid into Alex's pink chair. "Brought snacks," she announced, digging into the plastic grocery bag. "I can't stay long. In trouble with my granddaughter. I'm not supposed to leave the house *unattended*. I got in trouble."

"For what?" Amara asked.

Lenora looked at Amara, then into the bag again. Amara knew she had heard her.

"I made sandwiches," Lenora announced.

Pine cleared his throat and gazed out over the porch rail. There was a young woman in a green polka-dotted bikini cutting between their house and the next. She was wearing a ball cap and carrying a striped red, white, and blue canvas bag. She had to live nearby. They saw her all the time.

"Want a sandwich?" Lenora pulled one out of the bag.

It was unwrapped, and Amara couldn't immediately identify what it was. On top of that, the smell was questionable. "No, thank you. Not right now."

"Well, just let me know." Lenora dropped the sandwich back into the bag and wiped her hand on her chambray culottes.

She didn't have cancer, so technically she didn't belong on the porch. They'd discussed that the other day when she'd come up the steps and plunked herself down in Ellen's chair as if she belonged there. Amara and the others had assumed Lenora had been invited. Later, Lara had relayed the story about Lenora breaking into the house to make coffee for Ellen, and as she had talked, Amara had gotten the strangest feeling. A feeling that Lenora had the right to be there and that she was needed. By whom, Amara didn't know. But they'd taken a vote and agreed that Lenora was welcome anytime she wandered in.

At least when Ellen wasn't around.

Because of Lenora's dementia, Ellen was concerned about the older woman's safety. It was a valid concern, but it didn't negate the feeling that Amara got that Lenora's place in the universe was on that porch. At least for the time being.

Amara leaned back and closed her eyes for a moment, enjoying the feel of the sun when she tipped it back just so. "How are you today, Lenora?"

"Good. Good. Making fried chicken and lima beans and dumplings for supper. Lester loves my fried chicken."

"I imagine it's good."

"Trick is to soak it overnight in buttermilk. The chicken." Lenora squinted. "What's that?"

Amara opened her eyes and held up the box. "My new iPhone. Alex is going to turn it on for me when she gets here."

"I don't need a new one. My grandson gave me his." Lenora dug around in her plastic bag and pulled out an old calculator. "See." With great concentration, she turned it on and hit several keys. The screen lit up with numbers. "Works just fine."

Amara patted Lenora's hand. The joy she saw on her friend's face brought joy to her own face. "Well, aren't you lucky, then."

33

Ellen set a plate of cheese, crackers, fruit, and nuts on a teak table between Lara and Grace. She was hoping Lara would find the charcuterie board tempting enough to eat something. She was worried about her. Her daily vomiting had lessened, but she looked gaunt, with dark circles under her eyes.

"It's so nice to see you today, Ellen," Grace said, her tone grandmotherly. "Why don't you sit with us for a few minutes?"

"Join us." Pine tapped the back of Ellen's blue Adirondack chair.

Amara echoed his invitation. Alex sat on the top step, her back to them, looking at her phone. Rose gold wireless earbuds protruded from her ears.

Ellen hesitated. She always felt a little awkward when she sat on the porch when everyone was here. Lara and her friends had become so close. Ellen didn't feel like she fit in and not just because she wasn't going through cancer treatment like they were. Each and every one of them, even the teenager, seemed to have life and themselves figured out, and the more time she spent with them, the more self-conscious she felt in their presence. Listening to them, she realized how lost she had been.

230 / Colleen French

And not just because of the divorce or Tim remarrying. It went deeper than that.

At the same time, she desperately wanted to be there, to be a part of the group.

Everyone needs a tribe.

"I don't know," Ellen hemmed. "I want to make a brine for pork chops I'm grilling for dinner, and I have rough draft papers to grade. My students—"

"Your students can wait," Lara interrupted, pushing her sunglasses up on her head. She had leaned over her chair and studied the cheese plate.

"I better not," Ellen said. She wasted away most of the previous day sitting with them on the porch. But it had been so enjoyable—once she'd relaxed. And she had a few ideas she wanted to jot down in her journal. She had been thinking about characterization and had found herself writing details about the people who gathered on her porch. Details like the love she heard in Grace's voice each time she spoke of her dead husband, Barrett's father. And Pine's always cheerful attitude. And the way Alex fit in so well among the adults. And how Ellen kept forgetting that she was a boy . . . no, that many people in society wanted her to identify as male. As Lara had pointed out more than once, Alex was more of a girly girl (if there was such a thing) than she or Ellen would ever be.

"Come on," Amara encouraged. "We were just talking about what we would pack in a picnic lunch for the beach. Anything you like." She gestured. "The world is your oyster. Anything on earth, the cost is no object. What would it be?"

"You're planning a picnic?" Ellen asked.

"Not a real picnic, it's a game," Lara said impatiently. "Maybe we'll have a picnic sometime, but the point of the question, Ellie, is to reveal something about yourself by your choices." She rolled her eyes and reached down at her feet, coming up with a drink that looked like a vodka and soda.

Their gazes met and Ellen could tell Lara was daring her

to say something. Instead, Ellen exhaled sharply through her nose, giving a little sound of disapproval. She walked into the kitchen, letting the screen door slap closed behind her. If Lara wanted to drink alcohol and risk interfering with her chemo treatment, that was her choice, wasn't it? She was a grown woman.

A grown-ass woman, as Lara liked to say.

Inside the house, Ellen's internal dialogue continued as she retrieved the ingredients she needed to make the brine for the pork chops. She was so busy grumbling under her breath that she didn't even hear Pine come into the house until she looked up and saw him standing at the end of the counter looking at her.

"Can I get you something?" she asked.

"Nope. But you can tell me something." He slid one hand into the pocket of his khaki shorts. He was wearing a teal madras plaid shirt and his floppy bucket hat.

"What's that?" She offered a quick smile.

"You were just going to say something. Outside." He tilted his head in the direction of the porch. "Then you walked away."

Ellen could hear Amara, Lara, and Grace talking, but she couldn't quite make out what they were saying.

"I wasn't going to say anything else."

Pine frowned. "But you *wanted* to say something else."

Again, she smiled, mostly because he was making her feel uncomfortable. Pine did that to people, she had observed. He asked direct questions and wouldn't allow you to dodge them.

He took a step toward her. "You made that sound. I know that sound." He waggled his finger at her. "Gwen makes the same sound when she wants to say something to me but won't. And I've heard you do it before."

She was quiet.

"Say it," he told her. "If not to Lara, who I'm guessing you intended it for, then at least to me. Something she did upset you."

Ellen set a bottle of peppercorns down hard on the counter. "She shouldn't be drinking vodka. It could affect her treatment," she blurted.

"Okay." He nodded. "So why didn't you say that? Why—"

"I don't—"

"No interruptions." He pointed at himself, then her. "I talk, then you talk. That's how folks converse. And right now, I'm talkin'." His tone was kind but firm.

Ellen pressed her lips together.

"You're her best friend in the world. Her words, not mine." He was holding his finger up at her again. "And friends tell each other what needs to be said. So why didn't you say it?"

She looked down at the floor. "No one listens to me."

"No one listens to you? Oh, boohoo."

Ellen was so surprised by his words that she stared at him, crossing her arms over her chest.

"Come on, Ellen, you're better than this."

She didn't know what to say, so she passed on her turn.

"All you do is boohoo! Woman, you got a chip on your shoulder that must weigh a ton."

She was beginning to get that scratchy feeling she felt behind her eyes before she teared up.

Pine took a step closer. "No, no, what you've got is a bunch of chains. Like Dickens's Jacob Marley. Not the kind made by bad things you do. Chains you created out of fears that are holding you down, pulling you back, keeping you from this wonderful world out there. They're not real. They're in your head. You're feeling sorry for yourself when you created these problems."

"I don't feel sorry for myself."

Pine gave a laugh that was clearly without amusement. "I don't know anyone who spends more time feeling sorry for themselves. And you've got no reason. No reason to cry! You want something to cry about, I'll give you something. How about you're a black man drafted and sent to the jungle to kill people? Sent to the jungle to crawl underground, waiting to hit a booby trap. How about you come home after serving your country only to find your country doesn't want you? Doesn't want to give you a job or let you have a house? How about you have a beautiful wife and kids burn up in a house fire while you're working a double shift in a fertilizer plant?"

Tears ran down Ellen's face. She knew Gwen was his second wife and that the first had died, but she had no idea he'd lost children, too. And in a house fire? She couldn't even imagine the horror. The pain.

And yet Pine was still smiling. How?

When he spoke again, his tone was gentle. "Aw, honey, I'm not tryin' to make you cry, or feel bad about yourself. But it's time you stood tall and got on with your life. So your parents died, so your father was a bastard, so your husband divorced you." He opened his arms wide. "Things like that happen to everyone. Like it or not, it's part of life. It's time to let all that stuff go, real or imagined. Cut those chains. You are smart and capable and a good-lookin' woman. And you've got people who care about you. You got Lara and you got us out there on that porch." He took another step closing the distance between them. "And you need to start living the life you've been given before it's gone."

Ellen stared at her bare feet and the seashell-pink toenail polish she was wearing. She sniffled.

"Ah, come on, now. Stop your cryin'; otherwise, I'll feel bad. You don't want to make an old man feel bad, do you?"

Ellen looked up at him. "I knew Gwen was your second wife, but I had no idea you had lost your first wife and children in a fire. Pine, I am so sorry."

"Thank you. It was a long time ago. Still hurts every day. I still miss them every day," he told her, not breaking eye contact. His eyes filled with tears, but he went on. "She and my three little ones. We were staying with her sister, the place caught fire, and they didn't get out. None of them. That was back in the days when we didn't have smoke detectors like we do now."

"I'm so sorry," Ellen whispered because she didn't know what else to say.

"Thank you." He wiped at his eyes. "I really didn't mean to pick on you, Ellie. Can I call you that?"

She found a smile for him, this one genuine. "You can."

"So how about a hug then, Ellie? We still friends?"

"Of course we are," she murmured. And then she allowed him to wrap her in his arms, and she felt herself relax for what seemed like the first time in a very long time.

34

Ellen walked across the front porch with bags of groceries in the crooks of both arms and a sack of fresh produce from the farmer's market on her shoulder. Lara had said she was craving fresh, local sweet corn, which was beginning to ripen in Delaware. Ellen didn't know that Lara would actually eat it, but it was worth a try.

Her phone in her pocket vibrated. A voice message.

From Tim.

He'd called again.

She lowered one of the bags to the floor and pulled out her phone at the front door. She hesitated, then listened to the message.

"Hey . . . I didn't need anything," Tim said, sounding hesitant. "I just called to say hi."

He called to say hi? He hadn't called to say hello to her in ten years.

"So, um . . . Christopher told me what was going on with you. And Lara. That you're at the beach house. I hope she's okay."

There was a pause; then he said. "So . . . give me a call sometime, if you want."

Call him if she wanted? She stared at the phone for a moment and realized . . . she didn't want.

She deleted his voice mail and picked up the bag again. As she opened the door, she heard voices. She was surprised to find Lara and her friends all sitting in the living room in front of the big-screen TV. No one ever used the TV that Tim had insisted on buying the summer before the divorce. She and Lara hadn't turned it on once in the month they had been there. A couple of times they'd watched Netflix together, but it was always in Lara's bed on her laptop.

The blinds were closed, and the lights were off, and it was cool in the living room. They'd taken her advice when she left for the grocery store. It had been so hot outside with no breeze that she'd suggested they might all like to adjourn to the living room for a while.

Music blasted from the speakers Tim had installed around the room. On the screen was a strikingly beautiful black woman in a long, colorful gown and big blond hair, strutting down a runway.

The Porch sat enthralled by what was on the screen. They were all there: Lara, Grace, Amara, Pine, Shorty, and Alex.

Pine was clapping his hands and cackling the way he did. "Work it, girl!"

Ellen had to smile. They all seemed to be thoroughly enjoying themselves. "What are you watching?" she asked, stepping into the living room area.

No one responded. Everyone was talking at once. There were glasses of iced tea and what looked like homemade lemonade resting on the coffee table and end tables. Also, a big bowl of cheese puffs.

Growing up, there had never been food or a drink in her mother's living room, and Ellen had always followed the same rule. The funny thing was, seeing them all with drinks didn't even bother her. She wondered why she had ever set such a silly rule to begin with. What did she care if someone spilled iced tea on the ugly floral couches her mother had bought two decades ago?

"Welcome to the main stage of *RuPaul's Drag Race*," the stunning woman on the stage announced, her hands on her shapely hips.

"Lara?" Ellen put the bags on the floor and walked into the living area where the TV was mounted above the closed-in fireplace between built-in bookcases. There had been a coal stove there when her mother had been a girl. There had been a coal stove used for cooking in the kitchen as well.

Ellen watched the screen, intrigued. Men and women were sitting at what appeared to be a judges' table.

Lara, who sat beside Amara on the end of one of the two couches that faced each another, turned. She was still wearing her blue cold cap and was wrapped in a blanket. Her face pale, no eyebrows to be seen, she barely looked like herself today. Except for her big smile. "Hey, Ellie. You're back." She returned her attention to the TV.

Ellen couldn't look away from the screen, either. None of them could. The woman in the gown was so poised. So gorgeous. "What on earth are you watching?" she asked, smiling.

"*RuPaul's Drag Race*," Lara answered, not looking at her. "Alex's idea. We were going to watch a movie, but we couldn't agree on anything."

"Isn't she gorgeous?" Alex exclaimed from her perch on the arm of the recliner that Shorty was sitting in. "I'd love to make myself a gown like that," she said wistfully. "The orange ruffles are to die for. I just don't know where I would wear it. Maybe the cancer ball, but it's not until February." She made a face. "Not sure I'll be available."

"I bet you'd look pretty in something like that," Shorty told her, reaching for a glass of lemonade.

Ellen shook her head, still smiling. "Drag race? I don't see any cars."

Pine laughed so hard that Ellen thought he was going to fall out of his chair.

Grace reached out from the other couch and brushed Ellen's arm. "They're drag queens, luv. Alex was telling us all about them, and we decided to see for ourselves."

Ellen's mouth fell open as she stared at the stunning black woman again. "That woman is a . . ."

"A man, dear," Grace finished for her.

"A queen," Alex corrected.

"That's RuPaul." Amara.

Somewhere in the back of her mind, Ellen knew the name.

Music blasted from the speakers. "First up, Kenya Michaels!"

Ellen watched as another woman—a man—strutted down the runway in a short hot-pink froufrou dress and long blond hair with dramatic bangs.

"Sit down." Lara patted the edge of the couch, scooting over a little.

As Ellen sat down, it occurred to her that a month ago she wouldn't have. She had groceries sitting in the entryway. Frozen edamame for a salad she wanted to make. She would never have left groceries on the floor to watch TV before.

But it wasn't about the TV. It was about Lara. And the porch friends.

A woman, a man . . . Ellen wasn't exactly sure how to refer to him/her strutting down the runway in a dress with colored plastic balls glued to it. And a gumball machine tucked under his/her arm. She laughed as she realized the plastic balls were gumballs.

"You've never heard of *RuPaul's Drag Race*?" Alex asked in fascination. "What big rocks have you all been living under?"

"Hey, hey!" Shorty called, raising a big hand. "I knew who RuPaul was and I knew about the show. My nieces told me all about it. They watch the show and follow different queens on Twitter."

"Wait, wait!" Alex exclaimed. "You're not going to believe Sharon's dress." She flapped a hand. Alex was wearing a pair of denim cutoffs, a tank top, and a blond wig Ellen hadn't seen before. She wore the wig pulled back in a short ponytail. She looked like any other fifteen-year-old girl on the boardwalk, right down to her flip-flops.

One without terminal cancer.

The thought brought a lump up in Ellen's throat, but it also made her smile.

Didn't everyone on some level just want to fit in?

"This dress is way outside of Sharon's comfort zone," Alex went on. "But that's part of what makes Sharon so good. Ru asked for girly girl, and that's what Sharon went for." The teen held up both hands. "I'm not saying anything more. I don't want to give anything away."

Ellen turned to Lara. She looked so happy. She rested her hand on her knee. "You doing okay? Anything I can get you?"

"Nope. I'm good." Lara checked her watch. "Only six more minutes with this effing cap and I'm done for the day." She met Ellen's gaze. "You notice I didn't say 'f—'"

"I did notice," Ellen interrupted with a smile.

"This is such fun," Amara declared to no one in particular. "I've never watched TV much. Had I known this was on, I'd have watched every season."

"You know they have a drag show at one of the bars on the boardwalk," Shorty said. "Sunday nights."

"You've gone?" Amara asked. It was Thursday. She was wearing her red head scarf.

"No." Shorty laughed. "It doesn't start until midnight. I'm in bed by eight most nights. My niece and her friends went last time they came to visit, though. Said it was a hoot."

"I'd like to see it," Grace said thoughtfully. "But I don't know if I can go somewhere at midnight. I'd have to sneak out of the house like Alex."

Everyone laughed, including Ellen.

"Wait! I have an idea!" Alex grabbed the remote and leaped up off Shorty's recliner as she paused the show. "We should have our own drag show."

"What?" Pine demanded.

"All of us! I could make dresses." Alex was so excited that she was flapping her hands. "And do everyone's makeup!"

"I see how Pine and I could do it, but how are the ladies going to be drag queens?" Shorty asked.

Alex pressed her hand to her forehead dramatically as if Shorty had just said the most ridiculous thing. "Drag isn't about whether you're male or female, gay, bi, trans. It's about being beautiful, feeling beautiful. And having fun!"

"A drag show!" Lara threw up her arms. "I love the idea!" She sounded almost as excited as Alex did. "We could use the front porch as our stage. The audience could sit in chairs on the lawn." She looked at Grace. "I bet Barrett would come. Wouldn't he?"

Grace caught Alex's hands and squeezed them, smiling up at her. "I don't think he'd miss it for the world."

35

Ellen walked out of the pantry to find Alex leaning over the sink, her hands pressed to the edge of the countertop. Out in the living room, Ellen could hear everyone talking over one another. They'd just started another episode of the TV show. She had boxes of books in the attic to bring down and go through, but she was half-tempted to ditch the task and watch a little more with them.

At first, Ellen thought the teen was looking intently in the sink for something. A lost earring? An errant eyelash? Nowadays, Ellen was always finding false eyelashes on the bathroom floor or on the porch when she swept away the sand after everyone went home. But as she got closer, she realized there was something wrong. Alex was gripping the side of the counter so hard that her knuckles were white.

Ellen walked up behind the teenager and pressed her hand to the small of her Alex's back. "What's the matter, sweetie?"

Alex slowly stood upright, taking a trembling breath. "I'm okay," she whispered. "Sometimes, they just hit me like this."

Ellen looked at her face. She was very pale "What hits you?"

Sweat had beaded on Alex's forehead. "Headache," she managed, her voice raspy.

Ellen wrapped one arm around the girl and led her to a stool on the far side of the counter. She'd thought about taking her into the living room so the teenager could lie down but decided against it. She suspected Alex had come into the kitchen so no one would see her like this. She didn't want to ruin the fun. "Sit down. Let me get you a cool cloth for your head." That was what her mother had always done for Ellen when she was Alex's age and had frequent migraines.

Alex dropped onto the stool and leaned forward, resting her forehead between her folded arms. "I'll be okay in a minute. This happens sometimes."

Ellen surprised herself by giving Alex a quick hug; then she went to the kitchen drawer where she kept clean dish towels. Grabbing a yellow-striped towel, she turned on the faucet, letting the water get cold before she soaked the cloth. Returning to Alex, she offered it to her. "Put this on your head. Do you want to lie down? We can go upstairs if you'd rather not go into the living room."

Alex slowly sat up and accepted the wet cloth. She rested her elbows on the countertop and leaned over, pressing the dish towel to her forehead. Next, Ellen brought her a glass of water. Alex took a sip.

"What can I do for you? . . ." Ellen hesitated. "Do you want me to call your parents?"

"No. Please don't call them." Alex looked up through her long fake eyelashes. "They'll want to take me to the hospital. Then later, they'll talk about what an inconvenience leaving work early was."

Ellen sat beside Alex. "Sweetie, I know you're a smart girl. And I know you understand your cancer. A headache like this could mean—" She couldn't finish the sentence.

"A brain bleed." Alex said it for her.

She spoke the words so easily that Ellen felt a tightening in her chest. This was so unfair. So damned unfair. How could such a beautiful child be dying from such a horrendous disease? *And how could she be taking it so easily? So gracefully.* **Those were even bigger questions.**

"Would that be such a bad thing?" Ellen asked, keeping her voice down to protect Alex's pounding head as much as to keep the others from hearing them. "Maybe you need a scan."

"Only if the headache is on for a while. And even then." Alex exhaled slowly and sat up a little straighter. "I think I'm about done with scans. There's never good news. And I hate having to stay overnight at the hospital. If I go, my parents will leave me there."

Ellen wanted to tell the girl, "Of course they won't." Instead, she just sat there and listened. Waited.

Alex met her gaze. She was a little better now. A little color was returning to her face.

"That's what they always do," Alex said softly. "They take me in and then they find an excuse why they have to leave. It's always something about work. Or they have to go home to let workers into the house. My mom has remodeled the whole house like three times since my diagnosis. It's so lonely in the hospital at night." She took a drink of water and went on.

"When I was younger, I used to notice that all the other kids in the pediatric ward had a parent staying with them at night. The nurses will even bring a cot if you ask." She shook her head slowly. "But mine never did. Not that I really would have wanted my mom or dad there. They're kind of rude to the staff. But . . . it would have been nice if they had *wanted* to stay with me. You know?" She looked up at Ellen, and even with the false eyelashes and glamorous long hair, she looked like a little girl much younger than she was. A scared little girl.

Ellen put her arm around Alex's thin shoulders again. She smelled good, like coconut and . . . youth. And cheese puffs, which almost made Ellen laugh. Which of course was totally inappropriate at the moment. "Do you get them often? The headaches?"

Alex leaned forward and rested her head on her arm on the counter. "More often than I used to." She pursed her lips that were a glossy red from the cherry lip balm she'd been passing around in the living room. "It's the tumor."

Ellen searched her pretty green eyes. She could see pain in them, but not just physical pain, emotional pain. "Is there anything that can be done?"

The corner of Alex's mouth turned up into a halfhearted smile. "No, Alyssa. That's why they call it inoperable."

Alyssa? Ellen felt a moment of panic. *Was Alex's brain bleeding causing confusion?*

Alex must have seen the concern on Ellen's face because she laughed and said, "I call you Alyssa because you remind me a little of Alyssa Edwards. A drag queen." She sounded sheepish now. "Season five. I have secret names for everyone."

Ellen wasn't sure how she felt about having a drag queen name, but she knew this wasn't the time to discuss it anyway.

Alex took another deep breath and sat up, still holding the dish towel to her head. "See. I'm already feeling better."

"Don't you think you need to call your parents? They have a right to—" Ellen stopped and then went on, rephrasing what she wanted to say. "If you were my daughter, I'd want to know, Alex."

"You have a daughter?"

Ellen shook her head. There was a commercial break for something called a lace wig in the living room. Grace and Amara were talking about what they liked to eat for breakfast. She tuned them out again. "Just a son."

"Are you disappointed?" Alex asked, but she went on before Ellen could answer. "My parents wanted a boy. They got me." She smirked. "Can you imagine how hard it must have been for Kenneth and Imogene to find out their boy child was actually a girl child? Only with a penis. A little one, albeit." She pinched her thumb and forefinger together.

It was the first time Ellen had ever heard her make a reference to being transgender. And she felt . . . honored. "I can't imagine how hard it must be for you," she heard herself say. She was surprised she was able to say aloud what she was thinking, what she'd been thinking since she found out. "Being a teenage girl is hard under any circumstance with all the changes that take place in your body as you go through puberty." She leaned forward to rest her elbow on the counter, her chin in her hand so that she was almost eye level with Alex. "I know it was hard for me."

Alex shrugged.

Ellen hesitated, unsure if she should say anything else, but she thought about what Barrett had said about writing about what you knew in your heart. Maybe she wouldn't be able to write about the things closer to her heart if she didn't learn to speak them. "Did you know I knew?"

Alex sat up. "Sure. Lara told me."

"Is that okay that she did?"

"It's not like it's a secret. It's out there. I have a YouTube channel." Alex set the wet dish towel on the counter. "I'm fine with it. I just don't walk around telling people."

"Because you're afraid they'll judge you?"

Alex looked at her for a moment. "No. What do I care what people think? I know who I am. I just . . . I'm like any other girl. Did you talk about going through puberty with people when you were my age?"

Ellen thought about it for a second. "No, but . . ." She stopped and started again. "Alex, I don't have the right vocabulary, so anything I say, if it's offensive, I don't mean it to be."

She waited.

"I guess I just assumed that because you were born with . . . male parts—" Ellen exhaled, feeling flustered now. She didn't want to hurt Alex for the sake of her own curiosity. But it wasn't precisely curiosity. It was more about wanting to under-stand her, to get to know her better. She was such a kind, sweet girl with such a love for life and for those around her. Ellen groaned and pressed her hand to her face. "Oh, I don't know what I'm trying to say."

Alex unfolded and refolded the wet towel. "I kind of think I know what you're asking. I don't talk about how I was born because that's . . . just how I was born. It's who I am. I don't know any different. In my brain, I've always been a girl."

They were both quiet for a moment, a quiet that was com-fortable for Ellen.

"Anyway," Alex said, "I'm just trying to figure things out like any other fifteen-year-old girl." She got off the stool. "I feel better now. The headache's almost gone." She blew out through her mouth. "Every time I get one, I wonder if it's the big one." She shrugged. "Guess it's not today." She hooked her thumb in the direction of the living room. "I think I'll go watch the rest of this episode. I love the lip syncs. I've seen this one like a mil-lion times, but I love seeing Dida Ritz and the Princess lip-sync for their lives. It's a Natalie Cole song." She slid sideways across the floor, putting out her arms, lifting her chin high. "This will be an everlasting love," she sang. Then she looked over her shoulder. "You coming?" She offered her hand.

And Ellen took it, wishing she'd had a daughter. One just like Alex.

36

Ellen walked through the soft sand toward the house, her goggles on her head, her towel over her shoulder. She'd had a good swim, but she was so tired that her legs felt heavy as she trudged. She'd bent her own rules and swam a good two hundred yards farther than she usually did.

To punish herself?

To delay going back to the house?

Probably a little of both. She and Lara had had words. Ellen had walked out on the porch on her way down to the beach to swim and found her and her friends all excitedly talking about their drag show. Ellen wasn't sure they actually intended to have a drag show. Maybe it was like the plans to take a trip into town for fries or caramel popcorn or shaved ice. It didn't matter if they did it or not. They were having a good time talking about the drag show. Planning it. And Alex was in her glory.

Before her swim, Ellen had walked out onto the porch to find Lenora. In Ellen's chair. She had been sitting there with her hands together, her feet not touching the floor, looking from one person to the other, enjoying being a part of the fray.

Seeing her, Ellen had curled her finger at Lara, signaling she needed to speak to her. In private.

Lara had exhaled impatiently and gotten out of her chair. "Anyone want anything?" she had asked.

"I'll take a new pancreas if you've got one in the pantry," Amara had quipped.

Everyone had laughed.

When Ellen had first heard someone crack a joke like Amara's, it had made her uncomfortable. She was dying of pancreatic cancer. It wasn't funny.

But if that was how Amara chose to deal with her diagnosis, making jokes, what was wrong with that? Every person with a cancer diagnosis had the right to choose how to handle it. Just as anyone had the right to choose how to handle any other event in their life. And Ellen had concluded that she found the way The Porch dealt with their illnesses admirable.

"What's up, Ellie?" Lara had asked, following her into the kitchen.

Ellen had set her towel and goggles on the counter. "Lenora's here."

Lara had glanced through the screen door, then back at Ellen. "She sure is."

"Sitting in my chair."

"You weren't sitting in it. I think there might be a coup. Everyone thinks she should have her own chair."

"She's not supposed to be here," Ellen had told Lara. "I talked to her granddaughter about her coming into the house without being invited. Her family is trying to curtail her wandering. You asking her to join you all will only encourage her to keep coming."

"You talked to her granddaughter?" Lara's temper had flared. *"Why?"*

"Because she was breaking into my house. Because . . ."

Ellen had looked away. "I was worried she'd get hurt or lost or . . . I don't know." She had looked back at Lara. "She was breaking into my house," she repeated

"But you said you enjoyed her company."

"I do. I did. But what does that have to do with this? Lenora keeps turning on all the burners on the stove to make a pot of coffee. And she doesn't remember to turn them off. She could burn herself. Burn down the whole house."

"If you're down here with her, she isn't going to burn down the house." Lara had frowned. "I can't believe you ratted her out. You want me to tell her to go home?"

Ellen hadn't been able to meet Lara's gaze. "I guess if she's with you, she's safe."

Then Lara had just walked away.

Ellen reached the dunes. The grass had grown so tall now that she could no longer see the pilings the beach house stood on. From where she stood, it looked like the back porch was resting in the sand.

When she returned to the house, she'd decided she'd apologize to Lara for being bitchy about Lenora. She still thought she had a responsibility to the elderly woman to keep her safe.

But Ellen knew that wasn't the only reason it upset her to see Lenora laughing with Lara and her friends on the porch. It had perturbed her because Lenora, who half the time didn't know what decade it was, fit in with the porch friends.

And Ellen still didn't.

And she wanted to. She just didn't know how.

She was halfway up the steps before realizing that the laughter and excited voices she had heard when she left the house had gone silent. They were still all there. She had seen Amara's big hat and Lara's blond hair from the dunes.

When she reached the top step, she looked around. Everyone who had been there when she left was still there: Lara, Amara,

Shorty, Grace, Lenora, Alex. She looked from one to the next. They had all been crying. Even Shorty.

"What's the matter?" Ellen asked.

Lara looked up, her cheeks streaked with tears. "Pine's dead."

37

Saturday night, Lara went to bed at six o'clock without eating. The disagreement she and Ellen had had over Lenora the day before was forgotten, Pine's unexpected death eclipsing their difference in opinion. Feeling very alone, Ellen cleaned up the kitchen and wandered out onto the porch. There, she sat for a long time, enjoying the cool evening breeze on her face, thinking.

She felt so bad for Pine's wife. She couldn't imagine what Gwen was going through right now. That morning Ellen had ordered a big snack basket from her and Lara and the porch friends and had it delivered thinking Gwen's house would be full of family. People always dropped off casseroles, but no one thought about snacks. Every occasion, happy or sad, needed snacks. They had also sent a case of wine from Barrett's friend's store because, as Lara had pointed out, a lot of people don't eat much after a death in the family, but everyone drinks.

The gifts seemed like such a small gesture in the face of Gwen's loss, but the widow had texted Lara when they arrived to thank everyone. Lara said they had texted back and forth the usual things people say when a loved one dies and then Gwen had promised to let her know as soon as arrangements were made for the funeral.

Ellen couldn't stop thinking about Pine and the impact he'd had on her, despite only knowing him a month. He had been such a larger-than-life character and full of joy, a joy that spilled into others' lives. He was a man who had faced many odds: being born black in the forties in the South, going to Vietnam as a teenager, the deaths of his first wife and children, and then the cancer that would ultimately kill him.

He'd had a heart attack. It happened with cancer patients sometimes, Gwen had explained to Lara. He'd lain down for a nap, and when Gwen had gone to wake him an hour later to bring him over to the beach house to be with his friends she'd found him dead. He'd just fallen asleep and not woken up.

Ellen took a sip of Chardonnay, trying to think about some of the things he had said to her, things that made her laugh. Things that had made her consider her own life and the choices she had made, the choices she could make now.

Suddenly she was afraid she might forget.

She went into the house and grabbed her laptop. She'd been keeping random notes: details of the lives of those on the porch, but also just her thoughts. Her observations. Others' thoughts and observations.

She found the page of notes on Pine, added a few random things he had said, including the silly knock-knock joke he had told the first day they met. Then she typed:

Life Lessons from Pine

She thought for a moment. What was her one takeaway? That:

Tragedies did not make a tragic life.

She thought about what he had said to her in the kitchen the other day when he had talked frankly with her: "You want something to cry about, I'll give you something."

She thought about all of the reasons Pine had had to cry: being born a black man in the South, being drafted, losing his first wife and his children in a house fire, his cancer.

Then she listed the reasons why she didn't have something to cry about:

> **A good job**
> ~~A home~~ *Two* **homes**
> **A son**
> **Lara**
> **The porch friends**
> **Half a brain**

She poured herself another glass of wine.

> **A nice ass**
> **Knowledge of Restoration England history**
> **The ability to roll her tongue**

The last made her laugh out loud.

And it felt good.

Thinking about Pine's death led her down the path of thoughts of her father's death. And how sad she'd been, but also a little . . . What was the word she was looking for? Then it came to her.

> *Relieved.*

She stared at the word on the page. And almost deleted it. But she didn't, because if she was honest with herself, she *had* been relieved. She and her father had always shared such a strained relationship. And while she had loved him, loving him had been hard. That was the truth.

It was her truth.

> **You don't have to like the truth. But you have to
> accept it.**
> **Acceptance of the truth in ourselves . . .**
> **Why is a truth so hard to face sometimes?**

She was staring at the question she'd posed to herself on the computer screen when her phone vibrated. A text.

She picked it up, thinking Lara might need something. Sometimes Lara texted her from her bedroom when she didn't have the energy to get up or holler to Ellen. She said it was a skill she learned from her daughters when they were teenagers.

But it wasn't Lara.

It was Tim.

You unfriended me?? he'd texted. Two question marks, she noted. He was upset.

She stared at her phone. It reminded her of Pine's new iPhone that he'd only gotten to use for a few days. He'd been so excited that it was space gray. The name had delighted him as much as the actual color.

Text bubbles appeared on the screen. Then another message:

Tried to send you a FB message. And called.

Ellen was surprised not by emotion caused by Tim's texts, but her *lack* of emotion. She wasn't angry at him anymore. She wasn't even all that sad.

She thought for a moment about how to respond, then texted:

I didn't want to see photos of your travels. With your girlfriend.

She sent it before she chickened out.

The seconds that ticked by before he responded seemed to pass like hours.

Can we talk?

Christopher all right? she texted back.

He's fine. In CA for the weekend.

If their son was fine, why did Tim want to talk to her? They had agreed six months ago (when, granted, she was acting a little crazy when the girlfriend had come into the picture) not to talk anymore. At least for a while.

But he had been her husband. If Tim wanted to talk, shouldn't she talk to him?

But she didn't want to talk to him. Not tonight.

Need something? she texted.

No. Just missing you.

Her mouth went dry. Tim missed her?

Six months ago, even a month ago, she'd have done anything to hear him say that, but tonight . . . She thought for a moment and then wrote:

Tonight's not good.

She thought about telling him that a friend died, but she didn't want to share that with him. She didn't want to share anything with him. She hit the send key.

He responded a second later.

Talk soon?

"Maybe," she said aloud without answering him. And then she held up her wineglass and made a toast to herself.

38

As Ellen pulled her car up in front of the hospital, she glanced at Lara in the front seat. Her friend looked small, tired, sad. She'd been this way all weekend. She hadn't even wanted to walk down to the beach to watch the Fourth of July fireworks set off on the town's pier. Something they had always enjoyed together in the past.

They hadn't seen any of the porch friends all weekend. Everyone had family holiday events to attend.

Lenora had appeared on the porch on Saturday morning and sat with Lara. Ellen, who had been cleaning out kitchen drawers, had made the decision to pretend she didn't know Lenora was there. If she acknowledged the older woman's presence, she felt that she'd have to tell her to go home. But Lara enjoyed Lenora's company and was so upset about Pine's death. How could Ellen get in the way of any comfort Lenora could offer Lara? So Ellen let it go but kept an eye on them through the kitchen windows.

Mostly Lara had napped in her chair on the porch. Lenora had occupied Pine's chair, looking out over the ocean, talking. Later, Lara had told Ellen that Lenora had rehashed conversations they'd had with Pine on the porch. And accurately. But other times, the old woman's mind wandered between decades. She'd referred to Lara and Ellen by her sisters' names and talked about her brother, Joe, and when he would be home from France.

Still in the passenger's seat, Lara exhaled loudly, bringing Ellen back to the moment.

"I guess I need to go inside. Get this over with." Lara ran her hand over her messy bun. "I'm getting so I dread the effing cold cap more than the infusion." She glanced at Ellen.

The look on Lara's face made Ellen realize how much her friend needed her. Even more now than when she had started chemo. Pine's death wasn't just about losing him, it had brought the reality of Lara's mortality front and center, and she was scared.

And it was time Ellen stepped up. Because for most of their lives, it had been the other way around; she had needed Lara. Lara was always the strong, protective driving force in their relationship and Ellen had clung to her, going along for the ride. Now it was Ellen's turn to be strong and protective.

And she could do it. She could be here for her. Be present in Lara's needs instead of her own. This shocked Ellen. The realization that she'd been selfish all these years. She wondered how many times Lara had needed her and she had been too caught up in her own woes to realize it.

Ellen reached out and laid her hand on Lara's arm. In the simple gesture, Ellen felt a surge of emotional strength that surprised her. "You think you should skip your treatment today?"

Lara drew back her head in surprise, looking at her through the big blue lenses of her favorite sunglasses. "Skip today? Sweet Mary, Mother of God. I'm usually the one who wants to play hooky. You're the one who tells me every morning that I have to go so that I can check one more treatment off my list."

"I'm just wondering if you could use another day of rest. What's one day?"

258 / *Colleen French*

Lara smiled faintly, and then she glanced out the windshield.

Together, they watched Grace get out of a car with an *Uber* sticker in the back window that had pulled up in front of them. Grace had said that if she couldn't drive anymore, she'd find her own way to and from the hospital some days. She had said she wasn't ready to have her son "pushing her in a pram" yet.

Grace was wearing a T-shirt with Supreme Court Justice Ruth Bader Ginsburg's face on it, and below it read *Dissent*. She was also sporting a pair of purple knee-length pants of the type that Ellen's mother had called clamdiggers. Grace spoke to the driver through the window and then slung her bag over her shoulder and made her way to the door.

Lara looked back at Ellen. "It's tempting, but nah, I'll go. The oncologist is supposed to stop by. I told you that the last blood tests and scan looked good."

"I've noticed you're barely limping anymore."

"The pain is pretty much gone." Lara blew out her breath. "Another week and I might be done with chemo, for now at least. Then maybe radiation. The doc here is going to talk with Dr. Gupta at Penn and they'll decide if that's the best course of action. If we do that, I'm taking a week off before I start that crap."

"You're allowed to do that?" Ellen asked.

The look Lara gave her as she tilted her head, even wearing the sunglasses, wasn't hard to read. Lara was in control here, and she meant to keep that way.

And good for her.

The thought surprised Ellen. Maybe this wasn't the best choice in terms of the treatment of the cancer, but if it was best for Lara as a person, maybe it *was* the best.

Right then and there, Ellen promised herself that she wouldn't argue with Lara no matter what she chose to do in the next stage of her treatment. She'd support her choice.

"If I get a few days off, we can do something fun. I haven't been to Assateague Island since the girls were in middle school."

Lara moved her bag from the floor of the car to her lap, preparing to go. "Wouldn't it be fun to go see the wild ponies? We could take a picnic dinner. I know! We could get drunk on the beach."

Ellen poked her in the arm with her finger. "You can get drunk on the beach, and I'll carry your sorry ass home," she teased.

"Sorry ass!" Lara laughed. "You said another naughty word, Ellie." She leaned over and kissed her cheek. "Love you, sister by another mister."

"I love you, too," Ellen murmured. Then she watched Lara make her way into the hospital and thought about how hard it was going to be for her, for everyone at chemo, not to have Pine there today. Knowing they would never hear him laugh again.

She took a deep breath and started the car. As the pulled forward, though, Lara's water bottle rolled out from under the passenger's seat. It must have fallen out of her bag. Easing her car around the drop-off circle, she parked and grabbed the water bottle. She'd just run it in.

Inside the cool, quiet hospital reception area, she checked the map next to a station that offered free masks and hand sanitizer. The new hospital was a warren of hallways, and she was never great with maps. She used her GPS to navigate everywhere. Noting the direction she was supposed to go, she took the third hallway on the left. Staff in white coats and bright scrubs on cell phones passed her. She was beginning to wonder now if she should have taken the second hall. Then, ahead of her, she saw Grace walking slowly, her bag in the crook of her arm.

Ellen wondered why Lara hadn't caught up with her. Maybe Lara stopped at the ladies' room? She was about to call out to Grace when the older woman halted at a door, opened it, and went in.

The sign above read *Volunteers*.

Ellen braked hard. Why on earth was Grace going in there?

260 / Colleen French

Didn't she have to have her treatment before her volunteer duties?

Then the answer hit her.

Grace wasn't going directly to chemo because she wasn't taking chemo.

As she thought back to all of the signs, Ellen couldn't believe what an idiot she had been. It had been right in front of her face: Grace and her afternoon pink gin and tonic, her good appetite, the little sprouts of hair appearing on her bald head beneath her hats and scarves. She was doing better, at least for the time being, because she was no longer getting the drugs that made her sick.

Or killing her cancer.

Grace had gone to the hospital every day since Lara arrived, but not to get chemo. She went to distribute food and drink and barf bags, to use one of Alex's favorite phrases.

Ellen stood there, her arms at her sides, Lara's water bottle hanging from her fingers. All she could think of was Barrett and how devastated he would be when he found out.

What was Ellen's responsibility in this?

Did she tell him?

39

Ellen stood at the porch rail, looking out into the darkness as she sipped her glass of wine, a Cabernet. She heard the waves crashing, but she couldn't see them. Behind her, the house was bright with lights, and the sounds of voices and someone rinsing dishes in the sink drifted through the windows. She kept thinking she heard Pine laughing, that cackle that made her smile every time she'd heard it. She'd only known him a short time, but the ache in her chest was so heavy that it felt as if she had known him for years. Her whole life.

She and Lara had gone to Pine's memorial service in a local church he and Gwen had attended. The rest of The Porch had gone, too. There had been a reception afterward, but the group had decided ahead of time that they would be too tired to go. That, combined with the fact that they all needed to avoid crowds because their immune systems were compromised, sealed the deal. They would come back to the beach house for a little while, instead, they had decided.

Ellen had assumed it would just be the porch friends coming, but they had all brought someone with them, a spouse, a niece, a son in Grace's case. Alex's parents had even stopped by, though they'd made a quick retreat. Shorty and Brenda would take Alex home later. And then there were others from the hospital whom Ellen didn't know who had shown up: patients, two nurses, an oncologist, a receptionist, and two men from Maintenance.

The house was bursting at the seams with people who had loved Pine.

Ellen was glad she had ordered the tray of lunch meats and salads, and some bite-sized baked goods from Leeder's Bakery. She'd also loaded up on bottles of wine, some liquor, and some mixers. Which was a good thing, because everyone seemed to be imbibing tonight, even those who shouldn't have been. She was glad it was a Friday night because she imagined Lara would be in no shape to go to chemo in the morning.

"Not get the memo, luv?" Grace said, coming up behind Ellen. Ellen looked at her. "Sorry?"

The older woman leaned on the rail to look out over the dunes. "Did I not say that right?" She chuckled. "All these years in the States, and I still get the idioms wrong."

"That's the right phrase." She looked at Grace, thinking about what she'd discovered at the hospital Monday. It was all Ellen had thought about all week. A part of her was upset with Lara for not telling her, but if Grace had asked her to keep it a secret, Lara would never have betrayed that trust, not even for her sister by another mister. "Not my story to tell," that's what Lara always said in these situations. Ellen hadn't even told Lara she knew.

"What are we talking about, Grace? What memo?" Ellen asked.

Grace indicated Ellen's modest sleeveless black dress. "The proper funeral attire."

"Ah."

The Porch had all worn their brightest clothes to the service to honor Pine. And because he would have expected no less of them.

Ellen took another sip of wine.

She was a little tipsy.

She hadn't eaten all day. She hadn't even sampled the mini lemon meringue pies from the bakery that had been included at no cost by the owner because they had been Pine's favorite. Seeing the crowded memorial service, hearing so many people talk about Pine, she was astonished by how many lives he had touched in their little beach town.

"No one told me," Ellen said, checking the level of her glass. "I didn't know until Lara came down the stairs in that striped gypsy skirt and lime-green blouse of hers that we weren't supposed to wear black. I've always worn black to funerals. I bring this dress with me every summer, '*just in case.*'" Balancing her wineglass on the rail, she made air quotations around her last words. "Because you never know and who wants to be caught without funeral clothes in their possession. How ridiculous is that?" she asked, letting her hands fall to her sides.

Grace stared out into the darkness again. "Organizing our lives, planning, always being prepared. We all do it on some level. Some more than others. It's comforting. It gives we human beings a sense of control in a world that we have very little control over."

As if rejecting Ellen as she had the dress, the fabric suddenly felt itchy. Suffocating. She scratched under her armpit, fighting the ridiculous urge to step out of the dress. Standing there in her lace bra and matching bikini panties she'd bought recently seemed better than the dress. She hadn't intended to buy herself pretty underwear. She'd gone to get Lara a smaller size of denim shorts because her friend had lost so much weight that her bony hip bones couldn't hold up her favorite pair anymore. Ellen had seen the matching black bra and panties and bought them on impulse. And smiled to herself the rest of the day, thinking how much she liked them.

Grace rubbed the small of Ellen's back. "You bringing that dress did not cause Pine's heart failure, luv. It was the drugs he took for the cancer that probably weakened his heart."

"I know, but . . . suddenly so much of what I do, what I've always done, I feel like it's stifling me." She groaned as she pressed the heel of her hand to her forehead. Despite the cool breeze coming off the ocean, she was hot and sweaty. "Now I sound like Lara."

"You know she just wants what's best for you."

"I know." Ellen tipped her glass. She needed another. But how many had she had? She'd lost count. More than her glass and a half, for sure.

"I see the changes, you know," Grace went on. "In you."

Ellen was quiet. Conversations like this one made her uncomfortable. But she wanted to hear Grace's thoughts. What she thought was important to Ellen because she respected Grace. Liked her.

Likely loved her.

"You always drink white wine so you won't stain anything if you spill it, even though you prefer reds. You told me that the first week we met." Grace's voice seemed to float. "But tonight, you're drinking what you enjoy."

"A special occasion," Ellen heard herself say. She was thinking about Grace walking through the volunteers' door at the hospital. If Grace had stopped chemo, then she was going to die. The unfairness of it hurt. And made her angry. The injustice not just of Grace's illness, but everyone's. And Pine's death? He had been such a vibrant man and touched so many lives. Why did he have to die?

"Grace, I saw you. At the hospital on Monday." Ellen didn't even realize she had spoken until the words were out of her mouth.

Grace didn't say anything, though Ellen knew well that she had heard her.

"I ran into the hospital to take Lara her water bottle. I went down the wrong hall, and I saw you. You weren't going into the oncology department." She turned to look at Grace. "You stopped taking chemo, didn't you? You go to the hospital every day, but instead of getting the drugs that could . . . prolong your life, you put on one of those smocks, and you pass out cookies. Why would you stop chemo that could prolong your life?" she asked softly. Desperately.

"There are fates worse than death, Ellie." She spoke slowly as if she wanted to be sure Ellen absorbed every word.

For later. When she was gone.

There are fates worse than death.

Ellen fought the tears welling in her eyes.

"Which is why Lara is right," Grace continued. "You need to find your own happiness. You need to continue to make the changes you want to make. That I know you can find inside yourself. Because you're a good person, Ellen. You're smart and kind and giving—"

"When I'm not being an uptight— I don't know what."

Grace pursed her bright lips that were thick with red lipstick. "Grimalkin."

"*Grimalkin?*" Ellen laughed. It wasn't funny. None of it was. But she couldn't help herself.

Pine would have laughed.

For all she knew of the afterlife, he was laughing right now.

"Like the cat in Shakespeare's"—it took her a moment to grasp the name of the play—"*Macbeth?*" Ellen asked. "The cat that helped the three witches see his future?"

"One and the same. It's a word my Scottish grandmother used to use. It means 'bitch.'" Grace whispered the last word in her ear.

Ellen laughed, covering her face with her hands. She *did not* need any more wine. "I don't mean to be a bitch," she finally said when she found her voice again.

"I know, luv."

They both stared into the darkness again. The wind kicked up, and the breeze cooled Ellen's sweaty face. She could still hear the sounds of those in the house, their voices blending into one. There were tears for the loss of Pine. Laughter for who he had been. "Barrett doesn't know, does he? That you've stopped treatment."

Grace hesitated. "He suspects, I think, though we haven't discussed it. But I'm feeling good right now. Better than I have in months." She pressed her hand to the small of Ellen's back again as she turned to go. "Please don't mention it to him. It's my job, as his mum, to tell him when the time is right."

"Not my tale to tell," Ellen whispered.

40

Ellen stood at the rail for a while after Grace was gone. Then she decided she needed a walk to clear her head. She left the glass where it was and took the stairs. She was halfway down before she realized someone was sitting in the semi-darkness at the bottom.

"Hey."

She knew the voice before she reached him. Barrett.

She glanced up at the rail where she and Grace had been standing. How long had he been there? Had he heard his mother and her talking? She looked back at him. He'd worn khaki pants—the first time she'd ever seen him that he wasn't wearing shorts—and a turquoise polo shirt that had made his gray eyes seem grayer by the light coming from the porch above.

"Hey," she said, not sure if she should just pass him or stop. Maybe he was here because he wanted to be alone.

He stood. "Let's go for a walk."

She glanced over her shoulder at the brightly lit windows of the house. She saw people moving around inside. She heard their voices. She was the hostess. *Did she need to stay?*

"They'll be fine." Barrett kicked his loafers off in the sand.

She noticed he wasn't wearing any socks. Of course he wasn't. He was too cool for socks.

He was so far out of her league.

Wasn't he?

"Coming?" he asked.

She followed, leaving her black flats behind.

As they took the path over the dunes and crossed the soft sand, she tried to think of something to say. But what? She knew better than to bring up the weather.

They had reached the wet sand, and he headed south, away from town. She walked beside him. The cool air and the chilly water on her bare feet cleared her head.

"I heard you," he said.

His voice startled her.

"Talking to Mum."

Ellen stopped to look up at him, realizing what he was talking about. "I'm sorry," she whispered.

Barrett looked down at her. She wasn't wearing her watch, but it had to be after ten. The moon was rising, casting light across his face.

"Ellie— Can I call you that?" he asked.

"Sure."

"Ellie, don't look so serious." He slid his hands into his pockets. "I knew."

"You *knew*?"

He shrugged. They were almost beyond the beach houses and condos, now. "I live with her. I knew something was up within a week of her refusing further treatment." They started walking again. "All of sudden, she started eating like a horse and knocking back bottles of pink gin."

His tone bordered on being disrespectful. Wasn't it disrespectful to make fun of your dying mother? Yet she had seen Barrett and Grace together. She knew how much he loved her. How much she loved him. Their relationship wasn't the typical mother and son relationship.

But that wasn't a bad thing, was it?

"I suspected right away," he went on. "She was so damned happy all of a sudden. But then my suspicions were eventually confirmed. Wanna sit?"

"Sure."

They walked away from the water so they could sit in the dry sand. They were beyond the last house now, and the only light was the reflection of the moon.

"When I was a freshman in high school, I was having a hard time. You know, struggling through puberty, unhappy with the rules, not doing well in a new school. We moved all the time because of Dad's work. I went to eight different schools in thirteen years. Anyway, I started skipping. Not every day. But when I didn't think I had it in me to go. And one day, my mother dropped me off at school and I walked in the front door and out the back. I went downtown and bought a comic book and a soda. I had my whole day planned. I was going to the beach. I had my bathing suit and towel in my backpack. So, I was standing at the cash register paying when I looked up and saw my mother through the storefront window. She only hesitated for a second on the sidewalk, but long enough to make eye contact. Then she walked on." He sat down in the sand.

Ellen grasped the hem of her dress and sat beside him. They both dug their bare feet into the sand that was still warm from the hot day.

"I knew I was busted," Barrett continued. "I knew she was going to kill me. I spent the rest of the day quaking in my flip-flops. In my house, my father was the teddy bear, my mother was Count Dracula." He stretched his feet, wiggling his toes.

She could smell the scent of him on the ocean air. It wasn't cologne or aftershave lotion or even his deodorant. He just smelled . . . masculine. And the fragrance of him, of his skin, made her heart flutter.

"I knew she'd wait until dinner to throw the net over me. In front of my father. And I knew the punishment was going to be bad. No food or water for a month. A couple of weeks in Alcatraz."

Ellen smiled to herself. He sounded like a writer. "It's been closed for decades, you know."

"My mother would have convinced them to open it just for me. Anyway, I still remember what we had for dinner. Bangers and mash." He looked down at her. "Ever had it?"

She shook her head.

"A British thing. It's big, fat sausages cooked until they're about to burst with goodness. And mashed potatoes with this onion gravy that . . ." He pointed at her. "You know what? I'm going to make it for you. There's no way to describe it adequately." He returned his gaze to the outgoing tide and the waves crashing on the beach. "Anyway. I walked into that dining room of hers with all the doilies and fancy china, and I knew I was dead meat." He paused, creating just the right dramatic effect. "And then . . . we had dinner. We talked about the wasp nest on the corner of the house, Dad's . . . I don't know. Hemorrhoids. Mum asked me to take the garbage out after dinner. And that was it." He opened his arms wide. "She never said a word about me skipping. And she hasn't. Not to this day. But I knew she knew. And she knew that I knew."

"Did you start going to school every day after that?" Ellen asked.

He laughed, throwing his head back. "Of course not."

They were quiet for a second and then he went on. "Ellie, the point is, sometimes you have to let the people you love make their own decisions. Even if you don't agree with them. Mum's made a decision she's good with. She's not ready to talk about it with me. Who knows, maybe we'll never talk about it."

"She doesn't have long, does she?"

"Probably not. She's already got mets to her liver, and I don't know where else. Next will be her brain."

"Oh, Barrett," she whispered.

She was gazing up at him, trying to wrap her head around what he had told her, when he jumped to his feet.

"Want to go swimming?" he asked.

She glanced at the water, then back at him. "Um . . . I guess I could go back and get my swimsuit."

"*Swimsuit?*"

He pulled off his polo, baring his chest that, like him in general, was pretty hunky. When his thumb caught in the waistband of his jeans, she looked away. She could feel her face growing hot. Was he going skinny-dipping? She heard his shorts fall to the sand and waited for his underwear to drop. But he walked away, down toward the water.

So maybe he was kidding about the skinny-dipping. Perhaps he was wearing his— She looked up just in time to see his bare, white butt in the moonlight. And she didn't know what came over her, but she giggled. Apparently, Barrett Faulkner did not wear underwear.

He reached the water's edge, and, in the shadows, she couldn't see him naked anymore. "Come on, Ellie! You're not going to be a chicken, are you?" He began to cluck.

She stood, trying to decide what to do. She knew she shouldn't go skinny-dipping with Grace's son. With a man eight years and a generation younger than her.

But she *wanted* to.

"You know you want to!" he called. "You went to a funeral today. A friend's funeral!" he called to her. "If Pine was here, what would he tell you to do?"

Ellen reached back and touched the zipper of her dress. Taking a breath, she slid it down and dropped her dress in the sand.

"Thata girl!" Barrett turned away from her and ran through the surf, dove in, and disappeared into the dark water.

Ellen peeled off her new panties, unhooked her bra, dropped it onto her dress. And ran into the ocean, welcoming the cold water on her warm, naked skin.

41

The following morning, Ellen looked up from the stool at the counter as Lara walked into the kitchen. "Hey, sleepyhead," she said, closing her laptop. She'd gotten up to see the sunrise and made coffee. She wondered if she had been hoping, subconsciously, that Lenora would show up?

She had not.

And Lenora hadn't come to Pine's memorial service or to the house afterward, even though Lara said she had written the information down on a piece of paper for her to take to her granddaughter. Maybe Miranda hadn't been able to bring Lenora to the service. But maybe the elderly woman was ill. Ellen hoped not.

Instead of having coffee with Lenora, Ellen had cleaned up from the night before, and then she'd sat down and started typing in her journal. They were just random thoughts, observations about Pine. About the other friends on the porch. Their reactions to his death. Their thoughts on their own mortality. She'd also made notes about Grace and Barrett and their opinions on death, and life.

"Morning." Lara dropped down onto the stool next to Ellen.

"Hot tea?" Ellen asked. Lara had stopped drinking coffee a week into her treatment. It was too harsh on her stomach.

"Please. And an ice pick so I can give myself a lobotomy." Lara lowered her head to the counter and groaned. "I had too much vodka last night."

Ellen ran her hand across Lara's back and got up to put on the teakettle.

Lara watched her, her chin nestled between her arms on the counter. "You cleaned everything up already."

Ellen glanced around as she filled the kettle with tap water. The counters were covered with dishes drying on dish towels. There were three bags of trash and recycling sitting on the back porch waiting to be carried downstairs. "I've been up awhile."

"I could have helped," Lara said. "Once I got my ass out of bed at the crack of"—she glanced at the clock on the stove— "ten-ten."

"I didn't mind." Ellen opened the tea canister on the counter. "Earl Grey or Irish Breakfast?"

"Earl Grey."

Ellen dropped the tea bag into a buttercup mug and walked over to the side of the counter opposite Lara. She leaned down, resting her head on the heels of her hands, so she was eye level to Lara. Her mouth twitched in a smile. Suddenly she was bursting to tell Lara about the night before. "Guess what I did last night."

"What? Drank red wine? I heard. You wild thing, you." Lara was teasing, but it was in good fun, and Ellen heard, in her voice, her understanding of what a big step that was. "Grace was so proud of you!"

Ellen stood up, her hands on her hips. "I did that, too, but I *also* went skinny-dipping." She paused for dramatic effect. "*With Barrett.*"

Lara jumped off her stool with a squeal, throwing her arms in the air. It was the fastest Ellen had seen her move in weeks. "Get out of town! No, you did not!" She was grinning ear to ear.

Ellen grinned back, pleased she had pleased Lara. Not that she had done it for that reason. Lying in bed earlier, she had considered the reasons why she *had* done it. Ultimately, the only conclusion she'd been able to make was that she did it because she had wanted to.

Lara came around the end of the counter and wrapped her arms around Ellen. "Is he as hunky naked as he is with clothes on?"

Ellen giggled with her. Suddenly they were both middle schoolers tittering over a little butt crack they saw when a lifeguard dove into the water. "I can't believe you would ask me such a thing." She tried to look shocked. Then met Lara's gaze. "He is."

Lara grasped Ellen's arms, looking into her eyes. "Did you have sex with him? Please tell me it was hot as I think it would be."

Ellen pretended she was horrified, but she couldn't stop smiling. "Have sex with him? It was Pine's funeral!"

"So? I don't think Pine would have minded."

Just what Barrett had said about them skinny-dipping.

Ellen crossed her arms over her chest. "I did not have sex with Grace's son."

"Why in God not?" Lara rolled her eyes. "Wait, let me guess, he was too drunk? You were too drunk?" She sighed. "Okay, okay. Good call. You want the first time the two of you are together to be amazing. Everyone knows alcohol and sex don't mix well. But honestly, sweetie, you shouldn't have been swimming if you were drunk. That would be a lousy way to start my weekend, having the sand-cleaning machines pick your bodies up this morning."

The kettle began to whistle, and Ellen went to the stove to pour the water for tea. "I was not drunk. A little tipsy when we left the house, maybe, but we took a long walk. I was fine. I had all my faculties. And I don't know that he'd had anything but a beer."

Ellen thought about the conversation she and Barrett had had about his mother. About him knowing she was no longer taking treatment. But she didn't say anything. That fell into the category of "not my tale to tell," as well. "It just kind of happened."

"Did you at least make out?"

Ellen carried Lara's tea to her and set it down. "We did not. He was a complete gentleman. He didn't stare at my breasts. He didn't even act like we were naked. We just . . . *swam*. Talked. When we got out, he went first and put on his shorts. Then he"—she smiled to herself thinking of the moment—"he turned around so he wouldn't see me. And handed me my dress. And picked up my panties and bra when I almost forgot them." She bit down on her lower lip.

She felt so like a teenager right now.

And it wasn't altogether a bad feeling.

"He asked me for my number. And texted me later so I'd have his."

Lara narrowed her eyes. "Please tell me you're not holding out on any juicy details. You didn't even kiss?"

"No." *But I wanted to kiss him*, Ellen thought.

Lara reached over to dunk her tea bag. "It's a start. And a little naughty. Tell the truth, didn't it feel good? To be a little naughty?"

Ellen thought for a moment.

"Come on," Lara dared. "Admit it. At least to yourself if you can't admit it to me. It felt good to step outside all those invisible boundaries you've drawn around yourself. That box you've built. No one was harmed, nothing bad happened, except the two of you had a good time together."

Ellen stared at her bare feet for a moment and then looked up. "It did feel good."

"That's my sister by another mister." Lara grinned and

pulled the tea bag out of her cup. "I think we should do something today. Something fun. Like play putt-putt."

"You feel up to it?" Ellen asked.

Lara opened her arms. "I feel like celebrating. I'm all done with chemo, at least for now. And I'm done with that freakin' cold cap." She held up her finger. "You hear that? I didn't say it."

Ellen went to the sink for a glass of water. "I can't believe Amara is breaking you of the habit. I've been trying for almost forty years."

"It was costing me too much money."

"Good point."

Lara took a sip of tea. "You know what. I think I'm hungry."

"I can make you breakfast. Eggs? Pancakes? What do you feel like?"

Lara thought for a moment. "French fries."

Ellen raised her eyebrows. "French fries? Like hash browns?"

"Like delicious, greasy Thrasher's fries with plenty of vinegar."

Ellen laughed. She'd never had boardwalk fries for breakfast in all the years she'd been coming to the beach house. "You want to go to the boardwalk and have French fries for breakfast?"

"Yup. You in?"

Ellen shrugged. "I'm in, sister."

42

Later in the week, Lara took the car to the hospital for an appointment with her local oncologist. Ellen had offered to go with her, but Lara had insisted it wasn't necessary. After the appointment, she intended to go to the infusion department to see if there was anything she could do to help Grace and Alex, who had pretty much taken over the volunteer team there.

After Lara was gone, Ellen sat down at the counter to check her work email and grade some papers. She had considered working on the porch, but that had been an abysmal failure the previous day. Instead, she had spent most of the morning just sitting and staring at the ocean. And watching YouTube videos demonstrating how to curl her hair overnight without heat or styling products. And done the Sunday *New York Times* crossword puzzle.

Ellen opened her laptop. She planned to read her email, grade the latest assignment from the class she was teaching. Then she would make herself go up to the attic for a couple of hours. Which she hadn't worked on since Pine's death.

It was weird, but the closer she got to completing the task that she'd come to Albany Beach to accomplish, preparing the house to sell, the less enthusiastic she was. But not for any of the reasons she'd had when she began the job. When she arrived at the house, all she'd seen was the tedious work that needed to be done: cleaning out the attic, painting the porches, caulking the showers, replacing the broken ceiling light in the laundry room. And the bad memories. The day she and Lara pulled into the driveway six weeks ago, she'd been playing the tape in her head of Tim asking for a divorce.

A divorce that she was beginning to see was best for both of them. So often couples stayed together for the sake of the children. But Christopher was an adult now, an independent adult, who'd responded when she broke the news to him, "About time." She'd been crushed by his words at the time. Looking back, she knew he hadn't said it to hurt her feelings. He'd said it because he'd been a firsthand observer of his parents' marriage from the beginning. And he had seen the truth in it, maybe before Tim had. Certainly before she had.

Thinking about Tim reminded her of his texts. She supposed she should call him. But not today. She had other more pressing things to do.

Ellen glanced at the screen of her laptop. She had a stack of messages from students and one from her boss to respond to. The same parent who had complained about one of her baby's grades was now demanding that Ellen change his latest grade. And the parent was a big donor for the university. Ellen's boss was asking if she could make an exception this one time.

The email angered Ellen. And maybe hurt her a little.

She'd been a professor for more than twenty years. She was good at her job and she knew it. Her boss knew it. Why wasn't he supporting her? She had a whole list of reasons why he should. The student hadn't done the assignment correctly. He'd known her grading system. It wouldn't be fair to the other students not to grade his paper accordingly.

There were easier emails to respond to, mostly from students locked out of the online site they used. But she was restless. She kept looking out the windows, which were closed. July had hit full force, and now it wasn't only hot but humid as well. As humid as July in New Orleans. So the air conditioning was on in the whole house, probably would be for the remainder of her stay. She intended to put the house up for sale in late August and return to Raleigh the first week of September.

She watched the fish wind sock out on the porch whip in the wind. She'd miss the beach when she went back to her home in Raleigh. She'd miss the porch.

So why not enjoy it while she could?

She scooped up her computer and moved outside, making a pact with herself not to go on YouTube. She made it through two students' papers before she found herself gazing over the rail, breathing in the briny air, feeling the sun's heat on her face. The porch had become her absolute favorite place at the house. This place where Lara and her friends gathered. It was where she and Lenora had drunk coffee from the old percolator and watched the sunrise.

Lenora.

Where was she?

Had her wandering come to roost? Had she gotten lost? Been caught breaking into someone else's house? Had Miranda grounded her? Was Lenora sick?

Ellen sighed and opened up another student's paper.

Then she closed her laptop.

Considering her next move only for a second, she carried her laptop back into the house, grabbed her sunglasses, and went out the front door. She walked down the street, onto the next block, making a beeline for Lenora's granddaughter's house.

At the front door, she rang the doorbell.

No one answered.

She rang again. Still nothing.

As she went down the steps, concluding no one was home,

she caught a glimpse of a brown mixed-breed dog lying in the grass, around the side of the house. Was the dog outside alone? It didn't seem likely.

"Hello?" Ellen called as she approached the dog cautiously. She couldn't believe she was doing this. Lenora had stayed away. That was what Ellen had wanted. This was so unlike her. She usually minded her own business. She certainly never crept around people's houses.

The dog barked, but only halfheartedly, and rested its head in the grass.

"Lenora?"

A pair of bare feet stuck out from behind a flowering pink rhododendron bush. They were not Lenora's wrinkled, knobby feet.

Miranda leaned out from behind the bush. "Hey! Ellen." She stood. "Just doing a little weeding. Kids never do it the way I want them to. Day off," she explained. She wore jean shorts and a yellow bikini top.

"Hi, Miranda. I, um . . ." Ellen cleared her throat. "I was looking for . . . I was wondering how your grandmother was. Lenora didn't make our friend Pine's memorial service. I wanted to make sure she was okay."

Miranda wiped her sweaty brow with the back of her hand. From the backyard, obscured by trees and bushes, Ellen could hear the sounds of children playing. Lenora's great-grandchildren.

"She's fine. She's not here right now. She'll be sorry she missed you. She rode over to the farmer's market in Lewes with my husband to get a watermelon. I'm sorry I didn't contact you about the funeral. Granny took the paper with your friend's number on it and squirreled it away somewhere. And I didn't know which house was yours on Pintail. I asked Granny, but you know how she can be. She started telling me about a house she'd lived in when she was a teenager. Out in the country."

Miranda wiped some grass off her knee. "Honestly, I don't think her dementia is as bad as it appears to be sometimes. She's what she would refer to as *ornery*. I think she manipulates fact and fiction to suit her needs. She didn't want to tell me where you lived, so she didn't. Her PCP says it's not uncommon—the manipulation. It's a way of self-preservation, she says. Self-care for some seniors."

"Was Lenora sick over the weekend? Is that why she didn't come?"

Miranda leaned her head one way and then the other. Her red hair was piled up in a knot on top of her head the way Lara wore hers.

"Not sick, just . . . Granny's been in a bit of a funk." Miranda exhaled. "Would you like to sit on the porch? It's hot out here." She gave a wave in the direction of the flower bed. "I'm over this weeding thing."

Ellen considered the invitation. She'd enjoy chatting with Miranda on her porch. But she had to get those papers graded and reply to her boss's email. "I'm sorry, but I can't. I work from home, and I need to get back to it. I just wanted to check on Lenora." She slid her phone out of her back pocket. "And maybe exchange contact info. Just in case your grandmother . . . shows up again or something?" she added.

"Great idea. I left my phone on the step. It kept falling out of my pocket." Miranda turned away, then back. "Oh, and I have what I suspect is the key to your house."

"My key?"

"I think so. Attached to a piece of red yarn? I found it rolled up in a handkerchief in my freezer."

"The freezer?" Ellen chuckled.

"Granny likes to hide things there." Miranda gave a wry smile. "Which means it's not such a good hiding place. Last week we found her favorite slippers in there."

Together, they headed around to the front of the house.

They reached the steps, and Miranda picked up her phone, then went into the house. A moment later, she was back, handing Ellen the key, hung on a piece of red yarn.

Ellen stared at it in her palm.

"It is yours?"

Ellen nodded. She wondered where Lenora had gotten it. Had she been the one to hang it on the piece of yarn? Was it the key her mother had stashed inside a seashell in a flower bed? It had to be. Yet it had been missing for years. "Thank you," she said, closing they key in her hand. Feeling guilty, though why she didn't know.

"Sorry about the key. Anyway," Miranda said. "Granny's been out of sorts. Your friend Pine's death hit her hard. I offered to take her to the funeral. I had met Pine at the hospital a couple of times. A delightful man.

"I thought it might be good for her to go. To be with you and her other friends, but she . . ." Miranda hesitated. "She can't do funerals. Never been able to. When my granddad died, her husband, back when I was in college, she didn't have a service. She refused. My great-aunt, Doris—she was Granny's sister, gone now—once told me that after their stepbrother's funeral, Granny never went to another one again."

They both stepped into the shade of the porch roof.

"He was young, nineteen or twenty. And it was a military funeral. Died in France." She shrugged. "Apparently, Granny had some sort of breakdown afterward. I don't know what happened. But I think it was bad. Her parents sold their house where they were living and moved. I guess Granny couldn't stand to be in the house where they'd lived anymore." She shook her head. "Sorry, I can't remember the details. And there's no one to ask. They're all gone."

Miranda's words floated in Ellen's brain.

Brother.

Military funeral.

France.

Ellen frowned. "How old was your grandmother when her brother died?"

Miranda exhaled loudly. "Let's see. It was during World War Two. In the forties, so I guess she was ten, eleven, maybe? She talks a lot, as you know." She smiled. "But that's one subject she won't talk about—her brother dying. She mentions his name occasionally, but only in passing. When the kids or I ask questions, she changes the subject as if she never heard us."

"Was his name Joe?"

Miranda looked surprised. "It was."

"So he was real," Ellen murmured.

43

Later in the day, Ellen sat at the counter grading papers. Lara and her friends were on the porch, moping. It was just Lara, Amara, Grace, and Shorty. Alex hadn't shown up at the hospital to volunteer, but no one had been concerned. Sometimes her parents had other plans for her. Lara said they were expecting her anytime now.

After the interesting visit with Miranda, Ellen had returned home and made limeade and shortbread in case anyone was hungry in the afternoon. The sounds of the porch friends now drifted through the window Ellen had opened a bit . . . so she could feel a part of them while she worked. She'd hoped they'd decide to come in out of the heat and sit in the living room. Maybe they'd watch an episode of *RuPaul's Drag Race*. Ellen kept wondering who would be eliminated next. Was it going to be Milan or Jiggly? If they didn't watch the next episode as a group, she wondered if Lara would want to watch it together that night in bed.

Ellen's phone on the counter vibrated. A text.

She made a note on a student's paper, indicating a word needed to be capitalized. How did high school graduates not

know proper nouns needed to be capitalized? She knew the answer: they didn't know what proper nouns were.

She pulled off her reading glasses, rubbing her temple, and
picked up her phone. She was expecting to hear from the boy
who mowed her lawn back in Raleigh.

Was hoping to hear from u after the other night.

She stared at the phone for a second. Had her lawn boy
texted her instead of one of his girlfriends? But it wasn't from
the lawn boy. He was in her contacts.

Who is this? she texted back.

How many guys did you go skinny-dipping with this week????

She groaned, feeling the heat rise in her cheeks. She still
couldn't believe she'd done such a thing. Swimming in her underwear with Lara had been daring, but Friday night had been
madness. Temporary madness. All weekend, she told herself
it had been the wine, all the emotion over Pine's death, maybe
even her talk with Grace about living life. Ellen had decided to
set the whole event aside and pretend it never happened.

But he was hoping to hear from her?

Really? She couldn't resist a little smile. But what did she say
to him? She set down the phone.

Picked it up.

Set it down.

She really was in middle school again.

Was that a bad thing?

She grabbed her cell to respond, but she didn't know what
to say.

Bubbles appeared on her screen. He was texting again.

How about another swim?

She pressed her lips together, smiling.

He was flirting with her!

Even with her profound lack of flirting knowledge, she
knew it.

Right now?

His response was immediate:

Nite swims r more fun. Agree?

She chewed on her lower lip.

Grading papers, she responded.

My students don't know that the names of countries are capped

Oh dear

Again, the bubbles.

So no moonlight swim tonight?

U asking me on a date?

She stared at what she had just written. Backspaced.

C u tomorrow at the meeting?

It had been changed to Thursdays to accommodate a couple of regulars.

Only if you'll have lunch with me after

2 or 3 is late for lunch

His next rapid-fire text was an emoji of a mug of beer, followed by a question mark. She thought for a moment, then found an emoji of a glass of wine, held her breath, and sent it before she backspaced again.

He sent an emoji of what looked like the symbol for her Google calendar app. It took her a minute to figure out what he meant. And then she got it.

A date.

It was a date. A second date, if she counted the coffee she'd had with him.

The door from the porch opened startling Ellen and she set her phone down and stared at her computer screen.

It was Amara. Yellow scarf over her bald head . . . because it was Wednesday.

"Could you help me, dear?"

"Sure." Ellen looked up. The whites of Amara's eyes seemed very yellow today. Had they been that yellow before? She knew that jaundice was a consequence of pancreatic cancer, but Amara had seemed to be holding her own. That was what she'd said.

"I've got this new phone and Alex isn't here, Lara's on the phone flirting with some man, and . . ." Amara exhaled impatiently. "I gave someone at the hospital my number and he texted me, but I don't know how to"—she waved her hand over the phone—"add him to— Oh, I don't even know the word. I want to be able to text him later."

"You want to add him to your contacts. I'm no Alex, but I can show you."

"I'm not up for a lesson today." Amara held out her new iPhone. "Could you please just do it for me?"

Ellen laughed. "Sure." It only took her a second to add *Leon Parks* to her contact list. She handed it back.

"Thank you." Amara slipped her the phone into the pocket of her shorts but continued to stand there.

Ellen looked up. Amara was wearing a bindi today, a red dot on her forehead, but it was smudged. Amara had been a good friend to Lara since they came to Albany Beach. She wondered how much longer the older woman would live. She didn't want to think about anyone else on the porch dying; most of the time she didn't. But Pine's death reminded her that if Pine, whose prognosis had been good, had died, any member of the support group could die. At any moment.

"Still working?" Amara asked.

"Answering students' emails. Grading papers. And I need to respond to an email from my boss. I've got a bit of a situation, and I never handle this sort of thing well. I'm not sure if I just give in, or . . . don't."

Ellen heard a beep from Amara's pocket.

"Maybe that's Leon." Amara pulled out her phone. "No: Alex. She sent a group text." She squinted, read the text, and sighed. "Alex isn't coming today. The text says she has 'a thing.'" She looked up. "What does that mean?"

"It means she has something to do or somewhere to go. Teenage speak," Ellen explained.

"That's too bad. We were all looking forward to seeing her. She always brightens our day." Amara returned her phone to her pocket. "Want to tell me about your problem with your boss?"

Ellen hesitated. "I don't want to bother you."

"You don't want to bother me because I'm dying?" Amara sat down on the stool beside her and gazed into her eyes. "You know, Ellie, it's easy to forget that when people are dying, they're still living." She let that thought settle on Ellen and then went on. "I like hearing about what's going on in other people's lives. Come on, humor me." She raised the kohl-black eyebrows she had carefully drawn on. Which, like her bindi, were smudged. "No one out there feels much like talking today." She tilted her head in the direction of the porch. "I'm bored."

Ellen took a deep breath. And then told Amara the story about the student whose parent was an alumnus and heavy donor to the university where she worked and was demanding that her son's grade be changed. Amara was a good listener. She asked questions. She patiently let Ellen tell her far more details than were necessary.

And when Ellen was done, Amara shrugged. "What do you want to do?"

"Well, usually, I would say no. I'm not changing his grade. I don't do that."

Amara shrugged. "Why didn't you tell your boss that? Why are you hesitating?"

"I don't know," Ellen answered honestly. "Because that would have been my response six weeks ago."

"Okay." Amara waited for her to go on.

Ellen had been thinking about what Lara had said about the box she had built around herself. "I'm wondering if this is something to dig in about?" she asked herself as much as Amara. "I mean . . . How important is this grade? This student is taking this class to learn something. If he doesn't want to learn, or can't or whatever, is that my responsibility? And if this parent stops donating, other students will suffer. Students who want to *learn*. And my boss asked me to do him this favor. He never asks me for favors."

Amara squeezed Ellen's hand with her smaller brown, wrinkled one. "Your gut tells you to change his grade." She shrugged. "So change it. And next time you're in a situation like this, look at it the way you just looked at this now and decide the right thing to do. Maybe next time you won't change it. That old adage about rules being made to break. Sometimes it's true." She patted the counter. "I best get back and let everyone know Alex won't be coming today."

Ellen watched Amara get up slowly as if her bones were made of spun glass. "Thank you."

"You're welcome, dear." The door to the porch closed, and Ellen sat there for a moment. Amara was right.

No, *she* had been right. Her instinct had been right. Changing the student's grade, in this case, was the thing to do. She was a woman of free will, a woman with a brain, and she could make choices. Good choices, without the parameters of all the rules she had stored in her head.

Her phone on the counter vibrated and she picked it up. It was Barrett again.

Just 2 clarify. That's a no on the skinny-dipping?

She laughed aloud and texted back:

Not 2day

44

Ellen slid into her pool-blue chair on the back porch to join Lara and her friends and picked up the glass of wine she had poured for herself.

Her glass of *red* wine from a bottle of Malbec.

Barrett had insisted on buying the wine for her when they'd gone for a drink after the writers' meeting the previous day. They'd gone to a bar that looked like a cross between a bar and a library, which also sold liquor. There were shelves of wine and hard liquor to buy and books to borrow. There was also a massive walk-in cooler where patrons and customers, just passing by, could purchase beer brewed locally.

The bar was in an old building one street off the avenue. Similar to Barrett's bookstore, it had brick walls, old hardwood floors, and charm, all illuminated by pendant lights burning Edison bulbs. There was the standard polished wood bar with the standard personable bartenders: a cute blond woman and a tall, dark, and handsome guy with tattoos that were in good taste. But the cleverest feature of the bar was the half walls made of cardboard boxes of wine and beer, used to create separate seating areas. The Bibliotecha Bar was owned by Barrett's friend, who'd refused to take Barrett's credit card after Barrett and Ellen each had enjoyed two drinks and a plate of Old Bay crab nachos.

Barrett had helped Adam gut the building used for storage and remodeled it over the winter. This was the first summer The Biblio had been open. Barrett had tried to convince Adam that the man wouldn't stay in business if he gave away free beer and wine, but he threatened to cut up Barrett's credit card if he tried to hand it to the server again. In retaliation, Barrett had bought more than a hundred dollars' worth of booze, including the bottle of Malbec for Ellen.

She adjusted her sunglasses and took another sip of wine. She was having her own little private celebration. She'd emailed her boss the previous day, agreeing to change the student's grade, and had received a reply of thanks and praise in return. She still wasn't sure it had been the right thing to do. But she was pleased that she had been able to make a decision based on what she thought was the thing to do, rather than simply following the rules. She used rules, she was beginning to realize, to make decisions for her. So she didn't have to make them herself and risk being wrong.

But that was part of being human, wasn't it? To be fallible.

Shorty cleared his throat, and Ellen looked up. Lara was reading one of her romance novels. Amara and Grace were doing something with their new phones, and Shorty was sitting in his chair, staring straight ahead, his hands folded on his lap. He wore a pair of classic Ray-Ban aviator sunglasses that looked nice on him.

A pall still hung over the porch.

Pine's sudden death had hit them all hard. As Lara had explained the night before, no matter how often they talked about their *expiration dates*, whether they were in six months or sixty years, the reality of it was still hard to manage. And they all missed him desperately.

Ellen did, too. More than she had expected. She'd only

known him a month, she reminded herself. But how many times had he been in her house? How many times had she heard his laughter? Thinking about it made her smile. She couldn't stop envisioning the photos of him taken in Vietnam. How had he survived crawling through Vietcong tunnels, then died of heart failure? It seemed unfair.

Who said life was gonna be fair?

Had Pine said that to her? Or was she just imagining his voice in her head?

"What are you thinking about, Ellen?" Shorty asked, startling her. They'd never really talked before beyond pleasantries and drink orders.

But his question wasn't unwelcome. This was something she was learning to do. Answer truthfully when someone asked her a question about how she was feeling or what was going on in her mind. "About Pine. About how sad it is that he's gone."

Shorty stretched out his long legs, and she imagined what an imposing figure he must have been before he fell sick. She could envision him covered in soot at the site of the World Trade Center collapse, fighting to save people.

Shorty smiled at her, a lazy, slow-to-appear smile. "I don't think he wants us to be sad."

She considered that for a moment. "I think you're right. But easier said than done."

He leaned forward, resting his hands on his knees. "When I go, I don't want my wife or my children or grandchildren to be sad. I've lived a good life. Done what I wanted to do. There's no need for anyone to be sad."

Ellen studied him. The first time she met him, the day they'd painted the Adirondack chairs, she'd guessed he was in his sixties. She learned later that his cancer had aged him, that he was only fifty-two.

And wouldn't live to see fifty-three candles on his next birthday cake.

But she didn't know much else about him. "You were a 9/11 first responder. Is your cancer related to the World Trade Center bombing?" she asked.

"It is. Mesothelioma, that's what I've got. Affects the membranes of certain internal organs. In my case, my lungs. I was doing the chemo because Brenda wanted me to, but—" He shrugged. "The cancer is too far advanced. Doesn't matter what I do, I'm on my way out."

"Caused by exposure to asbestos, right?" she asked.

He smiled, and Ellen saw beneath his sagging skin to the handsome man he must have once been. How masculine by contemporary standards. A man's man, her mother would have called him. "It is. Happened to a lot of us who were first responders."

"Wow," Ellen murmured. "I remember reading about how slow our country was to acknowledge and take responsibility for the illnesses and deaths that came out of the rescue and recovery operation."

"And people are still being diagnosed with cancer for the first time after all these years," Shorty told her.

She nodded, hesitated, and then spoke what was on her mind because she wanted to learn to talk about her feelings *and* others'. "Are you angry, Shorty?"

He pulled his head back as if surprised by her question. "Why would I be angry?"

"Because your country ignored your suffering. Ignored your sacrifice. It's been such a fight over the years to get legislation to help men and women like you."

He thought before he spoke. "Nah, I'm not angry. I was doing what I wanted to do." He shrugged his big, thin shoulders. "I *loved* being a paramedic. When I went in there, to Ground Zero, I knew what kind of chances I was taking. I think a lot of us did. We knew it was dangerous, even when we were told it wasn't. But *someone* had to go."

She stared at him. "How can you say that so easily? You're going to die because you were there." She whispered her last words.

Six months ago, she would never in her wildest dreams have said such a thing to a dying man. She would have skirted the issue or spoken one of the often-used platitudes healthy people said to those who are dying. Phrases like "But you never know! You might live years longer" or maybe something about God. Always with phony positivity.

But going through this again with Lara, and now with the others on the porch, Ellen was learning that sometimes she just needed to acknowledge their truth. She honestly wanted to know what Shorty thought about his own sacrifice. Because that was what it was. He'd sacrificed his life for the lives of those he had saved, for the families of those whose bodies he had recovered.

He wheezed, then coughed. (Lara had said his wife had told her he was on oxygen at night, but he refused to use it during the day.) He was wearing a yellow T-shirt advertising the annual marlin-fishing contest in Ocean City, Maryland. She wondered if he had been a fisherman before cancer had wreaked havoc on his body.

"And you're not angry?" she repeated. "Even knowing we, as a country, weren't there for you?"

He shrugged. "I'm not. I'd do it again. Ride that rig right in the belly of the beast." He took a breath. "The way I see it, we're defined not by other people or other people's choices, but our own. When I tell you I loved being a paramedic, I mean I *loved* it. Even after the towers fell, I loved it. To my family's detriment. I worked fourteen hours a day, did extra shifts, never took my vacation days, missed birthdays and anniversaries." He shook his head. "You know, Ellie, you can be upset with other people's behavior and still be happy with your own. Does that make sense?"

Ellen pressed her lips together and tried to wrap her head around what he was saying.

"I'm not angry, and I'm not even sad." He opened his arms wide, grinning. "I'm the happiest dying man in town. Well, Pine was, but then I took the title." He looked down at some sand on the floorboards, then back up at her again. "Can I give you a little advice?"

She read the question as rhetorical and slid forward in her chair to listen.

"Look, I know your husband left you. That you didn't want a divorce, but that's on him. You loved him. Do you know how many people in the world never find love? Ever? It just didn't last as long as you hoped. That's all. My advice is to move on." He sat back in his chair. "Be yourself and be happy with the choices you make. Make choices you know you can be happy with. And the hell with what other people do."

"The hell with what?" Alex came up the steps from her perch where she'd been sitting and talking on the phone. She wore a white tennis dress with a daisy chain of silk flowers around her waist and a blond bob wig.

Ellen did a double take. The teenager was wearing heavy foundation, but even with the makeup, she could see a bruise on her cheekbone. "Alex, what happened?"

45

Alex covered her cheek with her hand to hide it.

"Is that a bruise?" Ellen asked, going into mom mode. She got out of her chair to have a closer look. "It looks like a bruise."

"Did someone hit you?" Lara set down her book.

Amara and Grace had stopped whatever they were doing. Everyone was looking at Alex.

"Nobody hit me," Alex snapped. "I fell."

"What were you doing that you fell on your *face*?" Grace asked.

Alex whipped around to Grace. "That's none of your damned business. If I had wanted to tell you what happened, I would have!" Her voice was so sharp that everyone went silent and stared at her.

Ellen went to the door. "Alex, could you join me in the kitchen for a moment?"

Alex pushed her sunglasses up on her head and looked at her in confusion. "Um, sure?"

Ellen walked into the house and held the door open for Alex, then closed it behind her. "You can't talk to your friends that way," she said. "To my friends." She hesitated. "You can't speak to people that way, Alex. You need to apologize."

Alex stared at Ellen for a moment, then lunged forward and threw her arms around her, hugging her tightly.

Ellen returned her embrace in confusion. She'd reprimanded Alex and she was hugging her?

"That's the nicest thing anyone has said to me in a long time," the teenager said, sounding as if she were about to cry.

"What is?" Holding Alex in her arms, she leaned back to study her. The teen's eyeliner was in black streaks under her eyes, and one of her false eyelashes had curled up on one end. She smelled of makeup and something fruity. Some kind of candy.

Alex held Ellen's gaze. "No one ever tells me I can't do something. I try and try to get my parents to holler at me. I say the *f* word, I steal money from their wallets, I say mean things to them, and they don't say anything."

With one hand, Ellen smoothed Alex's bangs back out of her eyes in a caress. "Why would you do that, sweetie?"

"To get them to react. To show me some kind of emotion. *Any* emotion." She sniffed. "My parents haven't raised their voices to me in more than a year. I haven't seen my mother cry in two years. When I was first diagnosed, she cried all the time."

Ellen didn't know what to say, so she said nothing.

"It's like . . ." Alex thought for a moment. "It's like I'm already dead." She bit down on her lower lip, tears running down her cheeks. "Or I never existed at all."

"Oh, Alex." Ellen drew the teenager closer and held her tightly. Alex lowered her head to Ellen's shoulder and Ellen gently rocked her. "I'm so, so sorry."

"I'm still here," Alex whispered. "Don't they understand?" She took a shuddering breath. "*I'm still here.*"

Alex cried softly against her shoulder, her whole body shaking. Ellen didn't say anything; she just held her. Ellen couldn't imagine what it was like to be a teenager who was dying. She *could* imagine how hard it had to be to have a child who was dying and there was nothing anyone could do to stop it. But she said nothing because right now she knew this needed to be about Alex and not her parents.

Slowly Alex quieted. Her body relaxed. Eventually, she lifted her head. "I had a seizure. At home, and I fell in the foyer and hit my mother's Stickley table on the way down. That's how I got this." She touched the dark bruise on her cheekbone that was more obvious with the makeup she had cried away, smearing it across Ellen's T-shirt.

"Oh, Alex," Ellen breathed.

"I had to stay the night at the hospital. Had a scan. The usual bullshit."

Ellen didn't reprimand her for the cursing. She felt like cursing herself. Instead, she grabbed a clean cloth napkin from a basket on the counter and offered it to the teenager.

Alex patted at her eyes. "You shouldn't rub, you know." She sniffed. "It's bad for your skin. You know, no one wants to say it, but my expiration date is closing in on me. Especially now that I'm not taking chemo anymore. Of course, last night, everyone, the nurses, the oncologist, my parents, the maintenance lady who emptied my trash can, tried to talk me into trying a different type of chemo. *To give me more time.* My parents threatened to make me. You know, because I'm underage and all and can't legally make decisions for myself. But I didn't buckle under the pressure. I hinted that if they tried to make me take chemo again, I would kill myself in a way that makes a big splash. It would be bad for their law practice."

"Alex, that's a terrible thing to do. You weren't serious, were you?"

"About killing myself?" She made a face. "Of course not. You know me better than that. But my parents don't." She fiddled with the wonky faux eyelashes.

Ellen ran her hand through her hair, trying to process what Alex was telling her. "Have you had seizures before?"

"Once, but it was months ago. It's how the tumor progresses. I had a little bleed this time, but eventually—" She dragged the back of her thumb across her throat and rolled her eyes toward the back of her head.

"That's not funny," Ellen chastised.

Alex laughed. "Sure it is. Anyway, eventually, the bleeds will get worse. I'll end up not being able to talk, walk, or breathe. And then off I'll go." She shrugged. "On to my next adventure."

Ellen felt like dropping to the floor and curling into a fetal position, then bawling her eyes out. Instead, she smiled back. "You might be the bravest woman I've ever known, Miss Divine." It was her drag name. Ellen had figured that out after watching *RuPaul's Drag Race*.

"More practical than brave, I think."

For a moment they stood there and looked at each other. And Ellen felt her heart swell for the girl in front of her who would never become a woman. She thought about how fortunate she was to have met Alex.

"Well," Alex said finally. "I guess I need to apologize and tell everyone what's what." She walked toward the door, the napkin bunched in her hand.

Ellen thought about handing several more to her. Those on the porch might need them when Alex told them about the seizure.

"You coming?" Alex asked.

Ellen forced a smile. "I'll be out in a minute."

Alex went onto the porch and Ellen went into the powder room off the kitchen. She locked the door and sat down on the closed toilet seat.

And had herself a good cry.

As she was blowing her nose on a piece of toilet paper a few minutes later, her phone vibrated in her jean shorts pocket. She slid it out to look at the screen.

It was an alert from the dating app Lara had signed her up for. She opened it and found that she had a message. She'd looked at it quite a few times since her subscription had started. She'd even had a couple of conversations via the app's messaging feature. So far, no one had been interesting enough to tempt her to go out on a date.

She opened the message. It was from Ron R.

I'm an adjunct professor at the University of Delaware. I teach freshman E110 and a couple of literature classes. It looks like we have some things in common: divorced after twenty years, one child. Still trying to figure out how to make a pot of soup for one. I live in Rehoboth Beach, not far from you. Want to get together for a cup of coffee sometime? Discuss Shakespeare or direct vs. indirect objects?

She smiled. And she seriously considered messaging him back. Alex's breakdown, her own, made her want to connect with someone. Instead of going to bed and crawling under the covers, which might have been her response to Alex's news, had it come a few weeks ago.

But Ellen wasn't sure she was ready to meet someone new right now, to put herself out there, as Lara called it. At least not today. And then there was the issue of Barrett. Was there an *issue* with Barrett?

She'd respond to Ron R. later, she decided.

Then, after only a moment of hesitation, she texted Barrett: A walk on the beach after u close the store 2nite?

He replied immediately:

Telepathic powers? Was just thinking I could use a walk. It was a shit show here today.

She used both thumbs to text the way Alex did, instead of her usual hunting and pecking. Come by my place?

Oh, he responded.

Oh? Her chest tightened in panic. Should she not have asked him? Had she just ruined any chance she had with him? Not that she thought she had a chance, but . . .

Bubbles appeared on the screen.

She waited, holding her breath.

At last his dialogue bubble popped up:

Now I understand. You meant did I want to go for a walk with u

Ellen closed her eyes. She'd done it. She ruined everything. What did she say now? Did she delete him as a contact and move on?

Then another text appeared. It was a smiley face emoji, one where the smiley face was laughing so hard that it was crying. She frowned. Then laughed at herself. He was teasing her.

He was teasing!

Good one, she texted.

See u around 8:30?

Sounds good. I'll leave my swimsuit @ home

Smiling, she got up, wiped her nose again, and went out onto the porch. It was clear by the looks on everyone's faces that Alex had told them about her seizure. And they all clearly understood what it meant.

Alex, who was seated on the arm of Amara's chair, looked up at Ellen. "That went over well," she said sarcastically. "Thanks for the advice, coach."

A part of Ellen wanted to cry again. But how could she not laugh? At such a beautiful child, so smart and funny. Her prognosis was tragic, but what Alex had said kept going through her mind.

She was still alive now.

She was still here.

Ellen rested her hands on her hips. She didn't know how much longer the teen had where she could come and go as she pleased. But however long that was, they all had to make the best of it. They couldn't sit around and be sad about Pine when Alex's time left was ticking away.

And wasn't that true for every human? They all had an expiration date. The timelines were just different.

A crazy idea went through her head. Something Alex had

said that hot day when they'd all watched *RuPaul's Drag Race* together for the first time.

"I have an idea," Ellen announced. "Actually, it was Alex's idea." She looked to the teenager, then back at the others. "I think we should have a drag contest of our own."

Alex shot up off the arm of Amara's chair, pumping both skinny arms. "Yes!"

Lara looked at Alex and then at Ellen. "In honor of Pine."

"Good idea," Shorty chimed in.

Grace held up a finger. "The Pine Abbott Memorial Drag Contest. He would love it."

"He would," Amara agreed.

Alex began to pace, holding her hands to the sides of her head. "There's so much to do! First, we need to pick a date and a location. Then we have to decide who will be the contestants. Do we offer prizes? So many decisions!"

46

Ellen sat in her chair on the porch, beside Lara, making notes in her journal. As she typed, she listened to Lara, Grace, Amara, Alex, and Shorty discuss their drag contest scheduled for the middle of August, which was only three weeks away. As they talked, the newcomer to the group, Leon, put in his two cents. Ellen had added him to her journal.

> **Leon Parks**
> **Age: 65**
> **Diagnosis: Testicular cancer with mets to lymph nodes**
> **Prognosis: Decent (Leon's words)**

"We need to sell tickets," Shorty insisted. "If this is a fundraiser for the infusion department at the hospital, let's make some money."

"No, we agreed we would just take donations," Amara argued. "We don't have time to sell tickets, and tickets take money to be printed. It's a waste of money."

"She has a point." Lara reached for her vodka and soda.

304 / *Colleen French*

She didn't have one every day, but when she did, Ellen kept her mouth shut. She didn't agree with Lara's drinking, but she was letting her *grown-ass* friend make that choice.

"Okay, so donations. Next issue. I don't know if this porch is going to work." Alex paced the floorboards.

Today she had on shorty denim overalls, a tank top, and glittery ballet shoes. And no wig. She'd taken it off and stuffed it in her bag, declaring it was too hot today for a wig. She had a full half an inch of light brown hair on her head now, and Ellen thought it was adorable. She kept her mouth shut about Alex's natural hair, knowing if she made a fuss, if anyone made a fuss, Alex, like any other teenager, would be annoyed.

"How about the front porch?" Grace asked. "Could we do it there?"

Grace looked so tiny in her chair now that Ellen worried that if she got any smaller, she'd disappear. Those first weeks Ellen had known her, Grace had been enjoying a honeymoon of sorts with her illness. Off chemo, she'd been feeling and looking better. But the honeymoon was over and the lung cancer that had spread to other organs of her body had begun to take its toll.

"Our guests can sit on the lawn," Grace went on. "They could bring their own lawn chairs."

"My dad says we should get sponsors. You think we should do that?" Alex was talking again. "Ask people for money? He says his firm will kick in a thousand bucks. I know we haven't decided for sure what we're going to buy for the department, but that's a good start toward it. With serious money, we could buy those iPads for people who can't afford one. So they can read or watch movies."

"If you're going to accept donations of that size, you're going to need some kind of program," Leon said. He'd started joining his friends on the porch two or three times a week and had fit in easily. Everyone agreed he wasn't a substitute for

Pine. No one wanted that anyway. But he fit in well, and even though he was a sixty-five-year-old bricklayer, he'd been on board with the idea of a drag show fundraiser in Pine's honor. Not because he "agreed with the politics," he'd told them. But because it was important to them.

"People who put up money wanna see their names in lights," Leon continued. He was average height, thick at the waist, bald, and red-faced, with big, bushy eyebrows and a handlebar mustache. Which was beginning to thin out. He wore an old, stained ball cap that advertised Parks & Sons Masonry, the business he had sold recently.

"A waste of paper," Alex injected. "People will just throw them on the lawn and then we'll have to pick them up."

"An ad in the newspaper, then," Amara suggested. "Thanking all the sponsors. That's what we'll call anyone who contributes big bucks. Sponsors."

"I just don't think the porch is the right place to do this," Alex continued to fret. "We've got what? Eight contestants already? And they're all going to bring family and friends. And now George from chemo asked me today if he could participate."

"The guy in a wheelchair?" Leon asked. "How's he going to strut?"

Alex gave him a look. "We don't discriminate around here, Lee."

Leon threw up his meaty hands. "Fair enough."

Alex stopped to gaze over the rail of the porch. "Do you think we need to rent a place? Like the high school auditorium?"

"I don't think that's an option, sweetie," Lara answered. "The school district isn't going to allow men dressed up as women to use their stage."

"You're not a man," Grace told Lara. "Neither am I." It was the most enthusiasm they'd heard from her all day. "But we're going to be wearing big wigs. This isn't about being girls or boys. It's about looking pretty. Loving yourself." She looked to Alex. "Isn't that right?"

Alex gave her two thumbs-ups.

It had been decided that Grace would be the MC. When The Porch had come up with the idea right after Pine's funeral, it had seemed like a great idea. Now Ellen was worried Grace wasn't going to be up to it in three weeks. Lara had expressed the same concern, but they'd agreed not to say anything until Grace did. She was so excited about doing it that neither of them had the heart to suggest she shouldn't. Or couldn't.

"I get it." Lara sipped her drink. "But not everyone has such liberal views around here. I think we say the word 'drag' and that will be a big no from the school. What do you think, Ellie?"

Ellen looked up. "Unfortunately, I think Lara's right."

"Fine, fine." Alex lowered her head, pacing again. She reached the end of the porch, and her head popped up. "I know! How about if we do it on the beach?" She grinned. "How cool would that be?"

"I don't think I can walk in the sand in high heels," Shorty said.

"We could build a boardwalk." Leon again. "I got a ton of wood I bought for the deck I never built. It's sitting in my warehouse."

"I think you probably need a permit from the town to have a drag show on the beach," Amara suggested.

Ellen's phone vibrated, and she looked down at it on the table between her and Lara to see who was calling.

At the same time that Lara looked at it.

Lara stared at the vibrating phone. "*Tim's* calling you?"

Ellen grabbed the phone.

"Why is Tim calling?" Lara asked.

Ellen jumped up, making a beeline for the house. "Hello." She walked into the kitchen and closed the door behind her.

"Ellen."

"Tim." She pressed her hand to her forehead. Why had she answered it? She didn't want to talk to him. She didn't know why she'd answered. She guessed because she'd gotten flustered when Lara saw it was him who was calling. She hadn't told Lara about the texts or calls.

"I was afraid you weren't going to pick up," Tim said. "I've been texting you and calling you for weeks. Why haven't you returned my calls?"

Ellen went to the kitchen sink and leaned her back against it. "Because . . ." She exhaled. She was surprised that hearing his voice didn't upset her. It didn't make her sad. Or angry. It just felt . . . like something from the past that was no longer her present. She kept her tone neutral. "Tim, what do you want?"

"I . . ." He sounded unsure of himself now. "I . . . I just wanted to talk to you, Ellen. I miss you."

She heard the emotion in his voice. He *did* miss her.

She pursed her lips. "Does your girlfriend mind you calling your ex-wife?"

"We broke up. Back in June."

"But you were traveling together in June."

"She left me in Mexico City."

Ellen was quiet for a second as she sorted through her feelings. "I'm sorry to hear that," she said. And she meant it.

"Yeah. Thanks. But it wasn't going to work out anyway. Which is why . . . which is why I was calling."

Ellen waited.

"I was calling because . . . because as I texted you, said in my voice messages, I miss you, hon. I . . . I wonder if . . . if I made a mistake. A terrible mistake."

She hadn't listened to his messages. "You mean in divorcing me?" Ellen asked, wondering if she was dreaming this. Surely Tim hadn't just called to say he wished he hadn't ended their marriage.

"Yes."

"Tim." She sighed, trying to sort through her feelings. There were too many.

"I know, I know. I totally screwed up. And I am so sorry. Can . . . can I come to Albany Beach so we can talk? I could be there tomorrow."

Ellen studied her kitchen: the stove where Lenora had made her coffee, the old icebox, a buttercup coffee mug left on the counter. Seeing each object made her smile. And made her realize how much she loved the kitchen. Loved this house.

Was she sure she wanted to sell it?

She turned around to look out the window at the friends on the porch. Her friends. "This is not a good time, Tim."

"Are things not going well with Lara's treatment?"

She pressed her hand to her forehead. "I can't do this right now." The back door opened, and Lara walked in.

"Okay, how about if I call another day. Or you call me," he suggested, upbeat. "When it's a better time."

"We'll see. Take care of yourself, Tim." She hung up.

Lara walked into the kitchen. The radiation treatment made her tired, but she was no longer vomiting and had begun to put on weight. The color in her face was coming back. She looked good. She looked like a woman who had beat cancer again. Or at least given it a beating. A term she had learned from The Porch.

"Have you been talking to him?" Lara demanded.

"Nope. But he's been texting me. Calling and leaving messages. This is the first time I answered." She met her gaze. "Guess why he's calling."

"Why?"

Ellen tilted her head. "He's having second thoughts about the divorce. He wanted to come to see me."

Lara walked toward Ellen, her bare feet padding lightly on the hardwood floor. "You have *got* to be kidding me. What did you say?"

"I told him this wasn't a good time."

A smile of relief crossed Lara's face. "Good for you." She was quiet for a second. "You said he's been texting and calling for weeks. Why didn't you tell me, Ellie?"

"Because, sister by another mister, my ex-husband is none of your business." Ellen's eyes widened when she realized what she had said.

Lara got a funny look on her face and then burst into laughter. Then she swooped in for a big hug. "This is not the girl I came here with," she murmured in Ellen's ear as she squeezed her tightly. "I'm so proud of you."

47

Ellen sat cross-legged in her Adirondack chair, making notes in her journal. It was early evening, that magical time when the sun was low in the sky and the oppressive heat was sinking into the sand. Wind chimes Gwen had gifted The Porch in remembrance of Pine rang in the breeze. It wasn't the gentle tinkle of metal most chimes made. The sound was deep and melodic, almost like a gong, reminding Ellen of Pine's laughter.

Hearing footsteps on the stairs, she called, "Lose something?" Grace and Lara had left in Ellen's car in search of fake eyelashes for the drag show and new orange socks for Grace because . . . because she wanted them.

The footsteps grew closer, and Barrett appeared. "Not unless my mother counts." He walked onto the porch, dressed in what Ellen had come to think of as his uniform: shorts, a T-shirt, and flip-flops. His hair was slightly shaggy and even blonder than a few weeks ago, bleached by the sun. He glanced around. "Please tell me she didn't try to walk home again?"

Ellen cringed. "I guess she didn't text you? She said she was going to. She and Lara went shopping. Lara's going to drop her off at home afterward."

"I was hoping that the new phone would improve her communication skills." He looked at Ellen. "How was she today?"

Ellen tilted her head one way, then the other as she studied him. "Okay. She was annoyed she didn't feel well enough to volunteer at the hospital again today. Leon, Amara, and Alex had to give her a blow-by-blow recounting of what everyone said and did when they all got here."

He slid his hands into the pockets of his shorts. "So Alex was able to volunteer. That's good news."

Ellen took a sip from her wineglass. "Lara says Alex is getting headaches more often, but she hasn't had another seizure. I don't ask Alex. She's having such a good time organizing the show. Making the dresses. This is her dream come true."

"Mum's worried about her. She's afraid Alex won't make it until the show."

Ellen inhaled sharply. She tried not to think about Alex's prognosis, or Grace's, or anyone's on the porch. It made it too hard for her to live in the moment, in *their* moments, which were still full of laughter and telling tales and bringing show-and-tell items to share memories. "You think it could be so soon?"

"No way to know," Barrett answered.

Ellen gave that thought a push to the side. She'd contemplate it later. "Hey, you want a beer?" She hooked her thumb in the direction of the kitchen. "I think Lara has a couple in the fridge."

"How about a glass of wine?" He pointed to the bottle on the table beside her.

"I didn't know you drank wine." She started to get up. "I'll get you a glass."

"I'll get it myself. I know where they are." He opened the door and glanced over his shoulder at her. "You think I don't drink wine? Just how uncivilized do you think I am?"

She laughed and refilled her glass with Pinot Noir. When he returned with a wineglass hand-painted with seahorses, she watched him take a chair across from her. Lara's. Ellen passed him the bottle.

"Whatcha doing there?" With a nod, he indicated her laptop that she'd closed when he showed up.

She watched him pour the wine and debated whether or not she should tell him the truth. She hadn't said anything to anyone except Lara. She wasn't even sure why. Maybe because she was afraid that her premise for the book would dry up like every other. But she was trying not to let her fear get in her way anymore. "Working," she answered. "Writing."

He raised his brows. "Are you? Good for you." He pushed the cork back into the bottle and raised his glass. "Cheers."

She smiled and touched her glass to his. "*Yamas.*"

"You speak Greek?" He sat back and sipped his wine. "*Nice.*"

"I do not. However, my dad, the late, great Joseph R. Tolliver, could toast in multiple languages." She took another drink. "I can do it in Japanese as well." She lifted her glass again. "*Kanpai!*"

Barrett stared at her. "*Wait.* Are you saying you're the daughter of Joseph Tolliver, as in *Edmund's Folly* and *The Last of the Greats*?" he asked, naming two of her father's best-selling novels. "I thought your name was Ellen Edmundson. Ellen Edmundson pays for all of those books you buy in my store. Did you steal someone's credit card?"

She rolled her eyes at him. "I did not. I'm Ellen *Tolliver* Edmundson. I'm thinking about dropping the ex's name."

He sat back, seeming impressed. Which tickled her a little. And scared her. She'd been fighting it for weeks, but she liked him. *Really* liked him. He was all the things she wasn't.

And yet he seemed to like her.

"It would be a good name to put on a book cover of your own," he pointed out.

"You think so? I didn't know if that would be too . . . *presumptuous*. To use his name."

"It's your name, too, Ellie." He set his glass on the broad arm of the chair. "You have as much a right to it as he did."

"I worry about what the expectations would be. Would everyone expect another Joseph R. Tolliver tome?"

"If they did, that would be their problem."

They were both quiet for a moment. The shadows were lengthening on the porch. The wind had shifted, and there was the faint, earthy scent of the bay in the air—the smell of the mud flats, the reeds, and the brackish water.

"Why didn't you tell me that you were Joseph Tolliver's daughter?" He almost sounded hurt.

"Because I didn't want you to think . . ." She let her sentence trail off.

"You didn't want me to think *what*?"

This was one of the reasons she liked him. He never avoided hard questions. It also made her uncomfortable.

Was feeling uncomfortable always a bad thing, though?

"I didn't want you to think I thought that I was a writer."

He looked at her as if she were nuts. "But you *are* a writer. You've been published in *The Atlantic* and *The New Yorker.* Good stories, by the way. I liked the one with the carnie grand-mother with the tattoo masquerading as an upstanding pillar of the community."

She tried to hold back a grin. *He thought her writing was good!* "She wasn't *masquerading*. She *was* an upstanding mem-ber of the community by the time she was a grandmother." She reached for her glass. "And thank you," she added as an after-thought. "For the compliment. It means a lot to me, Barrett. How did you ever find them?"

"Where did I find them? The Internet." He stretched out his legs. "Wanna talk about what you're working on?"

She shook her head slowly. "Not yet."

"Your novel, right?"

She picked up her glass so she had something to do with her hands. "It is a novel. . . ." She hesitated, asking herself what *was* the book about. "A forty-something woman looking for a change meets a group of strangers and they become friends, and through the friendships, she transforms her life."

He hesitated, thinking. "Fiction or nonfiction?"

"Fiction." She tilted her head one way and then the other. "But based on some experiences."

Again, the hesitation. Ellen got the idea that he understood what she was saying. That the book would be loosely based on her own journey. She was thankful he didn't ask her directly.

"Simple. I like it." He flashed a grin. "Let me know when you do want to talk about it. I think you'll find me easy to bounce ideas off."

She pointed at him. "Thanks for the segue. I've been trying to figure out how to get out of this conversation. I need your opinion on this drag show. I don't know what your mom told you, but it's taken on a life of its own. I thought they were going to wrap a sheet around themselves and strut through my living room. Now it's a fundraiser with formal gowns and lace wigs, and they've got *sponsors*."

He laughed. "So I heard."

"You going to participate?" She raised a brow.

"Me?" He pointed at himself. "Dress in drag? No, ma'am. I have size fourteen hooves. Nobody sells heels that big around here."

She laughed. "So with all the interest in the town, the original idea of having the show on my front porch isn't going to work. I think too many people are coming, plus with the rails, it's not exactly a great stage. I did a little poking around and no one is willing to rent their facilities for this. It's too big of a controversy in a town that makes it or breaks it during the three months of summer."

"Really?" He grabbed the bottle, filled her glass, and then poured the remainder into his own. "In this decade?"

She shrugged. "I'm just telling you what I was told. Anyway, the porch crowd keeps going back to the idea of holding the show on the beach. Leon wants to build some kind of boardwalk over the sand to create a runway. They've thought of a way to provide solar-powered lighting. And Lara found someone to donate an entire sound system and a tech to run it that night. It's a whole thing. But they can't have a show of any kind on the beach, can they?"

"I think the city technically owns the beach, so no, not without a permit."

She ran her hand over her face. "That's what I was afraid of. This thing is supposed to happen in less than three weeks, they've got donations rolling in, and they don't know where they're going to have it."

He lifted his broad shoulders. Let them fall. "I bet I can get a permit to use the beach. Right out front here." He pointed in the direction of the ocean.

She looked at him over the rim of her glass. "You *can?*"

"I got a guy."

She laughed. "You got a guy?"

"He works in the city hall. Owes me a favor."

She leaned toward Barrett. "You really think you could get permission?"

"Yup, for that and whatever else you need. A bonfire, maybe?"

"I don't know about that. But would we be allowed to have a little party afterward?"

"I bet that can be arranged, too. I'd suggest sending the mayor a personal invitation. She likes that sort of thing. And she'll probably want to get in on the photo op when the check is presented to the hospital."

"Barrett, that's wonderful. Thank you so much."

"You're welcome." He finished his glass. "I better get home. Half the time, Mum can't remember what she's done with her house key anymore." He stood.

Ellen followed him to the steps. "Is . . . has the cancer reached her brain? She said it might happen."

He nodded, looking out over the porch rail toward the ocean. His voice was tight when he spoke. "I think so. How would I know, though? She refuses to have any more scans."

"Thank you, *Alex*," Ellen muttered.

He chuckled. "Nah, I think this decision was solely her own." He ran his fingers through his thick, slightly curly hair. "Anyway . . . we'll know soon enough. She'll lose her ability to talk or walk, and off she'll go."

The same thing Alex had said.

Ellen sighed and laid her hand on his chest. She didn't tell him how sorry she was because she knew he knew. They'd talked about his mother's eventual death several times in the last weeks.

Barrett put his arm around her, and she moved closer, intoxicated by the scent of his skin and warmth he radiated. His embrace felt so good as she rested her head against him that she wanted the moment to last forever.

She looked up at him. He looked down.

"What's going on here?" Ellen heard herself say.

"Here?" he asked, toying with a piece of hair that had fallen from her ponytail and brushed her forehead. "You mean between us?"

She felt as if she could barely breathe. She nodded. And that she could breathe deeply for the first time in a very long time.

"I don't know," he said. "Do we need a definition?"

She squinted. "Are we dating?"

"You want us to be dating?"

"You're asking me?" She laughed. "Barrett, I have no idea what I want."

He laughed with her. "I don't, either, these days. I don't necessarily mean about you; I just . . . My mother's going to die and I try not to focus on that, but it's all I can—"

He was unable to finish his sentence again, but he didn't need to. Ellen knew what he was thinking.

"I guess I'm trying to wrap my head around that right now,"

he continued. "And I feel like my brain is going to explode. I can't dissect what we've got here right now. What we could have. All I know is that I want to spend time with you."

"It's fine. You're right. We don't need a definition. How could we date, anyway? Lara's almost done with her radiation treatments. She plans to go home to Pennsylvania at the end of the month. I'll likely be back in Raleigh by Labor Day. With this house up for sale."

He was quiet. He just looked at her, his nose almost touching hers.

"Are you listening to anything I'm saying right now?" she asked.

He shook his head. "Nope. I'm just imagining what it would feel like to kiss you."

Ellen searched his gaze. Then she closed her eyes and kissed the first man, other than her husband, that she'd kissed in twenty-odd years.

48

Ellen gave the gallon-sized paint can a nudge with her bare foot and drew the brush across the top rail of the front porch. She'd been putting off painting the porches all summer. She didn't know why today was the day she'd chosen to do it. She'd woken up and just decided she wanted to paint.

Whether she sold the house or not.

She still *intended* to sell it. That's why she'd come to Albany Beach—to get the house ready to sell. She'd made an appointment for the Realtor to take photos the following week. But the idea that she didn't *have* to sell it right now kept working its way into her mind. Most of the time, she was able to tuck the thought back into an obscure place where she didn't have to look at it. But it was still there.

And she didn't *have* to leave Albany Beach.

She could work from here. All she needed to grade her students' papers was her laptop. And she could work on her book there.

And fall was the best time in Albany Beach. That was when the water was at its warmest and there were fewer tourists.

She dipped the paintbrush into the paint and brushed the

bright white onto the rail. She'd only wanted to paint the back porch, but she'd been so happy with how it looked that she'd moved to the front and was halfway done. She planned to finish painting and then start dinner. She'd picked up salmon and was going to make it the way Lara liked it, covered in slices of lemon, and cooked on the grill in an aluminum foil packet. She'd been counting down the weeks and now she was counting down the days until Lara would leave. Her sister by another mister had completed her radiation treatment and would follow up with her oncologist in Pennsylvania. Her Lara was going home, and Ellen wanted to treasure every minute they had left together.

Ellen's phone vibrated in her back pocket and she let it go to voice mail, determined to finish up the painting. Then it rang again immediately. *Butt dial?* she wondered uneasily. Then a third time—the *it's an emergency* signal.

She dropped the paintbrush, trying to get to her phone in the back pocket of the jean shorts. She glanced at the screen as she raised it to her ear to answer. Lara was calling. She, Grace, and Alex had gone with Shorty's wife to buy out all the fake eyelashes they could find in Albany Beach.

"Hello?" Ellen said.

"Ellie, it's Alex." She sounded scared.

Ellen's breath caught in her throat. *Something happened to Lara.* Otherwise why would Alex be calling from Lara's phone? "What's wrong, sweetie?" she asked, her voice shaky. "Is Lara okay?"

"I'm using her phone. I can't find mine. I think I might have left it at the store." She was talking so fast that Ellen could barely keep up. "It's Grace. She fell in the five-and-dime. We had to call an ambulance. I thought she was dead, Ellie. We're in the emergency department at the hospital."

"Did you get ahold of Barrett?" She dropped the lid onto the paint can.

"He's on his way now. Can you come?"

"I'll be right there."

49

Ellen stood in the emergency department waiting room, fighting to keep her emotions under control. The room was half-filled with strangers, some waiting for patients, others waiting to be patients themselves. But she barely noticed anyone or heard their voices or the cry of a baby being shushed by her father.

Grace was all right, except for a fractured arm, but Ellen knew this was the beginning of her decline. She could see it in Barrett's face as he stood in front of them.

They were all there. Alex had called Shorty, Amara, and Leon to join her, and Lara and Brenda had picked them up after dropping Alex at the hospital. They had been lucky enough to have Pine's wife, Gwen, working, and she had taken over Grace's case. Grace was having a cast put on her arm and then she'd be taken to a room for an overnight evaluation. She had refused any scans and only allowed the X-ray for her arm because it was obviously fractured. They'd each had the opportunity to go into the exam room and say hello, but then everyone, including Barrett, had been ushered into the waiting room.

Barrett would be notified once she had her cast and had been taken to her room.

"I think it's smart she not go home tonight," Shorty said, the concern obvious in his voice. His wife, Brenda, stood beside him, and he held her hand. "Even though I know she doesn't want to stay."

"But she can go home tomorrow, right?" Alex asked. She was wearing a pair of linen shorts, a cute lime-green tank top, and a blond wig pulled back in a ponytail. "I know she doesn't want to be here. We were talking about it yesterday. About whether or not we should do some kind of interview with Hospice now, while we 'still have our cookies.'" She pressed her lips together. "Her words, not mine."

Barrett massaged his temples with the thumbs and forefingers of his hands. "I promised her I'd take her home tomorrow morning. I'm going to pick up some things she needs and come back and stay the night with her."

In the bright LED lights of the waiting room, he looked like he had aged ten years since the last time Ellen saw him. Her first impulse was to touch him in some way—to hug him or hold his hand the way Brenda was holding Shorty's. But she and Barrett hadn't shown any physical displays of affection in front of the others, and she didn't know how he felt about it. She also didn't know if anyone knew they were sort of seeing each other. Though Lara had her suspicions that something more was going on between Ellen and Barrett than friendship.

The thing was, Ellen still didn't know what was going on between them.

Luckily, everyone on the porch had been so busy preparing for the drag show that no one had had time to talk about anything else when they were together. And Ellen and Barrett hadn't seen each other more than a couple of times alone. With them both working and writing, all their spare time was being spent helping The Porch get ready for their fundraiser.

"But Grace isn't going to be able to MC tomorrow night for the show, is she?" Alex asked in a small voice.

Lara put her arm around the teen and hugged her. "I don't think so, sweetie. Maybe she'll be able to come but . . ." She left the sentence unfinished.

"What are we going to do?" Alex asked the group, opening her arms. "We have a lot of people coming. We accepted all those donations. We can't back out."

"Maybe you could do it, dear," Amara suggested.

"Me?" The teen shook her head. "I'm terrible at public speaking. And I'm the wardrobe mistress. I have to help everyone with the gowns and their makeup and, and— No, I can't do it."

"Shorty?" Lara asked.

Shorty grimaced. "I'd get so nervous, I wouldn't be able to say a word. Plus, you saw me in those heels Gwen found at the secondhand store. I may have to go against RuPaul and wear flats to keep from falling on my face."

"And I'm too unsteady on my feet with or without shoes," Amara said. "My doctor says I should be using a walker."

"And I'm too fat and ugly," Leon put in. He had come to the hospital alone because he was alone. He was divorced, and his children weren't a part of his life. He'd told Ellen he lost them all because he'd been a workaholic for forty years. He'd never had time for them, and now they had no time for him. "Even in that pretty, sparkly dress Alex made for me."

Alex reached out and squeezed the retired mason's hand. "I think you look beautiful in it, Leon. Gold is your color."

He winked at her. "Thanks, kid."

"But what are we going to do?" Alex fretted, addressing the group again.

"Don't worry," Amara said. "We'll think of something."

"We can't cancel." Alex's voice was rising in pitch. She was on the verge of tears. "And we can't postpone. If I have another seizure . . ." She didn't finish her sentence. She didn't have to because everyone knew what she was thinking. Ellen was thinking the same. If they didn't do it this weekend, neither Grace nor Alex might be able to participate. They could be too ill. Or dead. That went for any of the friends on the porch.

Barrett was rubbing his temples again. "I'll do it," he said quietly.

Ellen turned to look at him in surprise. He was wearing old shorts and a dirty T-shirt. He'd been cleaning the kitchen and bathrooms at the bookstore when Alex called him. He didn't look like a man who would wear a gown, but if there was one thing she'd learned that summer it was to expect the unexpected from the people she had met.

"You'll be our MC?" Alex squealed and clapped her hands.

Barrett glanced at the large clock on the wall, then at his mother's friends. "I'll do it if no one else is willing to do it. This is too important to Mum to cancel, or whatever."

As she looked around, it occurred to Ellen how mismatched everyone on the porch was. In any other place and time, these people might never have met. She wouldn't have met them if Lara hadn't had a relapse. If Ellen hadn't impulsively offered to take care of her for the summer.

The idea that she could so easily have missed the whole summer and everything it had come to mean to her made her dizzy.

Alex threw her arms around Barrett and gave him a quick hug before spinning away. "Yes! That would be amazing." She looked to Lara and Ellen. "No offense, but it will be *way* better if our MC is a dude." She turned back to Barrett. "Grace's dress won't fit you, but I can have one made for you by lunchtime tomorrow."

"Grace should still be able to come, right?" Amara asked. "She'll want to wear her dress Alex made and the wig. She was so excited about having all that hair."

Despite the seriousness of Grace's situation, Ellen had to laugh. Alex's father had contributed Ellen didn't know how much money to buy wigs for all the contestants, as well as the

324 / *Colleen French*

fabric for Alex to make the dresses for everyone on the porch, including her, though Ellen and Lara had passed on the wigs. Alex promised to bring her teasing comb instead because she insisted everyone had to have big hair. Big.

"So it's decided." Shorty put his hands together. "And now we should all go home. We've got a big day tomorrow."

One by one, the porch friends said their good-byes and drifted out of the waiting room. Brenda offered rides to those who needed them. Alex didn't want to go, she didn't want to leave Grace, but Ellen reminded her that she needed to go home and get to work on Barrett's dress. Lara went to get Ellen's car, and soon Barrett and Ellen were standing alone together in the waiting room. There were a few others there, but Ellen was barely aware of them.

"Hey," she said softly to Barrett. "You okay?"

"I'm okay." His voice caught in his throat, and he took a deep breath before he went on. "I keep thinking we'll have more time together. I've been telling myself that since Mum's diagnosis. This seemed so far away, and now, the months, the days, are passing like seconds."

Ellen looked up him and moved closer, wrapping her arms around his neck and giving him a hug. He closed his arms around her waist.

"You're a good son," she said quietly.

He smiled. "She's been a good mum. Better than I deserve."

She rested her head on his chest, enjoying the feel of his arms around her and the comfort they gave. She looked up at him. "You sure about doing this MC thing tomorrow night?" She dared a little smile. "I kind of hope so. I'd love to see you in a tight gown."

He chuckled, smiling with her. "Mum already told me I'd have to do it for her. She's too unsteady on her feet. I was hoping someone else would volunteer."

Ellen traced his collarbone with her finger. It felt so strange to have a man other than Tim holding her in his arms. But it was a good kind of strange. "You're a good sport. This show is important to Alex. Not that it's not important to all of them, but this is Alex's baby. She told me it's going to be the shining moment of her life."

He laughed, but there was sadness in his voice. "That kid. Not even for my mother would I wear high heels. But for Alex, I'd do anything."

Ellen looked up at him, smiling even though she wanted to cry. "You're going to wear high heels?" she teased. "I can't wait!"

50

Tears welled in Ellen's eyes as she stood in the sand in her bare feet, looking out over the crowd. She'd had her doubts that The Porch would be able to pull off the fundraiser, especially after Grace's hospitalization, but she'd been wrong. The drag show benefit had been an overwhelming success. Full-time residents and visitors had come, toting their beach chairs and their wallets. Donations had been generous, and the mayor of Albany Beach had told her that the show would go down in the town's history as one of the best events ever held on the beach. She'd pressed Ellen to commit to a second annual Pine Abbott Memorial Drag Contest so the city could advertise it in their calendar for the following year, but Ellen wasn't up for making any further commitments tonight beyond getting herself a glass of wine.

A crowd of fifty or sixty still remained standing and sitting in groups around Leon's runway, talking and laughing. Under the solar-powered string lights that twinkled like stars, the attendees and participants shared snacks and beverages from the coolers they'd brought from home. And though the event had been in remembrance of Pine, the mood was light and joyful.

It had become a community party, the way Pine would have wanted it.

Ellen's gaze drifted over the crowd until she settled on a very tall woman with gorgeous long blond hair in a shimmering gown. The woman turned and caught Ellen looking at her and smiled. The beautiful woman was Barrett. Ellen still couldn't believe he had shown up in the gown Alex had stayed up all night making for him. He had acted as the show's MC without so much as a single falter. He'd even joined in when the participants had performed a closing lip-sync number to Aretha Franklin's "A Natural Woman" blasting from the sound system.

Barrett said something to the woman standing next to him, excused himself, and walked toward Ellen. Ellen saw now that Grace, in a wheelchair, was among the group, dressed in a long gown and the wig she had wanted so badly to wear, crowned with a sparkling cubic zirconia tiara. She looked good tonight. Happy.

Ellen watched Barrett sashay toward her along the make-shift boardwalk. As he walked, one hand on his hip, he swayed in an exaggerated motion.

She was laughing so hard by the time he reached her that she had to wipe away her tears. "I cannot believe you did this," she told him, grinning broadly.

"What? Wear a gown and a wig?" He patted the enormous Dolly Parton–style creation.

"And makeup, and those false eyelashes." She leaned closer, squinting. "Are those *rhinestones* on your lashes?"

"Too much?" He fluttered his eyelashes. "I worried it was too much. Leon was the one who said they made the outfit."

Ellen shook her head, still unable to contain her laughter. Her joy. Spending time with the men on her porch, Barrett included, had expanded her definition of masculinity. When she first met Barrett, he had seemed to be the epitome of the pretty blond beach boy, but he was much more.

She'd been wrong about him and she was ashamed that she had judged him wrongly.

How often did we misjudge people?

How many friendships in a lifetime did we miss out on because of narrow-mindedness?

Fear?

A man had to be truly secure in his identity, Ellen had learned, to do what Barrett and Leon and Shorty and the other men had done that night. Her father, who had formed her early notions of masculinity with his tweed and bourbon and chauvinistic attitudes, had not been much of a man at all. He had been insecure, narrow-minded, judgmental, and just . . . mean. She saw that now, and she realized that those early impressions had been another one of those boxes Lara had told her she'd built around herself. Trapped herself inside.

"I can't believe Alex made that gown in a few hours," she said, studying the silver lamé that looked like a shining waterfall on him "She's an amazing seamstress. It fits you perfectly."

Barrett cupped his fake breasts with both hands. "There was a big argument at the last minute about the size of my boobs. Leon wanted me to go full thirty-six triple Ds, but I thought the gown called for something a little more subtle." He turned sideways so that she could see his silhouette. "What do you think?"

She laughed. "I think you went with the right size. And your makeup is perfect. And your hair"—she shook her head, still shocked by the fact that Alex was such a great seamstress and makeup artist—"it's gorgeous."

"So's yours," he said softly. He touched a pin curl that was damp from the heat and humidity of the summer evening. "And that's all yours. Nothing fake here."

Ellen patted the hairdo Alex had created for her that was a cross between a beehive and sixties-style *I Dream of Jeannie* ponytail. "Thank you."

"You look beautiful," he said, meeting her gaze. He took a step closer to her. "How do you feel about kissing another woman?" His gray eyes twinkled with mischief.

"I don't know. I've never tried it," she answered in what she hoped was a sultry voice.

He leaned down and pressed his lips to hers. Ellen closed her eyes and, for a moment, there was nothing in the world but the two of them and the sound of the waves. Their kiss was long and delicious.

Only someone calling Ellen's name brought her back to earth. She looked over her shoulder in the direction of the beach house.

"Aunt Ellie!" It was Lara's daughter Vera, who was home from Paris and had brought her sister with her to stay the weekend with them. "Aunt Ellie, there's someone in the house who's looking for a Band-Aid. I couldn't find any in the bathroom." She traipsed across the sand in a maxi dress with a sweaty bottle of beer in each hand. "You see Christopher? He was here a minute ago," she fussed.

Ellen looked up at Barrett. Even with her wearing the platform shoes Lara had loaned her (she'd refused to wear four-inch heels and kill herself in front of two hundred people), he was much taller than she was. "I better see what's up. You're not leaving, are you?"

"Nope. Mum's hitching a ride with Gwen when she's ready to go."

"It was so good to see your mother tonight. I'm glad she felt well enough to come." Ellen caught his hand with hers. She didn't want to leave him, but if someone needed a Band-Aid she felt obliged to go.

"She wouldn't have missed it." He pointed toward the house. "Why don't you put out that fire. I'll catch up with you later. Maybe a walk on the beach when the place clears out? I'm going to get these damned shoes off." He lifted the hem of the gown to show her the heeled sandals that made him close to six foot five. "They're killing me."

"I meant to ask you." She backed away from him. "Where did you get size fourteen high heels on such short notice?"

He shrugged. "I went down to the bar on the avenue where they have the drag shows. One of the girls loaned them to me. Trixie. Supersweet girl" He glanced around. "She's here somewhere."

Ellen was still laughing when she climbed the steps to her back porch. There were several people she didn't know sitting in the Adirondack chairs in conversation. She smiled and said hello as she went into the house, noting that the fact that she didn't know them didn't bother her one bit.

She found Lenora sitting on one of the stools at her kitchen counter.

"There you are, Doris!" Lenora said as if she'd been looking for her. "I told Miranda you were around here somewhere."

"Lenora! I'm so happy to see you." Ellen rushed over, surprising the older woman and herself by giving her a big hug. "I've missed you," she told her.

"Missed me? I haven't gone anywhere. Been right here the whole time." She poked her gnarled bare feet out from under an orange flowered maxi skirt. "Got a blister on my toe from my sandals."

The bathroom door opened, and Miranda came out.

"I found Doris," Lenora announced to her granddaughter.

Miranda smiled. "Ellen, good to see you. The show was so much fun." She giggled. "Neither Granny nor I have ever been to a drag show. Lara told us it was okay to come up to use the bathroom and get a Band-Aid. She thought there were some under the bathroom sink, but I'm not seeing any. She said there was a first-aid kit?"

"I think it's in the pantry. I'll grab it. I'm glad to see you both." Seeing Lenora, Ellen realized how much she'd missed the older woman. Missed her coffee, too. Ellen had tried several times to make it in the percolator, but it never seemed to taste as good as the coffee they had shared on the porch.

Was it the company and not the coffee?

"Thanks. I appreciate it." Miranda stood in the middle of the kitchen in a cute lavender sundress, her feet bare. "I suggested we get one at home, but Granny wasn't ready to go. And she wanted me to see her house. It was just like you described it, Granny." Miranda looked at Ellen. "Granny has talked about this house for so many years." She gave a sheepish laugh. "She *told* me this was her house, but I didn't believe it. I thought my mother had told me the house they lived in when they were little came down in a hurricane."

Ellen stared at Miranda. "She *lived* here?" She looked back at Lenora.

Lenora sat on the stool, picking at her blister. "Told you. Told you both. This is my house." She sounded like a parrot.

"She and her sisters and their stepbrother Joe all lived here with their parents," Miranda explained. "After Joe was killed in France, they sold this house and moved west of here to a small farm. I guess my great-grandfather and Granny couldn't stand being in the house anymore. Without him," she finished softly.

Ellen watched Lenora closely. She didn't seem to be paying attention to the conversation. She was focused on her blister.

Had Lenora really lived in this house? Had the buttercup dishes that had come with the house originally been hers? Had Lenora watched the sunrise from the back porch with her brother, Joe, before he was killed in the war?

Ellen took a step toward Lenora, still staring at her. "Did you really live here, Lenora?"

"Sure did." She looked up. "I told you that. Don't you re-member, dear? You're a little young to be so forgetful." She got up off the stool and padded barefoot across the kitchen floor. "My name's in here. I'll show you."

Ellen met Miranda's gaze as Lenora made a beeline for the pantry.

Miranda shrugged, and the two women followed her grand-mother into the pantry.

"Back here," Lenora told them, flipping the light switch.

Ellen stood beside Miranda in the doorway and watched the

older woman go to the very back of the pantry near the window where old aprons and a flyswatter hung from a hook that jutted from the floor-to-ceiling shelves. Lenora set the flyswatter on one of the shelves and pulled the aprons down one by one. "See," she told them, pointing.

Ellen was the first to reach Lenora. There on the wood, written faintly, was Lenora's name and a line. In fact, Lenora's name was written again and again, along with the names of her sisters and brother with the same marks one after the other, vertically.

Ellen gasped. "Holy hell," she whispered. Someone, Lenora's father or mother, had recorded the heights of their children as they grew.

Lenora leaned closer, squinting. She scratched the wood with a fingernail painted a bright pink. "Used to be dates, too, but they're gone." She backed past Ellen so her granddaughter could see.

Miranda used the flashlight on her cell to get a better look. "Wow. Granny, that's amazing."

Ellen turned to Lenora in disbelief. "Why didn't you show me this before?"

Lenora shrugged and walked out of the pantry. "Guess I forgot."

51

Two weeks later, after a round of hugs and then a second round, the porch friends said their good-byes to Lara. Alex was the last to go, and she and Lara were both crying as they released each other.

"You'll be back in a few weeks, right?" Alex asked, wiping under her eyes. She sported her favorite pink wig and wore hot-pink lipstick, which had left marks on Lara's cheek.

"The weekend after Labor Day," Lara promised.

"And if I can't come here, if I'm not able, you'll come to my house?"

Lara grasped Alex's hands and squeezed them. "I promise."

"And I'll see you tomorrow for lunch, Ellie? Fries on the boardwalk, and then we're going to the bookstore." Alex looked to Ellen. "You're not going back to North Carolina yet, right?" Her last words sounded desperate.

"I'm not going anywhere yet. I'll be there if you are. And if you don't feel up to it, we'll do it the day after," Ellen answered, glad she was wearing her sunglasses so the teen couldn't see that she was crying, too.

Alex's health was declining. While she hadn't had any more

seizures, she had told everyone that she probably had brain bleeds. She had some muscle weakness on the left side of her body, and they'd all noticed changes in her speech. But she was still their Alex, wearing her wigs and crazy faux eyelashes, even though she didn't need either anymore. And she still enjoyed the minor celebrity status she'd gained from the drag show. Apparently, her YouTube channel had *blown up*.

"I'll meet you on the boardwalk at eleven-thirty," Alex said, going down the steps backward but holding on to the rail because she had trouble with balance sometimes now. "Right next to Thrasher's." She blew kisses to them both and was gone.

"Sweet Mary, I hope I'll see her again," Lara said softly, watching the teenager go.

Ellen put her arm around Lara and hugged her, offering none of the platitudes she probably would have, had she not gotten to know The Porch.

Lara rested her head on Ellen's shoulder for a moment and then straightened, clapping her hands together. "So, what's the plan? Wanna go for a swim, have a drink, get takeout?" They'd already decided that for their last meal together for a few weeks they'd pick up crab cakes in town and bring them back. Dining in town was crazy busy because it was the last big week for summer vacationers in Albany Beach. Too many tourists, they'd both agreed.

"Your call. You're the one going back to Pennsylvania tomorrow."

"I want to do it all," Lara said enthusiastically.

She was feeling good. And while there was no way to know what her future held, her local oncologists had talked with Dr. Gupta in Pennsylvania and they had agreed that she was in remission again and that no further treatment was necessary for the time being. A week had passed since her last radiation treatment, and she had almost as much energy as she'd had the day she and Ellen arrived in Albany Beach.

Lara was okay.

Her Lara was going to be okay.

"Let's have a cocktail first," Ellen suggested. "You feel like walking over to pick up the crab cakes? Finding a parking spot any closer than our driveway on a Saturday is going to be impossible."

"I'd walk ten miles to get Crab Shack crab cakes." Lara pointed at her. "So how about a drink, a walk to get takeout, a little dinner, and then we'll go down to the beach. Maybe have a swim." Her forehead creased. "You going out tonight with Barrett, or are you in for a few episodes of *RuPaul's All-Stars*?"

Ellen drew her head back. "A date your last night here? Of course not. Except with you and RuPaul."

Lara held up her hand as she opened the door. "Just asking. There have been a lot of late-night walks here recently."

Ellen smiled but said nothing. She still didn't know what was going on between her and Barrett, but she was surprisingly okay with that. It just felt good to have someone to call or text or go somewhere with other than Lara.

A few minutes later, Lara joined Ellen on the porch again with their adult beverages. They dragged their pool-blue and plum Adirondack chairs together to face the ocean side by side. Ellen sipped on a glass of Malbec, and Lara had vodka and tonic. They sat for a little while in comfortable silence, nibbling on mixed nuts and enjoying their drinks.

"I'm excited to get home and go back to work," Lara said eventually.

"And see *Raul*," Ellen teased. Though Lara had never allowed him to visit, he'd kept up his calls, texts, and weekly delivery of flowers all summer.

"And see Raul," she admitted. "And my girls. Just having them here for the weekend wasn't enough. Oh"—she turned to Ellen—"did I tell you that when Christopher was here, Vera asked him about Thanksgiving. He said he had enough seniority at work now to ask for at least part of the weekend off so he can have dinner with us. It'll have to be at my place. Vera can't take off enough time to drive here or to Raleigh. I know that means you'll have to drive from Raleigh. I hope that's okay."

"That's fine." Ellen was pleased her son had made arrangements to meet his *cousins*. Though they weren't related by blood, he and Vera and Chastity had always been close. "I don't know where I'll be in November. I might still be here. If I am, I can be at your house in less than three hours, even in holiday traffic."

Lara pulled off her sunglasses. The sun had sunk in the sky behind them. "Two things." She held up her index and middle finger. "One, you just said you didn't know where you would be in November. You who plan everything including trips to the bathroom and stick with it. And two, you're thinking about staying here?" She laughed. "Who *are* you?"

Ellen set her sunglasses down on the arm of her chair next to her wineglass. "Nope. I don't know what I'm doing. I haven't decided. But I could stay here, if I wanted to. For as long as I want. I can teach my classes online and work on the book. I think it's going well. I finished the third chapter this morning before you got up."

"I wondered why you hadn't had the real estate lady here to take the photos. I didn't want to say anything." She smiled over the rim of her frosty glass. "And break whatever spell you seem to be under."

Ellen chuckled but didn't respond. Lara was right, though. She felt like she was under some kind of a spell, too, but the good kind. So much had changed in the three months she'd been there. The world hadn't changed. But *she* had. Not that she didn't know herself anymore. She just knew herself better. She knew which elements of her personality could still use some adjusting and she knew what parts of herself she wanted to keep just as they were. As she was.

"So, uh"—Lara popped a cashew into her mouth—"what's this mean for Tim and his plans for reconciliation?"

"I talked to him this morning after putting it off for weeks. I told him that I realized now that he was right when he left, that we didn't belong together as a couple anymore. I said that he would still always be the father of my son, that I'll still always love him, and that I hope he finds the happiness he's looking for."

Lara cringed. "How'd that go?"

Ellen thought for a moment, sipping her wine, and enjoyed the feel of the cool ocean breeze on her face. "Surprisingly well, though he was pretty hurt. I think he thought I was going to go running back to him."

"Hm. I have to admit, I was a little worried. It would have been so easy to do, Ellie. To go back to the life you had. The life you were familiar with, even if it wasn't the life you wanted anymore." She reached over and squeezed Ellen's hand.

"I still feel like a little bit of a failure," Ellen admitted. "When I married Tim, I really meant until death does us part."

"I know you did, sweetie. But this, what you're doing, writing your novel, staying in Albany Beach until you figure things out, exploring a relationship with Barrett, this is a lot harder than going back to Tim. I'm so proud of you." Lara held Ellen's gaze. "Of course, you know if you stay here, it's going to get harder."

Ellen understood what she meant without saying it. Their porch friends were going to die, some sooner than others. But their cancer would likely take them all eventually. Grace had told them that afternoon that she had an appointment the following week with Hospice to discuss her plans to die at home with Barrett and her porch friends at her side. To hear her talk so calmly about her death had been heartbreaking. But it had also made Ellen proud to call Grace her friend and thankful for the lessons she had learned from the older woman. The lessons she had learned from them all.

Ellen was still marveling at how much she had learned about

living from those who were dying when Lara got up from her chair.

"Ready to roll?" Lara asked, downing the last of her drink.

Ellen smiled up at her. "Ready to roll, sister by another mister."

EPILOGUE

Monday morning, the house was so quiet when Ellen woke before dawn that, for a split second, she regretted every choice she'd made in the last three months. Lara was gone, back to her life in Pennsylvania. Ellen was alone, and she would always be alone, a tiny voice in the back of her head warned. Lara had her own life to lead and Ellen had told Tim there was no chance of reconciliation. Barrett was too young, too smart, too good-looking, too damned cool, to ever want anything more than a few kisses and a walk on the beach from her. At that moment, she regretted every decision down to changing that student's grade.

But those fears were the fears that lingered in that state when a person was still half-asleep.

They weren't justified.

Once she was awake, once she pushed her cat off her and climbed out of bed, she knew she'd made the right choices. And if she hadn't . . . that was okay.

Mistakes, fears, wearing false eyelashes, they were all part of living life to its fullest.

Ellen brushed her teeth, washed her face, and headed downstairs, noting that the days were getting shorter and that sunrise, according to Mother Google, was fifty-two minutes later than when she arrived the first of June.

She was halfway down the stairs when she realized there was light coming from the kitchen. And the heavenly smell of coffee.

She walked into the kitchen to the sound of the percolator's *blup, blup, blupp*ing. And the sight of Lenora taking the buttercup mugs from the cabinet. The elderly woman was barefoot, wearing pink squishy rollers in her hair and sporting her trademark flowered housecoat.

"Lenora!" Ellen exclaimed, not knowing how she got into the house. Not caring.

Lenora turned around, smiling her bright, denture smile. "I was wondering if I was going to have to wake you up. The sunrise is going to be a beauty this morning. No clouds. I didn't want you to miss it, Doris."

Ellen watched as Lenora turned off the flame beneath the percolator and then walked up behind her to turn off the other burners she'd lit. Just as Ellen was about to chastise Lenora for her dangerous habit, she thought about what Tim had said to her that night, right there in the kitchen when he'd told her he wanted a divorce. He'd said that to live freely, to truly live, you couldn't be afraid to make decisions fearing they might be dangerous or wrong.

Actually, it was Ben Franklin who had spoken those words, she reminded herself with a smile.

There was no doubt in Ellen's mind, there were risks to Lenora wandering around town in her state of mind. Randomly making coffee for strangers, leaving the stove on. But she realized, for Lenora, it was worth the risk. She also realized that Lenora was perfectly happy in her state of constant confusion, upheaval, unknowns always ahead of her.

Ellen saw a vast ocean of unknowns in front of her now. But if Lenora could do it at nearly ninety years old, she could do it. And she would embrace it as Lenora did.

"Coffee?" Lenora asked, pushing a mug across the countertop toward Ellen.

"Thank you." Ellen picked up the buttercup mug with the tiny chip on the handle and took a sip. The coffee was hot and strong. She blew on it. "Tell me something, Lenora, how did you get in the house this morning?" she asked.

The older woman shrugged. "Key."

"But where did you get the key? Miranda gave it to me and I hung it up in the—"

Ellen halted midsentence. She remembered the night of the drag show when they walked into the pantry to see the marks of Lenora and her siblings' heights on the wall. The key had been hanging on its piece of red yarn from the hook inside the door.

Ellen could see the key hook through the open pantry doorway. The key was gone. She turned back to Lenora. "Did you take my house key from the pantry?" she asked, curious, not angry.

"Sun's about to come up." Lenora shuffled past Ellen, toward the door that led to the porch. She took a loud slurp of her coffee. "You coming, Ellie?"

THE SUMMER I FOUND MYSELF

ABOUT THIS GUIDE

The suggested questions are included to enhance your group's
reading of Colleen French's *The Summer I Found Myself*.

DISCUSSION QUESTIONS

1. Do you think Ellen's invitation to Lara was altruistic? Why or why not?

2. Considering their differences, why do you think Ellen and Lara were still friends after all these years?

3. How do you believe Ellen's parents affected the person she was in her forties?

4. Was Ellen in a midlife crisis? If so, what caused it?

5. What was Ellen's relationship with the beach house at the beginning of the book? The end?

6. Who was your favorite person on The Porch? Why? Your least favorite? Why?

7. What purpose did Lenora serve in the story?

8. What did you think about Alex? Did anything about her surprise you?

9. Which character on The Porch had the most to offer Ellen on her journey? Why?

10. Did you learn anything about yourself or your beliefs by reading this book?